MAGDA, STANDING

MAGDA, STANDING

CHRISTINE FALLERT KESSIDES

BOLD
STORY
PRESS

WASHINGTON, DC

Bold Story Press, Washington, DC 20016
www.boldstorypress.com

This is a work of fiction. Apart from the well-known historical persons, events, and locales that figure in the narrative, all characters are the products of the author's imagination. Any resemblance to actual persons, living or dead, is entirely coincidental.

First edition: May 2023
Library of Congress Control Number: 2022922475

ISBN: 978-1-954805-38-5 (paperback)
ISBN: 978-1-954805-39-2 (ebook)

Text and cover design by KP Design
Author photo by Ioannis Kessides

Cover image: Pittsburgh skyline circa 1910

Printed in the United States of America
10 9 8 7 6 5 4 3 2 1

In memory of Betty, Ralph, Edna, Margaret, and CJ.

For Norm (the original Richy).

And for Gil and the Aunts,
whom I never had the privilege of meeting.

1916

1

Magda was tall enough now to look eye level at the principal. A twinge of anxiety and anticipation replaced awe and intimidation. It was as if he held a key to her future.

"Excellent grades," he said, handing Magda her tenth-grade report card. She relaxed the breath she'd been holding. His stiff, high collar pinched his plump neck, squeezing out a tight smile. "You should be a teacher someday, like your aunts. Please give them my regards."

"Thank you, sir," Magda bobbed a curtsy and turned away to leave the line of students in the auditorium. Her aunts were her heroines, but could she become something more? Maybe something even they hadn't been able to imagine, like making her mark somewhere far from Pittsburgh. She opened the little booklet. A's in all classes but civics, but she had been sick for that final exam. Magda pressed the card to her heart through the rough pinafore dampened with sweat in the June

MAGDA, STANDING

heat. She walked back to her chair, sharing a grin with her best friend, Lucia.

When she'd begged to start high school two years ago, Papa had relented but warned her not to expect to graduate; it wasn't a priority for the family. But how could he object now to completing her studies? If she kept up the good grades, maybe she could go on to college. Maybe even medical school.

Good grades still might not be enough to convince him, but if she got an award, she'd surely have nothing to worry about.

After handing out the last card, the principal made the announcement everyone was waiting for: "And now the students admitted to our high school honors society for 1916. Please rise as I call your name." The students all knew the principal based the selection not just on grades, but on his own estimation of "leadership potential" and other factors he never explained. It wasn't an objective decision, but Magda needed this. She bit her lip.

"Magdalena Augustin." At the sound of her name, she stood abruptly, loudly bumping the empty chair in front of her. She reddened as students seated in the first rows turned to stare and lowered her head for a quick sideways glance at the others whose names had also been called. In the class of one hundred, about a half-dozen girls and at least twice the number of boys were on their feet. She exchanged smiles with the girls standing closest to her and across the aisle with one or two boys who looked over. She noticed some of the heads that didn't turn to acknowledge her. The light applause sounded especially weak from the girls' section of the room.

The students milled about noisily after dismissal, talking excitedly about various parties to celebrate the year's end.

Mary Alice came up and gave Magda a quick hug. "Congratulations! Can I see it?" She pointed to the small collar pin the honorees had been given, still clutched in Magda's hand.

"You deserve it," said Paulina, with a peck on Magda's cheek, "but it would have been nice if he included more of the girls."

Magda's excitement dimmed a little—she had to acknowledge that. She glanced over to Margaret, who stood aside with Christoph's arm around her. Margaret's gaze passed over Magda, and she didn't return Magda's smile. They had an unspoken rivalry. No doubt Margaret deserved the honor, too, but everything would go her way in any case. Girls like Margaret, whose family was comfortably well-off, faced no resistance if they wanted to continue schooling, which to a point could lead to a more advantageous marriage—the very last thing on Magda's mind.

As usual, she rode the trolley toward home with Lucia, who chatted about her plans to spend several weeks with cousins near Conneaut Lake, just north of Pittsburgh. Magda's family never took a vacation, but she looked forward to spending as much of the summer outdoors, with friends and a good book, as her regular chores allowed. Magda squeezed Lucia's hand as they parted near their houses; she always tried to go into hers alone. Her heart beat fast, despite the slow pace of her steps.

Papa had completed his milk deliveries, and he and Mama sat in the kitchen when Magda entered. Crumbs of bread and cheese speckled the table. Dirty dishes from breakfast lay encrusted in the sink. Magda handed her report card to Papa first with a small flourish. "The principal announced I'm in the honors society!"

Without a word, her father put on his glasses and read the card, rubbing his beard. He showed it to Mama, who gave it a quick glance and a wan smile. Magda's heart pounded louder when she saw his frown as he handed it back.

"Magdalena, you are a good girl and you make us proud. Hard working and smart, like all of our family. But—"

Magda's fear burst out of her throat. "No, Papa, you won't say—?" Her fingernails cut into the card.

"I already said that you do not need to finish the high school. You can learn the rest of what you need to know by reading, as we all did, while you help your mother here."

Magda stared at her father with wild eyes. "No, I can't! I want to learn more."

"Hear me out, my girl." But why couldn't he listen to *her*? "You've already got more schooling than the rest of us."

It was true that Magda's parents only finished six years of primary, back in Germany. Instead of attending high school, her brothers Tony and Fred had gone to learn trades and her sisters, Kitty and Willa, took paying jobs with their domestic skills outside the home. While Magda didn't envy the working lives of her siblings, it seemed they'd at least found paths that satisfied them. Her choice—her need—was to continue school.

"Papa, you always wished you could have gotten more education!"

"And yet, I didn't. My family needed me. Your mother needs you to take care of the baby and the house. More useful experience for when you have your own family." Papa looked away when he said this, as if he didn't want to see the heartbreak in Magda's eyes.

Magda turned, pleading, to her mother, who was gazing down at little Richy on her lap. Her hair was uncombed, and she still wore a soiled house robe. She didn't return Magda's frantic stare. Mama had been especially quiet and sickly since the child was born two years ago. Most of the time, Mama seemed detached from her own life, as if it was something happening to her, beyond any of her control. Exactly what Magda would refuse to accept herself.

Magda had been the youngest for almost fourteen years and had gotten used to a bit of freedom. With older sisters, she had been able to escape many household duties. By studying diligently, Magda had hoped she could plan a life much different from that of most women and girls in the community. Certainly, different from her mother's.

Magda clenched her fists and leaned towards her father. "Doesn't it matter what *I* want?" Her voice rose, and her face flushed in resentment. He didn't answer.

Her hands shook as she struggled to continue, knowing she had already violated one of the basic rules of the family: no talking back to adults. But her head was on fire and she couldn't stop. "I always brought home the best grades. And now you say I have to leave school for good? To stay home? How is that fair? Even the principal said he expects me to continue my studies and," she put the words into his mouth, "not waste my good mind!" It landed like a slap.

Papa rose from his chair, his hand rubbing his bad hip. "Calm down, Magda." His voice was hard, and he shook his head with the anger that Magda knew he was holding back in front of Mama. "Your brothers and sisters quit school to work because we needed the money when I lost my job at the mill. I could hire the woman to look after us for a while, but we can't afford to keep her any longer. We have many more expenses. We must take care of our own. Your mother isn't well."

So that was it? Magda was the unlucky one, to be shut in at sixteen and made to feel guilty, too, for objecting. Hot tears welled, but she refused to cry here. Mama looked sad and dazed. Whatever her thoughts about this decision, she would not say in front of them both. Everyone in the family was used to Papa having the last word.

Taking a deep, shaky breath, Magda reached for the toddler and took him from Mama, who didn't resist. "I'll put him down for his nap, then go to the baker." Her head ached from holding back the sobs that rose in her throat. She had to get away and think about what to do. The house was silent as she left. She let the door slam behind her.

———

The next day felt like the beginning of the end of Magda's life. She scraped Papa's shirt collar against the washboard. Two minutes each, Mama always said—the time it takes to say one Our Father and Hail Mary. The corrugated metal surface bruised her knuckles and the raw skin started to burn. She rubbed the rough soap bar against the collar again, but the dark stains refused to disappear. Papa's sweat mixed with the dirty air of the city made his shirt collars the worst part of the weekly laundry.

No, the baby's diapers were a messier job, and the sheets and towels took too much strength for Magda to wash by hand. Mama had said she'd let her avoid all that by convincing Papa to use a neighborhood laundress with one of the new electric washing machines. That promise was Mama's small gesture of compensation for his announcement the previous day. Papa had objected to the expense and only agreed because Mama said they would save water and soap, and that it would be temporary, for maybe another year or two. Mama rarely took such initiative and didn't seem to have challenged Papa's decision about school, but when she did express a quiet wish Papa often gave in—hoping, perhaps, to spark an uplift of her moods.

Thinking of Papa's words made Magda's stomach burn. Really, reading as an alternative to the classroom? That worked for him—Papa read two newspapers a day, American and German, and she knew he could hold his own debating politics with better-educated neighbors. She did love reading, but to feed her imagination, to see what was possible in the world and, perhaps, in her own future. Most importantly, she wanted options other than getting married and caring for a household—to be more independent and make a bigger contribution with her life. Maybe healing sick people and discovering a cure for whatever ailed Mama.

Magda was upset that she had not prepared a better argument. Papa always called America the land of opportunity, but evidently not for her. She didn't want to compare herself to most young people in the community, whose families may also have considered public high school an unnecessary detour from responsibility. She thought instead of her classmates: most would probably graduate within two years, especially the girls, and some would even attend college—a higher share than the boys, more of whom would rather join their fathers at work. But what could she have said? That she wanted a better life than that of her parents, maybe even better than the rest of the family? And that for all her efforts, she deserved more? But that would sound too selfish. Besides, his mind was already made up.

Now she would be humiliated in front of her friends. How could she ever face them again?

Magda finished hanging Papa's shirts on the line behind the house to catch the afternoon breeze. She decided on her first step: she would talk to her aunts.

She checked that Richy was napping in his crib beside their parents' bed. Mama was resting and didn't rise when Magda whispered that she was going to run an errand and would be back before long. She left the room before her mother could reply.

Stopping by the small bathroom, Magda splashed some water on her face, which was red and damp from the exertion. Disheveled braids barely held her thick brown hair, but she didn't want to take time to redo them. From the bedroom shared with her sisters, she grabbed her hat, which the aunts would insist was proper wear for a young lady outside the home. She slipped the money for the butcher Papa had given her earlier that morning into her pocket and headed downstairs and out the back door. She closed it gently, praying Richy's sleep wouldn't be disturbed.

The thick gray haze was typical of almost any day in Pittsburgh. A bit of blue might appear for a little while, but the smoke and ash from the iron and steel mills formed heavy, low clouds that combined with the mist lifting off the rivers. Soot would settle on windows, on doorsills, on white fences and white dogs, and on clothes hanging out to dry. Often, it was necessary to shake down the sheets, towels, and everything else before bringing them inside to be ironed. Worse were the particles of grit she sometimes felt herself almost chewing and swallowing. She would spit them out, or sneeze dark specks into her handkerchief. And many people, especially men who worked in the mines outside Pittsburgh and in the mills, breathed it till they coughed a blackish froth. Papa used to do that for years after he left that job.

Magda didn't feel sympathy for him now, only for herself. She strode along the steep brick sidewalks of Mt. Oliver, its streets lined with close-set houses and small shops, many seeming to be cut from, or clinging to, a hillside. Her heels fell hard against the uneven ground, and she swung her arms as if to warn passersby to step aside. She crossed the road and took a less direct route to avoid passing her elementary school and its church. She didn't want to see anyone she knew.

She arrived at her aunts' house with sweat running down her face, out of breath. Magda took several moments in the shade of a tree to compose herself, straighten her hat, and smooth her skirt. It took an effort to be decorous. She wanted to make the best impression, and the city's humidity was only partly to blame for her wilted appearance.

The aunts were well-known in the neighborhood. Theirs was the only influence in the family that matched that of Papa. Aunt Philomena, or Minnie to those close to her, was her mother's elder sister by six years. Aunt Matilda, whom everyone called Tilly, was two years younger than Minnie. They had come to America on the same crossing as Papa, but hailed from a different part of Germany. They supported themselves initially by tutoring other German families' children and, after taking certification courses at night, worked their way to teaching in public schools in the city. Minnie rose to become headmistress of her school, and Tilly was an assistant principal at hers—rather uncommon achievements for women. Magda noticed that everyone—the neighbors, the postman and policeman, and even the monsignor—treated both aunts with great regard, but they seemed to show a special respect for Minnie. Neither aunt had married. They owned their house and had taught other peoples' children but never raised their own. The aunts had always been a nurturing presence in Magda's life, and an inspiration. She was determined to find out what they could do for her now.

Magda looked up the high stairs from the street to the modest house of mustard-yellow brick. She slowly climbed the three levels of steps—ten, then eight, then ten. As she stepped onto the porch, she saw Minnie watching from behind the screen door. She pushed it open.

"Aunt Minnie! Did you know I was here already?"

"Hello, Magda. I thought we might see you today. Your father came by yesterday morning and we had a long talk."

Magda's throat tightened, but she tried to make her voice sound controlled and even.

"He couldn't have told you that I was admitted to the honor society." Magda had remembered to bring her report card, which she pulled from her skirt pocket dog-eared and a bit damp. Aunt Minnie took the card and waved her into the parlor—it wouldn't do to talk standing in the doorway. She lifted off Magda's hat and smoothed her hair with a slight gesture, then looked at the card.

"Very nice results. Come sit down, Tilly has just made tea and biscuits." Minnie put her arm lightly around Magda's shoulders and her voice was calm and low. Magda followed her across the foyer then suddenly turned around, remembering to take off her shoes and put on the scuff slippers that the aunts kept in a closet by the door for family visitors.

The sitting room felt cool even on days like today. The furniture was heavy but comfortable. A horsehair sofa, covered with a quilt that the aunts had brought from the old country. An upholstered chair and side tables in dark wood, deeply carved. Bookshelves lined with volumes in German and English. The main decoration was embroidered doilies that lay wherever head or arm would rest, and on the tables to protect surfaces from a vase or cup. Magda sat on a small rocker that she always felt was hers. This house and its owners promised refuge—a place where her dreams could be safe.

Tilly entered carrying a tray with a teapot, three cups on saucers, and a small plate of cookies. It seemed strange to Magda to feel that she was being served, as she was no longer a child.

"My dear girl, I made some of your favorite sweets," Tilly said. Possibly sensing Magda's discomfort, Tilly added, "It's the beginning of summer holiday for us, too, so a bit of indulgence is allowed." Both aunts had retired from their professional duties but still lived by the academic calendar.

Minnie usually struck Magda as the more dominant personality of the two—a bit severe, decisive and authoritative in her manner. Tilly was shorter and rounder than Minnie. The German community would describe her as gemütlich—good-natured. Tilly was more like a woman was expected to be—reserved and gentle by nature but equally intelligent, forceful in her views, and as determined as Minnie. To Magda, they seemed to complement each other perfectly.

Magda couldn't say Tilly was "motherly," since Mama was very different from her sisters as well as from other mothers she knew. As Magda got older, she increasingly found Mama puzzling and frustrating. She had been hospitalized years before, but no one talked about it. The family had lost two children very young, before Magda was born, but that was not uncommon. She wasn't sure that could explain why Mama often seemed in need of help, comfort, and understanding as if she were a child herself. The family had to support her in many ways—and now Magda was the one given this responsibility. Could someone she loved become a burden and weigh down her own life?

"So," Minnie said as she sat in her usual spot, the armchair by the window, "what exactly did your father tell you?"

The words poured out. "That I have to stay at home from now on, to help Mama with Richy. And for Mama. That I can learn enough just by reading!" She took a quick breath, then leaned in, almost spilling her tea. "But you both got more schooling. And then you worked, using your education. I want to be like you. Please, please, can you make him change his mind?" Magda's voice cracked as the pain struck anew.

Minnie and Tilly exchanged glances as Tilly poured their tea. Magda shot her gaze from one to the other, trying to read their thoughts.

"Papa said he was proud that I did so well in school. I always got better grades in science and math than Tony or Fred did. And he says I read and write better than Kitty or Willa—both in English and German." Magda paused for a moment to take the biscuit Tilly handed her. "Mama didn't say anything when he told me. She could have stood up for me, but then," Magda choked back a sob, "we all know she needs help and I'm the last daughter. Of course, I love her and little Richy, but... I... wish there was another way." Her voice broke again and she bent her head to hide her face in the teacup.

"Well." Minnie's dark eyes narrowed. Magda knew that when Minnie was angry, she could be stern, and when crossed—or delivering discipline to her pupils—she was formidable.

"I... I'm sorry, I don't mean to be selfish." Magda stammered, raising her head again with a quick look to both aunts, feeling a sudden wave of shame that she had voiced complaints about the parents she must honor and obey. About their sister. She must sound so ungrateful.

"My dear," Tilly said gently. "Your feelings are perfectly understandable, and you are right, besides. You need to continue your education. We will help you."

"Yes," Minnie stated emphatically, but then hesitated before continuing, "I argued with your father about this. If he were not our brother-in-law—if he were the father of one of my students—I would have tried harder to change his mind." Biscuit crumbs caught in Magda's throat. Why would Minnie say that? Did she accept that she should quit school now? Maybe the aunts had never objected when their older nieces and nephews didn't continue. Both Minnie and Tilly were very much present in the family when Magda was growing up, but she hadn't been part of the adult conversations.

"Of course, your parents love you and want what's best for you, for all their children—as well as they can provide that. Their lives have been difficult, more than Tilly's or mine."

"I know, losing two babies must have been so hard on them. Especially on Mama," Magda replied quickly. "But shouldn't that mean they would want me to become the best I can be? To be the first of their children to graduate?"

"I don't mean only losing the little ones," Minnie went on. "Your father escaped troubles in Germany, and your mother has struggled. . . ." Her voice faded slightly. Magda hung on mid-swallow, hoping her aunt would say more. "We want to help you understand your parents. That may be one of the most important lessons you can learn."

Magda looked from one to the other, expectantly. But what else would they teach her? Would they help her get her diploma? She was afraid to press them further. They sat quietly for several minutes, finishing their tea.

"But first," Minnie stood abruptly and smoothed her skirt, "I think you may need to go on back home for your mother and brother. Tilly and I will think some more about this. Give us a week or two to work out a plan. School is out for the summer. We can carry on your education another day."

Tilly gave Magda a quick hug and pecked her cheek. "Take the rest of the biscuits to your house," she whispered, "and no more tears."

Magda left the aunts with a lighter step than she had entered, still uncertain but more hopeful. They would help her continue her lessons, she was sure, though she didn't quite know how. As happened often in their presence, she came away feeling discreetly corrected, wisely instructed, and subtly challenged.

2

The next day was Sunday, honored by churchgoing and, almost as importantly, by family dinner. Magda heard her sisters' voices as she trudged slowly up the steep stairway to her house, tapping a bag of bread against the railing. Most times, she would take the stairs two at a time, and often she slid partway down, as her scarred knees attested. But long summer days could be draining, not exhilarating as she remembered as a child, and she still felt an underlying anxiety that dampened her usual energy.

"How long does it take you to go to the baker?" Willa complained as Magda entered the kitchen, grabbing the loaf from Magda with one hand and thrusting an apron at her with the other. "You have to help peel and grate more potatoes from the cellar, and please fill this bowl with kraut from the bin. I asked Kitty to make potato pancakes with the roast since they're one of Johannes' favorites, but that takes more time, so you need to help. This must be a special meal and we need to have everything ready before five when he comes. I'm so hot in this kitchen, I'll be damp from head to toe by the time he gets here and you know how that frizzes my hair!" At Willa's dramatic outburst, Magda sighed loudly, grabbed the apron, and ran upstairs to their room.

Willa had invited her new beau to meet the family for the first time, and only Magda knew how that had come about. At nineteen, Willa was closest in age to Magda and already a skilled seamstress. Her godmother, Susanna, Papa's distant cousin, had taught her to sew from the time she was five years old and said Willa took to it "like a bird to nest building."

Susanna had offered to teach Magda, but she couldn't sit still long enough to sew a straight seam and constantly pricked her fingers with the needle. After too many blood spots left on the old shirts used for practice, Susanna gave up, warning her, "You'll need to pay someone else to mend your husband's clothes or let him go into the world poorly dressed!" Serious faults, indeed.

Magda didn't care much about that, and she wasn't sure Willa did either. But once Willa had moved on to stitching nightgowns and slips with ribbons and delicate buttonholes, she became apprenticed at a dress shop downtown and was out of the house from seven in the morning to seven at night, taking a trolley car to work each way. Magda envied Willa's relative freedom, which their parents tolerated because she gave most of her wages to the family.

Then Willa met Johannes, a nephew of the proprietor. After that, Magda fell asleep many nights to Willa's enthralled reports of each sighting of Johannes. Willa let slip that she had gotten out of work early on some of the days she came home rather late.

Magda enjoyed the intrigue and kept quiet about the budding romance. Willa revealed that one day Susanna visited the shop near closing, just as Johannes entered the back door. Since Susanna might speak to Papa if Willa didn't, she finally invited Johannes to meet their parents.

"Why didn't one of you tell me about him before?" Kitty, Magda's oldest sister, scolded Willa and Magda when finally hearing the story. Kitty worked as a live-in housekeeper for a well-to-do German family across town, but came home every Saturday evening and stayed until Sunday night. Magda used to like sharing a bedroom with her two sisters, but she had come to appreciate the nights when she had the room to herself.

At twenty-eight, Kitty seemed to Magda more like another aunt than a sibling. She had worked for the Steinmetz family for over twelve years, running their household and supervising the three children when their governess was away. Magda admitted that Kitty demonstrated every skill that housewives were praised for—indeed, she managed domestic duties with far greater ease and finesse than Mama ever could.

Magda felt she had neither of her sisters' talents and was content with that. She recognized their accomplishments, yet couldn't see herself in their roles. But, like them, she wanted to gain some financial independence, to become knowledgeable and skilled in something useful, to be admired for it, and especially to have choices in her life.

On that muggy afternoon, her slip and long shirtsleeves clung to her skin from the exertion of her walk to the baker. In her bedroom, she peeled off the slip, pinned the sleeves high above her elbows, and pulled off her woolen socks. The full apron, with both a bib and skirt, would add another layer of cloth. She pulled it on without tying the strings and headed back down the stairs, hoping no one would notice if a rare breeze or shaft of sunlight exposed her efforts to get comfortable.

Like all houses in their neighborhood, the Augustin house was tall and narrow, with steep stairs between each floor. The brothers slept in the attic when they were home. On the second floor, their parents, the sisters, and baby Richy shared two bedrooms and a bath. The first floor contained the sitting room, dining room, and kitchen, from which rickety wooden steps led into the cellar.

On a day like this, Magda liked escaping to the cellar to sit on the steps and let the cool air settle on her arms and neck. Lit only by a kerosene lamp, the cellar had two high, dark glass windows. From the floor she couldn't see outside, but on the middle step she could look out and watch the neighbors in their small backyards. Sometimes, a dog, squirrel, or even the occasional raccoon would pass close to the window and Magda would meet its eyes. The cellar emitted a faint sweet-sour smell that wafted by as she passed the apple barrels and dried flowers that her mother used to weave into wreathes for the doors and mantelpieces. She walked carefully to the shelves in back that held jars of pickles, tomato jam, and spiced pears, many of them from Tilly. Magda pulled out the pin holding up her braids, shook them out, bent over, and swayed gently, letting the cool air caress her neck, ears, and forearms. Rising, she replaced the pin and sighed deeply, careful to inhale before lifting the wooden lid of the kraut bin.

Suddenly, she imagined this cellar as a prison confining the future of her life—her world. She remembered how older adults in the community, and some teachers and priests in elementary school, described the "sacred preoccupations" of women: *Kinder, Kochen, und Kirche*—children, cooking and church. Not for me, she thought.

"Maaagdaaa!"

Fred was in the kitchen when she came upstairs. He was the sibling whose company she most enjoyed. Fred had left school when he turned fourteen because he was "itching to work," and within a week got an apprenticeship with a printer downtown. He'd been employed there for six years and was already supervising some of the other staff. Fred kept his attic room, but the family didn't see him much these days. He often worked late getting out the newspaper, but just as often stayed out to meet his friends afterwards for a beer and pool or poker—as far as Magda knew. Fred enjoyed such a free life, she thought, with a twinge of jealousy, and she missed him when he wasn't around.

"*Meine Lieblingsschwester!*" he called to her, leaning in to tweak her nose with his ink-stained fingers. Fred teased her in German because they both thought the language sounded funny, like a barking dog. They had grown up with it at home— all the children in the Augustin household could read and understand German because their parents spoke it with each other and, less frequently now, to them. Papa said Magda had good pronunciation and didn't stumble as much as her older siblings. But none of them wanted to speak it unless required to. Fred was immersed in it these days because the print shop produced *Pittsburger Volksblatt,* the local German paper, as well as the Italian and Polish ones. It was the largest printer in Pittsburgh.

Magda heard the shrill voices of her niece and nephew from the street before they ran into the house, slamming the door. Her brother Tony's wife, Sabine, called to them, out of breath from the climb up the outside stairs, but Anna and Valentin were already in the kitchen pulling on their aunts' aprons. Sabine entered heavily, her face red and sweaty as she held her bulging abdomen.

"You must all have some lemonade to cool off," Mama said quietly, as she directed Tony's family into the sitting room. From there, the children ran to the small back porch where a basket of wooden toys and puzzles awaited them. Magda hoped she wouldn't be asked to entertain them—to ensure that, as Papa sometimes said, the children were "seen and not heard." She did love the little ones, but preferred to talk with Tony and Fred, and to hear the news they would discuss with their father. Tony had worked in a photography shop since he turned fifteen and learned the business both in front of and behind the camera. He and Fred gained privileged access to the goings-on in the city and even beyond since they knew many of the newspapermen. Both of them could get a press pass on occasion that allowed them to attend meetings around town, to listen to the local politicians, and to watch public demonstrations, when Magda thought their only qualification was curiosity.

A firm knock at the front door broke through the kitchen chatter. Willa gasped and patted her hair, leaving a flour and grease mark on her forehead.

"Johannes! He's early!" she exclaimed. Kitty helped her untie her apron as Willa wiped her face with a towel.

"Why don't I go and let him in," Magda said, eager to get out of the kitchen and meet the mysterious caller. "You run upstairs and freshen up."

She stepped to the entryway just as Fred and Tony reached it, each holding a beer glass. Pushing open the screen door, they put out their hands to a tall youth about Fred's age and Tony's height, huskier than either of them. He had Willa's blond hair but darker eyes.

After the young people had introduced themselves, Willa came down the stairs looking surprisingly refreshed. Magda could tell she had poured water on top of her head to cool off. Willa and Johannes beamed at each other, and Magda noticed their equally dimpled smiles. She could imagine without difficulty what their children would look like. They exchanged a quick arm's length hug that left about ten inches between them.

The five of them entered the living room, where Papa rose stiffly from his horsehair chair in the corner. He exchanged a solid handshake with Johannes. Magda thought handshakes among men must signify some code of strength and character. Too firm and long? Presumptuous. Too light and short? Weak. Her brothers shook hands quickly and casually. Friendly and nonjudgmental. But Papa would make his own test.

Magda brought Johannes a beer, which gave her an excuse to observe briefly before heading back to the kitchen to help Kitty. Papa asked Johannes how and when he and Willa had met. "Er—a couple months ago, at my aunt's shop, when I helped her carry bolts of cloth." He stumbled slightly and Magda saw Willa blinking her eyes at him. Perhaps they hadn't rehearsed this.

The dinner table was elbow-to-elbow with nine, not an unusual number for the household. Mama and Magda took their places at one end, with Richy in his high chair between. They were closest to the kitchen as they would spend most of the meal running back and forth to refill plates. Willa was in the middle of the main table, next to Johannes and across from Kitty, and the two brothers flanked their father at the far end. Sabine stayed at a small side table in the corner with her children, but Magda could tell she wasn't listening to their chatter.

As they all stood behind their chairs, Papa commenced saying grace with a combination of German and English phrases. Magda could recite most of them by heart and usually found her mind wandering while keeping an eye on the small cuckoo clock on the dining room wall. Two and a half minutes, as a rule. But on special occasions like this, he embellished the invocation with added prayers and even a reading from the Bible. Four minutes.

As he carved the pork roast, Papa looked at Johannes. "What do you do at the mill, and how long have you worked there?"

"I started stoking the furnaces two years ago, but now I work on quality control, checking ingots and beams as they move out of the plant." That sounded impressive to Magda, but Papa seemed less interested in the details of the work and more in the nature of responsibility. Was Johannes using his hands and strong back only, or his head? What would be the next step to advance? Papa sounded ambitious for the young suitor. He rarely asked his daughters how they spent their day, or what more they might want to do with their lives. His wish, never in doubt, was simply that they would all marry well—to Catholic boys of good families with solid, honest jobs—have babies, and live nearby.

When Papa paused in his questioning, Tony casually asked Johannes, "What do you hear in the mill these days about a possible slowdown? There are rumors—"

"Yeah," Fred said. "What are the workers saying about that? Sounds like things are getting tense."

Johannes squirmed in his chair. Any labor issues in coal or steel set the city on edge, and he probably didn't want to venture a view in front of their father without knowing his opinions. Magda thought that was the kind of subject her brothers knew about already, and maybe they were trying to deflect the attention from Johannes' own work—or test him.

Then Kitty broke in, "I'll bet we have many acquaintances in common. You went to St. Wendelin, too, didn't you? I thought I recognized you." Willa looked relieved. Gracious Kitty—no wonder she was so successful in running a household.

"Our paper may have to stop circulation for a while," Fred blurted out suddenly during another pause in the conversation. "Some of the delivery trucks have been pelted with eggs, and paint was thrown against stacks of the German paper outside the office. 'Go home to the Kaiser' was the latest graffiti."

"The same is happening in New York, St. Louis, Milwaukee—where our people used to feel comfortable speaking German on the street, not just in the beer hall," Tony said. War instigated by Germany had raged in Europe for two years, ravaging Belgium and France, and showed no signs of ending. "News of the Kaiser's army advancing has got everyone on edge. Some say all German immigrants should be suspected as spies."

"We left all that behind us," thundered Papa. "We are Germans in our memories of the beautiful forests, our churches and food, the music of Beethoven and language of Goethe. But 'our people' are of America now, no other country."

His shoulders and chin dropped as he fingered his knife, knuckles taut. Mama abruptly got up and left the table—she was easily stressed by conflict and would never address it. Magda exchanged glances with Kitty and saw Willa grab Johannes' hand.

MAGDA, STANDING

"If we have to join the war against the Kaiser, I want to be first to enlist," Fred announced, his voice strong and clear.

"Me too," Johannes added quietly.

Tony opened his mouth and then closed it as Sabine abruptly stood, shooting Tony an anxious stare. Willa turned to Johannes and then to Papa with a look of appeal.

"Many of us came over here to escape war and the constant threat of it," their father said firmly, looking to each of them, but especially to Johannes, who hadn't heard his lecture before. "It never settles anything. War feeds on itself and poisons the next generation to fight again—that has been Europe's history. I will not see my sons run into the lion's mouth." With that, he folded his arms over his chest and looked around the table, as if seeking one of them to challenge him. Magda couldn't catch Fred's eye, but she knew what he was thinking. He wouldn't argue with their father here and now, but he would make his own decisions. Johannes said nothing in response to Papa's tirade—but then, he was trying to make a good impression.

Papa had expressed the conflicting emotions—nostalgia and regret—as well as frustration, anger, and fear that followed mention of Germany these days. Magda sensed that her siblings, like herself, couldn't fully share the depth of these feelings, which lingered like a pall over the family and, in fact, the whole German community. Everyone was silent until Kitty brought her strudel to the table, and no more was said about war or politics.

Magda cleaned the dishes with Kitty, leaving Mama to retire upstairs with Richy and Willa to sit with Johannes and their father. Later, in their room together, Willa told Magda that Johannes had asked Papa for her hand.

"You might have told me first it was coming to that!" Magda cried. Although she and Willa hadn't been as close over the past year, Magda felt suddenly sad at the thought of losing her last older sister in the house. "But I like him," she was quick to add.

"Papa seemed to know much more about Johannes than he had let on. Susanna must have been talking to him and Mama," Willa replied. "Papa said he approves as long as we wait a year—oh, that is so Old World! And he wants Johannes to be able to rent a house for us and have some savings besides. If he has to do extra work on the weekends, maybe that will keep him so busy he won't think again of enlisting in other countries' wars. What an awful idea! I'm shocked he even mentioned that, but I can't believe he was serious."

Magda's sleepy "Hmm, hmm," kept Willa talking until they both drifted off.

3

Magda maneuvered the heavy baby carriage to the bottom of her aunts' stairs, stepping hard on the metal brake. She always imagined, in her bed at night, that she would let it go in a moment of absentmindedness and little Richy would careen down the steep slope to disaster. He smiled at her, blissfully unaware.

"If you only knew how unqualified I am for this," she murmured. She lifted him out and set down his solid form as she grabbed the railing to pull them both up the stairs. Everyone said he was big for a two-year-old, with a head of wavy, light brown hair matching hers. Poor thing, she thought, he'll never get it to comb down without pomade.

She was halfway up the stairs when she remembered the bag with his diapers, the talcum powder for his heat rash, and her notepad and textbook. She had left the paper and book in the carriage but realized with a silent curse that the cloths, pins, and powder still sat on the front porch of their house, fifteen minutes away. She was pretty sure Tilly could provide some soft rags and cornstarch if she needed to change Richy, which would certainly be necessary if they stayed through the afternoon. She didn't want to cut her lesson short. Fortunately, Richy had eaten lunch before leaving home and held his pacifier. Tilly would also have milk and biscuits, so they could meet his basic needs for the afternoon.

The aunts had proposed to tutor Magda in the essential subjects to earn her diploma. The plan was that Magda would spend the better part of each day watching Richy, keeping the house tidy, and preparing dinner so that her mother could rest. Magda noticed Mama taking spoonfuls of her bitter, dark brown medicine more often recently. Magda tasted it once when she was much younger—the only time Papa slapped her. It was labeled Laudanum, prescribed as a sleep aid according to her father, and he tried to control when Mama could take it. But Magda knew that Mama didn't wait for his approval and would often get agitated when the bottle was nearly empty, which always happened sooner than he expected.

Many days Mama didn't get out of bed for very long, but her naps and Richy's rarely coincided, so by evening Magda fought the temptation to turn in early herself. She had to stay awake to study and do homework, since the aunts expected her to complete her assignments. She hoped that if she made enough progress, and if the aunts could impress upon her father what a good student she continued to be, she might be allowed to return to school the next year.

Richy was certainly more entertaining than doing the cleaning, washing, or cooking, and Magda hoped that his energy might spark some of the same in Mama.

MAGDA, STANDING

"Come with us outside," Magda would beg her mother. "Let's leave the chores and take him for a stroll. It will do you good!"

"No, you go," Mama almost always declined. She seemed to realize that Magda's good nature had limits that would be rapidly strained by too much focus on housework. The monotony of dusting or cutting vegetables seemed easier for Mama than the active devotion and constant movement Richy required. Between Magda's lack of attention and Mama's lethargy, many of the household tasks were poorly done. Magda was sorry that despite her domestic confinement, she had little opportunity to be alone with Mama when they might have talked—really talked.

"*Hallo ihr Lieben,*" Tilly greeted them fondly as she opened the door. She embraced Richy with a loud and rather wet kiss on his cheek. She always gave Magda a quick hug, too—the only one of her relatives who did so, as it was not the way of the older Germans in her life. Very different from her Italian friends like Lucia, whose family, and in fact anyone visiting their house or who happened into their lives, was kissed at least once.

"I've made dumplings in broth, and you both can have your lunch while we discuss your English homework," Tilly said as she took Richy's hand.

Minnie came into the room and patted his head and Magda's shoulder lightly in greeting. "Ready for your lesson today? And you, my boy: lunch, then a nice, quiet nap."

Minnie believed in the discipline of schedules and planning for everyone of all ages and for all purposes. Magda could only come to the house to be tutored if Richy came along most days, and he still had very simple requirements, including play in the enclosure created for him among chairs and pillows in the sitting room. So far, he was what everyone called a "good baby"—quiet most of the time and easily entertained by his simple toys and books, but he was starting to explore the confined space. Magda thought he wouldn't like being hemmed in for long.

She knew she'd need to pick up the pace of her studies by doing more reading, writing, and math at home with the time left after dinner clean up and Richy's bath. It was fortunate now that she had a bedroom to herself. Studying alone was in some ways more tedious than in school, where she could have shared both the efforts and ideas with her friends, but she could also move more quickly through the textbooks when she was really interested. Thank goodness for Minnie and Tilly. She knew how fortunate she was to have them teaching her privately: Minnie for math, science, and history; Tilly for English, Latin, and civics.

Magda lowered Richy into the wooden high chair her aunts had acquired from a neighbor whose grandchildren had outgrown it. She tucked towels under and behind him for cushioning, and attached the small tray with a leather strap between his legs. Tilly brought out a steaming bowl of soup for Magda, who sat across the table to finish it well out of Richy's reach, while Tilly placed bits of warm dumpling on his tray.

The English lesson for today was a review of the pluperfect verb tense. Magda set her writing assignment on the table and read out several sentences, ending with:

If the girl had gone to school, she would not have married so young.

The baby had died before I was born.

If the baby had not died, the mother would be able to laugh.

MAGDA, STANDING

"Well, quite correct," Tilly said. "You have used the pluperfect appropriately for an activity that precedes another past activity, and to link two conditional phrases." Then she looked up at Magda and raised her eyebrows. "I sense the pluperfect is proving useful in expressing certain thoughts."

Magda gave a crooked smile.

"Life is full of 'what might have been,'" Tilly mused. "Sometimes, as in your sentences here, it is Fate—or as our religion tells us, the will of God—that marks the paths we face and those foregone. And sometimes, it is due to our choices, for better or worse."

She started gathering the empty plates, then continued, "I saw a poem just published a few months ago when I was in the library. It was titled 'The Road Not Taken.' It's by Robert Frost. He's quite a new poet, so I've never taught him before. Let's make that our assignment for this week: you go to the library and look up that poem. Mary will help you find it. Bring the volume back, and we'll focus next week's lesson on it."

Mary Gruber was a librarian and great friend of both Tilly and Minnie. She was one of the few librarians who allowed small children to come in, if the adult accompanying them could be quick and keep them quietly occupied while searching for a book.

"I will telephone Mary and ask her to set aside the volume for you, so you don't have to spend as much time looking," Tilly said as Magda wiped Richy's face and lifted him from the highchair. She had so little time to herself—every action needed to be planned around her little brother. That's what she found hardest about her life these days.

"Maybe Mama will let me leave Richy at home, if I promise not to be too long," she said. They all knew that Magda could spend all day happily lost in the vast reaches of Carnegie Library in Oakland, not even counting the trolley rides.

As she prepared to leave for home a little while later, after changing Richy and packing their things for the carriage, Magda turned to Tilly.

"Was Mama…Did Mama…make a choice she wasn't happy with? Or did she miss something in her life she had wanted—because of Fate?" Her voice trembled. She had never directly asked her aunts anything about her mother before. Mama was so different from them. Minnie and Tilly were never without purpose and always working, always moving, looking ahead. Magda's own sisters were the same, and she knew that she herself could be no other way.

Tilly looked at down at Richy and kissed him on the forehead as she put her arm around Magda. "That will be for another day," she said quietly. "I promise."

On Saturday, Magda went to confession, another family ritual. She did not leave the church mentally soothed or spiritually refreshed, as she was always told she should feel afterwards. Unburdening her thoughts to her aunts provided greater relief. Even if their judgments and demands could be hard sometimes, that was penance she was willing to accept.

The following Tuesday, after her math lesson was over and Richy still napped in the guest bedroom, Magda raised the subject.

"Aunt Minnie, can I ask you a different kind of question?"

"*May* ask, Magda. *Can* means ability, *may* implies permission requested. Of course, you may ask me anything."

MAGDA, STANDING

"Oh, sorry, yes, thank you, I forgot. Well, I went to confession to Father Magnus and told him about how I have to stay out of school, take care of Richy and the house instead. I said that I figured I broke a commandment at least in my heart, although I'm doing my best to obey my parents, but I don't really have a choice." She would have gone on, but Minnie raised a finger to interrupt her.

"And what did he say? Not the penance he gave you, but what did he say about it?"

"He said to 'Live the sacrifice.' That's just great! I feel like Isaac in the Bible story. We're told about his father Abraham putting him on the altar to be slaughtered, and then God finally changed his orders, thank goodness, but we never hear what poor Isaac thought about that."

Minnie's face lit with a smile. "That's an interesting analogy, indeed." She sat back in the rocker and looked out the window, then continued with a quiet tone. "Sacrifice can be a danger-ously pliable concept. Telling someone else their lot in life is a noble sacrifice that they must accept, that they will eventually be rewarded for it—that can lead to mischief." She stopped rocking and looked at Magda.

"But to choose to do something that is difficult, in order to achieve one's own goals—that is good, and necessary, if we are going to make something better of ourselves and our world. What's most important is what we set as our goals, our desires. Ask your-self what really matters to you. And what you need to do, to endure, even to suffer, to make that a reality. That is a good sacrifice."

Magda listened thoughtfully. "I don't know if Father Magnus sees it that way," she said.

"Maybe not," Minnie replied as she rose to the sound of Richy's wakeful cry. "But I would give him some benefit of the doubt. There is only so much advice he can give in the confessional after hearing a few dozen parishioners in one afternoon." She took a deep breath. "And he is a man—your father's age— and frankly, he has no *idea*," she leaned into the last word, "what you've been asked to do. What a woman's domestic life means, if she is unable to decide for herself." With that, she stepped forward and they went into the bedroom together to get Richy ready for the walk home.

4

After a month, Papa increased Magda's allowance to two dollars a week, surprisingly, without her asking. "Mama tells me you have been very helpful with Richy and the housework. I give you an extra twenty-five cents, but you must save it."

He didn't know the extent of her studies, which she mainly did at night in her room, but he considered that she was keeping the house fairly clean and tidy (the corners and under the sofa were something else, but he never looked there). He was content with the meals on the table—and thanks to Kitty cooking larger quantities on Sundays, at least the first two days of the week were covered. Luckily, Papa's work for the dairy helped the family to keep an icebox, so it wasn't necessary to cook every day. Papa didn't complain about leftovers when they were Kitty's cooking—and besides, food was never to be wasted. He took for granted that Richy was being safely tended, and Mama appeared more rested and calmer.

But then, there was the matter of clothes.

One morning, Papa couldn't find a freshly ironed shirt. Magda could see his frustration rising, but she stood her ground.

"Papa, here's one you wore only a short while the other day, it's still good." It would have looked better if he had hung it up after wearing, instead of leaving it in the dirty clothes bin where Richy loved to play. She hoped her father wouldn't notice that the missing button still hadn't been replaced.

"How do other households manage, I wonder?" he muttered. He had learned to curb complaints in front of Mama, who could dissolve with a harsh word. But he often seemed very stressed these days himself.

"They don't put a daughter in charge of everything, Papa," Magda replied, keeping her tone light and voice low, but her tight brow expressed her sharp feelings. She had to hold the line of being respectful while defending herself.

Lucia was the only person who always understood how Magda felt. They had been best friends since first grade and Magda felt closer to her than to her own sisters. Lucia's was a large family with grandparents, siblings, and a cousin who all lived in a house not much bigger than Magda's. They ran a prosperous grocery store and Lucia had met no resistance in going on to high school. There were so many adults in her home, including part-time hired help, that she didn't have to do many chores.

The girls made a plan of meeting regularly at the neighborhood soda fountain on Fridays when Magda didn't have class with the aunts, and Mama agreed to let Magda take the afternoon off. One Friday in July, Magda rushed down the drugstore aisle and saw Lucia sitting primly on a stool.

"Sorry!" said Magda as she slipped onto the seat next to her. "Since I made you wait, this one's on me." She plunked a dime on the counter and flagged the server for two glasses of Coca-Cola.

Although Magda could confide anything to Lucia, she was embarrassed when her drudging life became too apparent and interfered with their brief times together. She had left the house without even changing into a fresher dress, after confirming that Mama would be feeding Richy his supper. She felt so dowdy next to Lucia these days, who always managed to look pert with her glossy black braids and crisply ironed clothes.

Lucia reached out and patted Magda's hands, noticing their roughness with a slight frown.

"Let's think of some help for you," Lucia said. "I can speak to Mabel and maybe she can suggest one of her friends who also cleans houses or cooks. And can you talk to Kitty? Maybe she knows someone, too, since she hires help for the family she works for, doesn't she?"

Magda smiled warmly but pulled back from her friend's soft hand. "Thanks, Lu. But the biggest problem is how to pay them. And my father really doesn't want hired people around the house anyway. He thinks it will upset Mama, and I think he's right. She often sits in a dressing gown half the day and doesn't want to be seen by someone who will talk about her to the neighbors."

This was the first time Magda had revealed that much to Lucia, who had visited her house many times but didn't have much contact with Magda's mother.

"Maybe you can make arrangements on your own for more help outside the house, at least with the rest of the washing. Could you pay with some of your allowance? Then, if you can show your father that things are going better, ask him for another raise?"

Magda smiled at her friend, who revealed the entrepreneurial streak of a shopkeeper's daughter. She would have to think about how to negotiate paying a laundress to take in their clothes. People looked to make ends meet however they could, but all families were conscious of where they stood relative to others and how others viewed them, especially people they knew in the neighborhood, at church, and friends of their friends. Most people in their part of the city had come from the old country—some old country—and were determined to rise to a position of social respect, if not full comfort, in their lifetimes. It was a mark of some success to be able to hire someone, unless help was truly not required, as Papa seemed to think. But Magda was determined not to be taken for granted, even within her own house.

Sooner than they wished, Lucia needed to leave to help her father close the day's accounts at the grocery. "Don't tell our friends . . . about me," Magda whispered, not even wanting to mention what had been painful enough to relay to Lucia the first time she'd seen her after the last day of school. They hugged a moment longer than usual, Magda knowing she could trust Lucia, but wondering what stories would circulate among their peers.

Magda didn't want to give up the rest of her free afternoon, so when Fred came home early, she pulled him outside. "Let's have a little playtime ourselves for a change," she pleaded.

He grabbed his bag of sports equipment from the porch and they headed to the nearest park.

Fred threw the baseball to her and it landed with a satisfying *thwump* into the leather glove. Magda picked the ball out and threw it back to Fred, who caught it handily. They hadn't tossed around a ball for months. In fact, she had very little time alone with Fred these days. Some of her favorite memories were of them playing catch and of him teaching her to ride a bicycle.

"You still have a good arm, *küchlein!*" he said. "But I guess you're not planning to be the first girl pitcher anymore. We'll have to get Richy out here soon and see what he can do."

She gave his shoulder a not-so-gentle whack. Only a few years ago, she could spend hours with Fred on summer days and weekends after school, roaming the wooded lots, joining some of his friends fishing in the river, foot racing, and riding scooters down the hills. Those were her happiest times. Of course, her parents and aunts hadn't been aware of all those activities, and Fred always covered for her when she came home with a muddy pinafore, torn stockings, and hair threaded with twigs. When had everything changed? When Fred left school and started working, and they both became creatures of duty.

"Here," Fred said, gesturing for her to sit next to him on a bench at the edge of the park where the ground sloped steeply. From the bench, they could look out over the bluff to a sliver of the Monongahela River far below.

He reached into his pocket, took out a cigarette, and handed one to her. "Go on, you're old enough!" he said. She picked it up and let him light it. It was her first.

"If I come home smelling of smoke, I hope you'll make excuses for me!" she exclaimed. She coughed and made a face. "You know, I'm the one who has to run Papa's shirts through the extra rinse to remove the smell of his stogies."

"Those are totally different, *mein Liebling,*" Fred said, giving her his eye-twinkling smile.

"Cigarettes will make you look like a modern woman."

"And you the modern man?" Magda replied. "I have other priorities for now. I can't afford to start an expensive habit."

"What do you have to spend your allowance on?" Fred asked, "Assuming father is giving you something for your efforts."

"Nowhere near enough! I can't keep doing so much of the housework, and take care of Richy, and also study with Minnie and Tilly. I have to get help—and I'm going to hire it myself if I have to." She looked away, feeling her emotion rising.

Fred studied her a minute, then put his arm around her. "*Mashi*," he began with the nickname only he used, but she interrupted.

"And that's another thing! I feel like I've been bred to be the family servant. They named me Magdalena, which the sisters always said was a beautiful namesake because Mary Magdalene served Jesus to make up for her sins. I don't have time to commit any."

Fred ground out his cigarette into the grass. "I thought you were named for Papa's mother."

"And it gets worse. I just learned something: Do you know what *Magd* means in German?" Neither of them had studied the language formally, but she was picking up more words and phrases listening to their aunts chat with each other. "Maid-servant!"

Fred started, eyes wide, then after a few seconds threw his head back with a loud guffaw. "That's a good one! I can't believe it!" He held his sides and rolled over onto the grass.

Magda glared at him and stood up abruptly. But she never could resist Fred's ways of flipping her moods, or the temptation to wrestle like they used to. She knelt down, pushed him over, pummeled his back and sat on it till her own hearty laughter shook her off.

MAGDA, STANDING

———

Magda confided to Willa her desire to find someone to wash and iron the clothes. "Ask Elise Freund," Willa suggested, mentioning an acquaintance. Elise lived several streets over and was reportedly taking in laundry because her husband had died suddenly last year. She had a child who was close to Richy's age, so she needed the money.

A few days later, Magda decided to stroll over to the Freund house with Richy on the way back from her lessons. She lifted Richy from the carriage and helped him up to the front stoop.

"Yes?" The young woman stood in her doorway looking surprised and a bit anxious. As she held her son on her hip, the boy leaned down toward them so suddenly he almost slipped out of her grasp.

"Good afternoon, Mrs. Freund. I'm Magda, Willa Augustin's youngest sister. I was just passing and wondered if we could have a short chat?" She handed the woman a package of raisin biscuits that Kitty had baked last weekend. "Here's a little something for your boy."

The woman looked taken aback. "That's very kind. I'm afraid I haven't anything in return. I haven't made anything like that for so long." She reddened.

"I just thought you might like these. Richy and I were taking a walk," Magda tried to sound light and casual, "and I was hoping I could talk to you about something."

"Is there a problem?" Mrs. Freund's eyes darted around. She was clearly unnerved by Magda's visit.

"Oh, no," Magda replied hurriedly. She paused in the awkwardness they both felt. To pursue her question, Magda would have to pretend she didn't see that the woman was trying to withdraw.

"Oh look, the boys are trying to meet each other!" Magda cried, and lifted Richy to the other child's eye level. "What's his name?"

"Martin. I can offer you some tea. If you don't mind, I wasn't expecting company, and the house—"

"Oh, that would be very nice, thank you. We'll wait out here." She had noticed a strong whiff of laundry soap as they stood in the doorway. "Do you want to leave Martin with me while you prepare the tea? The boys can get acquainted!" She knew her voice sounded unnaturally cheery, but she was determined not to lose this opportunity.

In the few minutes she waited for the tea, Magda looked around the front porch and yard. The paint on all surfaces was chipped or faded, the screen door dented, and the two chairs and small table were rusted and covered with dust. The boys circled the table and then reached for the railing posts to pace the periphery. There was no gate, so Magda moved her chair to block the front steps.

She jumped to hold the door as the woman brought out the tea and a small plate of the biscuits. "Here, let me help you." In the light, Magda was surprised to see that she wasn't much older than Willa, but a few streaks of gray showed in her hair and her eyes looked tired.

"I don't want to take a lot of your time, Mrs. Freund, but—" Magda began.

"Please, call me Elise."

"That's a beautiful name!" Magda exclaimed. "Much nicer than Magdalena. I really don't like mine." Magda could have run on with that sore subject, but got down to business. "Well, anyway,

I can't continue in high school this year because I have to stay home to take care of Richy and help my mother with the house-work; she isn't well. But I find it really more than I can handle, since I'm also trying to do my lessons so I can still graduate."

Magda paused to take a quick sip of the tea. She took a moment to reach out and caress both boys, who were sitting on the porch floor watching each other, and nervously cleared her throat.

"I was wondering if you might possibly be willing to take in some of our laundry. Papa's shirts and pants, our skirts and blouses—the things that need ironing. I can only keep up with the small things."

Elise's eyes opened wider. "Your mother is asking this?"

"No, I am. This would be an agreement between us," Magda continued.

"I already have a lot of washing and ironing to do for another neighbor," Elise said quickly, leaning back.

"Maybe I can pay you as much as they do. And my brother could carry the laundry between our houses in the truck he drives for work."

Magda realized that she could be on the verge of offend-ing Elise. Germans didn't usually hire each other to do laundry and other physical chores—that was the role of more recent immigrants or colored women. Magda wanted to be careful not to give the impression she thought herself above the work. But Willa had said she heard Elise owned a mechanical wash-ing machine, which was rare in the neighborhood.

"You see, I need more time and energy at the end of the day to study."

"I left after elementary," Elise replied as she looked down at Martin and placed a small piece of biscuit in his mouth. "Then

I married as soon as I turned sixteen. You're smart to try to continue your studies. You never know what life will have in store for you." Magda imagined she was thinking of the death of her husband, and how difficult it would be to pursue any schooling now, while supporting the boy and herself.

"So, maybe—would you be able to take in the clothes every week—or even ... every other week?" Magda asked, flicking her tongue over her lips. "I could pay you—," she paused, having no idea whether she was about to offer an adequate amount. Her own allowance was hardly a point of comparison for someone outside the family. She should have discussed this with Kitty first, who would know what washer women were usually paid.

"—a dollar-fifty a week?" That was almost everything Father gave her. Elise reached down again to feed her boy another bite of biscuit, and didn't raise her head. Magda knew this wasn't going to work.

"A dollar seventy-five?" She swallowed hard. She would have to get by without spending anything on herself. "And," she added suddenly, fearing that Elise would still refuse, "how about I come by once a week and watch the boys together for the afternoon, to make it easier for you to do the work? That could be good for everybody!" she exclaimed with a burst of slightly desperate enthusiasm. Still no response. "Or ... two afternoons a week?"

Elise gave a very small, quiet chuckle. She settled her eyes on Magda's for the first time in their visit. "I guess we could try it for two months." Her look was less guarded, but it was only when they parted and the boys waved to each other that she broke into a wide smile that lit up her pale face.

Walking home, Magda reviewed her first business transaction. Firstly, the money—she hoped that her father would be willing to raise her allowance yet again in a month, if she could impress on him that his clothes were looking better. She wouldn't reveal that she had negotiated on her own to defer a household task to someone else—he might be impressed, or not.

How would she manage on her now very reduced funds? She didn't have much call to buy things for herself except writing supplies, which were rather expensive. She might appeal to her aunts for those, though she hated to ask them for money. They would appreciate her frugality if she did her writing assignments on used paper.

Minnie and Tilly were relatively comfortable, as teachers who had always worked and saved enough to own their own house. Magda thought the aunts may have helped her parents in very hard times, like when her father lost his job at the mill, but she also knew that it was not in the nature of her older relatives to borrow or lend money even for good purposes, and monetary gifts were also rare except on special occasions. "One has to take responsibility to live within one's means, but also work hard to increase those means," was a favorite saying of her father's. But her family was always generous with their time, and shared goods and services when possible—"charity in-kind," as the nuns called it.

Perhaps that was why Magda had surprised herself with the spontaneous offer to watch Martin. She felt some trepidation about the extra responsibility she had taken on without thinking. Caring for two toddlers was not such a bargain in saving time or effort.

"Let's see how it goes," she said to Richy. "I'll depend on you for ideas and modeling your best behavior."

"Want to play with Martin," Richy replied.

"I'll take that as a promise," she said as she kissed his fat cheek and they hurried home.

5

Magda wanted her friends to find out about her situation on her own terms. She hated the thought of them talking about her when school resumed at the start of September, just a month away. When she ran into Mary Alice after church one Sunday, Magda said with a casual air, "My parents need me to help at home, so I'll be tutored by my aunts for the coming year—well, probably not all year, just temporarily."

"Oh, I'm so sorry to hear that!" Mary Alice had replied, as if expressing grief over a death in the family. Magda didn't want such sympathy and thought that some of their classmates wouldn't miss her much anyway.

After receiving a warmly comforting note from Paulina a few days later, Magda decided to convey her own story not as a disaster but a kind of distinction, so she sent a carefully calculated reply.

MAGDA, STANDING

Dear Paulina,

Thanks so much for your letter! I do miss you, since taking care of Richy and the house doesn't give me time to socialize. I'm happy that you got a chance to visit your cousins in New York.

You asked me how I can do all my duties at home. That's a good question! I give my first attention to Richy, of course, until he goes to bed, and then to my studies with Aunt Minnie and Aunt Tilly. I try to do different tasks at the same time, if possible, and get my family members to help me. For example, yesterday I had to beat the rugs outdoors. Fred agreed to hang them up on the line, since they were too heavy for me. I gave Richy a small rug racquet and I took the other, and I showed him how to hit the rug with me. He had a great time! Afterwards we were both dusty and the rug was not very clean if one looked closely, but I crossed that task off my list. One thing I hadn't anticipated: he enjoyed that job so much he started hitting the furniture inside, and I had to put the racquet out of his reach and explain it was for outdoors only.

CHRISTINE FALLERT KESSIDES

Also, I try to think about my lessons while I'm doing something else. I've gotten pretty good at working out history and English essays in my head while preparing dinner or sweeping. I keep a pencil and paper in my pocket so I don't forget ideas. Then I write the assignment before going to bed. That's not so easy to do with math, since I can't really solve the problems in my head. Sometimes I get so distracted thinking about my homework that I forget to check on Richy. The other day, we were sitting on the porch and while I was looking at the math book, he pulled all the buds off Mama's favorite flower bushes! And he scribbled all over an essay that I had to copy again. I think this is going to get harder. But I hope it will only be this way for at most two terms, and that I can come back to join you all.

Well, I'm sure you don't really want to hear more about my life! Please tell me everything that is happening when school resumes, what you are studying, how the girls are dressing, and who are the couples this year!

Your friend,
Magda

MAGDA, STANDING

Mama watched her fold the note and slip it into an envelope. They were sitting in the dining room—just the two of them and Richy, having already finished dinner—and waiting for Papa to come home. "Do you miss your school friends very much?" she asked.

"Yes, of course!" Magda replied, surprised because Mama rarely asked her how she felt. "It's hard to find time to see each other, and most of them don't have telephones." The Augustin house had a telephone only because Tony and Kitty paid for it to keep in touch with their mother.

Mama rubbed her arms. "I had one very good friend once, back in our village. Her name was Cressa. We had such good times together."

"Oh!" Magda had never heard about this and leaned in closer. "And you had to leave her to come here?"

"She left me." Mama lowered her head, but her face showed no emotion, and her voice didn't change. "Well, it was a long time ago." Mama rose suddenly and went upstairs. Magda saw that a small window had opened and, just as quickly, closed.

On an unusually balmy day in late August, Magda entered the aunts' house, thinking it was rather a shame to spend it indoors on a chemistry lesson. She didn't see either of them inside and walked up to the sitting room window. Richy pointed excitedly at Tilly and Minnie kneeling in the vegetable garden.

"There they are!" he cried.

Magda took his hand and they headed down the basement stairs and out the back door.

"Hello, my dears." Tilly beamed from under her large straw hat. "The classroom is outdoors today. We're going to study acids and bases in the garden."

Puzzled, Magda turned from Tilly to Minnie, who usually gave the science lessons.

"This one's mine," Tilly said, anticipating the question. "I always found a way to give a horticulture lesson to my students, even if it had to be in Latin class."

Minnie rose from her knees stiffly, took off her hat and gardening gloves, and handed a small round trowel to Richy. "I'll happily leave it to you. I'm going to Schutz's for some wurst before he sells out." She tapped Magda affectionately on the shoulder and headed indoors.

"I read the chapter in the chemistry book," Magda said. "But what are we going to do now?"

Tilly took a small packet of paper strips out of her pocket. "I'll give you the section in my gardening book to read later for your report. I forgot to tell you about it before, but I wasn't sure if the rain would stop early enough to let us work outside today. We're going to test the acidity of different samples of soil from the yard, and of fertilizers, and make a chart. We'll look at chemical changes after adding nutrients such as egg whites and coffee grounds. That's useful research for deciding which flowers and bushes to plant in the different soil conditions."

Tilly pointed to a side table where she had arrayed several small glass jars and a pitcher of water. She handed Magda a spoon and demonstrated mixing small quantities of soil and water, marking the jars with a wax crayon.

Magda watched curiously. "But how will we know—?"

"We'll dip these treated strips—litmus papers—into each jar. The papers turn red when soil is more acidic or blue when it's alkaline." She looked at Magda. "You must record every-thing in your notebook."

Magda was intrigued and set to work after tying on the apron Tilly gave her. The yard wasn't large, but each tree or plant stood in a slightly different patch of soil—some covered in fallen leaves, others by acorns, roots, or petals.

Richy dug with concentration, repeatedly filling and emp-tying a small bucket with damp soil. He would need to be washed down when the lesson was over.

"*Tante*," Magda broke their silence after some time as she collected different soil samples in the jars, "What made you think of this lesson?"

Tilly took off her straw hat, rose, and sat heavily on a nearby chair while Magda continued. "Well, it's a long story."

"Oh, please!" Magda cried. "I promise it won't distract me."

Tilly gazed up at the sky. "At our family home, we kept a lovely small garden full of flowers and vegetables. Our mother would tend it with so much love and care. When she passed, I took over. Minnie, too, sometimes, though she was less inter-ested. But after a while the plants weren't doing so well. I was afraid I didn't have the green thumb, as they say here. But not wanting to give up, I made a plan to speak with the agricul-tural agent from our region who visited the villages to advise farmers."

She took off her garden gloves and rubbed her hands, pensively.

"Well, Herr Gunther was a busy man and wasn't very interested in the small problems of an amateur gardener, especially a girl. He cared more that the crops in the region were plentiful enough to feed the people and, of course, the army, and to produce the tax revenues, because he answered to the government. When I went to see him with a small basket of some of my sad plants, still clinging to their soil, there was a young man talking with him. I recognized him as the assistant pharmacist from the next town, Basil Fourmann. We had gotten medicines from him when our parents were sick."

She paused and Magda's ears perked up. This character definitely sounded more interesting than the agricultural agent.

"Basil was a chemist and very clever. He not only mixed medicines, but also provided chemical ingredients for small businesses in our town such as food shops and studied treatments for some plant diseases. The agent was consulting him that day, and they were discussing the results of testing Basil had done in his laboratory." She paused again to hand Richy a glass of water. "As I stood waiting for them to finish, the agent turned his back to me, thinking I was a minor nuisance perhaps, and would go away. But Basil looked at me and saw that I was interested in their conversation, so he drew me in. When the agent left, Basil sat me down, looked at my plant samples, and offered to examine the soil in his laboratory and research the problem if he could."

"And then?" Magda asked, a smile playing on her lips.

"That was the beginning." Tilly sighed softly. "A year later we were engaged."

Magda took a sharp breath and dropped her pen. Richy looked up, startled. "Oh, *Tante!*" she exclaimed gleefully. "I had no idea!" Her delight faded, as Tilly didn't smile. After a few moments, Magda asked, crestfallen, "What happened?"

"I was sixteen when we met," Tilly continued. "Basil was twenty. We planned to get married as soon as he received his full license as a pharmacist. And then . . . what so often happened back in the old country. Even though there was no war at that moment, the new German empire pulled in young men for service in other ways. Basil was promised that if he enlisted, he would obtain his license much sooner and could save money to open his own laboratory."

She paused for several minutes. Magda held her breath and reached her arm out to Richy, who had come over and was pulling her to get up.

"He was not in combat, but assigned to ensure basic sanitary conditions for the troops. Bismarck wanted to keep a large standing army, even after defeating France a few years earlier. Basil wrote me that there was so much to do to keep them healthy. Many of the village boys hadn't been vaccinated even for smallpox, which had killed so many during the last war. He spent most of his time just trying to ensure clean water supplies. He said the greatest risk in war and with any army was not so much bullets or bombs, but disease."

She lowered her head and her voice. "But he couldn't protect himself. He died of dysentery after about a year with the troops. It was so unexpected and sudden he didn't even have time to write to me after he got sick."

Magda reached across and took her aunt's hand.

Tilly's soft eyes filled with tears. "He was my only love. Perhaps a bit unwise, too eager to advance his career, he didn't need to join the army. But he did it for us, so we could marry sooner."

After a minute she stood. "To answer your question, whenever I work in the garden I think of Basil. This lesson always makes me recall the first time we met."

Magda rose and threw her arms around her aunt, and Richy joined in, gripping their legs. As she drew away, she noticed

Tilly fingering the small pin that was almost always on her bodice—a blue enameled cornflower in a gold frame.

Magda touched the pin and looked questioningly. "Yes," Tilly replied. "This was Basil's gift to me before he left, for our engagement. He said the blue matched my eyes."

For the first time, Magda imagined Tilly as a young girl like herself, and wondered what it would be like to carry that kind of love, and pain, for so long.

MAGDA, STANDING

6

The next Sunday afternoon, voices in the Augustin house rose and fell like waves flowing from room to room. On the porch, Anna and Val called out to each other with alternate shrieks and giggles as they played their games. Sabine sat on the swing nursing little Arthur, born in early August. She shushed his occasional cries and soothed or scolded the others gently with her soft voice. Sabine was such a natural, Magda thought. Although these children were Richy's nieces and nephews, the family called them all cousins.

In the kitchen, Kitty and Willa kept up a rapid-fire discussion of the merits of a gas stove compared to the wood and coal-burning ones. The family Kitty worked for owned the latest labor-saving appliances and gadgets, and she was usually a strong advocate, but a recent accident in the news—a woman had been badly burned when her gas stove exploded while she prepared dinner—made some people wary of them. Willa was planning her marital household—mainly a mental list of what she would eventually like to have—and Kitty was a major source of ideas, few of which Willa and Johannes would be able to afford anytime soon. Mama sat in the corner quietly shelling peas, seeming to take little interest in the conversation.

In the sitting room, the men's voices could be heard in a forceful debate. Magda tried not to get tied down in the kitchen so she could gravitate towards the men to listen. She would have simply sat there if it were only her family members this Sunday—despite Papa's quizzical looks, which she read as "Shouldn't you be helping your sisters?"—but Fred had brought home a colleague to join them for dinner, and she didn't want to be conspicuous. She chose to busy herself in the dining room, where she could answer her sisters' calls if needed but still follow the men's conversation while staying partially out of sight.

"The Kaiser will stop at nothing!" Papa declared. "Sinking the Lusitania last year was the worst thing, with so many innocents lost, but our merchant ships are now constantly at risk. I believe he wants to provoke us into the war." The women's voices fell silent. People still talked about that maritime disaster. A German U-boat torpedoed the massive ocean liner and over a thousand people drowned, including many women and children. Most were not Americans, but the ship had traveled from New York and was well known in the States. People still suffered nightmares about the Titanic, only three years before the Lusitania, but at least that was not a deliberate attack.

Suddenly a deep, unfamiliar voice answered her father. "I wish we could stay out of the war, but I fear it will draw us in. Our country is totally unprepared for the battles raging across the ocean. That I know."

Magda started. She had to see who spoke with so much confidence. She stepped into the doorway and caught the speaker's glance as he turned his head. Fred's friend was broad shouldered, with a shock of blond hair and piercing blue eyes.

He continued as if he had heard her question. "I can say that because I was at the Marne in September 1914 as a stringer for the *Pittsburgh Press*. I was attached to the British force. Good thing the Brits had pitched in at that point; the French were badly outmanned, but together they checked the Germans. Their generals, Moltke and Kluck, saw what they were up against. But so did the Allies. The armaments of this war exceed those of all others. Men are being plowed down." The room was silent for a few moments, and Papa signaled to the speaker that he shouldn't continue in that vein with Magda in earshot. As the guest rose from his chair and turned to acknowledge her, she noticed that his right sleeve was pinned up.

"Excuse me, I didn't mean to disturb," Magda mumbled, flushing red. "I need to get some napkins from the hutch." She moved quickly to the high chest along the wall, opened the creaky top drawer, thrust a handful of linens under her right arm without counting them, and pushed it closed with a jerk of her hip—an ungraceful move that she'd been chided for many times, but it was quick and efficient. She was about to run out but instead, turned to the visitor and raised her free hand. "I'm Magda. I'm sorry, I didn't get a chance to meet you when you arrived." Fred reached his long arm around her back and said, "Ah yes, my little sister!"

"I'm Conrad Hecht. Con. Very pleased to meet you." The young man stood at least a head taller than anyone else in the room. He gave her a studied look but smiled with his eyes. He put out his left hand and shook hers.

She decided to sit and join them. She was surprised when Con asked her father, "Were you in the war back in Germany in 1870, sir?" He certainly was self-assured.

"Oh no, I wasn't old enough. But I came of age in the mythology that grew out of it—that Germany was destined to be *the* military power in Europe. We were taught in school to believe nothing less. But, fortunately, there were other influences in my life. My parents wouldn't let me or my brother wallow in dreams created by big heads in tall helmets. I am not well educated, but I knew a man must decide for himself what makes a worthwhile life. And so, I came to America. At that time, we were between wars in Germany."

They all rose as Kitty signaled from the doorway that the meal was ready. The conversation over dinner reflected a concerted effort to steer away from serious talk of the war in Europe or national politics. The young adults politely let Papa direct the discussion, but every subject seemed to gravitate towards the forbidden. Magda knew he wanted to shield Mama especially, but that he thought all the women also needed protection from worrisome news. As if they couldn't read the papers or listen to neighbors in the shops. Magda wanted to know everything. She would find some time to have a separate conversation with Fred.

Since her father seemed in a reminiscing mood earlier, she decided to pursue it. "Papa, why did you leave Germany when you did?"

He hesitated before answering, then looked up from his plate. "Our farm in Blankenbach was too small to support both my brother Rolf and me. When our parents died, I thought I could make it work if I bought some new equipment and seeds. I borrowed money to pay for that, but for two years we had a drought and we made almost nothing. I thought we would do better in America.

"We couldn't get a good price for the land, just enough to pay the creditor and for one ticket to America. We decided that I would come first and save to bring Rolf later. I was almost twenty and Rolf was sixteen, and I knew we could find honest work for our labor. In those days, Germans had to get a permit from the government to leave the country. We were required to put a notice in the paper first—an 'Intention to Emigrate'—so that people wouldn't leave without paying debts. I had paid back my loan, but the lender claimed that I still owed him much more."

Papa seemed far away and his voice dropped.

"Then I decided to leave without the permit. Many young men did in those days. I traveled at night from our village to Hamburg and paid some bribes along the way. But I got on a ship." He stopped to chew a bite of meat slowly.

"I was afraid, even after landing in Baltimore, that German agents would find me and send me back. The money the lender said I owed wasn't so much, but the German government was making examples of people they said flouted the law. I was anxious to get away."

"Why did you come to Pittsburgh?" Con asked. Magda and her siblings knew this part of the story, but the conversation shifted towards the guest now.

"We'd met some people on the ship who were coming here, and a large group of us traveled together—including my wife's sisters. I found work and sent what money I could to Rolf. He paid the man to finally end his claim, but the government records still showed that I had left illegally and we weren't able to change them. Rolf wasn't allowed to emigrate because of me."

"Whatever happened to Uncle Rolf?" Magda struggled to recall the little she had ever heard about him.

"He found a decent job with a factory in our town, and decided to stay. He married and has a family. Two sons and two daughters, the last I heard. He has had a good life, I think, but we've not written to each other for several years. I hope his sons aren't in the Kaiser's army, but they probably are."

With that unsettling thought, the conversation split apart and settled to a low hum as the meal ended. Magda's mind was on what Con had said earlier about the war. He seemed pensive as well. She imagined he must think that small talk didn't matter much when he had seen the fighting up close. She watched his reactions from the corner of her eye, until she found the excuse of picking up his plate. Something about his serious mien made her say out loud what was on her mind. "Were you injured over there?"

"Yes, I was. I wasn't supposed to be a target, but I was in the wrong place at the wrong time."

"I'm sorry!" She felt her face redden and feared it was rude to have asked the question of a near-stranger and guest. Why couldn't she be more tactful and reserved? She should have waited for Fred to tell her later, she thought. Con seemed to sense her regret.

"I don't mind your asking . . . Magda." He paused before saying her name, as if he was underscoring their momentary connection. As if he wanted to remember her. This time, she blushed to her ears, but not from embarrassment. And for the first time, her name sounded good.

7

On the afternoons Magda took care of both Martin and Richy, she was so exhausted that she wondered if she should have offered to switch roles with Elise—at least the laundry didn't throw tantrums or risk tumbling down the stairs. But it was fun seeing the boys' personalities unfold, and she had become friends with Elise. On fair days, Magda watched the boys in the backyard of either house or on the small porches, striving to keep them out of the way when it was too wet to be outdoors. After the first few weeks, Papa had agreed to raise her allowance by another twenty-five cents, most of which she gave to Elise.

"I've been thinking," Magda said to her as they sat down to share tea while the boys puttered with a wooden Noah's ark set that Magda had found in her attic. "Wouldn't it help if my brother Fred came over and repaired your porch gate and the broken parts of the railing, so we could have the boys play there more safely? That would make a better place for Martin when he's playing alone too."

Elise reddened and Magda realized that she had spoken too frankly. "I'm sorry, I didn't mean to criticize. It's just that, well, I'm sure Fred would be happy to help and houses always need something—they're like kids, aren't they?" She forced a chuckle.

"I haven't been able to afford any repairs since my husband passed," Elise said quietly. "I'm lucky we can stay in the house at all. His uncle had left him the house but we still had to take a loan on it, since it was in very bad condition. Alf was trying to replace some roof tiles when," she paused and turned away, "he had his accident. Sometimes I hate living here, thinking that the house killed him. It's only because Alf held a bit of life insurance that I could pay off the loan, but there's nothing left of that now. The house isn't much, but it's Martin's inheritance."

They sat in silence for several minutes. Magda was struck that however often she felt sorry for herself, Elise's life had been more difficult.

"Are your parents living?" Another intrusive question perhaps, but Magda's instinct was to learn more. "Your husband's parents?"

"Not his mother. She passed away before we were married, but his father was kind to us. He bought us the washer for our wedding, thank goodness! But he died the year after Alf's accident. My parents are still in Johnstown. I haven't seen them since before Martin was born. They didn't come to Alf's funeral. They cut me off when I married him. They said I could have done better." With shaking voice, she continued, "A few months after Alf died, they wrote to say they would be willing to take the baby and raise him, but I would never allow that as long as I'm alive!"

"How could parents act like that?" Magda burst out. "I'll never understand that kind of behavior. I think that's worse than anything their child could have done." Too late, she was overstepping again. She should keep such opinions to herself.

Elise smiled slightly and squeezed Magda's arm. "Anyway, it's sweet of you to offer, but I can't be beholden to your brother. And besides, it may be a problem having a man at the house. Neighbors talk."

"He's not a man—he's my brother." They both laughed, and the boys looked up at the sound of their merriment. "Anyway, let me ask him. I'm sure he'll be happy to help. And Richy and I can chaperone, don't worry!"

Fred wasn't at the house for dinner the next two nights, but as soon as he showed up, Magda cornered him.

"Hey, listen, sis," he said, "if I needed help filling my time card I would hire you as a secretary."

"And I might accept, if the pay was good enough. But this is something you could do that helps me help Mama, and helps Richy play with his friend, and you remember what the Bible says about poor widows and orphans, and ..."

"Okay, okay, cut the *schmalz*," Fred sighed.

The next Saturday, Fred spent the afternoon making repairs to the porch and railing. Knowing the boys would be fascinated to watch and want to participate, Magda borrowed a wooden tool set from Tony's children and brought it along. The following Saturday, Fred whitewashed the porch and front stoop. Magda brought some water paints and brushes, but such sedentary play wasn't enough to occupy the boys, and they ran all over the fresh whitewash. To let Fred finish the work, she took them to her house with the lure of candy, where she scrubbed them down.

Bringing Martin back late in the afternoon, Magda found Elise and Fred sitting on the back porch sheltered from the street, chatting and laughing over glasses of beer. The boy ran up and grabbed pretzels from a plate. Magda wished she could have stayed out of sight to enjoy the relaxed pleasure on Elise's face, sparked by her brother's easy charm.

"Magda!" Elise looked slightly embarrassed as she noticed her. "I can't thank you both enough."

"The house looks so bright from the street," Magda said.

"Fred even offered to paint the shutters," Elise replied, "but that's too kind."

"Not a big job," he replied, pouring more beer into their glasses to finish the bottle.

"Save some for Magda." Elise reached out her hand to stop him.

"She's one of the kids," he said with a wink at Magda. "I can come next Saturday to paint the shutters if it doesn't rain, at least the ones in the front, if you decide what color you want."

"I will only accept if you stay for dinner afterwards," Elise smiled. "I haven't cooked for company for quite a while, but I was always told my beef stew and apple pie could win a prize."

"To get my brother to stay out of trouble on a Saturday evening I'll happily keep the boys," Magda added.

"Oh no, you must stay for dinner too!" Elise looked uncomfortable again, and Magda saw that she really had not meant to invite Fred to dine alone with her.

As they walked home, Magda gave her brother a hug. "Thanks for being such a sport," she said. "Elise is one of my few friends these days, and I want to help her. She's had a rough time."

"Tony knew her husband," Fred remarked. "They were in the same class. A swell guy, he says. Really too bad what happened to him, leaving a young family like that. Her boy's a pistol, isn't he?"

Magda smiled to herself. She sensed Fred was gaining more than sympathy for the widow too.

———

Many days, Magda walked to her aunts' house with Richy by slightly roundabout routes to avoid the empty lots and storefronts where her former classmates often played ball or stood around talking. But she would be late for her lesson with Minnie and the weather was threatening rain, so she decided to take the most direct way.

"Hey, Magda!" she heard over her shoulder as she was almost beyond the grassy lot. She didn't have time to stop, but she also didn't want to leave them talking about her without a chance to have her say. The school year had started and she guessed everyone knew her situation by now.

It was Christoph and John. She had known them and their families since first grade at St. Wendelin's. She would have counted them as friends, but with some boys she thought their egos had grown even faster than their bodies. When she was walking with Lucia, it was like old times, but in her present circumstances she felt they would look down on her—even though she had always gotten better grades.

"Where're you headed?" Christoph asked as they walked up. He was now about three inches taller than John or Magda. "I hear you're keeping house like your sister," he smirked. His father was a lawyer and she knew his family kept a couple of servants.

Her breath came more rapidly. "I didn't waste my time this summer. I've been studying all the subjects. I've got a jump on you all."

"Hi, Magda," John called. She felt comfortable talking with him when she saw him at his family's newsstand or at church. She thought he was interested in getting to know Fred and maybe hoped for an introduction to the printing shop. John was nice enough when he wasn't with Christoph.

"What's it like taking lessons with your aunts?" John asked, scrunching his nose with a skeptical look. He knew their reputations in the neighborhood as demanding instructors and strict disciplinarians.

"It's good!" Magda tossed her head with emphasis. "I'll cover the same material as you this year. My aunts picked up the textbooks, and extra ones besides. They give me exams and papers. I can move ahead faster at my own pace." She was determined not to let any of her old classmates, least of all these boys, think less of her.

"Huh." Christoph was always more interested in sports than school, Magda remembered. She thought he sounded impressed, then he added, "Yeah, but are you taking lab classes like us? This week we watched the teacher dissect a frog in biology. Except the girls didn't want to look." He snickered.

"I doubt that," she retorted. "Maybe your own eyes were closed."

"Too bad you can't be part of extra stuff we do, like the math competition," John said. He was a much better student than Christoph, and Magda figured this wasn't an activity they would do together. "It's like a spelling bee but with algebra, and the best students form a team to compete with other schools in the spring. We'll be starting it next month."

MAGDA, STANDING

"I'm not missing anything," Magda snapped. "I've got to go." She looked up to make them think it was the darkening sky chasing her, but her mood was bleak as she turned away and felt her cheeks dampen before any raindrops fell.

Magda raced up the steps of the aunts' house two at a time. She hated to be late, especially on those few days when she didn't have Richy in tow, when her mother or sister-in-law was willing to watch him.

She opened the screen and witnessed a shocking scene. The cat was lying on the mat with a small pool of blood near his head. Tilly, whom the cat favored, stood with her hand covering her mouth. Minnie held her arm around her sister, who looked pale.

"Oh no!" Magda cried as the door fell shut on her back. "What happened to Caspar?"

"He was hit by a car and it threw him onto the sidewalk outside," Minnie said quietly. "The postman saw it and brought the body up here immediately. It happened just a short while ago."

"Poor thing! I thought he was so fast on his feet he could dodge anything."

"We did too," Tilly said, crouching down to stroke the cat's back where the spine was visibly broken. "*Mein armer Kleiner*," she whispered to him softly. My poor little one. "But he was getting up in years and not moving as quickly. He hardly ever brought us a bird or mouse these days." She wiped her eyes. "He was a good cat. We must bury him in the backyard with appropriate ceremony," she said to her sister.

Minnie looked at Magda. "Well, we couldn't have started the lessons on time today anyway under these circumstances."

"I'm so sorry. I left home early, but got a bit distracted when I ran into two of my former classmates. They were sort of bragging, but I told them studying with you is even better than school." She paused as the aunts started placing rags over the blood spots. "I said that I'm learning everything I would in class with the same books and assignments. But—"

"Yes?" Minnie wiped some blood from her hand.

"Well, they started talking about some things they'll do that I'm missing. Like in biology, dissecting a frog in the laboratory."

"Hmm," Minnie replied. She stood rubbing her chin for several minutes. She rolled the cat's body onto a large rag and wrapped him loosely, then carefully picked him up on outstretched arms. "Tilly, would you object . . . I don't think Caspar would mind, if he participated in a special anatomy lesson today?"

Magda looked at both aunts, startled. Surely not! Tilly seemed to understand her sister instinctively. She placed her hand gently on the cat's head and replied, "No, I wouldn't mind, but I will let you and Magda handle that. Caspar was always a curious creature and would understand."

Minnie resumed her brusque efficiency. "Very well. We need to move quickly. Magda, roll up the mat and follow me downstairs. Tilly, can you bring us a few more rags, a pan, and our sharpest knives?"

Magda stared at her aunt. "Do you mean—are we actually—?" It was almost unthinkable. Caspar had greeted her in the house since she was a young child.

Minnie called over her shoulder as she headed down the basement stairs. "Yes, my dear. You will learn more from dissecting a mammal than a frog. And you will have to write me a detailed laboratory report about it. Bring paper and pencils too."

The basement underlay most of the first floor and was as neatly organized as the rest of the house. Shelves of preserved foods, baskets of root vegetables, and items from years of residence and teaching—including boxes labeled by subject and year—were stacked along the walls. A wooden table serving as a general workspace stood next to a large metal washbasin.

Minnie ducked under some hanging sheets that had been brought inside to avoid the rain. She gestured to Magda to pick up some old newspapers from a pile on the floor used to wrap the trash, after directing her away from the collection of issues kept for their content. There was a place and purpose for everything. Magda spread the newspapers under Caspar on the table, and Minnie pulled a kerosene lamp closer for better lighting.

Tilly set down the knives, rags, pencil and paper, as well as a large book. "I found your anatomy text," she said to Minnie. "We don't have any veterinary works, but Magda, you can follow up at the library for that, when you write your report."

"Excellent, thank you, Tilly," Minnie said. Before Tilly turned to go back upstairs, Magda saw her wiping her eyes again. It was natural for both aunts to seize opportunities for instruction, but this lesson seemed too close to Tilly's heart.

"Are you sure, *Tante*?" Magda asked softly. "We don't need to do this." She wondered if Minnie's action was upsetting her more sensitive sister. Magda felt torn with her own curiosity, but it pained her to think Tilly might be hurt by it. She looked at Minnie.

"Of course, Tilly," Minnie said. "You decide."

"It's alright," Tilly said to Magda with a sigh, patting her arm. "It's in the cause of learning. But I'll leave it to you two. I have no problem slaughtering a chicken for dinner, but I want to remember Caspar wearing his coat."

"Then we'll give him a proper funeral afterwards!" Magda exclaimed. She turned back to Minnie, who nodded and proceeded to the task.

MAGDA, STANDING

8

Three days later, when Magda was at her aunts' house for lessons, Minnie lifted a thick book off her shelf. "We'll start this history next week," she said, handing it to Magda. The aunts kept a large collection of textbooks on many subjects, and what they didn't own they could borrow from former colleagues. Magda looked at the title: *Europe from the Middle Ages to the Modern Day, 500 AD to 1900.*

"That's a lot of centuries!" Magda replied, weighing the tome in her hands with exaggeration. "It weighs as much as Richy. Couldn't we maybe just focus on Germany and the US?" She knew Minnie would never take a shortcut in her lessons.

"Well, Richy and the rest of us are products of this history, so it is indeed in our bones," her aunt replied—the closest Minnie ever came to making a joke. "But the German people— we can't say Germany, since it didn't exist as a separate country until 1871, as I think you know—were in the thick of European events. We can, of course, find many instructive examples there, for good and for bad."

Minnie assigned her a chapter to read and related questions to answer. "Write one page maximum per question. Conciseness is key to clear thinking," were her typical instructions. They were practical as well. Since Magda had to meet the aunts' standards for grammar, sentence structure, spelling, and penmanship, one page could take her a full evening of work.

Once a lesson started, it became a lecture, and Magda felt she should be taking notes. She wanted to be serious about her studies and Minnie wasn't easily diverted. But this day was unusually clear and sunny for Pittsburgh. A light breeze had chased away the semi-permanent gray haze, and the air felt as crisp as October apples. They sat on the porch, Richy at their feet playing with a set of blocks that had entertained every child in the family. Magda felt lit from within, her spirits high.

"Aunt Minnie, why did you decide to leave Germany?" she asked.

"Well . . . many reasons. We did not have a bad life in the early years—Tilly and I enjoyed a happy childhood in Sasbachwalden. I remember roaming the deep forests around our little town. That could be somewhat dangerous; people often got lost."

"Did Tilly go with you?"

"Not so often," said Minnie. "She read too many stories about bears and wild boars. But I loved the outdoors and knew my way around.

"The threat we did feel was the heavy hand of the government. Bavaria was surrounded by Germanic kingdoms and duchies that didn't always get along. France held military ambitions, and there were constant disputes with the Austrians. We little people were there to pay taxes and give our young men to the army."

Minnie gazed into the distance. "The big player was Prussia—Chancellor Bismarck. He started wars to consolidate his power and influence. He defeated Austria and France. People like to join a winner, so the rest of the Germanic states, including Bavaria, joined what became the German Empire in '71."

"Was that a good thing?" Magda asked. "What did it mean for you?"

"Not good for us. I turned thirteen that year. Tilly was eleven. Our two older brothers had been drawn into those earlier wars. The war with Austria lasted only seven weeks, but long enough to kill our oldest, Adam. Herman, who was three years older than me, enlisted to fight the French in '70. He thought he was following a noble cause and would avenge Adam's death, but against a different enemy."

She paused, sighing deeply.

"What happened to my Uncle Herman?" Magda asked softly. She had heard about Adam, but didn't remember her mother ever mentioning the younger brother.

"He came back after a few months. He had suffered a head injury, and I think the shock of seeing so much killing damaged his mind even more. Tilly and I took care of him and your mother, who was about seven at the time. Later that year, he drowned while swimming in the river. We were never quite sure that it was an accident. He wasn't in his full mind."

"And your parents?"

"They ran a small bakery, as you know. They had both contracted tuberculosis in earlier years, but got sicker as they aged. Papa passed away just before Adam went to war, and our mother shortly after."

"You mean you became the head of the family—at thirteen?"

"Yes," Minnie answered matter-of-factly. "That wasn't unusual in those days."

"That must have been so hard for you! And then you decided to leave?"

"Oh no, not yet. We were too young to think of that. I went to work at the local school where Tilly and Sarah were enrolled. I was an especially good student and had just graduated, so the headmaster hired me to teach the younger children. Our father's brother, Constantin, took over the bakery."

"You and Tilly couldn't have kept the bakery? She makes wonderful breads and cakes!"

"In those days, it wasn't possible for children, especially girls, to inherit a business. Uncle Constantin didn't know much about being a baker, and he gambled. After a couple years, he closed the shop. And because he had his own family, he didn't give us much help after that.

"Tilly joined me at the school. We made some extra money helping other shopkeepers in the village with their accounts, and Tilly did sell cakes on the side. But it was a lean time."

She looked at Magda. "You see, your mother didn't have the same carefree childhood that I had. Or," she added, "that you have had."

Magda didn't feel that her childhood had been entirely carefree. But she didn't want the story to end, especially on that note. It was so rare to get Minnie talking about herself, especially her past. She took the chance to press further.

"But finally, you and Tilly did decide to leave. And not with Mama."

MAGDA, STANDING

"Tilly and I qualified as primary school teachers. By the time I was twenty-two and Tilly was twenty, we decided to open our own school with the support of our church, for children of the parish. But then the long arm of the Prussian bureaucracy got in our way."

She leaned over to pick up Richy, who was getting restless, and put him on her lap, rocking vigorously. Magda held her breath, afraid of making a further move that might interrupt the rest of the story. Minnie rested her head on the back of the rocker, then resumed.

"You may have heard your father mention the *Kulturkampf.*" Magda shook her head and her eyes widened. If her parents had discussed it—whatever it was—it would have been in rapid German, which she often tuned out.

"It was a political clash between the Prussian authorities and the Catholic church. Chancellor Bismarck invited the southern states to join the Empire, but he couldn't leave well enough alone, of course. Most of us were Catholic and the northern states, especially Prussia, were Protestant. That became a problem when his meddling bureaucrats decided they could tell the Catholic church and school officials whom they could hire and what they could teach. Well, I was willing to go head-to-head with our local priest and even take on the bishop, if necessary, but I wasn't going to be pushed around by *die Nichtswisserin* in Berlin. Ignoramuses!" she exclaimed, with a vigor that made Richy turn around and stare at her, grinning.

She stood and put the boy's hand in Magda's. "Oh dear, we should be careful what we say. I hope he won't start calling someone that name. I think he is ready for home soon, and you too." Her transformation from young woman back to headmistress was complete. "I'll walk with you as far as the trolley stop. I may meet Tilly there; she's coming back from town soon."

Magda wanted to learn more. "Aunt Minnie, are you afraid of anything now?" Some people found Minnie to be daunting, a word Magda learned from the vocabulary list Tillie had given her the previous week. Daunting meant "tending to overwhelm or intimidate." But Magda felt a better word for her aunt was dauntless—"fearless and bold."

Mama, on the other hand, seemed to find her life daunting.

"Now, why do you ask?" Her aunt looked at her quizzically.

"Because I can't imagine what it would be."

Minnie cocked her head as she buttoned her coat. She raised both hands to replace locks of gray hair that had slipped from her bun, then bent down to fasten Richy's shoes.

"I think I have been afraid of different things, at different times of my life," she mused. "I never feared risks from the natural world—at least, not until the sea crossing. Our ship encountered one of the largest storms to strike the North Atlantic in 1875. I'll never forget those hours. Waves rose over the ship, and at one point it was almost standing on end." She raised her hand to her chest as if to calm her heartbeat.

"Our quarters were in the third-class compartment, deep in the ship, and we could barely afford that. I felt safer standing nearer to the bridge above deck, to watch the storm. I always felt that I wanted to look straight at whatever threatened me, not let it catch me unaware. But the crew wouldn't let us topside, as we could be blown overboard. They locked the doors, reportedly to protect us and limit the flooding. We would have never had a chance to escape if the ship overturned. But we made it through." With a sudden shake of her shoulders,

Minnie returned to the present and Magda exhaled the breath she had been holding.

"How terrifying! But is there anything you fear now?"

"Well," Minnie took the question and rolled it over as if she were framing another lesson. "I believe that we are most afraid of the unknown. And once we grapple with understanding whatever it is, examine it in the light—or look whomever it is in the eye, and listen to them—we can often overcome the fear. Or, if we can't fully overcome it, we'll have a better idea how it may threaten us—or not—and how to face it."

Magda thought that Minnie's way sounded like simply not being afraid at all. "But what about," she pressed, "something that may come into your life in a way you can't control?" She took a deep breath. "Like Mama getting sick again and having to go back to the hospital while Richy is still so little and hardly knows her."

Minnie stopped and stroked Magda's cheek with a touch of her index finger. "We would still try to learn as much as we can about it, and prepare as best we can. And if we can't confront something to change it, then it is something we must accept. Sometimes that's the only way to deal with fear."

"But that's just the thing. I don't understand what's wrong with Mama."

Minnie didn't answer but sighed deeply. Magda didn't know if Minnie couldn't, or wouldn't, explain. She was clearly more comfortable in a teaching mode, not expressing the personal or emotional. But, as they reached the trolley stop, Minnie spoke again with a burst of passion.

"These days what I fear most is something beyond our reach. I'm afraid of the Kaiser's war—that this time, our new country will be drawn into it. War is the thing that terrifies me. Whatever the circumstances, it is beyond comprehension. Beyond acceptance."

———

Richy's hand tore out of Magda's as he raced up the steps to the house. Fred and Con were sitting on the porch, beer steins in hand. Richy had gotten to the stage where he preferred their company to women's. Magda was fine with that. But she would have liked to slip in at the back of the house. She felt disheveled from their walk and her skirt was dusty. She knew her face was reddening even more from seeing Fred's friend without warning.

"Hello, Magda." Con stood and nodded to her. He had a way of being formal and polite, yet familiar. "I haven't had a chance to tell you that I really admire your studying on your own. I know that's hard."

Magda tilted her head slightly to acknowledge his compliment, without knowing what to say. Was he teasing her?

"Thank you." She looked aside. "Oh, Richy! Fred!" Magda grabbed the boy, who was sipping Fred's beer. "Fred, how could you let him?"

"He's thirsty," Fred laughed.

"Here, little fellow, let's see if I can pick you up." Con stretched out his arm and as Richy grabbed on, Con raised it level with his shoulder and swung the boy carefully back and forth. Richy giggled and kicked in the air.

Was he showing off for her? He was very self-confident, but not in the way of the boys she knew.

He set Richy down gently. "That must be very tiring," she said, then regretted that she'd pointed out his disability.

"Not really. I like to make the best use of what I have left." He grinned at her, and Magda blushed again. "The calisthenics they gave me in the hospital are boring. I'd rather make a little fun out of it."

"More! Again!" Richy cried. Con swung him several more times.

"Now say thank you. Mr. Hecht has been kind; you need to get inside for dinner." Magda gave Richy a gentle push towards the door.

"Let me know if I can help you study sometime," Con said. "I actually finished my high school exams after returning from France, while I was recuperating. I had left before the last term, in '12, to work for the paper. But I wanted to get my diploma too." He swallowed the last of his beer. "I wouldn't be much help with the math or science at this point, I'm afraid. Forgot most of that. But my English is good if I do say so myself, and I think I can handle history and government questions. Not bad in geography either."

Was he bragging? But why would he bother? He certainly didn't need to impress her. Magda didn't know what to say. She could use someone to quiz her, and it would be nice to have company. But he was Fred's friend. Almost seven years older than her. He was just being kind.

If he worked with her, she would have to fix her hair and change out of her housework dress just to study. She would get even more upset with herself if she missed questions, because what would Con think of her? No, she couldn't let herself get derailed by anybody. But she would like to learn more about him too.

"Thank you for offering. Maybe sometime . . ." she murmured, sounding more flustered than she felt.

She had forgotten Fred standing in the corner of the porch. "Go on, then!" he urged. "I can recommend Con as a good teacher and Magda as a good student. Con taught me poker and I taught Magda everything she learned before she started school, and all the really useful things after that. Just don't study together on our game nights." Magda glared at him.

Con laughed. "I don't have sisters or brothers," he said gently. "And my parents passed away when I was in elementary school. I don't have anyone to tease or to tease me." He paused to pick up his hat and waved to Fred. "It's my pleasure to visit your family, and I'd be happy to help you if you want." He lowered his head to look at her intently, smiling but obviously sincere, and she almost forgot to breathe.

9

Sometimes on Saturday mornings, Magda rode with Richy on the trolley to spend time with Kitty in her employers' house on Mount Washington when the family was out. Then the three of them would ride back home together. Magda loved exploring the house discreetly, performing a task such as refreshing the flowers in the vases, which gave an excuse to look into most of the rooms. Many of the staff were given either Saturday or Sunday off and left the house as soon as they could, but most came back at night to sleep in their attic rooms. The kitchen alone was almost as large as the whole first floor of the Augustin house. There were multiple porches and balconies, fireplaces in every room, and tall ceilings with crystal chandeliers.

She kept a close watch on Richy, who could break the knick-knacks or simply get lost in the many spaces. On rainy days, they sat together with Kitty in the kitchen while she prepared the lists of menus for the week, organized the bills, and prepared the cash payments her employers gave her for the grocers and other purveyors, and for the junior staff.

Kitty had clearly inherited the aunts' efficiency and apparent ease with their work. She was respected and trusted, and skilled at her profession. Magda admired her elder sister and wanted to be like her in all these respects—but not as a housekeeper, no matter how impressive the setting.

"How's it going?" Kitty asked as she turned over the last invoice. "You seem to be managing well, even with Richy. I'm impressed that you've kept up studies with Minnie and Tilly. That must be challenging. I didn't attempt that when I was taking care of you."

"What do you mean, taking care of me?" Magda replied, puzzled.

"I guess you don't remember. It was from a few months after you were born until I turned sixteen and came to work for this family. Mama was in the hospital for part of that time. While she was there, Tilly and Minnie would come to the house after their school day—mainly Tilly, who also took time off from teaching to stay with us. I think that's why she didn't get promoted to principal later. She taught me most of what I know about cooking."

"You didn't go on to high school because of me?"

"Partly . . . things were bad then, when Papa had to leave the plant for his lungs. If it weren't for our aunts, I don't know what we would have done. They supported us. And it wasn't just you. You were an easy baby—not as active as Richy. I also had to walk Fred and Willa to school and back, and fix their breakfast and lunch while the aunts were at work. I didn't have to help them with homework. Minnie or Tilly would do that when they came over. All of us learned more than our lessons back then."

Magda sat quietly. "I never thought about it before—that I wasn't the first one Papa made leave school."

"No, but I didn't really mind. It's what I do now, and I like it. Although, I don't have to watch young children anymore. And Willa and Fred helped."

"Fred?" Magda asked. She didn't recall him ever doing household chores.

"He let you play with him and his friends when I was busy."

"I thought they wanted me to play with them!" Magda cried indignantly. "I kept up with them pretty well."

Kitty laughed. "Yes, you did. You always thought you were one of the boys." She looked at Magda sympathetically and took her hand. "I know it's difficult for you now—you're much more alone in your work at home than we were, and Richy can be a handful." They looked over at him as he rearranged potatoes, oranges, and apples among baskets on the floor and then rolled them like marbles one by one under the tables.

"Can you convince Papa to get me some help?" Magda asked. "Because continuing with school work is the only thing that I have for myself. I'd go crazy without it! But I need more time."

Kitty nodded. "I'll see what I can do." She leaned over to start collecting the fruit and vegetables underfoot.

"And, Kitty," Magda pressed, "I wish I understood Mama better. No one has ever told me anything. What's wrong with her? Why is she always so quiet? I think the laudanum makes her more so. What was she in the hospital for?"

Kitty looked down and sighed. "I don't really know either. And I don't think Papa understands it. Melancholia, that's all I ever heard anyone call it. An excess of melancholia. A beautiful-sounding word for sadness that won't go away."

The postman's footsteps on the front porch and the creak of the box outside as he left the mail were favorite sounds for Magda and Richy every afternoon. For her, letters were infrequent but much anticipated connections with girlfriends she rarely saw. Richy was fascinated by the postman's uniform and sack, and he always ran to the porch to greet him. She had discovered a game they both enjoyed: she would put some envelopes or papers in a small bag, place one of Fred's hats on his head, and tell him to deliver the mail around the house. He usually slipped them between the chair cushions or under the sofa, and then called to Magda to get them. The game was one of their favorites until Richy picked up the actual mail one day and hid the water and electricity bills under the carpet. Papa had a fit when he missed the due dates and had to pay a late fee.

Magda was thrilled to see a note from her old friend.

Dear Magda,

We missed you at Margaret's garden party last week. Her family's new house is amazing! They have windows across the front reaching almost from floor to ceiling, and as the day was warm, they opened them, and it felt like we were sitting outdoors. There is a balcony all around the house on the second level, and she showed us that she can step out from her bedroom—like in Romeo and Juliet! They have a long winding driveway, and their driver picked us up and drove us home in their LaSalle.

MAGDA, STANDING

I miss you in class even more. The days are long without my dear friend there to share notes and stories. And how I wish we could study together. Math this year will be the bane of me.

Mama says I can have a birthday party next month and invite anyone from the class—even the boys—but I'm not sure I want to. Look for the invitation in the mail!

Hugs and kisses,
Paulina

Magda bit her lip. She hadn't been invited to the party, which didn't surprise her. She was never close to Margaret, especially since her family had moved to Shadyside and she enrolled in a new private school there. Magda had heard that area was full of wealthy people and big houses. What could she have worn? She was tired of her best dress and owned nothing fashionable enough.

She would feel worse when she turned down Paulina's invitation. She needed some way to keep up with her old friends without feeling left out.

Minnie and Tilly came by the house to visit Mama most weeks, usually on Friday afternoons. Magda made a particular effort to clean the most visible parts of the house beforehand—dusting the bric-a-brac in the sitting room, scrubbing the sink in the kitchen, and wet-mopping the dark wooden floors that weren't covered with area rugs. Sometimes, she chose to stay and take part in the conversation, if Lucia wasn't free to meet her. It had

CHRISTINE FALLERT KESSIDES

become harder to make plans with other friends, since she felt increasingly distant from them as the school year wore on. It seemed forced if they asked her to join them for shopping trips to town or other outings—and such invitations were few. She didn't have money to spend on herself anyway.

When Papa came back from the milk deliveries, he sometimes joined the women's conversation for a while, although he usually preferred to go out and meet his own friends at one of the local *bierhallen*. Magda hoped the aunts would say something to him about her diligence in her studies, and how much progress she was making. She didn't need to ask them, since she knew they were pleased with her efforts, which reflected well on their skill as teachers too. It would give her satisfaction if he recognized that she hadn't allowed anything to hold her back.

This day, the aunts arrived carrying a favorite food of Mama's, *sauerbraten*, that Tilly had made. Tilly put the covered dish, wrapped in towels to keep it warm, on the table, and Magda put out four place settings.

"*Wirst du mit uns essen, Josef?*" Minnie invited Papa to join them. Usually, the adults would relax into German when they were together, and Magda understood most of it. Tilly pulled a tall, dark green bottle of white wine out of her canvas bag. "We're celebrating that Magda has completed a term's worth of work. At this rate, she'll finish high school ahead of her classmates." Tilly gave Magda a small wink.

"*Nein, danke,*" Papa replied absentmindedly as he put on his coat and prepared to leave. "Of course, we're very proud of our girl. She can do anything she sets her heart on, I'm sure." That was a high compliment from her father, although Magda wasn't convinced that he believed it.

MAGDA, STANDING

As the women sat down, Tilly started to serve the food, saying excitedly, "I've gotten all the details regarding the suffrage meeting tomorrow evening in town. Sarah, you must come with us. Magda has been studying the Constitution and the process of amendments for her civics lessons. This is an excellent opportunity for her—and for all of us—to hear from the president of the Pennsylvania Women's Suffrage Association. Even though the referendum was defeated last year, they haven't given up. It will be well-attended—we must leave early enough to get good seats."

Papa, who had almost reached the door, called out from the hallway, "What's that you say, Tilly?" He reentered the kitchen and stood over them. "I don't want my wife and daughter attending any suffragist events. Those have attracted a bad element, and even some of those women speakers are not well-behaved."

Minnie looked directly at him. "Josef, there's safety and power in numbers, and more so when the cause is just. You cannot deny that the vote for women is deserved and that time is on our side. Why, the reform has even been widely supported back in Germany, as you know, and when the day comes for a republic—hopefully even sooner once that awful war ends—women will get the vote there too. In the meantime," she poured a glass of the wine and handed it to him, "we're making ourselves well-informed and aiming to educate the rest of you. This country will depend on its women even more if we are dragged into war."

Papa's mustache twitched. He looked down at Mama. "Sarah, do you want to do this?"

She replied softly, "Josef, it might be nice to go out with my sisters and Magda. If I feel well enough tomorrow."

Papa swallowed the wine in one gulp and set the glass down. He opened his mouth to say something more, hesitated, then turned away to walk quickly out of the house.

Magda felt proud of her mother for speaking up to Papa, although she rarely went out. The women clinked their glasses in a toast to Magda's progress. She reflected on her aunts' way of making their views prevail: being prepared, knowing the facts, and not giving ground to blanket resistance.

—

The next weekday, as Magda entered the aunts' house for her regular math lesson, she asked, "Aunt Minnie, do you know the math chairman at the high school? I heard he started a competition. Do you think I could ask to participate? If I did well, it would be a feather in your cap too. You're such a good teacher! The winning team will get a small financial prize and might even travel to another city."

Richy ran over to Tilly, who took him out on the porch as Magda sat down at the dining table and opened her math book. Minnie stood, hands on hips.

"My, aren't we ambitious," she chuckled lightly. "Pursuing distinctions for both of us now?"

"Well, I thought ... maybe it would be a good way to study the lessons anyway, and ... I just wondered ..." Her words got softer and slower as she felt she might be overstepping again. The aunts were already doing her a great favor, and it really wasn't Magda's place to ask for more.

"It's not outside the realm of possibility," Minnie replied after a few minutes, as she sat down across from Magda and picked up her assignment paper. "I do know Harold Kreutz. In fact, I hired him for his first teaching job. I can ask him to share the coaching syllabus for the team. If it's on material we're already studying, we could do this. But you'll have to be tested by him. Once you qualify," she looked over her reading glasses with a firm set to her mouth, "—and of course you will qualify—you'll also have to find a way to practice with the team. It will be quite a commitment."

"Oh, yes!" Magda jumped out of her seat and gave her aunt a kiss on the cheek. Already, she was imagining the excitement of sitting among the winners. It would erase the embarrassment she felt having to leave school. She could tell that Minnie was energized by a competitive challenge, too, although she hardly needed the recognition.

There would be the matter of finding a way to extract more time out of her days. She would think about that on the way home.

⁓

The next Friday, Magda met Lucia for a stroll to window-shop and, as a rare treat, to see a short film at the nickelodeon. Magda told Lucia that she planned to compete in the math bee and that, regrettably, she would probably have to devote most Friday afternoons to preparing.

"Even so, I'm glad!" Lucia exclaimed. "I know you can do it. We girls need some potential winners to represent us."

"What will the others think?" Magda asked, chewing her lower lip.

"Oh, I expect Henry won't be happy for another star on the team," Lucia laughed. "But who cares? As long as he's captain, he can't complain. Most of the other students don't pay much attention and just think of it as a boring club."

"Does anyone say anything about me these days?"

"Well," Lucia sipped her drink and didn't look up, "some girls—I think you can guess who—say that you don't have time for your old classmates, that you think you're better than us, and will just want to show off to everybody."

Magda tossed her head and crossed and re-crossed her legs under the café table quickly, bumping it hard enough to make her Coca-Cola splash. Lucia reached across and grabbed her hand. "Don't let them bother you."

"I don't!" Magda retorted. "Still, if they only knew. How snooty can a housemaid be? I'm not the one who has a new dress for every holiday and gets driven around in a car."

"You're not a housemaid!" Lucia cried. "I always tell them that you're studying as much as we are, and that you'll probably join the class next year. That usually shuts them up."

"Actually, Aunt Minnie and Tilly say that at the rate I'm going, studying all year, I can probably graduate before the class. Won't they think I'm stuck-up then!"

"I think you should do whatever you want to do, and don't think about them at all."

Magda had to admit that she did think, often, about what her old classmates were doing and how they would view her everyday life. She didn't want to care, but she did. And she cared a lot to show them—and the teachers—how much she had achieved in her studies and that she was as smart and accomplished as the best of them.

These thoughts were not very helpful when she was struggling to learn a new lesson with little time and sleep. They did energize her when she was pushing a broom and scrubbing the pots. "This isn't the me I'll show them," she whispered. "They'll see."

10

Magda heard a loud commotion out in the street in front of the house. She ran to the window and parted the curtain. Her parents were standing on the lower steps, her father's arm tightly around Mama. Officer O'Grady was on the sidewalk, writing in a notebook. Several neighbors and people she didn't know were gathered around him.

Magda stepped out of the house and stood on the porch. Fred, who had the day off and had slept late, followed her and ran down to the sidewalk.

"Tell me exactly what you heard," the policeman said to one of the bystanders. "Can you describe the persons? How many were there?"

Papa turned around and saw Magda and Fred. "Take your mother inside," he said, soberly. Magda ran down and took Mama's arm, then walked with her into the house.

"What happened?" Magda asked. Her mother shook her head and Magda could see tears in her eyes. Mama let Richy run to her, but turned around to watch the people outside as Magda returned to stand with Fred. Papa talked longest to the officer, but the others added confirmation and details of what they had seen. Their father had taken Mama to a doctor's appointment in town and when they boarded the trolley to return home, a group of young men followed them. Hearing her parents speaking German, as they usually did with each other, the young men started jeering: *Go back to Germany! Your Kaiser wants you, we don't! If you drag us into this war we'll attack your houses. We know where you live! Get out of town!*

One of the culprits spat at them and another threw a lit cigarette at Papa before the group ran off the trolley when it stopped at the next block. A neighbor, Mr. Gruen, who had also been on the car, gave the best description of the perpetrators. He thought they weren't from the area and had been looking for ways to cause trouble for German residents. After several more minutes, the officer closed his book and promised to file the report promptly. "I'll ask at the station for more police to watch the trolley routes in this neighborhood," he said kindly. "It's fortunate I was there when you disembarked and that we have other witnesses. We'll find the rascals!"

Fred and Papa slowly climbed the front steps and entered the house. Papa went to Mama and enclosed her in a tight embrace as she continued to cry softly. Magda saw again how gentle and protective her father could be. He treated his wife almost like a child. "*Wir sind in Sicherheit, meine Liebste,*" he whispered, rubbing her head softly with his chin. We're safe, my dear one.

"This is happening all over the country," Fred fumed. Papa gave him a fierce look that said *Not now, not around your mother.* Fred motioned to Magda to follow him outside.

"Did Papa say what he did when the man spat on them?" she asked.

"He tried to brush the cigarette off his coat, then the bastard was gone. He didn't want to leave Mama sitting alone, anyway."

"What can we do, besides avoid speaking German in public?"

"We're not going to hide who we are. You stay with them," he called over his shoulder, "I'm going to look into this myself."

"Fred, that won't help—it'll just cause more trouble!" she pleaded. He was already running to the trolley stop a block away.

Later that day, Magda took Richy for a walk while Mama rested and headed straight for the aunts' house to relate the event. They shook their heads, worriedly.

"Oh, poor Sarah," Minnie said. "That was like the 'Germans Go Home' graffiti I told you about, Tilly, painted on Shutz's shop window. People are afraid, looking around for enemies, and some want excuses to fight."

"I'm really concerned about Mama." Magda's brow furrowed. "She's so distressed much of the time for no particular reasons I can see—and now this attack! She certainly didn't deserve that."

"We should go see her right away," Tilly replied. Both of the aunts rose and quickly put on their coats. Tilly picked up a loaf of fragrant rye bread she had made that morning to bring along.

"We'll take the car," Minnie said. The aunts had bought a Ford in the latter years of their employment but rarely took it out, preferring to walk the half-mile or so to most shops and Magda's house, or to take a trolley. The automobile signified important trips and was at the entire family's disposal. Magda sat in the back with Richy on her lap. Minnie drove in silence.

Papa was sitting in the living room, his head lowered to the German newspaper on his lap. He hadn't turned any lights on despite the growing dusk. Magda thought he was dozing, but he rose shakily as they entered. Minnie and Tilly each put a hand gently on his shoulders and murmured quietly.

"Thank you for coming. Sarah is resting. The doctor gave her a stronger sleep medicine when we saw him this morning, and she has taken it." The lines on his face were deeply drawn.

"People are increasingly afraid of war, as are we all," he continued, "and I try to be understanding. But this was simply aggression; shiftless youth playing at war. Against Sarah, of all people." His voice broke.

Tilly made them tea and brought out her bread with cheese. Minnie opened a bottle of cordial and poured each of them a small glass. Magda sat with Richy at the dining table, feeding him small bites with milk, from a seat where she could watch and listen to the conversation.

"What did the doctor say this time?" Tilly asked her brother-in-law.

Papa looked over towards Magda, shaking his head.

"Josef, I think Magda should be told, she is old enough and is helping to keep your household," Minnie spoke firmly.

Magda strode over to her father and kissed him gently on the cheek. "Please, Papa, I want to understand."

Slowly, his words cut through the silence in the room. Sarah's mental state—her melancholia—was getting worse. They all knew it, and her physical condition was becoming a concern as well. She was losing weight and had no energy to dress, bathe, or even to leave the bedroom most days. He was not sleeping in their bedroom, trying not to disturb her, but she often didn't sleep. He would find her wandering the house in the middle of the night.

"The doctor wants to commit her again," Papa sighed deeply.

"W-what does that mean?" Magda stammered, looking at the three of them.

Minnie replied to her. "Your mama had to go away, to Mayview State Hospital, on three occasions. First, after your infant sister died, in '90. She was there more than a year. Tilly and I moved in here and took care of Tony and Kitty. And then again, when we lost little Christian, the year before Fred was born. The third time . . ." she looked to Tilly.

"When you were about four, I think," Tilly said.

Magda's eyes widened. She had heard people call Mayview an insane asylum. "But I thought Mama had been in a hospital for tuberculosis! That's what you all told us."

Papa shook his head and looked sadly at Magda. "I'm sorry, but we didn't want people to know that your mother was in a mental institution. The first time, when she lost the baby, we could make excuses. Even the second time—"

Magda protested, "Couldn't people understand how sad Mama must have been?" She felt defensive of her but checked her voice as it rose, for fear that her mother would hear.

The aunts and her father sat quietly for several minutes. "We were all very sad, of course," he answered, "but your mother couldn't function afterwards . . . can't function, still."

"Well, what can the doctors do?" Magda persisted. She had always known in her heart that something was terribly wrong with Mama, but never felt she was allowed to ask. She looked to the three of them, each seeming to wait for the others to respond.

"It's her nerves. There is no medicine for that," Tilly finally replied. "In the hospital they made her rest and take therapeutic baths. It seemed to help a little."

"Medicine can suppress the feelings," Minnie said. "Tincture of opium—her laudanum." Her voice assumed a cynical tone. "Some of the doctors blamed her state on 'female troubles,' which is often an excuse, I think, when they just don't know. Some of them don't even see it as a problem for women to be so quiet and passive."

Magda's eyes grew wide. "That medicine is opium? She's taking it more often than she used to, I know. It calms her down too much, I think." She addressed her father this time.

He didn't look at her in reply. "It is supposed to help with her moods and her languor, which the doctors said were caused by a female condition that would go away as she left the childbearing years. But after Richy, she got worse." He looked embarrassedly away from the aunts as well. Such things weren't talked about.

"Josef, what are you going to do now?" Tilly finally asked. "Did the doctor say they would have to continue that medication? I have wondered sometimes if it was worse than the disease. She seems to have grown dependent on it."

Papa shook his head, lifted his hands and rubbed his neck. Magda had never seen him look so forlorn.

Suddenly, they heard steps on the floor above and a door open. Papa rose quickly and went to the stairs. He turned and gestured to Minnie and Tilly to follow him.

"Not you, Magda. Please stay down here with Richy." The boy had left the table and played at their feet, watching their faces.

Magda started to protest, but suddenly from the corner of her eye she saw Fred pass the side window to the back of the house. She opened the kitchen door and gasped.

"What happened to you?" Blood ran down the side of his face and his right eye was almost swollen shut.

"Don't worry, this is nothing," he said gruffly, grabbing a towel. "I found those creeps. I was pretty sure who they were and checked three other stops along the line. Mick Morrison, Matt McFail, and Ben Withers."

"How did you know them? And you took on all three of them yourself?" Magda asked, as she washed his cuts with soap and water. "Hold still!"

"They've been causing trouble for months. No, not alone. I picked up Paul and Pete Graf on the way—they were happy to help. Paul works out by boxing, he got in some good ones. Those bastards won't be harassing anyone again, the cowards. We made sure they'll have some scars that everyone can see."

"So will you," Magda said wryly. "Too bad, you used to be handsome." She gently tugged at his ears and hugged him.

Minnie entered the kitchen with a tray of empty teacups. "Fred, my goodness! What have you been up to?"

"Executing justice, *Tante*." He tried to grin and wink, but grimaced instead. "Matt McFail will carry the print of my fist on his nose for what he did to our parents today."

"That boy has been a bully since third grade," Minnie replied. "I had to give him a firm comeuppance more than once, and I was only too happy when his father, who wasn't much better, pulled him out of my school. But you shouldn't be stooping to their level. Did you report them to the police?"

"No," he said wearily, as he pressed Magda's hand in thanks, and started upstairs. Richy's eyes were wide as he ran up to Fred. She had almost forgotten the child was watching. Fred picked him up and the boy fingered the wounds gently, then threw his arms around his brother's neck.

"I'll give him his bath," Fred said. "And tell him all about it, blow-by-blow."

"Don't you dare!" Magda and Minnie exclaimed in unison.

Kitty came over early on Saturday to spend extra time with Mama. Later, the two sisters prepared dinner, talking quietly with the kitchen door closed so their parents wouldn't hear, while Magda fed Richy in his highchair.

"Papa hasn't said whether Mama is going back to the hospital or not," Magda said. "He hasn't really explained what the doctors would be able to do for her either."

Kitty stood at the sink, silent.

"Did you know she had been in a mental hospital?" Magda asked, with a slight accusation in her voice. "Did all of you know? Fred and Willa too?"

Kitty turned with a sympathetic look. "We knew it wasn't a regular hospital, but we didn't understand much. Not even the name. Papa and the aunts always discouraged us from asking."

Kitty pulled out a chair, sat, and stroked Richy's arms gently, as if to soothe herself with their softness. "When Mama came back the last time, she was really changed, and not for the better. At first, she didn't even know us. She had no energy and depended on us for everything. Her heart hasn't been strong since."

"She's still that way, it seems to me," Magda replied. "Why wouldn't it have made her happy to be back with us?"

"I think her emotions were not really her own anymore," Kitty replied, "If that makes any sense." It didn't make sense to Magda. Then Kitty stood up again. "You should ask Minnie and Tilly about it. They know more than any of us."

"I'm really sad, too, that Richy will not know his mother the way he should," Magda burst out suddenly. Mama was often a bit distant with the boy, as if he wasn't hers and she were just another relative. "It's not his fault, being the last child. And Papa doesn't pay much attention to him." She lowered her voice even though she knew the boy didn't follow her meaning.

"But he has you!" Kitty said with a smile, handing him a biscuit as Magda wiped off his empty tray. "And he has us older siblings, and his cousins. That's more family than many children have."

"Yes," Magda replied quietly, "but I wonder sometimes if I'm expected to adopt him. What about the rest of my own life?"

Kitty put her arm around Magda's shoulders. "Don't worry, we'll all help take care of him. But," she paused and looked at Magda directly, "I have to tell you something important."

Magda bit her lip while Kitty paused to stir the pots on the stove—bad news?

"The family is moving to New York in January. Mr. Steinmetz has gotten a big job on Wall Street. They've asked me to go with them."

Magda swallowed hard. "Of course, you should. None of us has ever been out of Pittsburgh."

Kitty smiled. "I'm not sure if it will make much difference to my everyday life. If anything, I'll probably be much busier running the household in a strange new place. Hopefully, I'll meet more people and see an exciting city, at least. And I'm not getting any younger. This is the closest thing to adventure I may have."

Magda suddenly felt chilled, as if the lights had dimmed and a draft filled the room. Being twelve years older, Kitty had been like a mother in many ways—someone Magda could talk to and ask for advice, although it was always "adult" advice. Magda had never known Kitty as a girl like herself. She was now almost thirty. Magda didn't think Kitty wanted to give up the chance of having a family of her own, but the opportunities were shrinking.

The soft click of the front door opening and footsteps on the landing made them both turn as Richy ran to the sound. Willa appeared at the kitchen door.

Seeing Magda's long face, Willa said, "So Kitty told you her news?" Magda nodded. "How much longer will we be graced with your weekend cooking, Kit?" Willa asked. Magda knew that Willa must be very sorry to see Kitty leave, although Willa was the most sociable of the sisters and held a wide and growing circle of friends.

"When will you tell Mama and Papa?" Magda asked, trying not to sound critical. But she felt oppressed by a sense that Kitty's move would only make it harder for her to cope. She knew Papa assumed that Kitty was helping Magda more than she was—he really only paid attention to the meals, and Magda had by now learned many of Kitty's recipes and could get by with some of them when the Sunday leftovers were gone. Magda couldn't complain of being left behind by her siblings, she just didn't want to be trapped or taken for granted by everyone.

"I'll tell Papa first, tonight, and see how Mama is doing before I tell her. I don't want it to upset her even more in her present condition. She doesn't really have to know yet that I'm moving. We can tell her that I'm temporarily out of town with the family while they're traveling, or something like that."

More secrets. Not exactly lies, but not truths. Always to protect Mama.

Magda thought she would need to protect herself too.

MAGDA, STANDING

11

To give Magda more time for her classes, Sabine agreed to spend the better part of two days a week at the house, bringing her children to play with Richy. Willa took one morning off work to do the same. Magda was greatly relieved and slipped out as soon as they arrived.

Minnie laid out two algebra books and a pack of paper on her dining room table. Magda looked, wide-eyed—it was a lot to study in six weeks, when the first round of the math bee would take place.

"Here we are, my dear," Minnie announced energetically. "I've spoken to Mr. Kreutz and he was pleased to learn that you want to compete for the team. We have much work ahead of us." She pushed forward one of the papers. "Ah, algebra. I always liked this subject. The study of unknowns. How nice to be able to discover something unknown from a formula."

Magda took the paper but didn't really look at it. Her eyes, suddenly full of tears, rose to meet her aunt's. Her tormented thoughts spilled out.

"Aunt Minnie, I am very excited about this, and I really appreciate everything you're doing for me. But I can't help thinking about the biggest unknown in my life. Especially since Papa said Mama may be going back into the hospital. I've asked Kitty and Willa, and they don't know anything either. What is melancholia? Has she always had it?"

She searched for her handkerchief in her pocket but couldn't find it. Minnie placed hers in reach. "I'm sorry, *Tante*. I don't mean to disrupt our lesson today, but I haven't been able to think about anything else these last few days. I don't think Papa will ever tell us. Kitty said to ask you and Tilly."

Minnie sat quietly and lowered her eyes. Magda feared that she had broken some unspoken rule. And clearly she had. The rule had been in place for much too long.

Minnie got up and left the room, returning in a few minutes with Tilly who was removing a long apron. She had been doing laundry in the basement. They both sat down at the table. Tilly reached for Magda's arm and stroked it gently.

"You are right to insist on an explanation, my love, we promised that. You all have been left in the dark. None of us understands fully, but you deserve to know as much—or as little—as we do. It's not easy for us to tell." She looked at Minnie, soundlessly asking if she wanted to start. Minnie gave the slightest nod, and began.

"I did tell you that when your mama was a girl, we faced some hard times after our parents died. We didn't have much support from our uncle and his family. Well, in fact, they could have taken Sarah in, since she was the youngest, but Tilly and I didn't want to let her go. Uncle and his wife were severe with their own children and had no ambition for them. There's no telling what life there would have been like for your mother.

MAGDA, STANDING

Tilly and I were determined to keep Sarah with us. But by the time we were both teaching, Sarah had finished the six years of public school in the village. We didn't have the fees to send her for further education."

"Couldn't you have taught her at home, like we're doing now?" Magda asked.

"We tried, for a while. But around that time she became . . . like a different person with us. Many young people at that age, around thirteen or fourteen, can be resistant to their elders, of course, but her personality changed. She withdrew into herself, and—"

"She almost stopped talking to us," Tilly broke in. "It was strange and sudden. She never seemed upset with us, just . . . closed down. And we couldn't get her to do even simple chores around the house. We were at school all day and it worried us that she was alone."

"Didn't she have a friend?" Magda asked. "She mentioned Cressa to me once."

"Yes, one girl she became very close to around that time." Minnie said.

"Crescentia," Tilly continued. "Sarah called her Cressa. She lived in our village with her mother, a seamstress. Cressa also finished school around the same time and came over frequently, especially while we were working. They took long walks together, which Sarah seemed incapable of doing with us. It seemed she was happiest with this one friend, which was some relief to us, but we were still concerned about her future. We wanted Sarah to further her education and be able to take care of herself, eventually. All she would agree to do was some sewing work, with Cressa, for her mother. She didn't really become more skilled, but at least it kept her occupied."

"When you decided to come to America, why didn't you bring Mama along? Why did you wait two years for her to come?"

Minnie shifted in her seat. "We have asked ourselves that many times over the years. Maybe it would have made a difference. Maybe not."

Tilly resumed. "The two of us decided we'd all be better off if we emigrated in 1880. Minnie was frustrated with the increasing regulation of her school. I bore a broken heart, as I told you, and was eager to leave. Sarah was about your age then, and around that time she informed us that she wanted to join the convent of St. Francis in a town not too far from our village. Two of the younger nuns from there had been visiting our church for the Easter holidays, for their annual alms request, and Sarah told us that she had talked with them and decided she wanted to live with them. Well, we were—"

"Shocked!" Minnie interjected fervently. "Sarah hadn't become more religious, as far as we could tell, although she wasn't confiding in us. We didn't think she was spending much time in church, and when we asked her to meet with us along with the pastor to get some advice, she refused. Tilly and I really knew no one we could turn to for help with her. Of course, we wanted her to come with us to America. We thought that might have drawn her out of her mood and given her something to look forward to: an adventure! But she refused. And we couldn't force her."

Magda found it hard to imagine her mother standing up to anyone, least of all her eldest sister. Tilly spoke next.

"We got our travel papers and made our arrangements. We had not yet bought our tickets, which we could only do when we got to Hamburg. Sarah insisted that she wouldn't leave with us but wanted to enter the convent. So, we put our trip aside for a few weeks and thought we'd go visit the convent with her. We didn't really think the sisters would accept her without an introduction from a priest or bishop—a kind of recommendation that indicated she showed a genuine vocation. She couldn't bring much money, either, and convents expected new members to give a donation, an important source of funding for their upkeep."

"What was it like there? Was it a pretty place?"

"We weren't invited inside, just to the Mother Superior's office. The nuns were mainly cloistered—they spent their days praying, tending their garden, making bread and honey they would sell to support themselves. They also made a nice cordial from berries that they sold in a small shop on the grounds, along with prayer cards and other small crafts." Tilly rose and opened a drawer of the hutch, taking out a small booklet with a hand sewn leather cover. She handed it to Magda, who opened it and saw a dozen pages of short German prayers written in a careful script, with painted flowers in the corners. "We bought that in the shop. You keep it.

"When we took her to the convent," Tilly continued, "to our surprise, the Mother Superior said they would accept her. She would serve as a novice for two years, and then she would take vows. We knew Sarah wouldn't get much more education, except in religious matters, but if nothing else, she could gain some domestic skills that might help her later, if she chose to leave. We felt she would be safe there, at least. It was what she said she wanted and frankly, we could see no other way out."

Magda sat unmoving, speechless. Tilly rose to put on the tea kettle while Minnie picked up the story.

"Just before we left for our voyage, we learned that Crescentia had entered that convent around the same time that Sarah did. Crescentia's mother told us that it had surprised her, too, when her daughter announced her vocation, but she seemed rather relieved, we thought. She found it difficult to support both of them on her meager earnings, and her daughter hadn't shown much interest in working or getting married."

Relaying the story seemed to have drained the usual energy from both of the aunts. They sat quietly, picking at threads in the tablecloth, rubbing their hands. At this moment they were not former professionals in charge of their lives; they were reliving their vulnerability.

"But then, Mama did finally come over here," Magda broke the silence, determined to force the story forward. Tilly responded.

"The Mother Superior wrote to us, in early '82, that Sarah seemed to be having a breakdown. She had not completed the steps of the novitiate and was unprepared to take vows. The Mother Superior reported that Sarah had stopped eating and was so weak and disoriented they were considering transferring her to an asylum. The Mother Superior said that she was not suited to the convent and would have to leave."

"That was the most distressing news we could have received. We felt helpless—we were so far away! We couldn't communicate with Sarah directly, but we made plans to have our cousin Sophie visit her. Sophie had written us earlier that she planned to come to the United States around that time, so we arranged for her to bring Sarah too. It was a risk; Sarah wasn't in good health and the crossing could be rough, but we sent Sophie enough of our savings so they could have a second-class cabin, better than we had had."

"And Mama didn't object that time?"

"She couldn't assert herself in her condition, and the alternative was to be committed, with no family around. Sophie proved to be a godsend. She was a second cousin of our mother and lived in northern Germany most of our younger lives, so we hadn't seen much of her. But she had been recently widowed, without children, and decided to leave for the US. She took Sarah under her wing and it was the best plan we could have hoped for."

"If that was in '82, Mama was about eighteen," Magda struggled to place herself in the strange situation. "But what about Cressa, did she stay with the nuns? Wouldn't she have helped Mama there?"

"We don't really know," Minnie replied. "We didn't ask Mother Superior and she probably wouldn't have told us about another sister. They were so private. When Sarah and Sophie arrived, we took the train to meet the ship in Baltimore, and brought Sarah back here."

"She seemed improved, but still not very communicative," Tilly said. "We did ask her later whether her friend was still at the convent. She simply told us that Cressa had left, and that was all she would say. None of us ever brought it up again."

A long pause. Magda wanted to get up to use the bathroom but feared breaking the story's spell. Minnie rapped the table suddenly and set the terms in her usual way. "Let's have some of that apple tart you made last night, Tilly, it's past lunch and we all need to take a minute's break. We aren't putting you off again, Magda. It's a lost day for algebra, but this is just as important for you."

"Thank you," Magda whispered, and went to the kitchen to help.

A short while later, unable to swallow her questions along with the food, she blurted out, "So, how did Mama get along here? What did she do when she arrived? And how did she react to meeting Papa?"

Tilly smiled. "Those were some of the happier times. Sarah seemed to recover her health and good nature, although she was still more withdrawn than we would have liked. She hadn't studied English in school so we enrolled her in a class, and put her to work assisting the teachers of the younger children in the German school where we both taught. We lived in a small apartment for years to save for this house, but we were happy together, and life was getting better each year."

"We had many friends, others who had come over from Germany—and other countries, of course. We met your father on our ship, as you know. We often got together with him and his friends. We urged Sarah to join us, or we invited people to our apartment so she would be included. She had become exceedingly shy, we thought. Your father fell hard for her. She was quite beautiful, you know, although we have no photos of her before she married. She still has lovely eyes. You have her eyes."

"Did you want them to get married?"

Minnie spoke next. "Oh, yes. We were impressed with Josef. He is a good man, your father. More traditional than we are, but honest. We thought it a good match, as did our group of friends. We strongly encouraged Sarah to think the same. She resisted at first, but not as stubbornly as before. I think she wanted to get out from under our guardianship most of all." Minnie took a deep breath and looked away. "I don't know—I have wondered, over the years, if we pressed her too hard. But I don't think she saw other paths for herself."

"She was twenty when they married, not too young. Many of our friends were marrying around that age," Tilly said. "I don't feel we rushed her, and she was rather eager to move out of our household and into her own."

MAGDA, STANDING

"Did she seem to be in love with Papa? Like he was with her?" Like you were with Basil, Magda wanted to add.

"She was not swept off her feet, but that is not always the best position to start a marriage," replied Minnie. "It seemed to us that she was content to marry him, and not long after your brother Anton came along, and then Kitty."

"Was it losing the baby at birth that made Mama have a breakdown again?"

"That was certainly part of it, but we'll never know for sure. She did get better, for a while."

Magda broke in, "And then—so many more of us! Christian in '93, and then Fred, Willa, and me. If Papa worked in the mill all that time, he probably wasn't home much. It must have been hard on her—almost one child after another."

Tilly shook her head sadly. "Little Christian, lost to diphtheria. I think that was an even greater shock to your father. Minnie and I spent much time with your family in those days. We took turns living in the house—there wasn't room for both of us—and we paid a Polish woman to help care for all of you."

"Sometimes we thought Sarah was going to be able to manage, but she seemed to relapse with each child. It wasn't actually giving birth that was so difficult—in fact, each delivery was fairly uncomplicated and quicker than most, so the midwife told us. She just became weaker—less capable—and more withdrawn over the years."

"And then Richy! She must have thought she was done having children by then."

"Yes, Richy surprised all of us. A reminder of how little control we women have in our lives. But, fortunately, you children who survived are all healthy, strong, and smart, a source of pride to your family. And the little one is a delight, isn't he?"

Tilly folded her napkin and Magda realized that the tale was coming to an end, for now.

"Back to my first questions," Magda hurriedly pressed on. "Do you know what the doctors say about Mama's condition? What can they do for her if she goes back into the hospital?"

Minnie sighed deeply. "Not really, my dear. The mind is a mystery. And your mama's heart isn't strong either, we know that. She has taken a medication for her heart, digitalis, for years. Beyond the laudanum and more rest, I don't know what other treatments there are."

She stood up. "Now it is time, you must head for home. Sabine probably needs to leave for her own house."

Magda gave each of the aunts a strong, lingering embrace, picked up the algebra papers, and quietly left. Her mind was full on the walk home. The more she learned about Mama, the less it seemed she knew her.

12

When the family sat together for Thanksgiving dinner, Willa and Johannes made an announcement.

"Sir, Willa and I feel we've saved and waited long enough, and we want to marry next month. We'd like your permission." Johannes didn't often speak up at family gatherings, but this was clearly important to raise before all of them, including Minnie and Tilly.

"We found a very nice apartment we can afford on the first floor of a house in Carrick," Willa added quickly. "Only a short trolley ride away!"

"Well, I respect your request," Papa replied. "You have my blessing." Magda was a bit surprised that he consented so quickly.

Everyone stood and embraced or shook hands to congratulate the couple. Fred had invited Con for the holiday dinner, and when Magda passed his chair, he raised his hand to shake hers. "May I congratulate the sister of the bride too?" he said, grinning. She noticed he hadn't eaten much of the turkey on

CHRISTINE FALLERT KESSIDES

his plate. "May I cut it for you?" she asked quietly. She wondered why she hadn't thought of that the last time he'd joined them for dinner back in October.

"Yes, thank you." She wondered if he'd hesitated to ask before. "Fred did it last time," he said. "But this gives us a moment." He winked and she felt her cheeks turn the color of cranberry sauce.

Willa told Magda later, as they readied for bed, "I didn't want to delay, to be sure that Kitty and Mama would both be here for my wedding. And Johannes keeps saying he thinks we'll join the war in a few months and he could get drafted. Oh, I hope he's wrong! Anyway, he just doesn't want to wait any longer. You know men!" She gave a deeply dimpled grin. Magda didn't "know men" much, but remembering Con's wink made her ears burn.

Plans for the wedding were already well underway. The couple had spoken to Father Magnus to reserve the church hall for the week before Christmas. Kitty was going to prepare some dishes for the reception, and the aunts agreed to pay for the cake. Johannes asked a friend to bring a Victrola, and another would play the piano. They would keep the reception small and accepted only a modest contribution from Papa to help with the cost.

"Is your gown ready?" Magda asked, knowing that Willa was spending all her free time on it.

"Ready enough—simpler than some I've stitched, but I like it. I don't want to tell Johannes I need more time for that." They agreed Willa would make a few minor alterations to a second-hand dress for Magda.

The morning of the wedding, Mama seemed in especially low spirits, not sharing any of the animated excitement of the family members running through the house. Magda had to get her up and dressed with help from Tilly, who came over early so that Kitty and Willa could focus on other preparations.

"Don't be sad, Mama, Willa will still be close by," Magda said, trying not to sound as impatient and exasperated as she felt. Even Tilly couldn't say anything to staunch Mama's tears.

Minnie drove Mama, Magda, Richy, and Tilly to church in the Ford, while Fred drove Willa, Papa, and Kitty in a borrowed car. When they entered the church, Fred put his arm securely around Mama's waist, almost carrying her down the aisle, while Richy held her hand. People remarked later that they were touched that Mama was so emotional for a first daughter's wedding, and that her sons showed such affection. But to Magda, her condition wasn't at all a good sign.

Kitty moved a few of her belongings back home—things she didn't want to take to New York, like clothes she considered too unfashionable, some books, and a few decorative items that Mrs. Steinmetz had given her over the years. Magda looked through them listlessly, but didn't see anything she wanted for herself. She only wanted to keep her sister.

Kitty bustled more than usual overseeing the packing of the Steinmetz household, a larger job than anyone imagined. One Saturday evening, shortly before her move, Kitty spoke with Papa about a young woman who had worked under her supervision.

"Molly Green can cook. I taught her all the dishes you like. She can clean and iron your shirts, watch Richy, and help Mama on her difficult days." That's what they called it when their mother didn't want to get out of bed, or bathe, or brush her hair. "She's Irish and has only been in this country a year, but she learns quickly, works hard, and I trust her. I can't bring her to New York—I wish I could, but I'll have to hire other staff there. I think you should have her work here, at least while Magda finishes her studies."

"We can't afford—" Papa started.

"I knew that's what you'd say, but she won't cost as much as you think. We paid her $12 weekly and that included trolley fare. She can live here, so she'll be available to help even at night. We can start her at $9.50, with room and board at no charge, and—"

"Impossible. And I don't want another woman in the house."

"Papa!" Kitty sounded exasperated. "If only you were willing to try it, I think we could make it work for you."

"No, I'm not going to ask her." He was getting agitated. Kitty usually had a way with him. If he had a favorite child, it may have been she, with her sensible, businesslike manner. But he was adamant.

"It's not that I wouldn't like Magda to get some help, but your mother—she may need to go back to the hospital. It will cost us to pay for a decent room, medicine, and the doctors." He placed his hand on Kitty's shoulder, sighed deeply, and quietly left the room.

The sisters looked at each other. Their eyes glistened.

"I wish I weren't leaving town," Kitty whispered. "But there's really nothing I can do here for her. Or for him," she added, picking up her coat and purse.

"You'll be so far way." Magda spoke to herself as much as to Kitty. "It will leave such a hole in our lives. I'll never be able to visit you. Two train rides away, when would I ever be able to afford it?"

"*Liebchen*," Kitty gave Magda a soothing hug. "I'll save up for your tickets and you'll be the first person to come visit me. I promise."

A few days later, Magda met Kitty at the Steinmetz house. Molly Green was still employed until the family moved out, but most of their things had been shipped under Kitty's careful supervision. She had offered to ask Molly to watch Richy so Magda could spend the afternoon studying.

"Ah, what a hearty lad!" Molly exclaimed when she met him. "He's a big one for his age; sure and it's the German food." Magda took an instant liking to the young woman, who looked the very picture of health and energy.

Magda asked Molly if she had found another family to work and live with yet.

"I canna live in. I have my own boyo, a bit older. We stay with my cousin in Brentwood."

Kitty had entered the room. "You never told me you have a child," she said, her voice slightly sharp.

"Sorry, ma'am. You didna ask." Kitty's and Magda's eyes slipped instinctively to Molly's left hand, which was bare.

"And...does your husband live there too?" Kitty asked, a bit more softly.

Molly averted her gaze. "He's back in Ireland. We couldna both afford to come. And I couldna leave my Colin there."

"Does he send you money?" Kitty continued.

Molly licked her lips nervously. "When he can. Sometimes I send money." Clearly eager to change the subject, she swept Richy in her arms.

"And what does this little man want to do today? Shall we play hide and seek in the garden?" Her brogue drew out a long *aar* sound in the word. Richy wriggled from her embrace and

CHRISTINE FALLERT KESSIDES

took her hand, eagerly leading her outside.

"She may be good at housework, but I bet her heart's in caring for children," Magda remarked, taking out her books and settling into a corner of the kitchen.

Kitty watched them through the window and shook her head. "You think you know someone you're around all day," she mused. "I took her for an innocent sort of village girl a year ago when she started. She's only about nineteen, so she must have married very young, or . . ." Kitty wasn't judgmental by nature, but she was responsible for the Steinmetz household and her employers put great stock on respectability. "Best I found out about this now."

"Well, she looks to me like a serious young mother who's probably had a hard time," Magda protested. "Imagine crossing the ocean in steerage with a little child. I have enough trouble keeping Richy clean and fed in our own house."

Magda was beginning to think she could weigh some of the burdens other people carried, which she understood at least in part because of her own. She didn't feel so sorry for herself these days. She knew that she had risen to her tasks well— most of the time, at least—but she was starting to understand other people much more than she used to. It made her feel less alone.

"You're growing wise," Kitty said softly, as if reading Magda's thoughts, and gave her a kiss on the head.

The sisters glanced outside, then resumed their work to the distant calls of Richy searching for Molly in the garden.

MAGDA, STANDING

1917

13

On a cold January afternoon, Richy bounced on Magda's lap and leaned his face towards the window of the trolley. She reached her hand in front of his soft lips just in time. Inside and out, the windows were gritty with street dirt. Smoke from the iron and steel mills hung so heavily over the city that the streetlights remained on all day.

Magda leaned against the hard seat back and looked around. She hadn't been downtown for months, or anywhere much beyond home. When Elise had pointed out that a few of Papa's shirt collars were wearing thin, Magda jumped at the chance to go shopping to replace them. He gave her the money, saying only: "Make the trip brief." Magda slipped a bit of her meager allowance into her purse in case she saw a small item for herself. Perhaps some hair ribbons, although there was nowhere special to wear them. At the last minute, Magda decided to take Richy along so she didn't have to prevail on a neighbor to watch him. The negotiations over trading favors were tedious,

MAGDA, STANDING

and she desperately wanted a change of scene, however short and mundane.

The trolley wheels shrieked to a slow stop at Liberty Avenue and Fifth. In the rush of pedestrians crossing the intersection, she was surprised to see several soldiers in brown uniforms. But what caught her eye was a large red and white banner spread across a shop front: American Red Cross Volunteer Center. It was a few blocks from her destination, but she felt a surge of curiosity and excitement. Without further thought, she scooped Richy off her lap and moved quickly to the exit door. They managed to slip out just before the driver reached for the handle.

The curb was covered with the gray slush that was Pittsburgh's winter carpet. It rose almost to the top of Richy's high shoes.

"No more ride?" he asked, looking up at her. She adjusted his cap and mittens that were attached to his coat sleeves. She had never taken him on foot into a crowd before, and suddenly realized that they would have to walk the extra distance to the store. But the bright flowing banner was all she focused on.

She opened the door and they stepped into the Volunteer Center. What had once been a restaurant was now converted into an open space with tables full of strips of cloth, papers, pins, small bottles, and other objects. A wide table was positioned in front, a few feet from the doorway. A middle-aged woman with a handmade Red Cross badge looked up.

"May I help you?"

As Magda reached up to straighten her hat, Richy's hand slipped from hers.

"I saw your sign outside. You need volunteers?" She glanced at a handwritten poster on the table.

CHRISTINE FALLERT KESSIDES

The woman looked Magda over, her eyes resting on Richy warily. "Yes. We need women to prepare materials to support our medical personnel and civil defense needs." She spoke stiffly, as if she had said these words too many times to think about them. Then she leaned forward with a more direct look at Magda. "We welcome young women who wish to help the cause, but they cannot bring their children."

"Oh, this is my brother." As Magda reached down to take the child's hand again, he ran over to the closest table and grabbed the corner of a cloth. Spinning around with his brilliant smile, he pulled the cloth slightly, causing pins and bottles to spill on the floor.

"I'm so sorry! I mean we're so sorry, he's just excited to be here," she blurted, mortified. "Let me pick them up!"

"No, no, please leave them alone, I'll do it, the supplies must be kept clean. As you see, we can't have children in here." The woman shooed them both out of the building.

Hot tears welled in Magda's eyes. Richy sensed her distress and patted her hand apologetically. "Never mind," she sniffled. She noticed his shoes had darkened from the melted slush and realized that by the time they walked to the store at Penn Avenue and Stanwix Street and back, they would be soaked. The January chill was a danger. Should they just wait for the next trolley home and give up the errand?

Hearing the volunteer center door open behind them, she quickly turned away and took several steps toward the car stop.

"Magda Augustin, is that you?" The voice was unmistakably that of a former neighbor, Mrs. Ubinger. "I thought I recognized you. I haven't seen you for several years, you've grown up so nicely, my dear! And is this mischief-maker your little brother?"

MAGDA, STANDING

Magda reddened as she acknowledged the woman, who was wearing the official Red Cross badge and apron under her open coat. "Yes, I'm so sorry. It was a mistake to go inside with Richy, but I wondered—"

"Oh dear, I don't want to keep you both standing here, it's too cold. I can see Richy's shoes are wet. Were you heading home? Do you still live in Mt. Oliver? I have a car and can give you a lift."

Magda felt like crying with both embarrassment and relief. But she quickly explained what had brought them downtown, and confessed that she would have to leave without completing the errand.

"That's not a problem, Magda. This will give us a chance to catch up. Stay here while I bring the car from around the corner, and I can wait for you outside the store. You don't want to go home empty-handed."

Magda didn't know any women who drove themselves around town. She realized it would have been another risk to take Richy into the store, as he was getting fretful. Mrs. Ubinger offered to sit in the car with him and let him play with the steering wheel. She even had a small package of biscuits in her purse.

Magda ran into Joseph Horne's, a large and fashionable department store, where she would have loved to spend an afternoon with Lucia. She quickly explained what she needed and bought the first two shirts and replacement collars the salesgirl brought out in her father's size, spending all of his money and her own.

"Are you interested in volunteering for the Red Cross?" Mrs. Ubinger asked as they pulled away from the curb. "I've been working there for several years, and we'll be getting much busier in the coming months, I fear. You're old enough, I think."

"I'll be seventeen soon," Magda answered as the woman continued without pausing.

"We'll need seamstresses, nurses, administrators, drivers, and all manner of assistance if we get drawn into that European war. And even if, pray to God, we can avoid that, the ARC is already contributing to the war effort in Britain and France, indirectly."

Magda explained that she was intrigued by the idea but couldn't really consider it yet, given her studies and duties at home. These she relayed selectively, emphasizing what she thought might make her sound most qualified. "I'm completing high school—my aunts are tutoring me." This elicited an admiring nod. "I've been very organized about getting help from others too."

"And how is your mother?" Mrs. Ubinger's pointed question, and her solicitous tone of voice, startled Magda. She realized that many acquaintances had probably observed Mama's problems all along and understood what the family was coping with.

When they arrived at the house, Magda invited the woman inside but she demurred, to Magda's relief. She wasn't sure there was much to offer along with tea and she needed to feed Richy right away.

Mrs. Ubinger wrote her phone number on a slip of paper and handed it to Magda. "Call me if you want to go back downtown to meet with some of the other women. I'll be happy to introduce you and get you started."

"But, because of Richy—"

"That's part of my thinking, actually. We have many young women who might like to work for the Red Cross and we need their help, but we must also find arrangements for their

MAGDA, STANDING

children. In normal times we would not recruit volunteers who have young children, and some of our board would even consider marriage a disqualification, although I obviously don't agree with that. This is the modern day! And besides, the war upends many such ideas. Maybe you can help me come up with a plan for that."

Magda looked dubious. She didn't reply, except to express her thanks. If it meant becoming a nanny for the volunteers, she didn't think even a red badge would make that attractive.

"We'll see. Let's talk again!" Mrs. Ubinger called cheerily. "Get that good boy some warm food, and yourself too." She revved the engine and they both watched in fascination as she drove away.

The next several weeks were exhausting. In addition to spending at least an hour every night on math problems for the competition, Magda was trying to keep up with her other subjects.

She raced through her days cutting corners on housework. Whipping the dirt under the sofa and carpet (it could wait till she graduated). Leaving the beds unchanged, and just airing the pillowslips after a quick swing on the outside line to make them smell almost clean. Appealing to Willa—who had cut back her hours at the dress shop since marrying—to help cook and take Richy for several hours. When Sabine came to the house with her own children in tow, there wasn't much extra quiet time.

While neither Willa nor Sabine had really cared about going to high school, they showed a grudging admiration for Magda's efforts. The math bee, however, was a puzzle to the family. Why did Magda want to take on this extra work, and why did she need to compete so publicly? Magda realized none of them thought that she, as a girl, would make it through the rounds and reach the winning team. Only the aunts believed in her. In the little time she could daydream, she saw herself regaining the admiration of her former classmates and teachers. A girl who wasn't even attending the school, and look what she had achieved! Winning might even help her get a scholarship for college.

The next round of the math competition, against a neighboring school, was a week away. On a mild late-winter day, she decided to try keeping Richy occupied outside in the backyard with his toys and the makeshift tools he used to dig in the flowerbeds. Mama had lost interest in the garden, so Magda figured that if Richy demolished it but was happily occupied, she could replant it later. She would have to wipe him down afterwards, but she hoped to get at least a solid hour of study before that.

She laid out her exercise sheets on the porch table and opened her textbook. Her aim was to finish each problem first as best she could, then look at the book's answer key.

Ten minutes later. "Can Magga play?"

"Richy, you know I have to work here now. You have your garden tools. Dig over there."

Five minutes. "Firsty. Fowers want a drink. Richy wants a drink too."

Magda quickly went into the kitchen and poured both of them a cup of apple juice. She really wanted coffee, but couldn't take time to brew a pot. Maybe later she would see if Mama wanted some. She cut a slice of bread, buttered it and broke it into small pieces, and added a handful of raisins onto an old plate. Richy didn't need lunch yet, but he was always hungry and eating was a good distraction. "OK, you can have a picnic. Bring teddy." She spread a large towel on the ground.

Now she needed to bring him in to wash his grimy hands, which meant letting him track in dirt or taking off his muddy shoes. She wet a washcloth with soapy water and gave him a quick wipe before he touched the food. He happily went back outside with the drink and snack.

"Magga have a picnic too?"

"Not right now. Later, after my work. You and teddy can do it."

Twenty minutes and only two problem sets later, Richy had exhausted the potential for solo play in the backyard. Its dimensions were small, just a rough square the width and depth of the house. On one side, a narrow walkway led to the front of the house where there was no yard to speak of—just a terrace and steps to the sidewalk. Magda walked to that side hoping to see anything that might entertain Richy. She saw a leaf rake with missing tongs, a small bucket, and some cans of old paint.

"I want to play with Magga." Richy gave her a series of looks ranging from sweet appeal to a threatened outburst. She could match him in temper, but knew that would make the morning a total waste for study. She also didn't want to provoke one of his crying fits and disturb Mama. If she could just have another half hour of peace, maybe she could take him to the aunts and continue studying there, although this was supposed to be their afternoon for marketing.

"Here." She demonstrated raking the dead leaves from the side path into the backyard and urged him to make a nice pile. It worked to capture his growing sense of independence, and he happily took over the rake. She returned to the porch and resumed studying to the rasp, rasp that assured her he was just around the corner.

Magda managed to breeze through three more problem sets but got stuck on the last one. She felt ready for some exercise and closed the book, thinking she would make lunch and then take Richy for a short walk. At nearly three, he often resisted napping, and she found that her only respite most days was to lie down with him to read stories and count the short rest against her evening sleep. Maybe the fresh air today would tire him enough that she could finish the math unit, or review one of the other subject lessons after lunch. Then again, maybe she should continue while he was quietly occupied.

He was certainly very quiet.

She stepped down from the porch and ran the few steps to the side yard. Richy wasn't there. She ran to the front of the house. He wasn't there either. He hadn't entered the front door—it was locked.

"Richy? Richy? *Richy!*"

Where could he have gone? She was sure he hadn't crossed the backyard to the side fence's narrow opening. She would have seen him. And he couldn't have run past her into the back door, so he wasn't inside the house. But when was the last time she had looked up from her work? When was the last time she had heard him make a sound? The thought made her head swim. Sweat started dripping down her spine.

She didn't see him up, down, or across their street. She ran to a nearby intersection busy with midday traffic of horse carts, the trolley, and occasional cars. Should she go over to the next

MAGDA, STANDING

street in case he was heading that way? But if he wasn't there, should she try the next door neighbors? Should she return to the backyard and look over the fence? Maybe he had somehow crawled out that way.

"Richy? *Richy*! Where are you?!"

Only Mama was in the house, and Magda didn't dare let her know that Richy had disappeared. If she called too loudly, her mother would hear her.

She ran in increasingly wide circles across the street, into the side streets, the back alley, and into backyards. No sign of Richy. Her Richy. She was responsible for him.

What was he wearing? She tried to remember how she had dressed him that morning, or rather, how he had dressed himself ("I do it!"). She usually let him choose his own clothes. Oh yes—she recalled he was wearing his favorite red shirt and brown pants.

Tell people to look for red.

She quickly knocked on the closest neighbors' doors to ask them to help her search. Although all the women in the area were housewives, they may have been out shopping. Only two answered, but said they couldn't help.

"I'm so sorry, I would, but I can't leave my baby."

"I'll keep an eye out for you, but the plumber is arriving soon."

She stopped on the sidewalk and took a deep, shaky breath. Richy was used to strolling around the neighborhood with her, so maybe he would be able to find his way back to the house if he hadn't gone too far. Most of the neighbors would recognize him, surely, if they saw him walking by himself, but did they all know he was an Augustin? Would they bring him home? Could they call the house? Few owned telephones.

What if the wrong kind of person found him?

CHRISTINE FALLERT KESSIDES

She would have to go inside, but whom should she call? Papa couldn't be reached when he was delivering the milk, although he would be home soon. Fred was at work. Willa didn't have a phone. Sabine? Maybe she should just call the police. Would they take her seriously, just a flustered girl?

She wanted to make one more run around the neighborhood in a larger radius first, but she felt about to throw up. She held her forehead and bent over. Suddenly, a police car rounded the corner. She ran out into the street and stepped in front of it.

"What's wrong with you, lassie?" It was Officer O'Grady, who usually covered the neighborhood on foot.

"My brother's gone missing," Magda was wheezing, barely able to breathe.

"The little lad? How long ago since you saw him?"

She was mortified to admit that it must have been over an hour since she last heard the scratching of the rake. The officer would think her a neglectful idiot. He'd be right.

"You stay here in case he comes home. I'll drive around the neighborhood and contact the neighbors on the back streets."

Magda let the tears flow. Richy would be scared to be away from home alone. He would be hungry and cold. The temperature had dropped since morning and he didn't have his coat.

He would be looking for her and thinking she had deserted him.

She decided to go into the house, call Sabine, and have Sabine reach Willa's closest neighbor with a phone. She couldn't handle this without her family's help. The phone was in the front hall—what if her mother heard her? There was no avoiding it: Mama would find out.

MAGDA, STANDING

As soon as she got the words out to Sabine, the operator who'd connected the call broke in with "Dearie, I'll tell everyone with a telephone!" For once, Magda was glad that woman was such a busybody.

It was now mid-afternoon. Officer O'Grady and another policeman who joined the search were scouring the neighborhood and circling by to check in at the house. Papa had come home about an hour earlier, then Sabine arrived. She had managed to contact Tony at work and he eventually reached Fred. Magda met each of them at the door. Papa listened soberly and told her to stay there in case Richy came back on his own, while he went upstairs to sit with Mama. He asked Sabine and Tony, when he arrived, to go to each neighbor on the side streets.

Magda wondered if they would ever trust her again.

Finally, Fred appeared, explaining that he'd been across the city making newspaper deliveries and had come as soon as he got word.

"Let's be Richy," he said to her, "Where would we go?"

Magda looked at him with renewed tears. "What are you thinking?"

"The police and everyone are looking for him like a lost dog or cat. He wouldn't just wander aimlessly like that. He's smart, and he knows his way around. Have you tried Elise?"

"But Fred, Elise lives half a mile away! And anyway, if she'd seen him, surely she'd find a way to let us know, even if she doesn't have a phone."

"Well, we can't just stay here. I'll tell Papa that you and I will drive over that way."

They climbed into the printer's van. Elise lived on the other side of Brownsville Road, a major thoroughfare in the area.

Fred pulled up to her house and Magda ran up the steps and banged on the door.

"Magda, whatever—?"

"I've lost Richy! He wandered away from the yard while I was studying."

"When?"

Magda explained through her sobs, ashamed. She was supposed to be capable of caring for Elise's only child too. How could she have been so selfish, so oblivious, so foolishly irresponsible?

Elise said that she and Martin had been inside all day because they both had colds, and they'd just gotten up from a long nap. "How can I help?"

The three of them made no effort to hide their drawn faces. Magda felt worse when Elise put her arms around her. Elise would never trust her again either.

"We should get back home," Fred said. "We need to check more places before it gets dark."

"Please, at least take the chicken pie I made this morning. Your family will need to eat, you won't have time for cooking when you get back. Martin and I don't need it. It's just outside where I put it to cool before we took our nap." She opened the back door off the kitchen.

There was Richy, lying asleep on the doormat, his face and red shirt covered in pastry crumbs.

Apart from a considerable thirst, a blister on each heel, and very dirty face and hands, Richy seemed none the worse for his adventure. Magda was another story. She held both arms tightly around the boy as Fred drove them home in the press truck. Richy stood on the floor of the back seat watching in fascination as Fred handled the gear stick. It was his first ride in the truck and his excitement clearly overtook any bad memories he might have of the day. If they hadn't needed to get home immediately to share the good news of their discovery, Fred would have given in to Richy's call to "Dive more, more, Fed!"

As for Magda, the knot in her stomach had now traveled to her head and her heart. The initial overwhelming relief turned to dread, thinking of her father's reaction—and everyone else's—to her negligence. She buried her face in the boy's dusty hair.

Papa met them at the door. "*Dem Himmel sei Dank.*" Thank heaven. He embraced Richy briefly, unused to the gesture, his body shaking, and turned away from Magda.

"Thank God!" Sabine and Willa were there at the front door behind him, enveloping Richy in their arms so that his feet didn't touch the ground for minutes, until he wriggled away to join his cousins.

"Does Mama know?" Magda whispered to Willa.

"She's still in her bedroom. I don't think so. Papa gave her a sleeping powder earlier. Don't worry about her." Willa looked at Magda sympathetically and hugged her tightly. Sabine turned to Magda then and wrapped her arms around her.

"I'm so sorry," Magda's sobs burst out of her tight throat. "It was all my fault. I was paying too much attention to studying math. I thought he was playing around the side of the house, and at first I could hear him, and then I couldn't, but by then—"

"Really, Magda, how could you have gotten so distracted?" Willa asked quietly.

"It's one of my worst nightmares," Sabine whispered, "but I can understand how it could happen. You were very lucky; Richy was lucky. We all are."

Magda walked weakly across the sitting room and sunk to her knees in front of her father, who had lit his pipe and was staring out the window. "Papa, I'm so sorry. I was selfish. I was only thinking of myself and my own work. I let everyone down." She tried to steady her voice but it broke.

Papa reached down to raise her chin. She realized suddenly it may have been the first time they had actually looked into each other's eyes for months. He appeared so old and tired. "I'm sorry," she whispered again. "I'll give up studying."

"I thank God," Papa replied softly, "that my family, that all the children, are safe. You must thank God, too, for his blessings to us." He didn't seem to have heard her comment, or it didn't merit a response. "I'm relieved your mother didn't have to know the boy was gone." He leaned back and closed his eyes.

That night, Magda sat up in her bed, holding Richy close as she read him a bedtime story. He slept in her room on one of her sisters' old beds now that they were both gone from the house, and Richy was too big to stay in their parents' room.

"I'm very sorry I didn't take you to see Martin today, but you must promise me you will never, ever walk away from the house by yourself again."

"Magga have important work. You were busy," he replied matter-of-factly.

"Not more important than you. You could have been hit by a car!"

"No more boy."

"That's right. And I would've never stopped crying! Magda would never be happy ever, ever again."

He looked up and stroked her face as if to wipe away tears. She put her head back on the pillow and closed her eyes. After a few minutes she opened her eyes and saw Richy looking at her with Fred's sly grin. Just as Magda realized her emotional dependence on the child, he was discovering his independence from her. Exhausted, they took turns giving each other a tight squeeze and fell asleep in her bed, a tangle of limbs.

As Fred relayed the story later, Richy hadn't considered himself lost at all—he was heading to Martin's house and knew the way. The boy became briefly famous, mentioned in a *Pittsburgh Press* article printed two days later, and enjoyed several gifts sent to him by readers, including a red wagon, a set of metal cars, and a wooden horse. People were impressed that a child not yet three-years-old had walked a half-mile on his own to find his playmate. The writer, a colleague of Con, agreed to write the story as an adventure from the boy's perspective, skirting the questionable role of his sibling caretaker.

The journalist also made Elise's chicken pie a feature of the story after tasting one to provide first-person details about its savory flavor and hearty nourishment. The local German delicatessen, Grundel's, offered to stock the pies and give her a nice price for each sold. The shopkeeper wanted to call them "Richy's Pie" to maximize the advertising appeal, but they all felt that was too much exploitation of what was, after all, a very close call.

Magda was sick in bed the next day with the worst headache and menstrual cramps she'd ever had—surely punishment from heaven, she thought.

"I'm going to quit the math bee." She blurted out the decision she had made on her way to the aunts' house as soon as she recovered. She didn't have to explain why.

"My dear," Tilly replied with a gentle hug. "Don't punish yourself. You have been wonderful caring for Richy and nobody blames you for this, really. We understand what you've been going through."

"But there was no excuse, *Tante*! I was so sure I could practice all the math exercises, *and* study for the rest of the courses, *and* take care of Richy, *and* the house. In that order, so it seems. And I was tired and impatient with him. I really just wanted him to stay quiet."

"Come sit down. We're having lunch. Where is he now? We wanted to meet the young Houdini!" Tilly's soothing good humor was the first warmth Magda had felt since the whole nightmare.

Minnie entered the room. "We must thank God for his mercy to us and protection of the little one," she said firmly and took her seat at the end of the table. "Pride cometh before the fall."

Magda hung her head. "I know," she whispered. "I was thinking only of myself; I wanted everyone to admire me. Now I just feel ashamed."

"I wasn't speaking mainly of you, child," Minnie said, patting her hand. "It may have been your idea to attempt the math bee, but it also appealed greatly to my pride as your teacher. I was thinking it would be such a success for both of us. But I should've been more considerate of everything else you had to do. I should have given more thought to how else we could help you."

"You could still compete, if you really want to," said Tilly. "We could come up with a better plan for taking care of your other duties for the next few weeks."

"Willa has Richy with her today. But it's too much for everyone to have me spend all my time on the math bee and work on the rest of my lessons as well. I don't want to give them up." Magda paused to chew a piece of bread. "I've been wondering. Do you think I could take the final exams this year and graduate early? Because I have something else in mind too."

She took a sip of buttermilk and leaned towards her aunts. "I want to join the Red Cross. They're looking for volunteers to help prepare for the war effort. I stopped in their office when I went downtown last month, and saw that they offer nurse's aide training." She bit her lip and sat back. "I haven't told anyone else yet. And I'm not sure how to make that work at home either."

The aunts looked at each other and Minnie spoke first. "Magda, I'm very glad to hear that you haven't lowered your sights. Ambition is a good thing, especially for a bright girl like you. What matters is having an ambition that justifies the effort—and this time, finding a solution that minimizes the disruption it will cause for you and your family. Let's think about this one."

"You can certainly take the exams at term's end if you focus on those now," Tilly added. "I've talked with the principal and he said the district plans to have the finals earlier. They expect many boys will want to enlist in the next several months, as it's looking more likely we'll be joining the war, sadly. He doesn't want them leaving school without getting their diplomas, if possible. I took the liberty of telling him we thought you should take the exams as well, that you would be ready." She glanced at Minnie, who nodded, then back at Magda. "I suggested you could take the German exam instead of Latin. He agreed. We'll need to look at the schedule and map out your remaining lessons."

Magda looked from one aunt to the other, thinking her heart would burst. She still wanted to succeed in ways many of her peers hadn't, to make people think well of her, and to become qualified to attend college later. That might have to wait, if there were a war. But she knew this time she would have to plan more carefully and not simply put herself first.

MAGDA, STANDING

14

As soon as Richy fell asleep, Magda took her books and looked for an empty spot in the house to study. Usually, she went to Fred and Tony's old room in the attic, which was undisturbed but also drafty and musty. She could have made the effort to dust it thoroughly and air it out, but it seemed one more task that could be deferred—even if she would have been the sole beneficiary. Final exams were three months away and she still needed to learn much of the material. She was putting a price on every minute of her time and didn't devote any of it to negotiating with herself.

The house was unusually quiet. Papa was at work, one of the occasions when his boss asked him to go at night to transfer the milk and cheese from the farm trucks and large tanks to prepare the deliveries for the next morning. He always said he preferred the early day shift because driving the horse-drawn cart reminded him of his boyhood, and he enjoyed greeting his customers, but he did whatever the supervisor requested.

When her father worked the night shift, he normally slept the following morning. But that evening he told Magda that her mother would be leaving for the hospital the next day. He asked her to prepare them a good breakfast before they departed.

Magda spread out her study papers on the dining room table. Timelines of European and American history. An annotated list of the amendments to the US Constitution. But her mind kept wandering to what would happen in the morning.

At the sound of soft footsteps, she raised her head with a start. Mama stood in the doorway with a shawl over her long white nightgown.

"I don't sleep," she said, sitting down at the table. "Your Papa gave me the sleeping powder before he left, but it's not working anymore." She pulled some of Magda's papers to her. "What are you studying now?"

"History and US government. For final exams in June."

"I never read about America in my school. Only a little, here, for the citizen test. *Ich weiss so wenig.* I know little." Mama's English was rough and her accent thick. She didn't interact with many people who couldn't interpret or compensate for her broken language.

"Did Minnie and Tilly try to teach you about America before you left Germany?"

"Oh, they try many things with me. I did not want to be a student. Not like you."

Magda closed her book. She couldn't concentrate anyway, and she needed to know more.

"Mama, the aunts told me that you . . . that you went into a convent. You never told us about that! Did you really want to be a nun? What did you plan to do there? Would you have become a teacher or just stayed in the cloister?"

Mama's eyebrows rose in surprise at the questions. She pulled the shawl closer and fingered her long braid. She was quiet for several minutes.

"I ... I was looking for something. I couldn't think—nothing seemed right. Nothing felt good. I couldn't be like Minnie or Tilly. But I was afraid to be alone. Afraid of my own thoughts." Her fingers separated the strands of hair and she pulled on them as she talked. "I was never like you or your sisters, or the boys. You are all so ... sure and, how to say, *fähig*." Capable.

"Minnie and Tilly also said your best friend went to the convent at the same time. What was she like?"

Mama gazed across the room but her attention didn't seem focused.

"Cressa. Yes. You would have liked her. She was like you. She was full of the life that I did not have. She had no fear. She understood me better than my sisters."

"She sounds wonderful. I wish I could have met her. But she doesn't sound like someone to become a nun in a strict convent."

"No." More silence for many minutes. "*Bitte*, would you make me some hot milk?"

"Of course." Magda got up quickly and poured enough milk for both of them into a pan. She didn't want to make herself sleepy, but to fortify herself for the study hours ahead. It took a while to get the pan warm. Most times she would do something else while waiting and find the milk boiling over, but now she watched it carefully. She wanted to get back to Mama and her story.

"Here you are," she placed the cups on their saucers. "With cocoa and sugar too."

"*Danke sehr, mein süßes Kind.*" My sweet child—what Mama used to call her. Magda hadn't heard it for many years.

CHRISTINE FALLERT KESSIDES

She sat down and wrapped her hands around her own cup, feeling a chill. "Tell me about Cressa, please."

"Going to the convent was her idea. We want to live together, but we have no money and girls not married could not live by themselves. Cressa's mother wanted her to marry a boy in the village, but Cressa said no. And so we made a plan."

"And the convent accepted you both?"

"Yes. The convent needed workers. We did not take vows yet."

Another long pause.

"What was it like there?"

"For me, not too bad at first. I was even a little happy. I worked in the garden. They grew beautiful flowers to sell. But for Cressa—too much *streng*, how you say, strict. She got into trouble with the Mother many times. She wanted to leave, but she did not tell me. Maybe she was thinking I am better off there. One day she left. I did not know where she went."

"Without even telling you? You must have been so sad. She was your best friend! Your only friend?"

"In convent we were not allowed to have friends. They say our happiness only comes from God and the community." Magda poured the remainder of the cocoa from the pot into Mama's empty cup.

"That was the first time I wanted to die. I thought . . . I have nothing to live for. But such thoughts are sinful. I could not live any more, and I could not make myself die."

Magda felt a glimmer of understanding of her mother's suffering.

"Then you came to America."

"I let other people take charge of my life, since I could not." Mama replied. "I let them tell me what to do, like in the convent. It was better for me that way."

MAGDA, STANDING

"And you met Papa."

"He is a good man. He tries to take care of everything. Life is not easy for him, but every day he hopes something good to happen. What I find so difficult. I—I feel every step is so big. I fear too much."

"I guess you didn't want so many children," Magda said softly. "Things would have been simpler for you if all of us hadn't come along." She was number seven. She was afraid to finish her thought. Could Mama have possibly not wanted her to be born? "But losing the baby, and then Christian—maybe that was the worst thing?"

Mama stood suddenly and came over to Magda's side of the table. She leaned over and wrapped her arms around Magda, whose eyes filled with tears.

"You children, all of you. You are all the life I have had. All that is good with me. I am proud of each of you." Mama had never spoken like that before. Magda pulled away and looked at her. Mama's eyes were dry and her face was calm. "But, yes, every time one of you was born, I felt more ... *überwältigt*."

"Overwhelmed?"

"Like I was torn apart and couldn't get back together. Thank God, my sisters were able to help us. And your father. He always tried."

It struck Magda that she couldn't remember how long it had been since she and Mama last touched. She stroked Mama's hands and saw how rough the nails and skin were. Her hair obviously hadn't been washed for quite a while, and maybe they wouldn't do that for her in the hospital. "Come with me," she said suddenly, pulling her mother around the waist and drawing her upstairs. "I want to give you a shampoo—like you did for me when I was little."

Mama let herself be led into the bathroom and Magda untied the drawstring at the neck of her nightgown and wrapped a towel around it. "Now just wait another minute."

She ran downstairs and picked up the kettle, which fortunately was full and still warm on the stove. She brought it to the bathroom. Gently, she helped Mama kneel down at the large clawfoot tub. Magda blended the water till it was tepid and poured it over Mama's salt-and-pepper hair. She placed some liquid soap in her hands and massaged it gently into Mama's scalp, running her fingers along the long strands. Neither of them spoke.

After rinsing with the warm water, Magda rubbed rosewater lotion into her mother's hair and carefully combed it out. She placed a clean towel over Mama's head and led her to her bed.

"Now, let's take care of your hands."

Mama let Magda hold each of her hands to massage them gently and file the nails. She took a scented cream of Willa's and spread it slowly on Mama's arms. Then she stroked her hair with the towel and spread it out to dry on the pillow.

Mama closed her eyes. Magda leaned in and inhaled her mother's scent until memories of her childhood overtook her. Days when she sat on her mother's lap and rested her head on her soft shoulders. The smell of laundry soap and the rosewater rinse she'd always used.

Mama took Magda's hands and kissed them. "I try to sleep now. And you want to study. My good girl." She rolled to her side.

Magda tried to focus on her books for a little while longer. Her mind kept wandering to two girls her own age. One cocky, rebellious, determined to have her own way. The other lacking confidence, fearful, following anyone who might help her find herself. Magda knew she wasn't either of those girls, but sometimes she could be both of them.

Papa woke her very early the next morning. Richy got up shortly after, despite Magda's efforts to tiptoe out of the room to dress in the bathroom. She went downstairs to make breakfast for everyone.

Mama was quiet and withdrawn, not reacting much to Magda's efforts to be cheerful or to Richy's questions to Papa about the milk horse. Magda wondered how much her little brother would miss his mother when she was away.

They finished the eggs and warmed-over potatoes, drank the coffee and milk. "Should I pack sandwiches?" Magda asked. Papa said it wasn't necessary, but she put some bread and cheese in a paper bag for him anyway and filled a thermos with the rest of the coffee.

Minnie and Tilly entered the front door. They would drive Papa and Mama to the hospital and stay as long as he wanted. The aunts bundled their sister into her coat and checked her small valise, which, as they suspected, hadn't been packed with much care. No one knew how long she would be in the hospital this time or what she might need.

At the door, Magda threw her arms around her mother and kissed her cheeks and neck. She lifted Richy and told him to give Mama a big hug and kiss too, which he did in a rushed, little boy way. The adults hurried down the front steps into Minnie's car, with her at the wheel. Papa closed all the doors firmly. The last click sounded like Magda's childhood memories being locked away.

Papa didn't come home until after dinnertime. He looked dead tired. He sat heavily on a dining room chair and asked Magda to pour him a beer. She removed his dinner plate from the oven and placed it in front of him. He ate slowly.

"How did it go?" she asked tentatively, when he had finished most of his food. "Did the doctors say how long she would have to stay?"

He didn't answer until the glass was empty.

"They don't know. They want to wean her off the opium. They gave it to her at first as a tonic for her melancholy, but she has become dependent. Too many patients in her state take an overdose, they say, which can be fatal. But they think there is a chance she might improve without it. There are risks either way."

Seeing Magda's skeptical look, he went on.

"Laudanum did help her, for a few years. I think it makes her more listless now and disturbs her sleep."

"Why can't she just stop taking it then, and stay here with us?" Magda couldn't resist pressing him.

Papa turned his head away. "It's a difficult thing to withdraw from that drug. She has to be under a doctor's supervision." His shoulders shook. She threw her arms around him and felt his heaving breaths. "It will be okay, Papa," she whispered. "I know Mama understands that we want what's best for her, and she accepts that. She does. I know it."

After a few minutes he collected himself and looked across the room, but not at Magda. His eyes seemed unfocused and his fingers played with his unlit pipe. "I should not have married your mother. She never wanted to be married."

Magda started. "What do you mean? How can you say that?"

MAGDA, STANDING

"I was thinking only of myself. I told you that after I arrived in America I was afraid the German agents would find me and send me back. It was not unheard of."

Papa seemed far away. Magda shared his growing tension as she listened.

"But why—what does that have to do with Mama?"

"Oh, I fell in love the first time I met her, soon after she arrived to your aunts' house. But I was too eager. I fear I rushed her into agreeing to marry me. I wasn't earning enough to support both of us and had sent all my savings to Rolf. But I wanted to marry even so, since I was sure I would never be deported if I had a wife here."

Magda's mind raced over what she knew of her family. Her parents were married in '84, and Anton was born in '86. They hadn't been forced into a hurried wedding. "But why do you say Mama didn't want to marry you?"

Papa shifted in his seat and looked up. It was as if he suddenly realized he was musing out loud to his youngest daughter and expressing thoughts that he'd always intended to suppress. "I can't explain it to you, you wouldn't understand." He pushed away his chair suddenly and rose, ending his revelations.

Magda didn't want to lose the rare moment of confidence with Papa. "It doesn't sound like it was all your fault, that Uncle Rolf couldn't follow you here or even that Mama maybe didn't feel ready to marry. You always did your best, Papa. Mama told me she thought so. And she told me," Magda's throat tightened, "that she wasn't sorry she had all of us." Papa stroked her hair but turned away and left the room.

Magda saw that she was now the one needing to console and be understanding. Life often wasn't what it seemed, she thought. People weren't always what they seemed. Even those you looked up to had little control of their lives. As Mama had said, Papa always tried and meant well. That might be the most anyone could do.

MAGDA, STANDING

15

Magda and Richy both had their birthdays in April, but there wasn't any sense of celebration within the family. President Wilson had declared war against Germany and the Central Powers on April 6, and that was all anyone thought or talked about.

She didn't see much of her siblings these days. Fred was always out, and Tony was too busy to come by. When Sabine brought their children over to play with Richy, they would usually stay later to see Papa—but he often went from work to the hospital these days. Despite Mama's emotional disengagement, she had been the reason the family members made an effort to come to the house regularly, and her absence created an imbalance they all felt.

Magda and her siblings hadn't had dinner together since their mother left. Finally, their father, missing the tradition, asked everyone to come on a Sunday in late May. Magda baked a cake to belatedly celebrate her own birthday and Richy's, with twenty candles as the sum of their ages. But the latest news made it a somber occasion.

"It is bad enough Wilson let the Kaiser provoke him and declared war," Papa declared irritably as the men sat together before dinner. He had been a consistent advocate of the President's efforts to keep the country apart from the European conflict. But with unremittingly awful news about the desperate suffering caused to Belgium and France, destruction of towns and countryside, continued sinking of ships at sea, and the mounting loss of life on all sides, Americans had grown increasingly in favor of entering the war "to destroy the autocratic Germans and save the democracies of Europe." Papa still wasn't convinced.

"And now this selective service law!" Magda glanced into the sitting room and saw her father holding up a recent newspaper. He read the headline aloud: "It is in no sense a conscription of the unwilling; it is rather a selection from a nation which has volunteered its mass."

"That Wilson! We have not volunteered our young men. He should at least be honest about it."

Willa and Sabine abruptly paused their conversation in the kitchen as Papa's voice boomed through the house. Magda knew that all women had the draft on their minds since the government's decision was announced after weeks of talk and speculation. All men over twenty-one—that meant Fred and Johannes. Tony was thirty-one, just past the upper end of the draft, and he was married with three children, but he might not be exempted indefinitely.

"Johannes may be able to stay back because the army needs the steel mills to keep running," Willa whispered, her face pale. "But he doesn't want to look like a slacker." Already the papers reported disparaging talk about men who hadn't volunteered immediately when war was declared.

Magda stood in the dining room to be able to hear both conversations. Fred spoke next. "Papa, I have to tell you something. I enlisted last week. I resigned from my job, but the boss says I can have it back when I return—victorious, of course!" He chuckled dryly. He paused, but their father didn't reply. "I'm not like some of the guys who think going to war is a great adventure and they can't wait, as if they'll all come back covered with medals. I understand what you've always told us. But if those of us from German stock don't enlist and have to be dragged into this war, how does that look? We should be the first to go out and whip the old crowd for their aggression. Don't you think so?"

"Me too," Johannes broke in. "I enlisted on Friday. The older guys at the plant can make the steel, I want to use it against the Kaiser. And I heard we'd get some benefits, better assignments maybe, if we didn't wait to be drafted."

Magda looked at Willa, who was now white. Johannes must not have told her yet.

"I want to, but with the kids and another on the way, Sabine wants me to wait until I have to go," Tony said. "But this war could be a once-in-a-lifetime opportunity for a photographer. I've learned enough of the basics and I need a chance to apply it. It would be a lot more interesting on the front than taking family portraits every day."

Con, who held a standing invitation to family dinners, remarked quietly, "That's what I wanted—to be one of the first journalists out there, to make a name for myself. But if you get close to the action, the conditions are nothing like working here. Rain and muck, and no supplies when you need them.

The press photographers I knew probably lost five or six films for every one they could use. Sometimes dumb luck was in their favor when they got good shots. It wasn't in mine."

Papa fingered his pipe and looked down. "I don't blame you, any of you, for wanting to go against the enemy with other young men and do your part as you see it. Once war happens, it has a terrible logic that can drag you in. With each loss it is said, 'Do not let them die in vain!' and so it goes. However horrible the start, it demands an equal response, and soon there is nothing good or noble in it."

Magda called the men to the table. Con sat to Papa's right and Magda took Mama's place at the other end. From there, she could scan the table for anyone's needs, and watch Con without being obvious. They often exchanged smiling glances that, to Magda's relief, didn't raise her color every time.

Papa was uncharacteristically quiet while they ate, and the young people tried to avoid further talk of the war. Through the roast beef and up to the fruit and cheese, Fred steered the conversation to baseball and the prospects of the Pirates finally repeating their first World Series win of 1909.

"But you know," Johannes didn't resist noting, "most of the team might be drafted and the whole season suspended. Fans would have to depend on amateur teams, while they last."

"That wouldn't be so bad," Tony interjected, "since the Homestead Grays here are one of the best in the Negro league and really worth watching. But maybe they'll be drafted too."

When Kitty had been in the group, Willa found no difficulty talking about decorating the apartment. She tried to broach the subject with Sabine, but her voice faded when she came to the point about fabrics becoming harder to find because of the military's needs.

MAGDA, STANDING

The family never wasted food and every bite was finished, but Magda thought it wasn't just from habit, or hunger, or good manners this time. She felt there was something final about it. Meat would also become scarce and expensive, and probably other staples too. They might not have another meal like this for quite a while, with the table well laid and the places filled with most of the people she cared about. Mama was away, and Kitty. Soon Fred, Johannes, maybe even Tony.

Magda was determined that she wouldn't be left behind. She wanted to do her part too. And she wanted, finally, to have a say in what that would be.

―

"Fred, hold still!" Magda struggled to reinforce the button that was coming loose on his army uniform. "How can this brand-new jacket have a loose button already?" He hadn't wanted to remove the jacket and was in a hurry to go downstairs. "Let me at least give you a needle and thread in case this happens again. What will you do out in the field if you can't close your jacket properly?" She wrapped the supplies in a small piece of cloth and tucked it into his vest pocket.

"They'll probably court-martial me," Fred grinned.

"Let me look at you," she said. Fred stood proudly in his full private's uniform. "The jacket is so full of pockets! Think about what else you want to take from here, you have lots of room. Here, I bought you something for the journey." She reached into a drawer and pulled out a packet of his favorite treat, licorice, and some chocolates.

"Aw, thanks, Magda. I can trade this for cigarettes when we get underway."

"I expect you to enjoy it and think of me, not trade it! Although, I guess there'll be times when you'll want to. It's odd to think of—candy as money." She looked him over. "Such funny pants. Why the bulge on the sides, as if you were going horseback riding? And why do you have those wraps over your calves? Won't that make it harder to get your boots on and off?"

"They call them puttees. Who knows? I bet the army just patched together some scraps and this is what it looked like. I'll let you know if these serve any useful purpose." He stuffed the candy into one of the jacket pockets and picked up a small leather folder he'd set down on the bed.

"What's that?" She reached for it but he pulled it behind him, and they tussled for a few seconds as they used to. Finally, he let her look at it, a soft packet holding a pad of fine paper, some blank postcards and envelopes, a pen, and a slot for stamps. "This is lovely! Did you buy this for yourself? I'm sure the army didn't issue it."

He looked down and slipped it into the other jacket pocket. "Elise gave it to me. Sort of a thank you, you know."

"You'd better write to her, then."

Fred started to the stairs, then turned around. "But how do I look? Ready to put the fear of God into the enemy?"

Magda shook her head slowly as the realization of what he was undertaking hit her fully. Fred, who tackled any problem head-on and usually came out ahead, would become a small cog in a terrible war machine.

Downstairs, Johannes had arrived with Willa, who was crying. Papa gave both men a long embrace and Magda could tell he was holding in his emotions with difficulty.

"You look very handsome too!" Magda said to Johannes, affecting cheer in an attempt to counter Willa's sobs. "But it's not just the uniform. Maybe if we had told you fellas that ear-lier, you wouldn't have been in such a rush to join up." Tony had borrowed Minnie's Ford to drive them to the train station, and he arrived at the door.

Magda wondered what it was about war that made young men and old politicians think it was all about glory and virtue. Papa had spoken often enough about how it devastated the people and the land long after it was supposedly over—and that it was never really over. Aunt Minnie had made a point of ensuring that Magda read various historical accounts to gain perspective. "If women wrote history, we'd see a different side of the whole military business," she often insisted.

They all went out to the front porch and after more hugs and kisses than the family had exchanged in years, the young men loaded their duffle bags into the back of the Ford. Val was going along for the ride and Richy pleaded with Magda to go too. "Let him!" Tony said.

She held Richy's hand tighter. Of course, he was excited to be with the men, to see their caps and uniforms, to sit in the car and look at the trains, to feel the electric atmosphere, whatever the cause. Magda wondered: Would there be a scene like this for Richy someday? Surely not, if this was to be "the war to end all wars," as President Wilson called it.

"Well, alright," she said finally, helping him into the car and seeing him settled between Fred and Johannes. "But, Tony, make sure he doesn't disappear among the troops. And keep him close to you when they've gone."

"I'll be careful with the boys," her brother answered, laugh-ing, "or Sabine will do me worse than the Kaiser!"

The car pulled away from the house, but stopped suddenly as it approached the end of the block. Fred opened the door and ran across the road. As Magda raised her hand to shield her eyes from the sun, she saw Elise standing on the far street corner with Martin. Fred threw his arms around her and gave her a long kiss, then picked up the boy and hugged him too. After a few minutes and loud honking from Tony, Fred returned to the car and it drove out of sight.

"Well, I'll be!" she muttered to herself. Something she had failed to learn while studying.

16

On a warm day in early June, Magda entered the high school auditorium for the final examinations in an anxious mood. Not so much from fear of not being prepared, but from remembering the last time she'd seen her classmates together. Almost all the boys were taking the exams before deployment and many of the girls were doing so as well, hoping to get jobs that men were vacating. During the break, she heard the boys talking among themselves about their hopes to fly the new planes, or go to sea and battle the submarines. They didn't have much to say to Magda. She envied their anticipation of adventure, however misguided she suspected it might be.

"Are the others continuing for senior year?" she asked one of the girls from the honors society as they walked out together.

"Not many, I think," she answered. "The school is offering intensive summer classes so more of the girls can be ready to support the war effort in various ways. If they still want, some

CHRISTINE FALLERT KESSIDES

may try to graduate in the fall." Many things were going to change, that was clear.

Magda received her results a week later—she had passed all subjects and was given her diploma "with distinction." Over the next few days, she found it hard adjusting to the sudden lack of structure and couldn't sleep. It wasn't just that home life wasn't the same, but Europe's war—now America's too—added a cloud of menace that hung in the air like a more dangerous pollution.

Papa was preoccupied with daily visits to the hospital. Minnie or Tilly often went with him, but they all strongly discouraged Magda from coming along.

"Why not?" she asked. "I'm not a child. I know it's probably hard to see some of the patients there, but my peers are facing worse on the battlefield. Doesn't Mama want me to visit?"

But her father was firm. "This is not the time." He said she was not allowed more visitors and wouldn't recognize even family members for a while. She had everything she needed for now, he insisted.

The one positive development was that Magda started seeing more of Willa, who was five months pregnant and often came over to spend a day or overnight at the house for the company. "It doesn't feel as exciting with Johannes not here to share," she said sadly.

"At least you have something good to look forward to," Magda said. "And sewing the layette can be a new display of your talents! You could make more to sell privately. And when the baby comes, maybe Johannes can get leave—unless the war is over before the year is out, as some say."

"You're so practical, as always," Willa said, putting an arm around her sister. "I guess I can watch Richy more often. I just need to stay occupied."

MAGDA, STANDING

"That'd be wonderful!" Magda exclaimed. "Because ... I'd really like to join the Red Cross. This is a great chance to start training as a nurse's aide and get some medical experience quickly."

Magda had never mentioned to her family that she thought of entering a health profession. Going to university would be impossible anytime soon, especially with the expenses for Mama in the hospital. But if war was going to disrupt everything, why shouldn't she take advantage of it?

"Yes, volunteering, that's a good idea," Willa mused. "Several of my friends have mentioned that. They'll need a lot of sewing—making uniforms, bandages, and so on. Not up to my skills, but anything to get my mind off Johannes ending up in a trench somewhere."

The next day brought welcome news. "A letter from Johannes!" Willa exclaimed as she sat down with Magda for dinner. "He's in Baltimore. He says he was transferred from their train at Philadelphia and lost touch with Fred. He doesn't know how long they'll be there, but he's in an engineering unit with other guys who've worked in the mills and factories, and they're preparing construction supplies to be shipped abroad. Oh, I hope they stay there! It's not so far from here. Maybe he'll even get leave sometime soon."

Not wanting to waste another moment, Magda dug out the phone number she had kept for months. Two days later, she sat on the trolley nervously fingering her handbag. She wore her best dress and a new hat borrowed from Willa. It had been so long since she'd gotten this dressed up to go anywhere, apart from Sunday church. The dress hem rose a bit too far above the top of her shoes, which pinched slightly. She thought she should have stopped growing, but was now taller than Willa. She would ask Willa to alter another of the dresses Kitty had left at the house. Willa would know how to make it look more fashionable.

Stepping down from the trolley she walked the two blocks to the Red Cross office downtown. Mrs. Ubinger had set an appointment time for their interview. Magda pulled open the door and saw a room full of women, most of them wearing a white pinafore over their dresses with the Red Cross logo on the bib. A few girls around her age sat along the wall, possibly waiting to talk with one of the organizers. Magda didn't recognize anyone, but the headquarters served the whole city.

Mrs. Ubinger stepped out of a room in the back and beckoned Magda to follow. The office was lightly furnished but filled nearly to the ceiling with boxes of supplies and stacks of papers. She gestured Magda to one of the two chairs in front of the crowded desk bearing a small plaque labeled "Supervisor of Volunteers."

"Well, my dear, I'm so happy you're here, I was wondering when I'd hear from you and was about to call you myself." Mrs. Ubinger didn't waste her energy on small talk or even much of a greeting. "I wanted to discuss what you could do for us, separately from our general orientation of prospective volunteers. That's why I asked you to meet me first. I spoke with your Aunt Minnie earlier this month, at the funeral of a mutual friend—as you may know, we've known each other for years, from the church auxiliary when I lived in the same parish, and—"

"No, I didn't know," Magda interrupted, nervously wondering if things were being planned for her again. Aunt Minnie wouldn't do that, she was sure.

MAGDA, STANDING

"I asked her about you. She told me how well you completed your high school studies while managing your other duties." She leaned forward and began a speech that Magda thought sounded slightly rehearsed. "We seek an arrangement for the volunteers' children, as I'd mentioned before. We can't rely on informal family care when we need many women to support our fighting men from the home front. And there are many other jobs that women will have to fill while the men are away, both here in the ARC but also in offices, factories, and many services. Even the supply deliveries used to be done for us by men, but we women will need to handle almost all of this. That reminds me," she suddenly murmured to herself and grabbed a paper, scribbling some notes. "I will get in touch with the high school administrators to see if boys who haven't reached draft age can help with that. So," she looked up again at Magda, stressing her words, "tending the children is a critical need and I hope we can count on you."

Magda was taken aback. The woman didn't seem to care about hearing what she wanted or was interested in. Magda wished she had thought to discuss with the aunts how to present herself. She suddenly felt as if she'd been hauled before the school principal or the parish priest and given a test or a penance that she didn't feel should be hers.

"Um, thank you for your confidence in me, Mrs. Ubinger," Magda replied, her voice coming out weaker than she intended. "I understand that there is much critical work to be done. And I want to help the war effort to the best of my abilities. But..." Her mind raced. What was the best way to say this? "I was really hoping to be trained as a nurse's aide, to take care of the soldiers on the battlefield."

Mrs. Ubinger looked surprised and seemed to see her for the first time. "You don't consider it worth your time to take care of children?"

"Oh no, of course I do!" Magda replied indignantly, eyes flashing at the thought she was being deliberately misunderstood. "It's just that I've completed science and other courses to earn my diploma, and I would like to apply my education now." She would have said she was more qualified than many other girls her age, but feared that would sound arrogant. After all, what were Mrs. Ubinger's qualifications to be in such a responsible position?

"Hmm." The woman narrowed her eyes, but she sounded more curious than irritated. "Your aunt said you were very well organized and good at enlisting others to help you, including herself and Tilly. She also said you can speak for yourself about what you want." She shook her head. "I don't mean that I see you simply as someone to care for children."

Magda gave a sigh of relief.

"But you may not realize, my dear," Mrs. Ubinger pursued, "that being in the Red Cross is a bit like joining an army. You do need to take assignments that you may not always prefer. And, as to nursing, many young girls have romantic notions of being an 'angel' to our soldiers, saving their lives and perhaps falling in love with a patient or doctor." She made an exaggerated flourish with her hands. "You may not be aware that much of a nurse's aide job, at least in the Red Cross, is as much drudgery as that of the common housemaid—cleaning up, washing linens, serving meals, and so on, twelve hours a day or more. Especially in war zones. Our nurse's aides get a few weeks of training, but you may not have much opportunity to use your schooling in math or science."

MAGDA, STANDING

Magda felt defensive, not chastened. "I do understand," she retorted. "I've read about Florence Nightingale and Clara Barton. I know that nursing takes a special dedication and it often isn't pretty. Or safe. In fact, Edith Cavell is one of my heroines."

Mrs. Ubinger nodded. "We're all inspired by that martyr. Even before she flouted the Germans in Belgium and they shot her—those beasts—she was an exemplary instructor of nursing. If we had a patron saint of the profession, it would be she."

Magda took a deep breath. She needed to bring the conversation back to her own wishes. "As I haven't signed up yet, I'd like to think about it before making a commitment." The woman looked surprised. "I'd like to talk with my aunts and get their advice. It's a big decision for me, and I will have to check with my father too." Magda thought he would be inclined to tell her to stay home with Richy, and she would need to consider her approach to him carefully. She didn't want the same outcome as last year.

"That's a good idea, you do that," Mrs. Ubinger replied, and pushed back her chair. "They are wise women and I would respect their opinions. If they agree with mine, of course!" She smiled slightly and stood up to gesture that the meeting was over. Magda felt a strain in their goodbye.

Arriving home, Magda's spirits were lifted by a letter addressed to her from Fred. He had written from a train station in South Carolina.

> June 4
> Dear Magda,
>   Well, finally unbending after two days on a crowded troop train. No fancy sleeping or

dining cars on this one, but I wouldn't know anyway, this being my first train trip, right? Guys hanging out of the windows, sleeping in the corridors. We played cards, smoked and traded our supplies, but probably should have held on to them till we get overseas. I did manage to keep your licorice for myself, so far. Can you send me some of those Clark bars they started making in Pittsburgh? Two candy bars might fetch a whole pack of cigarettes. I can't tell you where to send anything yet, but hope to get an address once we start training.

Please give Richy a big hug for me. He should start learning to throw a ball soon, so you need to teach him what I taught you and don't let him get too henpecked. Tell him I'll play with him and take him to see a real ball game when I get back.

Please also give Mama a kiss for me and tell her I love her. I can't remember the last time I did that. I feel real bad that I was at work the day she left for the hospital. Probably she doesn't even know I joined up, so please tell her I'm traveling for work. Just to delay her worry a little longer.

I'll write again when we get to basic camp.

—Fred

MAGDA, STANDING

Magda had written Fred the day after he left, sent to a common postal number that families were told to use. She realized that the letter was probably in the bottom of a bin on an even slower train to wherever Fred's outfit would end up for training. Just to be sure, she sat down to quickly write another.

June 11

Dear Fred,

Your letter of June 4 arrived today. I so wish we had thought to take a photo of you in your uniform! Richy asks about you every day and it's not enough to talk about you, which we do — he keeps asking where you are and wants to go see you. If you have a chance, can you please have a photo taken and send it to us before you go overseas?

I haven't been allowed yet to go visit Mama during this hospital stay, but I'm determined to find a way there anyway and will carry your message.

Speaking of love, I am rather surprised, to say the least, that neither you nor Elise saw fit to let me know that you were so sweet on each other, when I was the instrument of your meeting! I am pleased, of course, but I hope you aren't both swept up by the excitement and emotion of this time. I keep hearing of couples that are hurriedly getting engaged and even married before deployment. And, although I trust you (despite you not letting me know about it), I hope you don't raise Elise's hopes with a too-hurried courtship. I feel protective of her—even from my brother!

Do I sound like an older relative now?

Sending you as much love and more,
Magda

She put the sheet in an envelope but didn't seal it, hoping that before tomorrow's post they might receive another letter with a more specific address.

Changing out of her town clothes, she went into the kitchen to prepare something for dinner. Often her father ate at the hospital, something the aunts may have brought when they were visiting together. Magda felt again the irritation of being treated like a child who wasn't allowed to see her own mother. She was certain that not only would Mama appreciate her visit, but it would make it easier to accept the long separation and even more, the not knowing that was always in the back of her mind.

As Papa still hadn't returned and the dinner hour was passing, Magda sat alone and ate without much appetite, mulling over her conversation with Mrs. Ubinger. There was so much she needed to work out. Would Sabine and Willa be willing to take care of Richy more often, and even let him sleep over at their houses as agreed this evening, so Magda could spend whole days downtown to take the training without major interruptions? Would her father agree to that in the first place—and what if he didn't? Would Minnie and Tilly be willing to step in again and support her—and what did she need to ask them to do, exactly? She knew they didn't feel up to taking over the care of Richy, but they did exert influence on Papa, and she felt certain they would help her make her case.

And, if she actually gained enough control of her time, what should she say to Mrs. Ubinger about her request? Her stomach tightened as she thought of all the uncertainty and potential disappointment ahead; this would require careful planning and a good dose of luck.

17

L ater that evening, Magda looked at the clock. It was almost ten thirty. Papa had never come home from the hospital at such a late hour. She tried calling her aunts' house, but no one answered. That probably meant all three of them were still at the hospital or returning home. What if they'd had an accident? She could try to call the hospital. She ran upstairs to her parents' bedroom and rifled through some papers on the dressing table. The room had become increasingly disorderly, and she saw that Papa had left out a stack of bills from the doctor. Her eyes scanned past the telephone number as she searched for details about her mother's diagnosis and treatment.

Suddenly, the front door opened and she heard low voices. They were back! She quickly shuffled the bills into their original pile, deciding to look through them carefully another time, and ran to the stairs. "I was getting worried," she called down.

MAGDA, STANDING

Papa stood at the foot of the stairs and looked up at Magda. "Your mother...our Sarah..." He bowed his head. Magda flew down the final steps and almost threw herself at Tilly, who stood beside him. "What happened?" she gasped.

Tilly and Minnie each put an arm around Magda's shoulders and held her close between them. "It was her heart," Minnie said, more shakily than Magda had ever heard her speak. "We knew she had a weak heart. The doctors thought she would be well enough to withdraw from the opium, but—"

Magda pulled away and stared at them, then at Papa, who had dropped his jacket and turned around slowly to face her. "Yes, my child," he whispered. "Your mama is gone."

Her face started burning and she struggled to catch her breath. She felt a surging rage at all of them: Papa, Minnie, and Tilly, the doctors.

Not angry at Mama now. For once, despite all the times she had resented her mother's weakness, her inability to manage the household, her absence from her life and Richy's, Magda felt only guilt.

She should have protected Mama more. Done more to help her. Sympathized more. Just sat down with her sometimes and rubbed her shoulders. Anything. But she could do nothing now.

Papa told Minnie and Tilly to go home. They looked exhausted. They had all stopped at Tony's house to tell him, and then at Willa's. That's why they were so late.

She resented being the last to learn, but she stifled her anger to tend to Papa, who hadn't eaten anything since breakfast. She put out his dinner plate, some cheese, and a glass of beer after they left. He picked at it, holding his head in his hand.

"What happened?" she asked quietly, trying to keep her voice steady.

"Her heart gave out, that's all," he replied, looking up at her finally. "I'm sorry I didn't let you go see her at the hospital. She was sleeping most of the time, and when she was awake, she didn't talk to us. It's best that you remember her as she was. In her good times," he added, his voice breaking.

"Did she at least have the Last Rites?" Magda asked, ready to burst out critically if the answer was no. She was sure that Mama would have wanted that. But she had never heard any conversation suggesting that her mother's illness was life-threatening, that she would ever be close to death from it. She had appeared healthy in most respects.

"Yes, Father Magnus went to see her last week and I asked him to give her the sacrament, just to be safe. She died peacefully, Magda. In her sleep. She felt no pain from her heart."

He pushed out his chair, placing his arm heavily on Magda's more to help him rise than as a gesture of comfort. "In the morning we will talk more."

Magda sat in the dark in her room, bereft but unable to cry. It was so unfair. She was sure that when they'd said goodbye, Mama expected to come back. Papa may have suspected that his wife was in danger, and yet Magda hadn't been allowed to visit. But her greatest concern was for Richy, who had known their mother so little. And Fred—she would never be able to pass along his message now. Magda knew she should say a prayer, but she felt like cursing God instead.

~

MAGDA, STANDING

The family decided to lay out the body in the aunts' sitting room. Papa had wanted the showing in his house as would be customary, but the women all convinced him that for Richy's sake it was better to have the wake elsewhere, and Minnie and Tilly were as deeply bereaved as anyone. "This was the least we could do for her," Tilly said to Magda, her voice breaking into sobs as they prepared the room for the round-the-clock sitting.

"I think you both did a great deal for Mama," Magda replied, kissing her aunt gently. She felt numb; her anger at the aunts, which had been a first wild reaction, hadn't survived the night. She remembered their conversation about how they had insisted their sister come to America, and had encouraged her to marry Papa. Maybe they regretted some of that, in a way. But Magda felt now that her mother hadn't regretted it. At least, that's what she had to believe.

She insisted on coming to the house before anyone else, to help Minnie and Tilly prepare. Magda had seen the bodies of deceased neighbors, family friends, and relatives laid out in their homes many times before, but they were always older or very sick people whose deaths were expected. She felt close to Mama at this moment and wanted to touch her again, before everyone else got there.

Papa had gone to the hospital and accompanied the body to the house. Magda and her aunts dressed Mama in her best outfit, the silvery gray dress she had worn for Willa's wedding. They braided and wrapped her hair around her head. She looked beautifully serene.

The immediate family, first only the other adults—Willa, Tony, and Sabine—gathered around the casket a short while later, holding hands as Papa recited prayers. Kitty's employer had paid for flowers and her train fare, so she would be arriving by evening.

Neighbors brought the children in later, before other visitors. Richy had been staying with Willa since the previous day. "He doesn't know yet," Willa whispered, "I thought it best for you to tell him." Under some circumstances, Magda might have thought Willa was unfairly passing on a difficult task, but now it seemed only right—an acknowledgment of Magda's special relationship to him. She took him to the garden out back, where he had often played during her lessons.

"Richy, I have to tell you something," she began, shakily.

"Mama's sleeping, long time," he said, matter-of-factly. Seeing her surprise, he added, "Anna told me." Tony and Sabine's firstborn was seven and proud of her status as the oldest grandchild. He swung his legs as they sat on the garden bench, playing with a stick he'd picked up.

"Oh—yes. You know Mama was often sick, and she was very tired. She went to the hospital to get better, but the doctors couldn't make her well." Magda paused, her throat tightening on her words. "Richy, Mama can't come back to us ever again. She has gone to heaven to be with God." She hated herself for using such a common explanation—not that she didn't believe it, but she felt no balm in the phrase now and it seemed so inadequate for the child.

"I know. But you take care of me. You won't leave," he asserted, looking at her directly with a confidence that clearly meant comfort for him. And almost a challenge to her.

Magda opened her mouth, closed it, and buried his hand in the folds of her black skirt. She hadn't thought this through. Of course, he would think that. She had been the most important person in his life this past year. Didn't he deserve some certainty that she would remain here for him?

"I will take care of you, yes," she replied slowly, measuring her words. "I love you so much. Mama loved you, too, very much," she added quickly, "and Papa does, too, and Fred and Kitty and Tony and Sabine and Willa and Johannes. And Aunt Minnie and Tilly!"

Richy swung his legs harder under the bench and sidled closer to her.

"And now that you're so much bigger, you can play more with your cousins, who also love you."

"Can I see Fred soon?"

Magda winced. Maybe she shouldn't have mentioned Fred right now. If he were here she thought she'd be sitting close to him for her own comfort, with her head on his shoulder. She felt her face ache with the pent-up tears she wasn't sure she could control much longer.

"Fred can't come home right now. You remember, he's in the army and he's very busy learning to march with the other soldiers. But he's thinking of us, and of Mama, right now, I'm sure. And when he comes back, he said he'll take you to a real baseball game!"

They sat quietly for a few minutes, Richy playing with the stick. "What do you think about when you think of Mama?" Magda asked softly. It didn't seem fair to have their conversation turn away from her so quickly.

"She rubs my head. Like that!" Richy reached up and stroked Magda's hair. "And sometimes I sit on her lap." His eyes roamed the yard, as if he was looking for something. "She makes me chocolate to drink, like you do." He looked up. "That's all."

Magda's eyes filled with tears. That wasn't all, she knew, but it was enough for now. She would make a point of collecting memories of Mama with Richy. Maybe walk around the house pointing out the places where she'd liked to sit and the things that were special to her: her favorite vase and tea cup, the shawl she wore around the house.

Richy jumped off the bench and gestured for Magda to get up too. "I'm thirsty. Can I have a drink?" Magda was grateful for this simple wish, his focus on the present moment and the brief distraction it meant for her. They would have other conversations about their mother, and about Fred, and Richy would learn to understand. Magda wasn't sure if *she* would.

Father Magnus celebrated the Mass for the Dead two days later. In his sermon, he referred to their mother's illness as "the glory and nobility of suffering." He went on to say, "Our sister Sarah never complained, and devoted herself to her family as much as her illness permitted. She is an example for us all."

Magda squirmed in her seat. Mama's suffering was so cruel, and what choices did she ever have? When did her mother have a chance to be really happy?

Later, as the neighbors and family friends milled about quietly and shared the food some had generously contributed, Magda felt a tap on her shoulder. She turned and saw Con standing there in a dark suit, his blond hair falling over his forehead.

"Oh! Hello," she stammered. "Thank you for coming. Fred would be grateful that you're here."

MAGDA, STANDING

"I didn't come only for him, but for your whole family. You've all been so welcoming to me. Your mother seemed like a very sweet woman. And, especially, I came for you. I knew you'd be giving your family special support, as you always do, and maybe you'd need some of your own. And for Richy."

Magda was dumbfounded. How did Con always touch a nerve in a way that warmed her all over? "Did you get some food?" she asked awkwardly. He shook his head.

"Later, perhaps. Let's step outside. It's too warm in here, isn't it?"

They slipped out the side door and walked to the bench behind the house. Magda sat back and leaned her head to touch the tree behind. She hadn't realized how tense she had been all day.

"It was a nice service, I thought." Con continued. "Many people like and respect your family, as I do." He smiled gently.

Magda felt a flush of irritation, recalling her internal argument with the priest's words. "I wonder," she said, "if people would have been as sympathetic if Mama's heart attack had happened at home. It was only because she was in the state mental hospital that some people may have realized she was really sick, not just weak and tired all the time, or maybe even lazy." She paused and looked at him. "That's what even I used to think, and sometimes," she choked up, "I almost hated her for it." She lowered her head into her hands.

Con put his arm on her shoulders. "We can't understand fully the pain in someone's mind." He sat back and glanced over the yard. "There is a lot of that in this war. The French and British soldiers have been months and even years in and out of the trenches, facing constant bombardment. When they come back, some of them are truly unable to talk, or sleep, or eat. I saw men staring at nothing for hours, maybe days, shaking uncontrollably. Some of their superiors and fellow soldiers think they're faking, just trying to get out of fighting by pretending to be crazy. But I think it's real. They're deeply in shock. And sometimes it doesn't get better even if they're sent home."

Magda suddenly remembered Aunt Minnie telling her about their brother Herman. She sat up, "Will that happen to Fred if he has to be out there for several months?"

"I'm sorry," Con shifted on the bench, "I meant to say something sympathetic, but I'm afraid I've upset you more. I've been thoughtless. Forgive me."

"No, I want to hear what you have to say," Magda replied. She didn't want him to think she was too delicate to handle any news about the war. "Please, always be honest with me."

"Try not to worry too much about Fred," Con said. "He's pretty tough, in a good way. Just keep writing to him." He paused and stretched his arm. "You know, working for the paper, I can get information about some of the troop movements. I'll try to find out where they're sending his unit, so maybe you can write letters that get there in reasonable time. A lot of letters will get lost, you have to expect that, but it helps to have a better address."

They stood and Magda looked at him warmly. "Could you come by sometime to see Richy?" she asked, feeling bolder now. "He misses Fred a lot, and my brother Tony is so busy. I'm sorry—of course, you're busy too!"

Con threw his head back and laughed. She liked his combination of earnestness and the kind, easy humor that always seemed close to the surface. "Yes, I'd like that. In fact, I was going to suggest that the three of us go for an outing soon.

Maybe to the natural history museum? Has Richy ever seen the Diplodocus?"

"Oh, my goodness, that would be wonderful!" Magda exclaimed, her voice rising like a child's. "I was there once for a school trip, years ago. We would love that. Richy and I haven't been much of anywhere, really, for the past year— except when I first went to the Red Cross office downtown a few months ago."

Con looked at her expectantly as they started walking back to the house.

"I want to join the Red Cross, but there are some complications," she said in a low voice. "I really want to train and work as a nurse's aide, and then go to a field station and take care of the soldiers. But they want me to help with child care for the volunteers here—women can't join in large numbers if they don't have anyone to stay with their children." She tried to keep her tone neutral, as she didn't want to appear complaining. But she couldn't make herself sound enthusiastic. It was important that Con see her as capable of more than domestic roles. "I don't know yet what I'll do. I have to think about it."

They reached the front of the house as clusters of visitors were leaving.

"I'm sure you'll be able to arrange a very good solution," Con said, "for them and for yourself. You've organized your life pretty well in the past year, as we've already seen!" He winked at her and she blushed. "May I come and pick you up—Richy and you—a week from next Sunday? I'll be working next weekend, so that's the soonest. About one o'clock?" She nodded and gave him a quick smile, turning away only when Papa called her to meet one of his friends.

Later that evening, Magda sat on the porch of her house drinking a berry cordial with Kitty, who was only able to stay in Pittsburgh for another day. Her employers were leaving for a vacation in the Adirondacks and she was expected to follow them to the resort town and manage their place there. "Maybe you should work for people who aren't so well off," Magda said, only half joking.

"It is a bit much sometimes," Kitty sighed, stretching her legs on the divan. "They pay me well, but I have little control over my time. I haven't gotten a week to myself for so long. In the nicest weather and around holidays, they're entertaining, or they want me to go with them somewhere. I'm looking forward to seeing the mountains—they say it's beautiful there—but sometimes I'd just like to settle into a little house of my own. I suppose I'll never marry, or at least never have children, but I would like to have a place to myself someday."

Magda had always admired Kitty's brisk self-sufficiency. It was hard to imagine her feeling deprived in any way. "Of course, you'll marry!" she insisted. "Isn't there a way you can find a suitable beau? Don't people sometimes put an ad in the paper?"

Kitty chuckled. "Spinster seeking bachelor? No, thank you! I may join a reading group at the library, if they gather on my day off, and do a museum tour occasionally. If I met a nice man that way, we'd have something in common." She twirled her glass and set it down. "Frankly, with the war, there's little chance of finding anyone eligible till it's over. And I don't want to dwell on my small complaints when there are much bigger problems in the world. New York isn't exactly paradise either. Did you know there were food riots there recently? People protesting the rising prices and shortages, and the worst is yet to come. They say whatever happens in this country is felt first in New York City."

Kitty reached over to hold Magda's hand. "I am so sorry I wasn't here when Mama went to the hospital—and I would have made sure we both were able to visit her there." Kitty sighed deeply. "We take so much for granted, but life is never a sure thing. And I regret that I didn't get a chance to say good-bye to Fred before he went off. Who knows when we'll both be back here together again?" She rose, gave Magda a kiss, and went inside.

Magda stayed on the porch a while longer, her gaze fixed on the crescent moon. Strange to think that capable Kitty fretted about too much restraint in her life. So often since leaving childhood, Magda had felt she needed to fight against an invisible current that would leave her cornered, like Mama. And now this war threatened to drain energies that could be devoted to more learning, to discovering and producing new things for the world, to strengthening families and love. She wouldn't let the war drag her down, or the people she cared for most. She would make it work for her.

18

Magda spent the next days trying to think of a response to Mrs. Ubinger's request. Come what may, Magda was determined to become a nurse's aide, but she was also intrigued by the woman's challenge. She couldn't delay much longer before replying, but she was, after all, still in mourning. Meanwhile, she decided to head over to see Elise. She hadn't shared a heart-to-heart with her friend since Fred left. Their arrangement to watch both boys had been disrupted when Elise gave up doing laundry to take a much better paying job as first assistant in Grundel's delicatessen.

"The service was lovely," Elise told her as they embraced and the boys ran to their play area.

"Thank you for the pies! You did so much work in the kitchen; I didn't have a chance to thank you that day."

"I was happy to help, and Mr. Grundel offered the pastries. I didn't even have to ask." When Elise was offered the job,

Magda was very happy for her, since she knew that taking in laundry was something she had done under duress during her first years as a widow. She would be better appreciated as a talented cook and baker.

They sat drinking root beer silently for a few minutes.

"About Fred—" they both spoke in unison, then laughed to the point of almost choking on their sodas.

"I hope—" again, from both. "You first," Elise said, when they caught their breath.

"I was surprised, since he'd never said anything to me—about anything related to a matter of the heart, in fact," Magda continued hurriedly. "I hope he's been a gentleman? You didn't continue my contract as chaperone!" She winked, aware that Elise was much more capable of handling men.

"I hope you aren't offended that you didn't know. Indeed, our feelings grew very fast. Well, we haven't promised each other anything. I said I'd write, and I hope he writes to me. I do care for him, but I know I need to protect my heart and my son's." Elise's voice trailed off as she looked at Martin.

"Let's agree, if either of us receives a letter with news to share, we'll let the other know," Magda replied, and Elise nodded vigorously. "Meanwhile, I need your advice and ideas."

Magda laid out her dilemma about the Red Cross. "They need an arrangement for everything on a large scale."

Elise started tapping her foot, a familiar habit when she was thinking. "The two of us agreed to share childcare last year, and it worked well. You first suggested taking Martin as a favor, but he enjoyed Richy's company so much that watching both on occasion was no trouble for me. And we might not have become friends without that." She paused to untangle the string that pulled Martin's toy truck. "Why couldn't something like that be done for more women and girls who want to work for the Red Cross?"

"What do you mean?"

"Well, I don't know, but suppose for every ten women who want to volunteer, at least half of them have two or three young children. Not all women will want to volunteer full time, and some may be happy to provide childcare as their service. Especially older women, and girls who are a bit too young to be considered for some of the other tasks."

"Yes, yes, you're right!" Magda leaned forward in her seat, pushing the glasses away. "And if I could get the Red Cross to credit this as a service, we could attract people to support the full-time volunteers like me."

"It will take a lot of planning," Elise added slowly. "Someone will need to manage the schedule for the children and adults, and the women will need to commit their time. They'll have to be very serious about it, so the children are properly attended to. And where will they take the children? They can't watch them in their own homes."

Magda chewed her cheek. She sensed Elise was becoming more reserved about the idea as she considered it personally. Magda recalled with chagrin her own failure to be reliable with Richy when studying for the math bee. Would women really put their children in the charge of others they didn't even know?

"Would you be willing to be a part of this—you and Martin?" she asked tentatively.

Elise tapped her arm affectionately. "I'd certainly consider it, when you work it out. I would love to be doing something to support the war effort and I don't have time for other volunteering. But the devil will be in the details, as with everything."

MAGDA, STANDING

Magda nodded with a knowing smile and called for Richy to leave. She realized that it was one thing to manage her own time and muster immediate family and friends to help her, and another entirely to mobilize a program with people who may not trust each other already.

Later in the evening, she stopped by her friend Lucia's family's store. They sat outside on the steps watching the people, trolleys, and horse carts go by in the warm dusk.

"I love the idea!" Lucia exclaimed. "Everyone would benefit—the Red Cross, women and girls who can't otherwise volunteer, not to mention the children. I would help if I could, but I only have Sunday afternoons free." The grocery was considered an essential service and Lucia's two brothers had enlisted, so she needed to work full-time for the store.

"I don't know—there's so much to think about," Magda replied, twisting a lock of her hair. "Before I propose anything to Mrs. Ubinger, I need to get an idea of whether enough people would be willing to share the care of children, and for enough time."

"What about the day-to-day organization—if someone is sick and can't watch the children? Since many houses don't have phones, you'd need to set up a messenger network or something like that. And what about those of us who don't have much experience tending to young children?" Lucia was the youngest in her family and had spent more time helping in the store than caring for young relatives. "How can you keep a roomful of little ones occupied and out of trouble—and for how many hours a day?"

Magda lowered her head in her hands. These were all good questions and everything was getting more complicated.

"I need to go for more advice—from my aunts."

"From your aunts!" Lucia exclaimed. "Of course. But one thing I can do, when you're ready, is call some of our old school mates together to talk about it and get them to sign up. When you know what you need and when."

Magda hugged Lucia, who was always so positive. The girls went inside and Magda put together a bag of groceries, paid Lucia's mother at the counter after thanking her for the food platter she had provided for the wake, and left the store.

Tomorrow, the aunts. She hadn't seen much of them since the funeral. They seemed to have closed themselves into their grief. Minnie and Tilly expect to be needed, she thought, and I need them now.

~~~~~

Richy ran up the stairs of Minnie and Tilly's house, waiting at the top for Magda. "You're making me feel old," she moaned. She didn't have his infinite energy, especially on such muggy days. She envied his short pants and thin, short-sleeved shirt.

She lifted him to reach the knocker and they entered the unlocked door. "*Hallo*," she called softly. The aunts were sitting on their porch out back, Minnie reading and Tilly knitting in the shade of a cloth awning. They looked cool, despite their black garb.

Magda hadn't had a chance to brief them on her conversation at the Red Cross and the complication it posed to her own wishes. She decided to lay it all out.

"When Mrs. Ubinger asked me to help with childcare for the volunteers, I understood how important it is, but to be honest, I was very disappointed."

MAGDA, STANDING

She paused. She was reliving the moment last year when she had appealed to Minnie and Tilly to save her. The two of them listened quietly, nodding, no doubt remembering the same.

"Well, I've been thinking, and talking to two of my friends. We have an idea, not quite a plan yet, but I wanted to ask your advice."

Magda expressed her thoughts about organizing a group of women and girls to share the care of volunteers' children. No one would be paid, but she hoped that the Red Cross would recognize everyone participating, and cover the cost of supplies and transportation. She stopped and held her breath, waiting for the aunts' reactions.

"Well, I think this can be done," Minnie responded with a firm nod. "Since everything these days seems to be on a war footing, there's no reason that tending to the children shouldn't be too. It's the only way women can step in to fill all the necessary jobs with the men away."

"Yes, I believe so!" Tilly added, enthusiastically. "It does require a disciplined commitment, like anything worthwhile for little ones. The women and girls should have some guidance in activities for them, and good resources like books and playthings, and a safe place. What about that?"

"Hmm." Minnie looked across the yard at Richy playing under the trees, then turned to Magda. "I'm reminded of the kindergartens we ran when we first arrived here, aren't you, Tilly? We knew them well in Germany. Kindergartens were the first schools Tilly and I could teach in over here, for the other German families. They're part of the school system now, but they were mainly for the immigrants when we first arrived, and we made the arrangements ourselves."

"Kindergarteners are usually five, but you could make a similar program for younger ones," Tilly said. "Mothers of babies are not so likely to think of volunteering, especially when still nursing. But you can set your own terms, after all." Her color rose as she set aside her knitting. "We could help you plan the work and activity schedule if you know how many women and girls are willing and the numbers and ages of the children. There are many books written now on educational practices for young children."

"Oh, yes," Minnie added. "Remember the article we read in McClure's on the pedagogical approach of that Italian woman, Maria Montessori? That's not so different from the kindergartens we knew. I think we could develop some lesson plans. But we'd need the right materials for children of this age."

Magda listened with growing excitement, but her questions mounted as well. "Where could we do this?" she asked. "It sounds wonderful to make it almost like a school, but we can't count on people having the children in their own homes."

Minnie rose with a bounce in her step. "I'll speak to the Monsignor. I'm pretty sure the church hall is underused these days—there are so few social activities with the war on, and this program can be the church's contribution to the Red Cross." She rubbed her chin. "He may say that young women should simply stay home and care for their own children. Hmm . . . I could suggest this as an extension of the parish school—although no, that would have to be cleared at the diocesan level. Too bureaucratic." She paced across the porch. "Better to put it as unofficial with him at first. Something to try out. If it works—and I don't see why it couldn't—we could say that it will be to his credit, something innovative. A visionary

MAGDA, STANDING

gesture for the war effort!" She smiled to herself and walked briskly into the kitchen.

Magda looked at Tilly and they exchanged wide smiles. "I've missed our lessons," Tilly said. "And Minnie has too. We've both needed something to put our energies into, after all the sad weeks with your mother. This is a good way for us to enlist!"

Magda felt the first surge of hope since her conversation at the Red Cross. She jumped up to give Tilly a kiss on her soft cheek and called Richy in for lunch. We're such a good team, she thought. In peacetime and in war.

Magda and Lucia decided that they would send a tea party invitation to some of their friends and acquaintances in the area. Magda didn't know many girls well enough to invite, but Lucia put together a list of twelve from the high school class and neighbors she knew as customers of the store.

"Won't they wonder why we're suddenly inviting them to tea?" Magda asked, biting her lip. "Is it right to present this as simply a social when we really want their help? What if we write out our plan and include it in the invitation?" She felt very nervous—she couldn't remember attending any event with more than one or two friends for at least a year, and had never hosted any kind of party.

"No, no!" Lucia cried. "They'll wonder even more that way. Everyone likes a social, let's just start with that, and then you can introduce your idea when they're all there and having a good time."

Finally, they decided to write on the invitation "A Tea for the War Effort." Magda was still skeptical. "They might not want to come if they think we're going to ask them for money."

"Don't worry," Lucia assured her again. "They'll come out of curiosity, if nothing else. And what choice do you have? You need to recruit a few girls for your program, and soon."

Lucia was right, of course. They wrote out the invitations for the following Saturday. Magda had the better handwriting, so she wrote the script, and Lucia decorated the cards with little watercolor flowers along the edges. They were lovely. Lucia offered to have the party at her family's house, which featured a large sitting room that opened onto a porch and wide backyard. Her mother agreed to provide Italian cookies.

"We've had to modify the recipes with the shortage of sugar," Mrs. Delarosa apologized. "I've added peach nectar and I think they're even better!"

Magda had planned to write Kitty for some of her recipes but there wasn't time, so she asked Tilly for one of her specialties—breadsticks with cheese and dill—even if they couldn't be made as flaky as usual, given the high price of butter. Along with tea, they settled on lemonade, adding watermelon for sweetness.

Magda hadn't spoken in public since her final civics test for high school graduation, when she'd been asked to give a two-minute reply to examiners' questions about the meaning of citizenship and the most important branch of the US government. She knew that presenting a plan to convince Mrs. Ubinger would be the real test, but speaking to these girls her own age was somehow more unnerving. Why did she feel so insecure about it? She hadn't spoken to most of them for over a year. Some would be dressed very well—and although she didn't like to admit that she cared so much, she would ask

Willa to help her find something nice to wear. It was probably her imagination that they thought less of her—certainly Lucia would laugh at her worries about that. Nothing should matter but getting the real work done for the country.

19

The week sped by as Magda prepared for the party while Willa helped with her dress. Laying out the actual plan itself was more work, but engrossing. She went one afternoon to Carnegie Library with Tilly to look up writings on Montessori education of young children. Evenings, she mapped out possible schedules for the program: how many children they could include, how many adults were needed for how many hours, and what the costs might be, such as food, trolley fare, paper, and crayons. She was determined that, if the party was successful in identifying at least a few volunteers, she would speak to Mrs. Ubinger early the following week.

On Friday, another letter arrived from Fred.

Camp Greenleaf, SC   July 3
Dear Magda,

I received two of your letters, both
yesterday, so they must have been routed
through Canada! At this rate, the war will
be over and we'll be picking up our mail on
the way home. But please keep on writing.
Some of the guys haven't gotten any letters
yet and are already worrying that their
girlfriends have forgotten them. By the way,
don't worry about me and Elise. Your brother
isn't a Casanova! Just keep an eye on her
and Martin for me, if they need anything.
Elise knows how to manage in difficult times,
I think, better than most people.

They've moved us to a different camp
for training. We're not supposed to say our
actual locations in our letters, although,
if an enemy wanted to track the army
through the mail, they'd always be weeks
behind us. Training so far consists of getting
up before dawn, marching till our feet are
blistered (please send more socks—smooth
ones, without darned heels), and digging
trenches over and over. Carrying our fifty-
pound packs is the worst part. I thought

I was strong, but all of us have aching backs. I never had to carry a rifle several miles, on top of all our provisions and ammunition.

The guys from Pittsburgh have been spread out between here and other training camps, so I lost track of Johannes but I think he's here somewhere. There are thousands of soldiers here, many more than the camp was built for, and we're sleeping shoulder to shoulder in tents. In my section are a few hundred guys from as far as Wisconsin and Missouri. Their whole outfit is German since there are about as many German immigrants out there as other Americans. A big fight broke out the other night when some of the local guys called them spies and enemies, and it took the officers to break it up. A few dozen ended up in the brig and our commander said he'd give a dishonorable discharge to anyone who fought with our own troops. Yours Truly did not get involved, you'll be happy to know, although I was sorely tempted to defend our patriotism. I did put some bets on one of the fist fights and made a little money on it (the Milwaukee Germans beat the Poles and Italians, by the way).

This is probably the longest letter I'll be writing for a while. I need to get more paper and you'll also be glad to know that I'm reserving my best stock for Elise.

Please give my love to Papa, Mama, and especially to Richy. —Fred

It seemed so strange that Fred didn't know yet about Mama. Magda hadn't the heart to write him immediately, the day after she died, but she had forced herself to do it before the funeral. She didn't want to take a chance that the letter might have gotten lost and he still wouldn't know, so she decided to write the sad news again.

July 12

Dear Fred,

Your letter of July 3 arrived today. You may have received by now the news I sadly wrote you last week, of our mother's death from a sudden heart attack. We didn't have any warning. I didn't even have a chance to visit her and give her your message. I'm so sorry. I was planning to go the day after I got your letter, but there wasn't time before we lost her.

We held the wake in Minnie and Tilly's house. Kitty was able to take the train down and told me she so regretted not having a chance to see you before you left. Many neighbors came for the wake and some people we didn't even expect. Your employer sent flowers, and your old friend Anselm from St. Wendelin's came too. I talked with him a while and he said he couldn't enlist or be drafted because of a stomach ulcer. Poor boy, he didn't look well, but he asked about you and said he wished he could be serving with his old pals.

Fr. Magnus celebrated the funeral Mass and said very nice things about Mama, that she was a "heroine and saint" for her suffering and such. I just don't feel it was fair of God to take her away so suddenly like that, when we hoped she'd get better this time and have more years to finally be happy. Every time I think of Richy losing his mother so young, I cry — more for him than for her.

I feel terrible giving you this sad news by letter. I'd asked Papa if the army could send you home for the funeral, but he said

MAGDA, STANDING

it doesn't work like that and anyway, there wouldn't be time. I'm sure he would have wanted you here. He is bearing up as well as can be expected.

I wish we could be together to comfort each other. I miss you so much.

All my love,
Magda

———

Saturday arrived with a rare spell of moderate weather for mid-summer. Willa had come the night before to take care of Richy so Magda could spend the morning helping to set up at Lucia's house. She slipped on the dress Willa had altered for her—a pale pink and white striped gingham with ruffled sleeves and hem, and matching hair ribbons from the supply of end pieces Willa collected from the shop. "Do these make me look like a schoolgirl?" Magda asked as she tied the ribbons to the end of her braids. She wanted to look a bit sophisticated, if that was even imaginable.

"It's not the ribbons—it's your hair!" Willa exclaimed, exasperated. "You either need to arrange the braids across the top—but that's like a Bavarian peasant—or take the extra time to pin your hair up like the Gibson Girl. Here." Willa expertly swooped, swirled, twisted, and tied Magda's long thick hair as she sat in front of the bedroom mirror, slipping multiple pins and a few tiny bows in with the locks. "If you want to look your age now you have to make the effort. Practice, it'll get easier!"

They looked at each other in the mirror. "I'd say you look rather glamorous, Miss Magda," Willa said with a wink and a peck on her cheek.

The guests arrived, and Lucia and Magda shared the greetings and hostess duties. Magda surprised herself by how comfortable she felt. The ice would have broken already if they'd been able to celebrate graduation, but with the war on, normal socializing had been suspended or at least minimized. In any case, Magda felt good in her new frock and hairdo, and reminded herself to find a special way to thank Willa.

An hour into the party, Lucia called everyone to attention with musical raps on the edge of a crystal glass. As agreed, she explained that Magda had something to talk about on behalf of the Red Cross.

"Thank you all for coming!" Magda started, her voice gravelly. She cleared her throat and took a deep breath. She had written out her notes but didn't want this to sound like a lecture. These were only young women like herself, not the President's Cabinet.

"Some of you—maybe many of you, actually—have been thinking of joining the Red Cross to become involved in the war effort. I have too. They will need tens of thousands of volunteers. I've learned that since women with young children can't volunteer for most of the necessary activities, there's a need to make arrangements to care for the children collectively—by young women like ourselves, pitching in with some older women to help. The children are part of the home front that our boys are fighting for, after all."

"What do you have in mind?" Mary Alice spoke up.

"Well, first, the supervisor of volunteers at the Red Cross downtown asked me to make a plan to care for the volunteers' children." Magda suddenly worried that she was sounding self-important, as she noticed some listeners exchanging glances. "I mean, she's been thinking about this herself, of course, and when I met her to sign up as a volunteer, she said this was a problem that needed to be solved rather urgently. I've been talking with several people about this, including my aunts who, some of you know, had a career of teaching and running schools. We think that a program could be put together for the children around ages two to four, not yet in kindergarten. It could become a nice educational activity for them."

She paused and finally took a deep breath. The faces were not hostile but some looked blank, puzzled, and perhaps skeptical.

"What do you want from us?" Helena asked. She was one of the old chums from St. Wendelin's who hadn't gone to high school.

"We'll need some women to participate who don't necessarily have their own children in the program, but are willing to work at least two or three days a week so we have enough adults to care for the children. That will permit the mothers to have those days off to do other volunteering with the Red Cross, if they wish."

"Why should we do this, rather than just volunteer at the Red Cross on our own?" Martha raised the question Magda most expected.

"I'm confident you would be recognized as their volunteers for the childcare," Magda stated, more assertively than she felt. She prayed Mrs. Ubinger would agree to that. "Everyone has different interests, of course, and some people may find children more fun than rolling thousands of bandages." That produced some smiling nods. Magda felt her listeners were softening. "Especially as we're planning to provide some structure—lessons and learning materials—so it won't just be playing, and it can be good experience for future teachers." She paused and looked around. She wanted to leave them interested, but not press them too hard now.

As no one spoke up again, she continued. "I was hoping that you would think about it, and let me know if you might be willing to help. We still have some details to work out—like the location and how to get a small budget for snacks and supplies. And to help the volunteers with their transportation costs, maybe." She shouldn't be raising expectations about that. "I still have to get the Red Cross supervisor to agree to this, but in order to even present the idea I have to know if there's enough interest."

"How many volunteers do you need?" Paulina asked, "And are you going to lead it? Someone has to be in charge day to day." Magda had braced for these questions too.

"Well, we'd start it as a trial program first," she replied. "If the supervisor agrees, I would be the organizer initially, but it would require a team to keep it running. My aunts will help us with planning activities and lessons for the children. If the program works, and the Red Cross wants to replicate it more widely, they would need to hire a director—someone other than me. My own plan is to become a nurse's aide, so I'm hoping to be able to start that training later in the fall."

The guests were getting a bit restless, so she thought it better to let them mingle. There were no more questions, but lively conversation took over. At least they were interested enough to talk with each other about it. Then Lucia stepped forward.

"Let's thank Magda for all the thought she has put into this idea. I know I'll participate, even if I can only get away from the store one afternoon a week." She then urged them to get

MAGDA, STANDING

another drink or bite to eat. The girls finished most of the food and then left in small groups after expressing thanks and telling Magda they would think about it.

"Well, I'd consider that a success!" Lucia exclaimed as she and Magda sat on the porch resting their legs on the wicker ottoman and drinking the last of the cooler with a dash of homemade limoncello.

"I hoped I'd come away with a list of names," Magda moaned. "How can this be a success when I still don't know if anyone will do it?"

"Listen, if enlistment in a good cause was so easy, Wilson wouldn't have imposed the draft, right?" Lucia laughed. "Don't worry. Talk to Mrs. Ubinger and tell her about your preparations. Say you have good reason to believe that some of these girls—maybe four or five, I'd guess—will do this, if the conditions are right. Get her to agree to do her part, to offer official volunteer status and a little budget to sweeten the deal. And don't worry about getting toys and playthings together—I'm sure we can collect those from neighbors. We can ask at the churches and at the store."

Magda warmly hugged Lucia and her mother. They insisted she go home without helping them wash the glasses and plates. Her head felt light as she walked the several blocks; she wasn't accustomed to spirits beyond the occasional beer or fruit cordial. Her mind was spinning too.

20

When the doorbell rang the next day, Richy opened the door and gleefully threw himself at Con, who swung him around on his arm in their usual greeting. Magda stood behind, touching her hair discretely and straightening the blue shirtwaist dress that was another of Willa's alterations.

"You look very nice," Con said with a grin. "I like your hair that way." Magda had never gotten a compliment on her hair and felt gratified for practicing the upsweep all week. "The dinosaurs will be honored by your visit!" His way of couching compliments in gentle teasing made them both feel less awkward.

She still wasn't sure if she should be telling someone that Con was taking them out—taking her out, but with Richy. Was it mostly for the child? Maybe she should tell Willa? No, she'd make too much of it. Definitely not Papa—no reason to, surely. But she might tell Lucia. Was there something to tell? She wasn't sure. She hoped so.

MAGDA, STANDING

Con let Richy drop the nickels into the trolley farebox and watch them fall through the glass. How did Con know how much her little brother would want to do that? They were all in high spirits, although when she thought of Fred shipping out soon, something she wanted to discuss with Con, she felt a shadow descend. She would wait to raise that later, after their outing. Nothing now that might spoil the enjoyment.

"How much does Richy know about dinosaurs?" Con asked.

Magda laughed at the question. "Nothing, I'm afraid. We don't have any in our neighborhood! I think there was one picture in a science book at school, but he's never seen that. He's heard about dragons from fairy tales, but I confess I don't know prehistoric or—what's the word?"

"Paleontology. I used to love going to this museum as a boy and getting books out of the library about dinosaurs. I'll give you a quick lesson." He pulled Richy onto his lap and explained what they would see.

"Like dwagons?" Richy asked, his eyes wide.

"Yes, but not alive now. They lived a long, long time ago and we'll see just their bones." Con held Richy's shoulders firmly. "If you feel afraid when you see them, remember they can't hurt us. In fact, they never did hurt people, they were never around people."

"Most importantly, Richy," Magda said, "you must stay with us!" This was the first time she was taking him into the city in months, but she felt they were safe with Con.

Walking into the natural history museum, their heads fell back as they gazed at the vast space, their mouths open. There was no other way to view it. Richy circled the Diplodocus warily but proved more excited by the tortoise shells and animal skins set out for children to touch. "He's fascinated by turtles these days," Magda explained, "because we see them in the park sometimes. But the dinosaurs—they're unforgettable!"

The museum branched off into so many rooms and corridors that Magda and Con spent their time following the child as he wandered into them, his attention shooting in multiple directions like firecrackers. Finally, they all found a bench to sit on in a shadowy corner to gaze at a large, bright diorama of a cave family. Richy sat for only a minute, then jumped up and put his hands and nose on the window, staring at the scene. Magda was about to call him back when Con reached for her hand and put it to his lips.

"It's OK, let him," he said softly. "He wants to get close. I can understand that."

Magda felt hot from her scalp to her feet and her heart pounded. "So . . . so can I," she murmured, then slowly withdrew her hand, rose and stood behind Richy. She looked back at Con on the bench, his eyes burning into hers.

Tuesday morning found Magda back on the trolley heading to the Red Cross headquarters. Under her arm, she carried a folder with carefully written plans, copied out three times just in case. As she entered the office, she slipped past a dozen or more women waiting to apply, or perhaps already registered and looking for an assignment. The well-publicized appeals for volunteers were having an effect.

After the receptionist waved her ahead, Magda knocked on the supervisor's open office door, and stepped inside. Mrs. Ubinger sat surrounded by a few other women all in starched white aprons, poring over typed papers with lists of numbers.

MAGDA, STANDING

"Oh, I'm so sorry to interrupt," Magda stammered. "The receptionist said I should come through for our appointment."

"We're just finishing, do come in." Magda took a seat in front of the desk. "The regional director is visiting the office tomorrow and we have lots to do to prepare," Mrs. Ubinger stated in her typical businesslike manner. "But first, I wanted to express my condolences on the loss of your mother, dear. I'm very sorry for your family. And I can understand if your father wants you to stay with him rather than join us in this sad time."

Magda was startled. She suddenly realized that in all her focusing on the childcare program she had completely neglected to discuss her interest and plans with Papa. He hadn't even been at home much in the past weeks, often taking dinner in his favorite tavern, and when he was home, he seemed rather inattentive, so they hadn't conversed much lately.

She decided to plow ahead and take her chances.

"Thank you, ma'am. I've given a lot of thought to your saying that you need arrangements for the volunteers' children. I've talked with several friends and neighbors about it, and with my aunts as well."

Magda proceeded to lay out the trial plan to organize shared care, with potentially about ten women or older girls and up to thirty children. The arrangement would free the mothers' time to volunteer in different ways for the Red Cross. She mentioned researching a suitable location and educational lesson plans. Magda stressed that the caregivers would want to have official volunteer status as an incentive, and that a modest budget would be required. After her somewhat breathless speech, she placed the paper on the desk in front of the supervisor. The points were all summarized in her best script on one page, a reflection of her tutors' insistence on brevity.

Mrs. Ubinger leaned back in her chair. "You've given this a lot of thought! But what about your wish to join our nurses instead?"

"I still intend to do that," Magda replied firmly, "but if you can support this program, I'd be willing to get it started and to participate myself in the beginning—maybe for the first two months. Then if it works smoothly enough, I'd like to hand it over to someone else and take the nurse's aide training. And then work in that function for the soldiers abroad."

Mrs. Ubinger studied the paper for several minutes. "Do you know several responsible girls or older women willing to do this?"

Magda swallowed. She hadn't emphasized the points that were uncertain, and was determined to maintain a positive tone. She had never been a salesperson before, but this was the moment for it. "I couldn't exactly sign up anyone yet, but I've gotten an encouraging response. They want to know that the Red Cross will recognize their efforts—and help defray their own costs, as I've indicated. But it will be a good arrangement for you, I'm quite sure of that."

Mrs. Ubinger narrowed her eyes at Magda and put the paper down. "You propose I make this a Red Cross program?"

"It must be! I know many other women are like me, wanting to help the war effort but concerned for the most vulnerable civilians at home. The children are our future—after all, we're 'making democracy safe' for them, aren't we?"

"Indeed! But I will have to discuss this with the regional director too. The organization is careful about its commitments and especially about recruitment, despite our great needs. We've seen some scandals when volunteers were poorly trained and supervised. If they work under our name, they need to be above reproach. We can't invite trouble."

MAGDA, STANDING

"Yes, of course." Magda felt a bit annoyed by the implication. At a knock on the door, Mrs. Ubinger dismissed her and said to return the following week. "We'll settle this then, one way or another," she replied. "And don't worry—I'll make your case. I like your idea. And your initiative!"

Magda decided that she had to talk with her father without further delay. Regardless of Mrs. Ubinger's response, she needed his approval to join the Red Cross. At seventeen, Magda was of age to sign up, but it was unthinkable to do so without at least discussing it with him.

She asked Papa to be home for dinner the next evening and cooked *bratwurst* with braised cabbage and *spätzel*, one of his favorite dishes. Meat was expensive and they ate it rarely these days, but she had been saving her allowance.

"That smells good. What's the occasion?" He sat with Richy on his lap. The boy picked out the noodles as they looked at a book together—very unusual, as Papa normally only patted him on the head when he came home.

"No special occasion. The butcher gave me some small pieces of *wurst*, just enough for the two of us and Richy. You seem thin these days and I thought you should have some meat."

Papa smiled weakly and pulled a letter from his pocket. "From Fred. He is to be sent overseas at the end of this month."

Magda gasped and grabbed the envelope. Fred more often wrote to her than to other family members, and she savored their personal correspondence, but she wasn't surprised that he would give news like that to their father first, out of respect. Still, she felt it was a typical approach in the family—saving the women's tender emotions—and it always annoyed her. She raced through Fred's scrawl to take in the news. The letter was dated August first, sent from the camp in South Carolina.

"Fred says they're going to France, but that's all he can tell us. And that he'll be with the infantry. That sounds dangerous. Is it?"

"Best not to think about it. No one will be safe over there, in any service. Look at Conrad, who was injured without even being in the fighting directly. I wanted us to resist this war, but as we are in it now, we must give it all we've got. That means no holding back. The Kaiser's forces will stop at nothing, and we have to give it our best. Without, I hope, stooping to such brutal behavior as theirs."

"So we give it our best men," Magda said quietly, dropping the letter on the table.

"If God so determines, yes," Papa replied.

"But God doesn't want his children to kill each other, surely! How could it be God's will for Fred or Johannes to be—" She couldn't finish the thought.

"We have to be strong, and pray for the end to come soon to this awful conflict," her father said, rubbing his forehead, "although I don't expect that." Magda saw that he was embracing Richy more tightly—perhaps thinking of Fred, and of Mama.

After the meal, Magda waited for Richy to get down from the table and play in the adjoining room, then broached the subject she couldn't delay any longer.

"Papa, I'd like to contribute to the war effort too. I want to join the Red Cross. I've looked into it, and spoken with them. I want to train as a nurse's aide to serve the troops. I can take the classes downtown; the course takes three months.

MAGDA, STANDING

It means I could start work early in the new year if I first help them set up a childcare program for some of the volunteers. I've already spoken with Willa and Sabine, and they're willing to take turns with Richy. He can even stay with them. Or, if you prefer, Willa said she could spend some days here every week, so you wouldn't be alone." Papa was looking down at his plate. He didn't say anything immediately, then wiped his mouth and looked at her.

"I was expecting you to say something like this," he said quietly, patting her hand. "I know you are not one to keep at home any longer, taking care of your old father and this house. You have done well, my girl, this past year. Your mama was so impressed how you took charge of the role we gave to you, and made it your own. She often said that of our children you were the one she would have liked to be, if her life could have been different."

Tears filled Magda's eyes. She opened her mouth but no words came out. How she wished she had tried harder to talk with Mama, to draw out her thoughts and whatever it was that caused her sadness and anguish. To simply try to get to know her.

"I don't want you to stay home for me. Take the Red Cross training, and do what they need you to do. But," he hesitated, "I would not like you to go overseas. There is enough you can do in our country, and Richy will miss you too much." He pushed back his chair, a sign that he was finished.

Papa's response was more accepting than she had expected, but still she was disappointed. Nursing the troops at the front seemed the finest role she could play, and she was able-bodied and unmarried—why shouldn't she go over there, if that's where she was most needed? Honestly, it even sounded a bit exciting to see Europe after having barely stepped outside Pittsburgh's city limits.

But she decided to bide her time. There were many uncertainties ahead, and she could make arguments later. For now, Papa was at least treating her as an adult. She was in charge of her own life. There was still her family to consider; she didn't want to subject Richy to any sudden shocks, and she couldn't imagine being away from him for very long. Decisions would be her own to make now. The realization didn't make her feel freer, but definitely more responsible.

21

Magda found herself thinking of Con day and night, reliving that moment in the museum. Did she imagine it? Misinterpret it? It was a very annoying distraction, she thought. He was really Fred's friend. He probably just missed family. She hadn't done anything to encourage him. He had invited her and Richy to ride the Duquesne Incline together on his next day off, and even suggested taking them to Kennywood before it closed for the season. She had never been to the amusement park on the city's outskirts, although she'd heard about it for years. Even if he just wanted company, and maybe he really wanted to spend time with Richy, she had to admit that being with him was exciting. It was truly enjoyable—and there hadn't been much joy in her life lately. She would need to talk with Lucia. It would help to get this off her chest—whatever it was.

Mrs. Ubinger telephoned Magda at home two days before their appointment. "We accept your proposal," she said, her voice sounding tinny over the line. "I can give the women ARC pins to wear, but not a uniform. We have to reserve those, especially at this stage. But I have approval for your budget of five dollars a week. I will need to know the names of each participant, both women and children, details on the location and hours, and a report each week of the activities, since this is a trial."

"Oh, thank you! I'll get you the information very soon." After hanging up, Magda leaned her head back beside the phone on the wall. This was going to happen. She was committed now, and the thought was rather unnerving.

Minnie and Tilly were pleased with the news, and didn't seem surprised.

"I finally got the Monsignor to agree to let us use the church basement," Minnie announced, beaming.

"Finally? Did he resist?" Magda asked

"Well, first he said that he thought the efforts of the parish women's auxiliary, collecting clothes and so on, were a sufficient contribution to the war effort. But I told him this is war; it is never enough! Then he argued that the children's noise would disturb daily services in the church."

"So, how did you convince him?"

"I told him I thought the Lutheran or Presbyterian churches nearby would be happy to grant our request. And that while the children would have to listen to the prayers over there it might not influence their young faith—although it would be too early to know."

Magda grinned. "Did you actually ask them first?"

"No," Minnie replied, "I was sure the specter of competition would be enough."

Magda turned to Tilly, who wore a broad smile. "I also have success to report. As you know, the public library doesn't like to lend out books for young children. They're more concerned about protecting the books than educating the young, in my view. But I prevailed on my friend Mary in Oakland, and I'll be permitted to borrow a half-dozen each week."

"The church basement will need a bit of work," Minnie said, "it doesn't have suitable furnishings for children and it needs a cleaning. Perhaps we can collect some rugs and borrow a few small tables and chairs from shops or even from other elementary schools."

"And maybe we can ask the Monsignor to place a request in the Sunday bulletin," Magda suggested.

The three exchanged conspiratorial handshakes. The aunts were living models of how to not take no for an answer, and how to reach a yes when the cause was good.

Magda and Lucia spent time later in the week going back to the friends who had attended the tea, and talking to a few other women. After three days of calling in person and by telephone, they collected a list of fifteen children, six adults, and two neighborhood girls who were old enough to help responsibly. If everyone held to the schedule, it just might work.

"We need a name for this," Tilly said one day shortly before it started. "We don't want people thinking this is just a place to keep children out of sight."

"What about play-school?" Magda suggested.

"Give that a try!" Tilly replied. "It has a nice sound, and is a good description besides. More emphasis on play than school, and that's appropriate for the little ones."

Over the next several weeks, the play-school got underway, slowly at first until everyone got used to the arrangements. Minnie and Tilly had said they would "drop in" occasionally, insisting they didn't have enough energy for little children in such large numbers. Tilly's visits were very popular as she created a regular story time, and she always seemed to leave with a higher flurry of enthusiasm than on her arrival. Minnie reserved her visits to chat with the women and girls and discuss the lessons, but over time she could be found with various children on her lap, deep in conversation or sitting quietly observing the activities.

After six weeks, Magda called a short meeting at the church hall with most of the participants to discuss the program and how it was working. The mothers were pleased with the extra time it gave them for other volunteer activity. Everyone seemed to enjoy the camaraderie for themselves and their children. But Magda had a specific reason for the meeting.

"I would like if we could find another organizer who could handle the scheduling—you know, when one of you is sick or we need to change a caregiver's days. It takes time to send notes or make calls to those of you with telephones. And someone who can buy the food for the children's lunch and prepare it. I think we need this person to be in charge every day, since I will start my nursing training soon."

She paused to see if anyone volunteered. "If none of you cares to do this organizing, I will speak to someone I know— Molly Green, who worked for my sister Kitty and the Steinmetz family. She has a young son and she may want to bring him to the play-school while she works. I think she'd be very good. She would need a small salary, though. And—"

MAGDA, STANDING

"Wait, I know her," one of the mothers called out. "She's unmarried and has a child. That's indecent. I don't want my girls to be with her. She would set a bad example!"

Suddenly the room erupted in chatter. Magda's face reddened in anger as she listened. Some of the women were agreeing, becoming agitated. Others sat more quietly, but it wasn't obvious what they were thinking or if they would defend the proposal.

"I think—" Magda raised her voice louder, "I want to say—" She clapped her hands to get their attention and walked to the center of the group. "This is a program meant to help each other." Magda spoke slowly, but forcefully. "It's for the good of the children, and to support our country at war. Should we be thinking of such irrelevant objections, if someone wants to join us and help?" She paused to let her words sink in. "And let's remember: whoever is perfect, let her throw the first stone." She tried not to look directly at the woman who had objected. Magda felt fiercely defensive of Molly, although she barely knew her.

The voices quieted down, and Magda wondered if she had been too abrasive. If the participants felt that she ignored or belittled their concerns, would they drop out and make the play-school fall apart? But fair was fair, and it wasn't right to be prejudiced against someone with a difficult life experience. And it was wartime, besides.

The next day, when Molly—who had taken on the family's laundry since Elise started working at the store—came to drop off the clean clothes, Magda mentioned the possibility of the play-school position as a two-week trial.

"You are too kind, like your sister!" Molly replied, clasping her hands together. "I would love to do something more than domestic work, and to be part of the Red Cross. And it would be so grand to have Colin with me every day."

She requested a modest wage of $7 per week. She was eager to be involved with a school, even a very informal one. "Ah, how I would love to be a teacher!" Molly exclaimed. "I dunna have enough education, but it was always my dream."

After letting the mothers' emotions subside for another week, Magda decided she needed to make the change happen. She proposed a small "administrative fee" to the participants—a dollar from each family per week—and explained that it would benefit everyone by having the program run more smoothly. Whoever still objected did not muster a rebellion, fortunately, and only one woman dropped out. Molly's delicious lunches and treats for the children, and her unfailing cheer, sealed the deal.

MAGDA, STANDING

22

on came to the house an hour earlier than they'd arranged for their outing to the amusement park. He explained that her father had contacted him saying he wanted to discuss Fred's deployment. Magda was also eager to ask Con what he might know about Fred's unit and where he might be stationed. She thought it would be a good idea for Con to mention to her father that he was taking her and Richy out again; not to ask permission, but to let him know. She suspected Con had thought of that too.

"I've asked around and looked at the wires from the communications office of the War Department in Washington," Con told them while they drank the last of the coffee Magda had been saving. There would only be weak tea most days now. "Fred is with the Sixteenth Infantry under the First American Expeditionary Force, and they're headed to northern France, near Belgium. France is where most of the action is now. That's as much as I can find out."

"It's too little, and too much," Papa said, twisting his pipe. "I'm sure Fred was impatient to get to the front. But if they're the first—"

"The first of the AEF, but the Brits and French will kiss them on both cheeks for finally coming," Con said, making himself sound deliberately more lighthearted than her father. "It's been really rough and those troops are exhausted. Some of them have been at it three years already."

"You'd think the Germans would be ready to quit too," Magda exclaimed.

"The soldiers may be, but the Kaiser has no qualms about reaching into the cradle for fresh bodies," Con replied. "They're taking boys who've barely shaved yet." He turned to Papa. "I promise to let you know if I learn anything more."

Papa thanked him. Con looked at Magda, who dipped her head slightly towards her father.

"Oh, and sir," Con said, as he stood to shake hands with him. "I hope it's alright with you that I take Magda and Richy on some outings, much to my enjoyment and I hope theirs too. And that if Magda agrees, I might take her to dinner sometime?"

Papa looked at Magda, rather absentmindedly, she thought. "Hmm, yes, go ahead," he replied as he tamped down his pipe.

As they left the house, Magda suppressed a giggle. "He was more hawkish with my sisters when they still lived at home. I guess he's too worn out to monitor me now."

"It's because he thinks so highly of you," Con replied, "or he doesn't think I'm much of a threat?" He was also laughing, but they looked at each other without a trace of embarrassment this time. This exchange had put their friendship on a different plane.

MAGDA, STANDING

Magda submitted her application to the Red Cross to train as a volunteer nurse's aide. She didn't actually know any women who worked as professional nurses, which required three years of hospital training. Even if she wanted to attain the more formal status, she couldn't wait that long. The newspapers were full of the desperate and immediate need for all types of medical personnel for the military. She wanted to get involved the quickest and surest way possible. She received her acceptance in the mail within a fortnight. She would have to report in a few days, pass a physical, and be vaccinated against smallpox and typhoid. She made plans with Willa, Sabine, and the play-school to ensure that Richy would be cared for, so that she could be available full-time for the training.

The Sunday before starting the program, she met Lucia in the afternoon. They hadn't had time for regular visits lately and possibly wouldn't again for quite a while.

"Won't you have weekends off?" Lucia asked, peeling an apple as they sat on her porch.

"I doubt it," Magda replied. "They may want us to do some practicing outside of class. I really don't know what it will involve."

"I heard some of the girls who were at our tea are taking that training too," Lucia stated. "Mary Alice, Paulina, Helena, and I think Margaret."

Magda's bite of apple suddenly stuck in her throat. Helena hadn't even gone to high school. Margaret? She was always seen in frills and curls—what did she think nursing would be like, more ways to make the boys look at her? The resentful thoughts came fast and hard, but immediately Magda was ashamed. Why did she always need to feel superior to her peers? Wasn't it a good thing that the others wanted to volunteer when the demand was so great? There was certainly enough work for everyone.

All she said aloud was, "That's nice. It would have been even nicer if they'd offered to help a little with the play-school too."

"Maybe they know they'd be better at wiping up blood than changing diapers. Although, if there are personal messes to clean, I'd rather do it for children than grown men!" Lucia chuckled.

Magda shifted to a happier subject. She told Lucia about Con—describing him as Fred's friend who was a newspaperman, who had become close to her family, and who was so good with Richy.

"And?" Lucia asked. "There must be more!" Her eyes twinkled as she looked at Magda.

"Well, yes, he's been very generous and kind. He offered to help me study for finals, although I didn't take him up on that. He's gotten us information on Fred's company from his contacts, being in the press and all."

"And ... ?"

"Okay, I like him. I like him a lot, actually. And ... he likes me too. Not like a sister, I mean. Or maybe he does just miss having a family. He's an orphan and doesn't have any siblings. I find that so hard to imagine, don't you? He's been on his own since he was about twelve—when his parents died and an uncle took him in—but his uncle's no longer around either. I know he appreciated that our family welcomed him at our house before Fred left."

"Hmm ... So, are you saying he has your sympathy and you're just being nice to him? And he to you?" Lucia's dimples deepened as a laugh played around her eyes.

MAGDA, STANDING

Magda knew she deserved to be teased. She sounded so foolish. She honestly had no experience with relationships. How could she? She'd had so little time for herself and no one to introduce her. Except, of course, Fred had introduced them.

"Do you want me to meet him? I'd like to. I can help you decide if he's a good beau for you. He sounds interesting."

"He is." Magda shook her head slightly. "I look forward to being with him and think about him a lot. But it does complicate things now if I have a beau—I don't have time! What about you? You haven't mentioned your neighbor Paul for several weeks. I used to see you talking with him after church. I know how much you like him!"

"He enlisted, of course. There aren't many fellas left here these days, are there?" It felt as if the sun had disappeared behind clouds. Lucia suddenly turned back to Magda. "Why isn't Con in the army? Does he have a deferment because of his work?"

"No, he's . . . handicapped." Magda hadn't actually spoken the word before. "He went overseas at the very beginning of the war to cover the fighting for the paper, and a shell exploded near him. He was very close to the front, but had thought he would be safe. His right arm was badly injured. It had to be amputated."

"Oh! I'm sorry," Lucia said softly and placed her hand over Magda's. Neither of them said anything for several minutes.

"Well, I want to meet him!" Lucia exclaimed, rising to her feet. "I want to meet anyone who makes my friend so befuddled."

They laughed, kissed, and agreed to find a Sunday afternoon when they would all be free.

"In the meantime," Lucia called after her, "I hope you keep Richy with you at all times as the responsible third party."

"Or at least as a major distraction, that's guaranteed!" Magda waved back.

———

"Well, here's some good news!" Willa held a piece of stationery that Magda could tell, from the paper quality and faint fragrance, was from Kitty. Magda read quickly through Kitty's account of the family's stay in the Adirondacks and their return to New York City in early September. Then, with Willa looking over her shoulder, they read the last paragraph.

> The best thing about our stay in Saratoga Springs, which is a more lovely spot than I had imagined, was meeting the regional postmaster. I had to make several trips to and from the local post office in the first few weeks as we settled in and arranged our household, and our paths crossed several times. He is a charming and refined man of thirty-six, a widower with two darling boys about the ages of Val and Richy. He insisted on showing me the area and we took some lovely drives around the lake and mountains with the children. I confess that I enjoyed this sojourn more than I'd expected. His name is Walter Lang. Because his duties encompass the Eastern region of the state, he may be able to come into New York in a month or two. His mother and sister live with him and help take care of the children. They are lovely women and we had very nice conversations when he took me to his house for tea . . .

MAGDA, STANDING

Magda and Willa looked at each other grinning, sharing a squeeze and a slight squeal. Kitty had hardly ever mentioned any gentlemen of her acquaintance.

"She seems quite taken with him," Magda exclaimed.

"And he with her, no doubt. Why not? Kitty would make anyone a perfect wife and mother," Willa added. "I'm so glad she sounds happy, but I hope this doesn't move too quickly. Especially as it seems Walter comes with a full family already. I know Kitty wanted a family of her own, but she shouldn't move from taking care of one household to another."

"Hmm," Magda reflected. She thought Willa might be thinking of her own case. She often said that Johannes' family could be helpful and embracing, but demanding and a bit suffocating too. Life becomes even more complicated when you leave your parents' house, Magda thought. She was very pleased with Kitty's letter. "Let's telephone her one of these days soon. I want to hear her voice when we ask her about him!"

"Yes, let's. And I'm glad for another thing. At least he's old enough that she doesn't have to worry about him being drafted. And he'd surely be exempted besides, given his position and family circumstances." Willa's mind was never far from worries about Johannes.

23

Early Monday morning, Magda arrived to start training in the basement of a dingy building near the Red Cross headquarters. There were no desks, just several large tables surrounded by relatively few chairs. A cluster of women stood around the room; by the time the instructor entered, Magda figured that about three dozen trainees were waiting.

"Good morning, ladies." The speaker blew into the room in billowing white sleeves and pinafore with the large ARC badge on the breast, a full gray skirt, and her hair tightly wound and topped by a short white veil. Standing at the lectern, she introduced herself as Nurse Elizabeth Kramer. "We professional nurses aren't called sister here in the States, but if you go overseas, you will hear the senior British nurses with that title." She did in fact remind Magda of one of the nuns from elementary school.

Nurse Kramer spent the first fifteen minutes citing the history of the nursing profession, giving due credit to forebears

Nightingale and Barton. "Dedicated women such as they have struggled to make nursing properly recognized as a true and noble profession. Some in the medical field have been slow to consider the women working alongside them as indispensable to the health and recovery of patients. But now, registered nurses such as I receive a minimum of three years of practical training—we do not simply read textbooks and look at pictures!" She paused and looked around the room. We'd better look suitably impressed, Magda thought as she stifled a yawn.

"With the US at war now, it has become clear to the leadership of the army and of the Red Cross that the numbers of fully trained nurses cannot be expanded quickly enough to meet the need. Hence, it has been decided to recruit nurse's aides—that is, assistant nurses—with the much-abbreviated training for which you have been accepted. If you complete this course satisfactorily, you will work under the supervision of a graduate nurse such as myself. Most of you will stay in this country, stepping into the work that does not require our higher level of training—such as serving soldiers' families and troops at the military bases here—thus freeing the professional nurses to work with the more medically demanding cases. If you gain sufficient practical experience and perform to our highest standard, some of you may be assigned abroad."

Magda reflected that if this introduction was intended to inspire the trainees, it felt like the opposite. Nurse Kramer clearly wanted them to understand the hierarchy. No room for feeling superior, that was certain. She looked around the room. The trainees had been standing throughout the introduction and none of them sat on the few chairs. There were slight rustles of movement as everyone shifted from one foot to another.

Nurse Kramer finally seemed to notice their discomfort. "You are probably wondering why we don't have enough chairs placed in this room for all of you. That's quite deliberate. As a nurse's aide, you will spend most of your working time on your feet—twelve or more hours a day, if you're in a wartime hospital or field station. You might as well get used to it now. Wear comfortable shoes." With that, she left the room.

At last, the women felt free to arch their backs and stretch. Across the room, Magda saw Margaret and Mary Alice, though not Helena or Paulina. They didn't see her.

Several minutes later, three Red Cross volunteers entered with boxes of papers and piles of folded white smocks, which they distributed to the trainees. Magda saw that the papers listed a weekly schedule of lessons, which she scanned eagerly. The thin smocks were to be worn throughout their training, until they successfully completed it and received their aide's uniforms. "Be sure to stitch the ARC badge on the right lapel of the smock," one of the volunteers called out over the rising din of conversation among the trainees. "Not on the left!"

They were told they could have a half hour for lunch, then the afternoon lesson would begin. Not having brought anything to eat, Magda wandered over to greet Margaret and Mary Alice.

"Hello! I heard from Lucia that you were coming here," she said, making a special effort to sound cheery.

"Well, it's not exactly what I expected," Margaret replied, not directly addressing Magda. "And they might have told us to bring lunch; I'm starving."

"Do you want to go out for some tea? Maybe we can do that and still be back in time," Mary Alice suggested, giving Magda a warm smile.

Along with a number of the trainees, they left the building and spread out to find a kiosk or cart where they could get some quick refreshment.

A boy on the sidewalk called out headlines of the day's paper: "Read all about it! First American casualties in operations in northern France!"

Magda grabbed the boy by the arm and gave him few cents for the paper. The other girls looked over her shoulder at the lead article. "It says they've been under shelling since early September in a place called Cambrai," she read aloud. She quickly read on silently, but the rest of the article's details didn't mean anything to her. Fred must have arrived in France by now. Con had said he was in the infantry. Surely he couldn't already be at the front.

But what did that matter? American boys were starting to die. It was undeniable now. Fred would be in the line of fire, and maybe sooner than later.

She bought a cup of tea and a roll with the change left in her pocket. Margaret and Mary Alice discussed the morning's session, but Magda didn't join their conversation. Walking back, she wondered silently how she would be able to concentrate now, between the headlines and her recollections of Fred's letters. It would be even worse for Willa, who feared for her husband, the father of her child. Magda reentered the training room determined to learn everything she could and get assigned to the front, despite her father's resistance.

A different nurse led the afternoon's lesson, held in a room with just enough chairs for the trainees. "Staying on my feet isn't so bad when there's reason to be moving around," Magda whispered to the woman sitting next to her, who introduced herself as Hilda. "But just standing to listen to a lecture is something else."

The instructor, Nurse Ackerman, started writing on the blackboard. "Ladies, you will learn eight principles that define the work of nursing. The first three are medical. To save the life of an injured person, the first and most urgent step is homeostasis—staunch the bleeding. Second, antisepsis—control of infection is fundamental to the healing of any wound. Preventing infection and maintaining sterile conditions for surgery are essential. Third is pain reduction; the initial resort may be aspirin, also our main weapon against fever. Morphine is the strongest medication we have for extreme pain, but it must be used sparingly. We must thank German chemists for those two, although I hate to admit it."

Magda was glad she had brought some paper and a pen; none was provided and many of the women were not prepared to take notes.

Nurse Ackerman continued, "The remaining five principles of nursing are of no less importance: hydration, nutrition, cleanliness, ventilation, and comfort, both physical and mental. These are the constant requirements for patients' recovery and health. If these basic elements—which we take for granted in our lives of relative ease here—are inadequate, there isn't much chance of success in healing." She paused to let her words sink in.

Magda looked around and noticed that all the trainees were neatly dressed, with clean clothes and shoes, and tidy hairdos. She would've expected nothing less, but she knew that it took a minimum of financial means to keep up appearances. The nuns in school had talked about working with families having limited access to soap and water, or even to a change of clothes.

Those women probably wouldn't have the freedom to volunteer, even if they wanted to. She imagined that the soldiers on the front must have even worse living conditions.

As if reading her mind, Nurse Ackerman went on, "As you heard Nurse Kramer say this morning, one of the greatest contributions the foundresses of modern nursing made during the wars of the last century was their fight against the pervasive filth and deprivation that soldiers suffered. Armies have been felled more by disease than by the weapons themselves." Magda thought of Tilly's fiancé. The instructor put down the chalk and asked if there were any questions. No hands rose immediately. Magda considered, but didn't want to be the first to ask. After waiting briefly, the instructor went on.

"The professionally trained nurses, under guidance of the doctors, are in charge of applying the medical elements of care. As nurse's aides, you will assist those above you in their duties and be charged mainly with the remaining tasks they may assign you. Do not think that they are any less important, as I have said. Providing nourishing food, safe drinking water, clean bedding, and keeping patients comfortable while maintaining a salubrious environment requires selfless attention, dedication, and effort."

When Nurse Ackerman paused to let her words sink in, Magda raised her hand.

"Yes?"

"I was just wondering, in the situation of a field hospital close to the front, how can we meet these conditions, such as obtaining enough safe food and water?"

"Excellent question. We often cannot, in fact. We have to make do with what we have. That means giving priority to the most serious cases and when necessary, sacrificing our own needs. Don't expect to eat full meals yourself or have the luxury of baths! In fact, you may have to get used to doing all your personal hygiene with one small bowl of water—per day."

A low gasp escaped in the room. Magda looked around. She saw Margaret and Mary Alice sitting in a nearby row exchange words as Margaret covered her mouth in horror. It would be hard to imagine her tolerating such primitive conditions, Magda thought. Then again, just thinking about it made Magda want to scratch.

She arrived home after seven, feeling more tired than she had expected from a day of classes. Willa was there, looking even more exhausted, as she was close to her delivery date. She had apparently not heard the day's news and Magda decided not to say anything, although she couldn't stop thinking about the fatalities so far away.

Willa had been generous to offer to help with Richy so that Magda could take the training, but it was obvious to both sisters that Willa needed more support herself. Magda thought again of Molly and, over dinner, proposed an arrangement that Willa agreed might suit all of them.

The next day, during a break in class, Magda called the church hall to speak with Molly. Magda proposed that Molly and her son could live with Willa and help her after play-school by cooking and watching the boys, in exchange for an additional wage, room, and board. "That way," Magda explained, "you'll be closer to the church and won't need to take the trolley back and forth to your cousin's, and Willa will get the help she needs." Molly responded that it was a "grand idea."

Willa still spent much of her time in the Augustin house with Papa, so the next evening Magda moved her own things from the second floor to the attic bedroom. The unfamiliar mattress was well-worn from Fred's weight, and she noticed a few cigarette burns.

Staring up at the steeply sloped ceiling, her thoughts flew to Fred and the risks he was facing. She wished she could talk to Con about it. Was that why she valued her friendship with him—that he was always so helpful and she could share her concerns? She would have called him right away, but there was only one phone in the boarding house where he lived, and it was late.

As her body settled deeper into the soft bedding, her mind ran over the lectures of the previous day. There was clearly nothing glamourous about being a nurse's aide. Cleaning house and preparing food was hard enough for her own family, let alone for dozens—or hundreds—of soldiers. What was she getting into? Would she be able to accept whatever assignment she was given? She remembered a Red Cross poster she'd seen around town with the slogan "Nursing Service is Military Service!" She was hopeful that if she performed well in the training and demonstrated her willingness to do hard work, they would let her focus on providing direct care to the soldiers. She wanted to be closer to what the men were doing. To save lives from the center of the fray. To not be so protected. To... To...

24

On Friday evening after class, Magda suggested to Willa that they try to telephone Kitty in New York. They hadn't received a letter from her that month, and the last one didn't contain much mention of Walter, so they wondered what was happening. Calls between cities were very expensive, but they decided this was important.

"Kitty, have you forgotten about us?" Willa asked, as she and Magda stood by the phone on the wall holding the ear-piece between them. "You tease us with news of your fella, then nothing!"

Kitty's musical laugh carried well over the line. "I was busy moving the family back to New York. It takes at least a week to close one house and open another. The girls started school, so that also created a lot of commotion here. And with the war, we've lost the gardener and driver for the family, and it's so hard to find supplies, and—"

"No excuses!"

MAGDA, STANDING

"Well, to put it simply, Walter and I write to each other about every other day, so that's why I haven't had time to write home lately. Sorry! Things are going well for us, but he's there and I'm here. We hope he can visit soon, but he can't leave his children for too long, so it may be only for a few days. And we were thinking that I might go up there for Christmas."

Willa and Magda looked at each other in surprise. Not come home to Pittsburgh? This must be serious!

Kitty asked about news from Fred and Johannes, and how the rest of the family was doing. Too quickly, they had to hang up, after exceeding their three minutes. Willa and Magda felt happy and relieved, but pensive, too, at the thought of Kitty possibly leaving them for good.

"We need to write her and ask more questions," Willa said, as if she were the older relative who needed to supervise the relationship. It was good for Willa to have some more distraction from her anxiety about Johannes and the imminent birth.

⁓

Magda was pleased that the syllabus focused on the medical priorities of nursing for two months, leaving the last month to study more general aspects of health and hygiene. The initial classes consisted of studying human anatomy—very basically and very rapidly. Posters portraying each major bodily system lined the classroom walls, and the trainees were expected to memorize the essential details: veins and arteries, the main bones in the arms and legs, the digestive system, the nervous system, and so on. It was a lot of work, especially since there weren't enough books and the trainees had to work in small groups. Magda felt somewhat prepared since she had studied biology and had enjoyed perusing Minnie's anatomy textbook, with its detailed drawings and descriptions. A few of the women in the class seemed almost entirely ignorant of major body parts—especially those of males.

"Haven't they ever taken care of a baby boy?" Mary Alice whispered to her, giggling.

At the end of the week, they took both a written and an oral test.

"Your grades each week will be considered in making your assignments at the end of the training," Nurse Kramer told them at the start of the exam. "We would like our nurse's aides to be as well prepared as possible in this short time, but if you don't pass each week, we can still find work for you, as long as you want to serve."

"I think that means if we don't study enough we can expect to report to the broom closet and be assigned a mop and bucket," Mary Alice sighed. "But you won't have any trouble," she said to Magda as they boarded the trolley going home together.

"You won't either," Magda reassured her. "But it would be easier, and more interesting, if we could see some of the lessons in practice. I mean, with real patients in a hospital. I hope we will."

Returning home, Magda spied a small envelope on the dining room table with Fred's unmistakable scrawl. "It's addressed to you," Willa said, wiping her hands on a dishtowel. "It came from overseas! Please, read it to me." Magda paused only to take off her coat and give a hug to Richy.

MAGDA, STANDING

France, September 20, 1917

Dear Magda,

I finally got the letter about Mama's passing. It was a shock, but I know she's happier in heaven. I wish I could have seen her again before I left, but I'm not in a hurry to meet her there just yet. I am sorry I couldn't have been there with you all for the funeral.

They shipped us out three weeks ago. All the guys were getting so restless, there's only so much basic training you can do and not go crazy with boredom. I'm glad we're among the first AEF units here.

The ship was no luxury cruise, believe me! It felt like we were cargo. Guys were sleeping in hammocks, three or four hanging vertically. The bum of the fella above me was an inch above my chest, and same for me and the poor guy below me. But we got here in one piece without meeting a U-boat, so I can't complain. I didn't get seasick, that was another good thing. Lots of guys did, especially when we went through some violent storms.

After landing, we traveled by train. I can say we're in northeast France, but

we're not allowed to give our locations—and
I don't even know yet where we are. The
signs along the road are illegible. I thought
German was a complicated language, but
French is totally unpronounceable! They
have twice as many vowels in their words
as they need, from what I can tell. Kind
of how German has too many consonants.
They should get together sometime, instead
of fighting each other, and mix up their
languages. Then they'd communicate better.

The view of France from the train was
nothing special, at least what I've seen so
far. I hope I get to see Paris, especially
the Eiffel Tower. What would you want me
to bring you? Some fancy perfume?

Well, I'll stop now and try to mail this
letter at the next stop. I'm not sure how
often I can write. Please ask everyone to
write to me, and tell me what you hear
from Johannes. I hope at least some more
letters find me—yours especially, of course!
Hugs to Richy, Papa, yourself, and everyone
else, Fred

"He sounds a bit like a tourist," Willa commented. "Like he's heading into some adventure."

MAGDA, STANDING

"I don't think he'd let us know if he was scared or anxious anyway," Magda reflected. "He finally received my news of Mama's death—so many months later."

"It's strange, having our family spread far apart like this," Willa mused. "My Johannes in Baltimore, Kitty in New York, Fred in France, you in . . . Where do you think you'll go, after your training?"

"I really don't know. But I hope over there with the troops. Papa said he doesn't want me to go abroad. Just being protective, maybe. I'm not sure it'll be up to me, in any case." That might be the best thing, she thought. If they needed her overseas, she could just tell him: "I'm in the army now!"

She was very pleased that Con called her to get together on Sunday, the only free day for both of them. She wanted to take Richy, because it was also the only chance she had all week to spend time with him, and she knew he missed her as much as she missed him.

"Of course!" Con replied, "I was going to suggest that." Magda was grateful that, as usual, she didn't need to explain her thoughts to him.

They rode down the Duquesne Incline, the small cable car that hugged Mount Washington, overlooking the city. Richy was enthralled, but so was Magda—she had only ridden it once before, when she was a little older than him. With so many men away, the crowds were sparse. "We'll do it again on the way home," Con promised Richy.

They took a trolley across the Fort Pitt bridge to the Point, where the Monongahela and Allegheny rivers meet to form the Ohio. A chilly breeze blew off the water in all directions as they walked to a small cafe. Magda had never taken Richy for a restaurant meal, only to pick up food occasionally at Grundel's, or for a lemonade or ice cream on one of their walks. She always wanted to conserve her modest allowance, and restaurants could be expensive. But Con insisted they have lunch, so they sat at a table by the window.

"What a lovely family," the proprietor exclaimed in greeting them. Magda hid a smile.

"I agree," Con answered him, "they are indeed a lovely family." She looked at him and blushed, impressed by his graciousness and annoyed with herself that she could never match it.

They ate potato salad and baked beans. There was no meat on the menu, but they were used to its absence. Richy was very well behaved, fascinated by the passersby and the waiters, and Magda felt as proud as if he were her own child.

After the meal, Con suggested they visit his newspaper office nearby. Inside a large brick building three blocks away, he led them to a large windowless room lined with desks topped by piles of papers and typewriters. Telegraph machines kept up a constant clatter.

"Where's your desk?" Magda asked. Con pointed to one that was much neater than most. "How did you learn to use a typewriter? May I see it?" She knew they were common in offices, but she didn't know anyone who owned one.

She sat at the desk with Richy on her lap. Con placed a sheet of paper in the roller and demonstrated by typing their names. His fingers were long and his hand wide, so he was able to reach across the machine and hit the keys accurately and quickly, then moved the carriage return. She wondered at the odd layout of the letters, which weren't in alphabetical order.

"The keyboard is arranged so the most-used keys don't keep hitting each other," he explained. "Typing is just a matter of practice—like playing a musical instrument, maybe, but easier."

"Did you know how to type before going overseas?" Magda wondered if he had learned only after losing his arm, but she didn't want to ask directly.

"Yes, but over there I usually wrote my stories with pen and paper and they were transcribed to the telegraph." He paused, then explained. "I was right-handed so it wasn't easy, learning to do everything with my weaker hand. But it's been over two years now and I'm getting much better."

Magda had noticed that Con rarely asked for help.

"How do you button your shirts?" Richy asked. That was something he was trying to learn. "I don't," Con replied. "Snaps, see?" He reached into his shirt and showed Richy the little metal discs. "A German invention, actually. If that country ever focuses its productive talent on manufacturing for consumers rather than the military, they'll get rich," he said to Magda.

She asked, "Will you ever get an artificial limb?"

"Maybe. There will be many more guys like me coming out of this war. Losing arms and legs. And we're the lucky ones. I'll wait a while. Sometimes the later models are better—like motorcars." He grinned.

They walked out of the office and strolled around the town a little while, then hopped the trolley for home. Magda asked Con very quietly about the news of first fatalities to the infantry division. "It's a mixed blessing that we can learn about the action overseas from the wireless within a day," he said. "You think you want to know everything right away, but it will become overwhelming. And the government is already censoring the news, trying to keep up morale. It's even taken control of radio, to use it only for the military. We're getting pressure to report only successes on the battlefield and nothing that sounds like a setback. Journalists want to tell the whole truth as far as we can, but as they say, truth is the first casualty of war."

Magda sat quietly, holding both Con's hand and Richy's until the trolley reached her neighborhood, and Con walked them to their house. They all exchanged a quick hug, and he headed back to the trolley stop in the gathering dusk.

The next several classes at the Red Cross were devoted to cutting, folding, and tying bandages for all purposes. The trainees had to practice on each other for hours. Then came splints: how to form them from various materials when proper ones weren't available, and how to position them. How to make and use a tourniquet. How to apply dressings and, just as important, how to remove them safely causing minimal pain and damage to injured tissue. The examinations would include a practical test with the stern senior nurses watching the trainees' clumsy attempts to demonstrate the techniques on a wooden dummy, or on a live volunteer.

When the need to practice intruded on the brief weekend hours they were both free, Con offered to help. "I was on the receiving end of some good nursing in Belgium, thankfully, so I can give you the patient's view," he suggested.

Sitting on a dining room chair with Magda standing, facing him on his right, he opened his shirt and slipped out the stump of his right arm. Magda suddenly felt her heart beating loud enough to hear. Her gaze lingered on his chest dappled with blond hairs peeking over the low neck of his undershirt stretched over well-defined pectoral muscles (she recalled the correct term). Con obviously did a lot of upper-body exercise as part of his physical therapy. She tried to keep her eyes on the site of the amputation, just above the elbow.

"How exactly did it happen?" she asked tentatively. "Was it horribly painful?"

"A shell landed near the entrance to the officer's hut where I was interviewing the captain of the unit. A large piece of shrapnel caught me cleanly. If it was a little higher it might have cut off my head."

Magda gasped.

"I didn't actually feel anything at first. Just bloody as hell. Sorry, I should watch my language."

"I'm not offended. I'll have to get used to worse, I suppose."

"Lucky for me there was a field hospital nearby. They whisked me over and I was in surgery by evening. The pain hit me later. Thank God for morphine, though. Be sure to learn that lesson well when you come to it."

"How long did you stay at the front before you came back home?"

"In the base hospital, about two weeks, then I caught a ship. A lot of men with such an injury have bad complications—infections, because of the dirt in the trenches. But, in my case, it healed pretty well. I can still feel pain and sensation from my right hand sometimes."

"How can that be?"

"It's a medical mystery. Instinctively, I still want to reach out and use my right hand first." He looked at her pile of practice bandages. "Okay, start winding one of them. I'll coach you if you get it wrong. I watched them do it plenty of times, and on the ship I often had to replace my own bandage."

Magda picked up one of the longest strips of gauze, positioned the end and wrapped as the trainees had been shown.

"Be sure when you finish that to use another one to tie down the patient's good arm too."

Magda looked up. "So he won't pull off the bandage and expose the wound?"

"No. So he won't be able to do this." He wrapped his long, left arm around her waist and drew her tightly to him. Because he was seated, her head was slightly higher than his. She placed her arms over his shoulders. She hadn't often looked down into his blue eyes. Or ever imagined that she would be the one to initiate her first kiss.

MAGDA, STANDING

25

Compared to the first month of classes, which Magda had enjoyed, in part because the trainees partnered together to practice the material, she found the antisepsis lessons more tedious. They were all about cleaning. Because there were no medicines to fight infection internally, it was critical to keep wounds as clean as possible. Depending on availability of supplies, the nursing staff might use castile soap, Dakin's solution, or saline on injuries to prevent and attack infection, and carbolic acid to sterilize equipment. For everything else coming into contact with patients, they were to use lots of soap and bleach, or just vinegar and boiling water, to minimize contagion. The instructors stressed that the stakes were high: "Infection is our greatest enemy!"

On a Sunday afternoon in late November, as Magda began to study the formulas for mixing cleaning solutions, she heard a knock on the door. Her friend Elise entered with Martin.

CHRISTINE FALLERT KESSIDES

"It's been ages!" Magda exclaimed, embracing them both. "I've been meaning to visit, but I've had so little time." She explained the intense schedule of her training, and that Richy was spending most days with his cousins. "But he'll be here shortly. Stay and I'll make you some cocoa. And I found a last can of peaches in the cellar!"

Magda felt guilty that she hadn't spoken with Elise since learning that Fred had arrived in France. Elise admitted she'd heard that news from him around the same time. Then she pulled a letter from her handbag.

"I received this yesterday," she said. "He's in the thick of it now, I think. The tone is so different from his previous letters." She pushed it across the table to Magda.

"Do you want to read certain parts to me? I mean, whatever isn't too personal?" She hoped that Fred was writing tender messages to Elise, but she couldn't imagine what effect being in war would have.

"No, I don't mind. You can read it."

Magda unfolded the thin sheet carefully.

Northern France, November 7, 1917

Dear Elise,

I'm writing this by candle in a bunker underground. There are actual rooms built here below the surface, about 8 steps down from the trench. We sleep on boards set into the wall, if we're lucky. That at least keeps us dry, but sometimes we just hit the sack on the bare ground and wake up in a

MAGDA, STANDING

puddle. This is one of the older trenches, so it's been partially rebuilt a few times. Some parts are better, some worse. They can't decide on the paint color or curtains! Very funny. But I guess I'm thinking of that weekend I painted your house. So long ago, and so far away. I must thank Magda for getting me that job.

The worst thing so far is the constant noise, the battering of guns and, sad to say, the cries of some of our fellows. We haven't had it as bad yet as it will be, so they tell us. The Brits and French soldiers all look pretty thin and gray-faced, clearly exhausted. They say we AEF look well fed and "in form"—for now, at least. I hoped to explore the neighborhood if I could get an afternoon off, but all the towns and villages around here have been hit hard and deserted. Not even a restaurant nearby for the famous French food. Not a park left to stroll in, or a church safe to enter. The local troops can at least go back home if they get leave, but we're too far away, so no chance of that unless we're unable to fight or the war finally ends.

CHRISTINE FALLERT KESSIDES

At night I try to dream that I'm with you. During the day, I try to think of you and it helps me feel a bit calm. I want to come back to you and Martin in one piece, but also make you proud. You deserve a man of sound mind and body, so I'm not taking any crazy chances. I'm making a list of all the good times we'll have together and places we'll go.

Well, I need to try to sleep for a few hours. Think of me too.

With love, Fred

Magda returned the letter. "He sounds sentimental, and that's new from him. If being away from you brings out the romantic in my brother, that's a good thing." She tried to sound positive, but the note raised her anxiety. He was near the fighting, and there was nothing reassuring about that.

"The letter took over two weeks to get here. I wish there was some way we could know sooner how he is. And if something happens to him, how long will it be till we find out?" Elise fretted. She was usually so reserved. Magda could see that her friend held her worries inside and, living alone with only her child, had little opportunity to share them and find reassurance. Magda felt guilty that she had been so preoccupied with her own activities. With her family close by, she never felt the lack of someone to talk with.

"Elise, I've been neglecting you, I'm sorry." Her friend shook her head and looked embarrassed.

"Don't worry about me, I'm very busy at the store. And since Martin started kindergarten, I've met some other mothers. But as a widow, living by myself . . . well, it's always a bit awkward, wondering what people think of me." Magda was surprised, yet realized that she really had no idea what it was like for a woman alone. Although Magda often itched for independence, she never envisioned herself truly on her own in the world. For a man, like Con, it would be much different.

"I have some news," Elise continued. "My husband's brother Emil—I don't think I ever mentioned him, he had moved out west shortly after we were married. He's a skilled carpenter. We fell out of touch, but he wrote to me several weeks ago. He brought his wife and two children back to Pittsburgh before he was drafted and they've rented rooms on the North Side. I haven't met them yet, but we have exchanged letters and she seems very nice. We've the same concerns now that everyone has: the men's safety and how to manage the shortages. I plan to invite them to visit soon. Maybe, if we get along well, I'll ask them to stay with me and Martin. It'd be good for him to be with cousins, and I think I'd like having the company. Until the war is over anyway, and Emil and Fred come back."

Magda felt relieved. Although Elise had always seemed so capable and self-sufficient—much like Kitty—she had probably been quite lonely.

Just then, Richy ran into the house, and he and Martin lightened the mood instantly, like sunbeams after a storm. Moments later, Willa entered with the pink bundle that was one-month-old Caroline. They all sat down to share Magda's turnip and potato stew, ingredients that were too familiar to everyone given the shortages, but the dish was well-seasoned this time with pickles and good conversation.

"How can we celebrate Christmas?" Willa sighed as they wiped the plates and the children's faces. "Nothing will seem festive without Johannes."

"The Red Cross is shipping parcels to the troops," Magda said. "They'll also deliver personal packages, and that's the surest way to get them there, I hear. Although it may take a month for parcels to get overseas, so we need to put them together soon."

They spent the rest of the evening making lists of what to send Fred and Johannes: chocolate, cigarettes, warm socks and underwear, preserved foods, writing materials, photos. Martin and Richy would add drawings. Just talking about surprising the men at a distant time and place was more satisfying than a rich dessert.

Christmas spirits were subdued in the city, with fewer decorations in the stores and on the streets. Families were cautious about spending on gifts when facing the hard economic conditions of wartime. But the children didn't know that. Modest efforts to bring cheer—including a toy exchange that Molly organized at the play-school—fed their excited anticipation. Magda felt the season as bittersweet: Mama and Fred were missing, but baby Caroline and Con's presence were blessings.

In the week after Christmas, a letter from Fred arrived, addressed to the whole family.

Northern France, December 15, 1917
Dear all,
    We're making the best of it here, but it's tough being away for Christmas. Some

packages have arrived and the fellas are good about sharing what they get from home—especially a cigarette and maybe a piece of candy (biscuits usually arrive in crumbs—but not a single one goes to waste). I'm guessing you may have sent me a package but it got delayed. It's not too late if you didn't! Sorry for begging, but I hope being impolite is the worst I can be accused of after this war. It's hard to keep our heads down and stay dry and warm. They say this is the coldest weather here in December for a long time. If you do send me anything, please add some woolens—socks, gloves, and earmuffs (the kind that can fit under a helmet). It would be great if Willa (not Magda) knitted me a scarf. No offense, little sister, but you're better at keeping the letters coming!

We spend a lot of time digging in and around the trenches, repairing them and bailing out the water when it rains. It's hard to keep small fires going since the smoke can give away our positions. We don't get much exercise, but a few times I was picked to be a courier and it felt really good to run for a few miles, behind the line of course. Although, my boots are not made for running and I had blisters afterwards.

The guys have tried to put up a Christmas tree, actually just a branch since almost all the trees around here are blasted and burnt. We don't have much to hang on it anyway. I think about you all sitting around the tree at home and singing carols. Remembering Christmas when we were kids—opening that one gift from Mama and Papa.

Hugs to everyone. And Happy New Year— which is only possible if this war ends very soon. Please pray for that.

Love, Fred

Con called Magda that same evening and asked if he could stop by. He had spent Christmas with her family, and Magda and Con had exchanged gifts. She gave him a volume of Robert Frost's poems, and he gave her a scarf and matching gloves, knowing that she had misplaced a favorite mitten downtown. He had asked the store to embroider an M on the scarf and on the backs of the gloves. "That won't keep you from losing them, but at least only Marys and Marthas can take them from the Lost and Found," he grinned.

MAGDA, STANDING

He arrived after dinner. Magda was at home alone with Richy, as Papa had taken a late shift at the dairy. She made Con some coffee that Kitty had sent from New York as a special treat and served a dish of dried apples from the cellar. Con let Richy climb on his lap and eat almost all of the fruit, then he brought out a colorful book with alphabet letters and pictures.

"You already gave him a nice Christmas gift!" Magda exclaimed. "You're spoiling him."

"I won't be here again for a while," Con replied, "so this is to remember me by."

Magda shivered. "Where are you going? Not overseas again?"

"No, but into a different sort of battleground. The paper is sending me to Washington. I'm going to report from there about the disputes between Wilson and Congress. It's a good move for my career."

Magda knew he was right, but she felt as bereft as when Fred announced he was leaving—maybe even a little more. "Of course," she said quickly, not wanting to spoil Con's obvious excitement, "that will be great experience, won't it?" She looked down at her coffee. "How long will you stay there?"

"I don't know exactly, but probably for the duration of the war. I hope, for many reasons, that will only be a few more months." He took her hand and kissed her palm. "And let's not forget, Miss American Red Cross, that you'll probably be leaving here for much farther reaches. I know that's what you want. And by the way," he added with a twinkle in his eye, "that's why my gift was something you can take with you—as opposed to something more valuable." He left that comment to her imagination.

It was true that Magda had spoken to him of her hopes to nurse the troops in Europe. But she hadn't actually thought about the separation. She would be going very far from her home, her family, and—she was now willing to admit—her beau. Temporarily, of course, but even the distance from Pittsburgh to Washington was more than she had ever traveled. Now they wouldn't see each other for many months.

"When will you leave?"

"Tomorrow morning, by train. I'll write as soon as I know where I'll be staying."

"Find a telephone," Magda replied, "and let me know you've arrived safely." She pulled Richy's arm gently to urge him off Con's chair. "Why don't you put your new book upstairs." Richy slowly walked out and she slid her chair over till their thighs and knees touched.

"I'll worry more about *your* whereabouts," he said softly, twirling a finger in her hair, "and I hope you find time to write me occasionally as you tend to all those boys who will fall for you too." He pulled her close and they kissed until Richy ran back into the room.

Magda thought late into the evening about Con's "too" and the touch of his whiskers on her lips.

1918

26

By mid-January, Magda's Red Cross training was completed. Paulina had dropped out halfway through, deciding she really wasn't cut out for it. But Magda, along with Helena, Mary Alice, and Margaret, passed the examinations and received their nurse's aide uniforms. The gray-blue dress, full-skirted and falling to the top of their high shoes, had long sleeves with detachable white cuffs. The ubiquitous white pinafore with ample bodice "makes us all look top-heavy!" Mary Alice complained. The white cap, they agreed, was less dowdy than a veil and more comfortable.

"I don't see how we're supposed to keep this uniform clean in the field hospitals," Magda protested. "Why don't they save some of this fabric for bandages and give us something simpler?" But as they frequently heard from the instructors, the Red Cross nurses and aides were to be "models of womanhood" and at all times represent the very best image of the mothers, wives, and sisters back home. Someone must have

MAGDA, STANDING

thought that flowing white uniforms made them appear more angelic.

The four girls had become better friends during the training, overcoming Magda's initial diffidence. Helena, despite having the least formal education among them, was quick to pick up on practical skills requiring deft fingers. Magda acknowledged that Margaret had shed her debutante airs—or Magda had shed that preconceived image of her. The trainees had gotten very little clinical exposure, but when they toured an operating room to observe major surgery, Magda felt queasier than Margaret did. When the aides were asked to help provide first aid to burn victims in a Homestead neighborhood where an explosion in the steel mill had spread fire to several houses, the young woman showed composure and compassion that Magda had to admire. "Margaret's a real brick after all," she admitted to Lucia when they got together for a rare Friday night Coca-Cola.

A few days after the training ended, Magda met with Nurse Kramer to receive her assignment.

"I see you've stated that going overseas is your first choice," the supervisor remarked, looking over Magda's file.

"Yes! I really want to care for our boys on the front." She winced at sounding like a poster on the trolley.

"The base hospitals in Europe are tending many civilians as well, you know. They're suffering injuries, disease, and malnutrition—especially the children. The needs are many and varied these days."

Magda prayed that Nurse Kramer would say the demand was greatest in the field stations and would assign her there. Then she could tell Papa—

"—and in fact," the supervisor continued, "we have a very urgent requirement right here at present. The University of

Pennsylvania is outfitting a base hospital in France, to be opened within the next two months. I need a reliable assistant to help oversee the packing of critical medical supplies that will be sent to Philadelphia and from there to the hospital abroad. The Red Cross is responsible for the assembly and shipment of all these materials from different sources. The nurses and doctors are only able to do their work if they have the essential materials, and we receive desperate requests every day from base and field stations that are running out of dressings, splints, ligatures, sterilizing equipment, and so on." She paused and spread her hands over a stack of telegraph messages. She leaned in and looked intently at Magda. "I've observed that you're good with details, especially with numbers, and you're well organized. However—" she paused and shook her head slightly.

Magda bit her lower lip. Spending the next two months in a warehouse? Disappointment must have been plastered all over her face. She braced herself for the rest of the explanation.

"I've also noticed that you're very competitive. You always seem to want to be first with an answer and to finish projects ahead of your peers." She narrowed her eyes and frowned slightly. "There isn't room for attention to one's personal achievements in this calling. As a nurse's aide, you will be closely supervised by graduate nurses who are strictly subject to a doctor's orders. One must be modest and self-effacing; your focus must be the patient. It is essential that staff at each level support each other, especially in the conditions of a field hospital or other emergency. No one should try to stand out, but only be part of a team."

The trainees had been given this message numerous times in different ways, although Magda wasn't sure what it meant

MAGDA, STANDING

in reality. Wasn't it a good thing to try to get ahead by learning more and excelling in the practice? Was it so bad to stand up and show some initiative? She felt her face burning with the shame of being singled out for what she thought was only her eager but, truthfully, ambitious nature. She fought rising tears and forced herself to look at Nurse Kramer directly, not letting her lips or chin quiver.

"I ... I'm sorry if I gave the impression that I was not respecting my proper role, Nurse Kramer. I never meant to put myself above my peers in any way that would harm our ability to work together for the patients' benefit." She needed a respectful way to challenge the superior's judgment, though she had to admit that modesty was not one of her strong suits.

The woman continued, "I'm not disciplining you, Magda, as I know you have meant well and are very able. But I think it will be good for you to have a first assignment that is perhaps not as dramatic as you might have wished. And, frankly, I thought of you because I know you can be relied upon. We wouldn't normally have someone as young as you do this kind of work, but I believe you are mature beyond your years, and trustworthy. Will you do this for us?"

Magda knew she had no choice but to accept readily, to show that she could put aside her own wishes. If it were to be temporary, she could tolerate it. She would have to—she was a trooper now, too, wasn't she?

"If that's what you think I should do, Nurse Kramer." Magda tried not to appear crestfallen. It was good to be thought worthy of what sounded like a big responsibility. "But, may I ask—" She hesitated, not sure if this was the right time, but she might not get another chance to press her case.

"Yes?"

"If the need is to prepare supplies for the new base hospital, could I be assigned to go with the staff as they set it up overseas? And serve with the nurses there?"

"I think that could be considered. Do your best and let's talk when the shipping is completed. You will report to the administrative officer, Mr. Hale, at the warehouse near the train station starting tomorrow." She pushed a paper with an address across the desk and turned back to her paperwork.

Magda walked out of the training center slowly, trying to control her emotions. She ran into Margaret and Mary Alice near the entrance.

"They're sending us out next week!" Mary Alice exclaimed. "We're going to France! Helena too." Seeing Magda's pale face, she asked, "What about you?"

Magda felt as if she'd been struck. "I'm . . . happy for you, I know that's what you all wanted," she replied in a monotone. "Nurse Kramer asked me to do a special assignment here for two months first. They need help managing the shipment of stores to a new base hospital in France. But I'll be going out there as soon as it's set up." She mumbled something about needing to leave for home, and walked quickly outside.

She was glad for the snowfall disguising her tears as she headed to the trolley stop. Did she really deserve to feel so crushed?

Magda entered her house with feet dragging. She could hear Tony's children in the kitchen. It wasn't a Sunday, and she was surprised that both he and Sabine were there, as well as Papa, for dinner. She greeted them and told them the outcome of her training—that she would still be in town a while longer. "Counting bandages, I think," she said, rolling her eyes.

"But surely that's important work or they wouldn't have asked you to do it," Sabine replied, always quick to see the best side of anything.

Tony had received a letter from Fred. "I didn't bring it," he said when Magda asked to see it. "He included some details about what they're facing now—really, just intended for me. He also wrote about talking to an army photographer there and gave me some tips on how to request that kind of assignment when I go. He did say he'd received the Christmas package and to thank you all for it."

Magda's disappointment carved deeper into her chest. She had so hoped to get closer to Fred very soon, geographically at least, to understand what he was going through. She would never really know if she didn't see it up close.

"Please don't talk again of enlisting," Sabine snapped at Tony. It was widely expected that the draft would be extended to men even in their forties, but the couple's fourth child had arrived just after New Year's and Tony was the sole breadwinner. Surely he wouldn't be forced to go?

He shook his head slightly as if to dismiss his wife's objection. Looking at Magda, he said, "Anyway, I've decided to change the spelling of our name before I register for conscription. It's too Germanic, Augustin. Many people are shedding their German names to avoid negative attention, and to make a statement. I don't want anything to do with that country or that culture anymore."

Magda raised her eyebrows. "Change it to what?"

"Augustine." He stressed the first syllable and sounded the end with an "ee." "That little letter gives it a very different sound—more English. I'm going to the courthouse to file the papers this week."

"Have you told Papa?"

"He said it's up to me."

"You'll have to write to Fred about it. He'll want to know."

Magda realized that if she wanted a different first name, in her new career she could have people call her something else. Maggie? Lennie? There was no point making everyone think she was Irish or Italian. She was too upset to give it further thought; there would be time enough when she was mindlessly packing boxes.

Liberty Avenue was bustling with traffic to and from Penn Station. Magda saw soldiers streaming in and out of the imposing rotunda. She walked past the station to a block of nondescript warehouses nearby and found the address she had been given. Entering, the warehouse struck her as almost more imposing than the train station. It was filled nearly to the ceiling with crates of all sizes. Seeing a small office to the side, Magda carefully touched her cap to make sure it was on straight, smoothed her uniform skirt and pinafore, and knocked on the open door. A small man with a receding hairline, wearing an eyeshade and garters on his sleeves, looked up.

"Mr. Hale?"

"Are you the accounting assistant I asked for?" He looked at her almost accusingly.

"I'm a nurse's aide," Magda replied firmly. "But Nurse Kramer at the Red Cross training center said you needed help with the supply shipments for the new base hospital, and—"

"Come along then." He interrupted, brushing past her without another word. He handed her a clipboard holding a thick stack of papers and motioned for her to follow him into the forest of pallets. She craned her neck to read the labels: blankets, hot water bottles, sheets, towels, sponges ...

On the far side of the room were several long tables. About fifteen colored women were arrayed around the tables, filling cartons with medical supplies, including small glass bottles and ampoules, syringes, rubber hoses, and surgical instruments.

"Girls!" Mr. Hale called, and the women ceased their movement to look up. "This is Miss Augustin. She's been assigned by the ARC office to oversee the shipments, starting this week. She'll be recording all the materials as the crates are assembled." He turned to leave. Magda wanted to sink into the floor as the women stared at her. What in the world was she doing here?

"Could I speak to you privately for a minute?" she whispered to him. "Excuse me," she said to the women, then turned to catch up with him as he headed back towards his office.

"Mr. Hale, please?"

He turned around impatiently. "Can you please tell me exactly what I need to do?" Magda asked in a firm voice.

"Record all the supply boxes. Make sure they're properly full before closure. Those forms list what goes out on the train each day." He jerked his thumb in the direction they'd just left. "They know how it works. You can ask them." His back was to her again.

"Will I be the only person here doing this? There are so many! How can I—"

"No, there are two other accountants and the movers. They'll be here later." He disappeared behind a tall stack of crates labeled "Lanterns."

Magda dug her nails into her palms to keep from screaming with frustration. She slowly walked back to the room with
the women.

They were working quietly as they handled the items, many
of them clearly fragile, with quick but careful movements.
They didn't look up again when she stood at the lead table. She
could see that most of them were much older than her. Many
were dressed in professional nurses' uniforms.

"Hello, everyone. My name is Magda. I'm new here, as you
can tell. I was asked to help with recording the supply shipments from here for the new base hospital overseas. I don't
want to disturb your work, but I hope you don't mind if I have
to ask you some questions so I understand what is being collected and packaged." She looked down for the first time at the
sheets on the clipboard. Each page seemed to concern different categories of supplies—various drugs, medical equipment
of many types, bedding, patient clothing, even foodstuffs such
as tea, oatmeal, and canned broth. It made her bleary-eyed.

"Perhaps you could tell me your names, and what you are
packing? And since you've been here before me and there's
no one else to ask right now, I'd appreciate if you'd tell me the
steps in your work." She'd never felt so out of her depth.

One woman, with graying hair tightly wound under her
white cap, spoke first. "I'm Marie. Look at your lists, Miss.
These here are aspirin bottles, and we pack them in cotton so
they don't break, then they use the cotton as part of bandage
supplies. They'll be wanting you to check the boxes before they
close to make sure they're done as need be. Then you check
them off your list." Magda looked down at the clipboard and
found the page specifying the number of aspirin packages to
be filled.

MAGDA, STANDING

The others around the table introduced themselves and showed Magda other items they were packing, including surgical implements and bottles of disinfectant. The delicate pieces were wrapped, and each unit counted. After inspection, the box would be closed with twine and a wax seal. Magda could see that the group worked together smoothly at a steady pace, each woman doing a separate task. After the boxes were completed and certified, they were stacked on the other side of the room and eventually taken to the rail yard and loaded onto the cargo trains leaving every few hours for Philadelphia.

Magda didn't want to stand there simply watching the women work, so she asked if she could take a box and help fill it until others were ready for her to close and check off her list. She could tell that her presence dampened the low hum of conversation that had marked the women's work when she arrived.

"May I ask—you are nurses, aren't you?" Several of the women in uniform nodded quietly, not looking up.

"I'm just surprised. I would have thought the Red Cross needed you in the troop hospitals. I want to be sent overseas to a field station—I still hope to go by March. I just trained as a nurse's aide and I know they really need staff overseas. I just expected—" She stopped herself, realizing that she might be about to embarrass them, and certainly herself.

"You're saying we're trained to do more than fill boxes?" A younger woman named Sally, possibly Kitty's age, spoke up. "Nice you noticed. We've been trained at Mercy, by the Hill. Some of us have even ten years' experience in that hospital. But the Cross and the army think we're not 'suitable' to care for the soldiers overseas, or they don't trust us to tell the enemy from the Allies."

"You mean they won't admit you as military nurses abroad? Why?"

"Where have you been?" Sally asked impatiently. "We Negro nurses are not—"

"But the army drafts men who come from German immigrant families like mine, as well as Austrian and Hungarian. If it trusts them—and of course it should, we're Americans now—why not recruit people who've always lived here and have the skills?"

The other women now looked at Magda, eyebrows raised, shaking their heads slightly. She knew the answer instinctively, but stating the illogic of it aloud made her sound ignorant and naïve. She had lived on the opposite side of town from most of the colored population, in her community where residents had largely chosen to live with people of a common background. Colored workers, mainly domestics and laborers, came and went as jobs demanded, but were largely unseen by people like her. Magda realized with a start that she was having the first real conversation of her life with colored people. These nurses were more highly trained and experienced than Magda, but more constrained in their opportunities than she had ever felt herself to be. She had been thwarted temporarily from pursuing her wishes for schooling, and mildly chided for her ambition, but she'd always seen that the doors ahead were only closed for a while, not locked. And she knew that there were always other doors.

Within a few days, Magda found her stride. She worked closely with the women packers and saw the lists filled with speed and accuracy each day. The two male accountants, who preferred to sit in the cramped office, took Magda's initial counts and completed the larger ledgers before the cases and pallets passed through the huge back doors onto waiting carts for eventual transport across states, seas, and countries.

After work one day, when the ledgers for Base Hospital No. 20 were almost filled, some of the nurses invited Magda to join them for a beer. They walked up Wylie Avenue and entered a small restaurant with musicians playing. Magda rarely had a chance to listen to live music, other than the German-style bands featured at church festivals and taverns. Con had invited her to a symphony concert at Carnegie Hall, but they couldn't go before he was called to Washington. She'd hear music on a gramophone and on the radio, always a bit scratchy and distorted. But these musicians played a different sound that seemed to enter her veins.

"Now you'll be leaving us for the front, Lady Liberty?" Magda had gotten closest to Sally, whose teasing sense of humor helped pass the dull days.

"I hope so. Not leaving you all, I mean, but I want to go to France. My brother and brother-in-law are serving there." She looked with embarrassment at the three women, who were so much better trained and prepared than herself. "I hope that soon you'll be going, too, if you still want to."

"Of course, I do," said Bella, who was about Willa's age. "Our menfolk are out there too. Not many of them allowed to do the 'glory work.'" She spoke the words with an exaggerated tone—she didn't believe in the glory of war any more than the rest of women waiting at home, but the denial of that prestige, however illusory, was painful. "Most of them are just moving supplies out there, like here, and doing the dirty jobs. But they take risks too; nobody is watching out for their safety."

"No matter. I'm applying again for the army hospitals here in the States," Sally interrupted. "The Red Cross and the army think they can do without us, but they sent all the white nurses overseas and the injured boys will start coming back. They don't need us graduate nurses filling boxes here, that can be done by others. Enough of that!" She shook her head and they clinked their glasses. They sat back to listen to the music, unfamiliar sounds that seemed to Magda alternately discordant, mournful, and moody. She tried to recall the music after she left, but found the tunes elusive. She would bring Con here when he returned, she decided.

Magda confessed to herself that the warehouse assignment had presented considerable opportunity for learning. Beyond her training, she now recognized a wider range of surgical tools and the drugs that were available. She saw the unimaginable scope of supplies needed for even a temporary field station to function near the front, so that wounded soldiers could be given both emergency care and minimal comforts. She realized the kind of organization that a war required, even far from the fighting. And she gained admiration for what unrewarded and unrecognized dedication really meant.

The last shipments from the Pittsburgh station headed to Philadelphia for Base Hospital No. 20 were completed in late March. The warehouse was still receiving massive supplies daily that other Red Cross chapters had funded and collected for distribution, but Magda was determined not to become trapped in logistics. As soon as she could get an appointment, she presented herself to Nurse Kramer.

"Well, I heard you did a good job, as I knew you would," the woman announced without a pause in shuffling papers on her desk. "I suppose you'll want to use your nursing training more directly now?"

MAGDA, STANDING

"Yes, I will. I mean, I do!" Magda replied, smoothing her skirt. She was braced to fight any suggestion of delay or deferral from getting sent abroad. "I hope I can go away with the staff of the base hospital, as we discussed. Or to some other field unit overseas. I could leave any time. I got my physical and inoculations with the rest of my class in January, so I'm ready."

The supervisor nodded. "I'm preparing the assignments for our latest class of trainees, so I'll let you know very soon. Come back on Friday." With that, she took a phone call with a dismissive toss of her head.

27

Magda spent the next three days in a flurry of catching up. On Tuesday, she brought Richy home from Willa's and took him to the park, where they met Elise and Martin, then on to Lucia's grocery for candy and a long overdue visit with her. She devoted the remaining mornings to helping at the play-school and spent more time with Richy afterwards. She invited the aunts to the house for dinner with Papa—the first time since Mama died.

The dinner was surprisingly lighthearted. They all needed distractions, and when Papa relayed some tales he'd heard from his friends at the tavern, the women laughed more heartily than Magda had heard from them—or anyone—in months. She had no trouble following their German. In one story, some village boys had outwitted the army recruiters back in 1870 by hiding deep in haystacks, then got themselves picked up and transported to the base to feed the army mules. Even Minnie dabbed her eyes.

MAGDA, STANDING

As Magda was washing the dishes, she heard a knock on the front door. It was nearly eight thirty—too late for normal visits or regular mail. Immediately, her throat tightened. Wiping her hands on her apron, she walked to the door, but her father was already opening it. The man standing there wore a badge on his lapel, which she could read clearly through the screen: US Government War Casualty Office. He handed Papa a telegram and didn't wait for a response.

Papa opened it shakily and read in silence. "It's Fred. He's been injured and they're sending him back to an army hospital in Baltimore." Papa looked up at the women. "It doesn't say how badly."

"Does it say when it happened?" Minnie asked, "Or when he's arriving?"

"Nothing more," he said, lowering his hand heavily and letting Magda pick up the telegram. "Perhaps they will tell us soon."

Suddenly, the thought of going abroad held little interest for her. "Papa, I haven't gotten my assignment yet. Maybe I can ask to be sent to Baltimore. Then I could see Fred as soon as he gets there. I'm sure I could find him, there can't be too many military hospitals in one city."

"Yes, do that," Tilly urged. "Maybe if he's well enough to travel you can even arrange for him to come home. Minnie and I could take care of him here."

After the aunts left and her father had gone to bed, Magda quietly telephoned Con. He was staying in a hotel, and she knew the front desk could reach him. It was much later in the evening than considered proper to call, but she needed to talk to him. She hoped that other people sharing her family's telephone line wouldn't be listening this late, so rumors might not spread so quickly about Fred.

"Magda! How are you? Is everyone all right? How's Richy?" Con's deep voice sounded immediately soothing and her shoulders relaxed a little.

"We're okay, all of us here. But we just got a telegram that Fred has been injured, and they're sending him to an army hospital in Baltimore. That's all we know."

Con was silent for several seconds. "I'm sorry to hear that. I wonder if he was in the battle at the Somme. We'd heard General Pershing offered some divisions to the French, ones most ready for combat like his, but that only a few American troops are actually taking part. It's still ongoing. If they're sending Fred home now, he probably was injured in the last ten days."

"Wouldn't they treat him in a hospital there? Like they cared for you? Why would they be sending him home so soon?"

"I'm sure they have treated him. They save many lives and patch up as many as they can to send back to the front. But some wounds take longer. If they're sending him home," Con paused, choosing his words carefully, "it means he can't fight again."

Magda's stomach dropped. "So it's bad, then?"

"Maybe so—or maybe like me. Maybe he lost his left arm and the two of us can make a matched pair." Magda tried to smile at Con's effort to allay her anxiety. There certainly wasn't much point in speculating about the worst.

"I miss you," she whispered. "I wish I had your arm around me now."

"Me too, dear one," he replied. "I'll send you whatever information I can get, I promise." The phone line suddenly spat loud static and broke off. Magda stood leaning on the phone box on the wall, her tears falling freely.

———

MAGDA, STANDING

The next morning, she headed over to Elise' house with Richy. Magda owed her the news, however difficult.

"I sensed it," Elise said softly. Her eyes glistened and she clutched Magda's hands.

"I was hoping to be sent with the next group of nurses abroad, but I've decided to ask to be assigned to Baltimore, or someplace close by. Maybe I can at least visit him until he can come home."

"Oh, I hope so too." Elise looked around apologetically. "I haven't prepared for a visit and the house isn't too tidy, but won't you please stay for a cup of tea?"

"Of course. Have you seen your sister-in-law?" Magda asked, aiming for a more positive subject.

"Yes, she came with her daughters a few days ago. We had a nice time. The girls are twins. A bit younger than our boys, but well-behaved. I invited them to stay with me here, starting next month before they have to pay their landlord again."

"What a big change for you and Martin!" Magda felt relieved that Elise wouldn't be alone, especially after the news about Fred.

They sat quietly while the children played. Elise got up suddenly, went inside, and came back with a small box. "Please give this to Fred as soon as you see him." It was a scapular she had made herself: an oval patch of thick felt about two inches long, embroidered with a cross and attached to a long round cord. "I was going to send it by mail. I would have given him a metal cross to wear, but I thought this might be more comfortable, and more personal. The prayers that go with it are just as strong."

Magda fingered it carefully. "It's beautiful," she whispered. She realized that she hadn't been able to pray much for Fred and Johannes since they left. It seemed to her less helpful for them, somehow, than focusing on ways to provide actual service to the soldiers.

She would only argue with God if she prayed: why did He let the Kaiser cause so much destruction, and bring shame to the German immigrants, who didn't deserve any of it? Why let His children kill each other? Who did He want to win? Surely not Germany, where people were suffering, too, and probably praying for victory just as those in the US and its allies. Sometimes she thought of the uncle and cousins she'd never met. What if Fred had to face them across a trench? Her mind was tormented, not comforted, when she tried to pray.

She didn't want to express her weak faith to Elise. She could see that for many people praying might be one of the few sources of relief they had. The nuns always said that God allowed suffering and evil to give mankind opportunities to do good, and that overcoming the bad things brought us closer to Him. At this moment, Elise's gift for Fred made Magda feel closer and more sympathetic to her.

"Fred will get this, I promise, and feel your gentle touch." She hugged her friend tightly and walked home slowly with Richy, who skipped and sang the whole way. If we could only keep the hearts of children, she thought. For them, she could ungrudgingly thank God.

Riding the trolley Friday morning to see Nurse Kramer, Magda worried about how to present her changed request. Saying she wanted to care for her brother probably wouldn't be convincing—putting the personal ahead of the professional.

MAGDA, STANDING

Should she offer to stay at the warehouse, on the chance that she could get away more easily to visit Fred in Baltimore, perhaps on a weekend?

As usual, the supervisor looked harried. "Oh, hello, Magda," she said, glancing up briefly. "I'd almost forgotten that you were waiting for your assignment. We've been so busy!" Magda felt deflated, but of course the Red Cross was processing hundreds, even thousands of volunteers.

"A slot for you overseas, I remember that's what we discussed when you went to the warehouse." Nurse Kramer tapped her pencil impatiently.

This was the opening Magda needed to shift the plan. She squirmed in her chair and searched for the right words as Nurse Kramer continued.

"But the fact is, we've sent so many graduate nurses, aides, and other medical staff to France and Belgium that we're facing a new problem. After months of our men fighting the enemy, we're getting the most seriously wounded coming back to the military hospitals here, which are very shorthanded. I don't want to disappoint you again, but—"

"I'm willing to stay in the States and work in one of those hospitals," Magda interjected quickly, leaning forward. "I understand. I've heard of more and more soldiers being sent back to places like Baltimore."

Nurse Kramer cocked her head with a quizzical look. "You mean you wouldn't mind?"

"No!" Magda replied. "I've been thinking the last few days that when the boys are sent back to recover, that's another kind of front. Besides, I want to start nursing as soon as possible, and travel to the field would delay me another two or three weeks, at least."

"Well, good, then!" The supervisor sighed her relief. "You'll leave tomorrow afternoon for Philadelphia with a group of our recent trainees and report to the military hospital there." She scratched a note and filled out a form as she talked. "But they will probably send you on to the Fort McHenry hospital in Baltimore, which is the largest receiving area for the most seriously wounded. I hear they're overwhelmed, especially now as many of the boys are arriving sick, on top of their injuries." She paused and asked, "You've had measles already, I hope?"

Magda nodded vigorously.

"I have to warn you: we didn't train you for some of what you'll see. Especially the psychological wounds. But you can handle it, I think. Good luck."

On her way home, Magda remembered how Con had described the soldiers with mental trauma. But her mind soon shifted to a more immediate source of concern—having less than a day to say her goodbyes. After all the waiting, she wasn't ready. She hadn't even started packing. Fortunately, the nurse's aides had been told what personal essentials to take, and to limit luggage to a small suitcase. The uniform alone would take up half the space. Assuming she would have little time to socialize, Magda thought she would limit herself to one simple dress, underwear and stockings, a nightgown, a change of cuffs and collar for the uniform, cloths and pins for her monthlies, and basic toiletries including soap and lotion. She had never given a great deal of attention to clothes or a "beauty regimen" as Lucia called it, referring to the ladies' magazines sold in the family store. More importantly, Magda hoped she would be able to take baths, but she knew her own comforts would be a minor consideration.

MAGDA, STANDING

She made a mental list of whom to see in the time left. She would telephone Minnie and Tilly and ask if they could drive her to the station, so she would have that time with them. She rarely asked them for transportation, but she thought they would agree. Willa had a phone now, so Magda could ask her and the children to come to the house for dinner and stay overnight. She would telephone her goodbye to Sabine and Tony if they were unable to stop by on such short notice. That left Lucia and Elise. She decided to spend the next hour or so visiting them if they were home, and if not, she would leave them each a note. She had no idea what her address would be, but she would promise to write as soon as she knew. She would telephone Con to let him know he shouldn't send letters to her house.

Fortunately, Willa and Papa were already at home when Magda returned from visiting her friends. Over dinner, she told them about her assignment.

"I think there's a good chance I can get to Baltimore. I'll do my best to find Fred. Maybe I can even take care of him there."

"That may be too much to ask of your superiors, but if you can just let us know where he is, and his condition," Papa said, his brow deeply furrowed.

Willa became very emotional at Magda's news. She dissolved into tears as soon as their father left the dinner table. "I'm glad you'll be nursing—I know that's what you want—but I'll miss you so much! And Richy will ask for you every night. I know he prefers you. So many people have left his life this past year, I'm not enough to make up for all of you. How I wish Johannes was still in Baltimore. He hasn't been able to tell me where he is now, just somewhere in France. Oh, I hate this war! I hate everything about it."

Magda tried to comfort her sister, but all she could think to say was, "Stay busy!" They laughed. "How's that for ridiculous advice to the mother of an infant, taking care of a four-year old, Papa, and two houses besides? You'll be too tired to worry."

"Thank goodness for Molly's help," Willa replied, squeezing Magda's hand.

Magda asked Richy to help her pack so she could spend some quiet time with him before his bedtime. He often seemed to observe and understand more than she gave him credit for, especially since she had been too preoccupied to spend more than a few hours with him for weeks.

"When will you see Fred?" he asked, playing with the clasp on her suitcase.

"I'm not sure. Soon, I hope. Do you want to give me something for him?"

He nodded and ran out of the room, returning with a baseball, three small metallic cars, and one of his toy soldiers.

"Oh, but not so much! And maybe he can't play ball where he is."

Richy looked at her thoughtfully. "Fred said he'd take me to a ball game when he gets back. And I want him to teach me to drive. So he remembers." He thrust the ball and one of the cars into a corner of the valise, putting the rest in his pocket. "Maybe he doesn't need the soldier."

"Okay, that works," she said. "And what about me? Will you give me something so I can think of you while I'm away?" There was little room left in her case, but a lump was rising in her throat. Willa was right. Richy's world had changed the most, and she still felt he was her particular charge. He ran out of the room again and came back several minutes later, holding a crumpled kerchief. She recognized it as one of Mama's

MAGDA, STANDING

that she had embroidered years before either of them was born. Richy used to clutch it for comfort before he fell asleep. She hadn't realized he still had it.

"Where did you find this?" she asked, her eyes filling with tears.

"It was behind my bed. You keep it."

Thank goodness for careless housekeeping! She threw her arms around him and let her tears fall into his thick hair. "This is the best gift you could have given me," she whispered. "I'll keep it with me every night!"

Richy patted her arm gently, as he used to do when she held him as a baby. "Come back soon," he said, and then skipped out the door.

Minnie and Tilly arrived early the next morning, wanting plenty of time to talk with Magda on their way to the train. Tilly brought two of her large pretzel rolls, a packet of dried fruit, and a block of cheese wrapped in a cloth bag. "You take these. You don't know what kind of food will be available on the train." Magda could see that both aunts, like her, were having difficulty holding back tears.

"We're so proud of you," Minnie stated, pressing an envelope with twenty dollars into her hand, "and I confess I'm a little jealous. If I were a decade younger, I'd be signing up with the Red Cross, too, to go back to Europe and try to undo some of the Kaiser's damage."

"I'm sure you would, *Tante*! And if there were more women like you still in Germany, I don't think he could've gotten this far. But anyway, I haven't done anything admirable yet. I just hope I can help some of the soldiers recover as they return."

Magda was going to mention looking for Fred again but paused, seeing Willa's drawn face. Bad news didn't always seem worse than no news. "I reached Con last night at his hotel," she told Willa quietly, "and asked him to inquire about Johannes' engineering unit. He'll try to find out where they're stationed and what they're doing, I'm sure."

Con had been pleased that Magda would be staying in the States, and relatively close to Washington. "Maybe I'll get an assignment to cover the military hospitals nearby and find a nurse's aide to interview."

As she entered the Pittsburgh station and hugged her aunts farewell, Magda felt overcome by the crowd, but even more by the realization that she was finally leaving home. Not across an ocean to a foreign country, but for the first time in her life, she would actually be on her own. "Don't even think of getting homesick," she muttered. With relief, she saw a sea of blue and white uniforms among the khaki, and found her place with the cohort of new nurse's aides who were also headed to Philadelphia.

MAGDA, STANDING

28

The train was slower than she'd expected, stopping in a dozen towns to take on more passengers, mainly other recruits headed for training camps. She had hoped to recognize someone in the group, but the crowded compartment made strangers become quickly familiar.

"I'm Jane," said the young woman who took the hard wooden seat facing her. "Maude," said another, squeezing into the end of the bench. "We're from the North Side. What about you?"

"Magda. South Side. Pleased to meet you."

All three wore the same uniform. This was their first train ride, and their first venture from home. Magda was grateful for the food Tilly had provided, which she shared with her new acquaintances who also offered their fruit and sandwiches. There was little for sale on the train.

At several of the station stops a boy came through the car selling warm drinks. After a while, a few soldiers followed him, jostling to get close to the aides. "Buy you a coffee, ladies?"

they asked. Magda was prepared to be very cautious around strangers, but she saw that Jane was more flirtatious than the soldiers. They all seemed like schoolboys, glad to be heading somewhere new, but aware there soon wouldn't be many opportunities to socialize. They reminded her of a younger Fred. She and Maude joined some lively card games and she bet a dime, thankfully winning it back. The players then shuffled themselves around the tight rows to let others play. "It would be nice if this were all we needed to do with the patients in the hospital," she mused.

They pulled into the Philadelphia 30th Street Station near midnight. Magda, along with many of the passengers, had dozed off and was jolted awake by the screeching brakes of the train. As they disembarked, a man called out orders for the soldiers to head one way, while a woman in a Red Cross uniform directed the nurse's aides and other medical personnel to a waiting van. After an uncomfortable ride, during which Magda's anxiety rose as they sat packed to capacity in the dark compartment, they stopped at what looked like a long metal hut. The aides were to spend the night in barracks built for the coming surge of wounded, and report to the nearby hospital early in the morning. "In case we had any doubts, we're soldiers now," sighed Maude to the others as they shivered in the April chill waiting for the washroom, clutching a thin blanket that constituted their bedding for the night. Magda swore to herself that she wouldn't complain; after all, the accommodations might look deluxe to men in the trenches.

Shortly after dawn, she and the other nurse's aides trudged across muddy paths to the imposing main hospital building where work assignments would be announced.

MAGDA, STANDING

"Ladies of the Red Cross!" A uniformed woman addressed them from the middle step of a staircase, facing the crowd of aides huddled in a reception area near the formal main entrance. "I'm Matron Haskell, in charge of the nursing staff here. Thank you for coming. I understand most of you have recently completed the training in Pittsburgh and will be new to your duties. We expect you to work hard and pay close attention to your superiors for guidance." She looked over the group, which Magda estimated to be about twenty aides. "We require half of you to stay here at the Penn hospital, but need the rest to continue on to McHenry in Baltimore. If any of you has a preference for that location, you may stand over to the side. I will assign the remainder myself."

Magda wasn't sure whether Fred would be sent to that hospital, and she didn't look forward to another crowded train right away, but she hadn't expected to be given a choice, so she decided to take a chance. She walked to the designated area and stood with a half-dozen aides there. She was pleased to see Jane in the group and slipped her arm around hers.

After calling out several more names, Matron Haskell directed the contingent for Penn to leave with a nurse through another door. "The rest of you will be taking this morning's eleven o'clock train for Baltimore. Be in front of the barracks at nine o'clock for transport to the station." On that cryptic note, she left them. Walking back in a light drizzle with only their coats for cover, most of the aides stopped at carts on the sidewalk selling tea and sandwiches of bean paste and cabbage.

"I hope they don't expect us to pay for our own food all the time," a girl named Lana said.

Magda nodded, worrying about the contents of her small pocketbook. "Maybe once we're registered among the staff they'll feed us," she sighed, then felt guilty for focusing on her own comforts. "At least this tea is hot and the bread isn't moldy!"

Once on the train, Magda was lulled to sleep by its slow, rickety movement over three hours. Feeling sufficiently warm, dry, and rested lifted her mood, along with the sunnier weather as the train approached Baltimore. Once disembarked, the aides mounted a cargo truck outfitted as a shuttle for transport to the hospital. It came to rest in front of a large fortress-like structure with a sign stating "US Army Hospital No. 2 at Fort McHenry."

The aides were ushered into a receiving hall and told to leave their luggage there so they could attend an orientation meeting before being shown to their accommodations. The meeting was a hurried lecture by a nurse matron who appeared tired and rather irritated, as if she had been pulled away from more important duties.

"You should all feel honored to be here," she began bluntly, not pausing to introduce herself. "This is one of the largest military hospitals in the States, 3,000 beds strong, and we're receiving many more thousands of invalid soldiers. Our staff includes some 200 doctors, 300 graduate nurses such as myself, the same number of medical orderlies who are military staff, and about 100 civilian aides, including yourselves." She paused after reciting what sounded like a memorized opening and consulted her notes.

"Always the same reminder that we're at the bottom of the pecking order," whispered Jane, sighing.

"This hospital receives patients directly off the troop ships returning to Baltimore harbor," the speaker continued. "We see many different afflictions, but the largest wards are those

MAGDA, STANDING

holding amputees, patients with head injuries, gas victims, and cases of neurasthenia." At the blank looks from some listeners on the last word, she added, "Shell shock. And, of course, many diseases of wartime, including pneumonia, measles, dysentery, and louse-borne infections such as typhus and trench fever. If the patients present with such diseases before transport they may not board ship, so they are typically acquired during the crossing, given the filth and overcrowding, and many arrive with multiple medical problems. Any questions?"

Magda's mind was overflowing with questions, but she decided to ask only one. "Will we attend lectures explaining these medical conditions and how they are treated?" She knew that large hospitals did a lot of teaching and discussed research.

"Not for aides to attend," the nurse sniffed. "You will get instructions directly in the ward and follow them. You won't have time to sit in any lectures. Keep your eyes and ears open and learn as you work. Your main responsibility will be to keep the patients clean, fed, and comfortable." With that, she left the room and was replaced by an administrative staff member who asked each aide to state her name, and gave their assignments. Magda felt her head spinning. When she was told "Amputees Ward 3," her initial thought was that it must be Fred's. Then she listened to some of the other assignments, including Jane's (Mental Ward 7) and Lana's (Infectious Diseases Ward 12). Few of the placements were the same.

The administrator explained the basic layout of the enormous facility, noting the building maps on every floor, and the locations of the laundries and kitchens. Magda was relieved to hear that the aides could take meals in the staff cafeteria and pick up their weekly stipends at the cashier's office—six dollars, of which two would be taken for room and board.

After confirming where to report for Ward 3 in the morning, Magda joined the group at a modest dinner in a rooming house a short walk from McHenry. There, she would share a room with three other aides, including Lana, Jane, and another she hadn't met earlier—Agnes, from New Jersey. They were all too tired after washing up to do more than introduce themselves and lay down on simple cots, made up with actual sheets, to sleep before starting work at dawn.

When the alarm rang the next morning, Magda could hardly lift her head from the pillow. She had a throbbing headache, sore throat, and fever. Several of the aides who'd traveled by train, including Agnes and Jane, complained of similar symptoms and felt too weak to get up. Magda had rarely been ill enough to stay more than a day in bed. The aides who were able to start work reported that many of the soldiers being shipped abroad, as well as those returning, were coming down with worse-than-usual seasonal influenza. It was attributed to the lingering cold weather and crowded conditions in the training camps and on all means of transport. But the outbreak wasn't severe enough to slow down the flow of troops and Red Cross volunteers. Magda was grateful that Mrs. Field, who ran the boarding house, was willing to check on the sick residents and bring them ice water and broth during the day, and that their unafflicted housemates were kind enough to do the same in the evening. After three days, feeling well enough to sit up, Magda picked up her stationery to write letters to Willa and to Con.

> *Fort McHenry, US Army Hospital No. 20, Baltimore*
>
> *April 8, 1918*
>
> *Dearest Willa,*
>
> *I'm very sorry I haven't written home yet. You must all be worried about me and think I got lost somewhere, but I simply wasn't able before now. After we arrived at the hospital in Philadelphia in the middle of the night, I was given an opportunity the next day to continue on to Baltimore. This is where I'll be working. I haven't had a chance to look around and I can't say what I'll be doing exactly yet, since I caught a bad cold on the way here and have been recovering in the boarding house with several other aides. We're much better, and I'll be starting work very soon.*

It was important to call it only a cold, knowing how Willa worried.

> *I'm with some very nice girls from Pittsburgh and other towns, and I'm sure*

I'll be busy soon. I wanted you to have my address and I would love a letter when you get a minute. I promise to write as well when I have more interesting news. Please let everyone in the family know where to reach me —

She wrote the boarding house address, which would be more reliable for mail delivery than the hospital.

Please give a special hug to Richy and tell him that I'll try to send him a postcard of the old fort here.
With love to Papa, Minnie, Tilly, and everyone,
Magda

She'd thought she owed the first letter to her family, and already the exertion made her want to sleep. But she so wanted to hear from Con that she copied out a similar text to him, adding the phone number of the boarding house and a bit more information at the end:

I chose to be sent here thinking this is where Fred may be, but of course I don't know yet. It's a large place and I plan to ask around as soon as possible. My first assignment will be in a ward of amputees.

MAGDA, STANDING

Perhaps they learned that I have special experience!

Please take care of yourself and write as soon as you have time.

With much affection,
Magda

———

When Magda reported to the hospital the next day, the same administrator gave her a cursory glance while flipping through the staff register.

"You've fully recovered?" she asked, not looking up again. "We don't want our patients getting sicker."

"Yes, I'm fine now," Magda said. She hadn't expected sympathy, but not to be treated as a threat either. The headache was not fully gone, but she couldn't stand the thought of being sequestered another day. "You told me last week I was to go to Ward 3. For the amputees."

"That's right, but not today. A new ship has come in and we need you down at the wharf to help patients disembark. There's a shuttle truck out back, take that. Then you'll need to report to the delousing station—the staff can direct you. That's the first stop for all the patients when they arrive."

Magda felt startled. She had imagined something like that, but avoided thinking about it. "Aren't they deloused before they make the crossing?" she asked, making a mental note to tighten her hairpins.

"Yes, multiple times. And this won't be the last. We don't want them bringing disease into the city. Well, go on!"

The morning was cool, with a breeze blowing off the Patapsco River. Magda stood with a group of nurses, aides, and orderlies as passengers in all manner of physical condition emerged onto the ship's deck. Most were soldiers, but some appeared to be medical personnel and others who had become wounded or sick in the line of war-related duty. Magda only had time to scan the first few passengers before being told to accompany a stream of wheelchairs and stretchers into one of several large tents set up in a lot next to hospital outbuildings. Down the center of the tent were three wood-burning stoves that tempered the chill as the orderlies and aides worked quickly to remove clothing. The worst items, stiff with dirt and bodily fluids, were dispatched at the end of a pole to a heap in the yard to be burned, while salvageable uniforms were placed in an enormous pot outside the tent to be boiled.

"Please go down to the far end, Miss," the senior orderly told her. The odor of unwashed bodies was strongest near the stoves. Following the staff's example, she picked up a soapy sponge for a boy close to her own age, his leg in a full cast, and scrubbed him behind a portable screen that gave an illusion of privacy and a bit of protection from draft. After rinsing the sponge in one of the large bins of water kept tepid near the stove, she rubbed him briskly with a small towel and then covered him with a fresh hospital gown and blanket. There wasn't sufficient time or warm water to be thorough in the effort, but the soldiers were probably cleaner than they'd been in months. Magda kept thinking how it would feel to Fred or Johannes to be in this situation, and she couldn't imagine cutting their clothes off and washing their bodies.

MAGDA, STANDING

"How are you doing, soldier?" she asked each one, sounding awkward to her own ears, but most of them tried to respond cheerfully.

"Been better, Miss, but glad to be Stateside finally. I'm sorry you have to see me like this!" Repeatedly, the patients apologized, gratefully. "I'm sorry. You're an angel. Thank you. I'm sorry I look like this. Thank you, Miss. Thank you."

This was like a baptism, she thought, as she scrubbed one soldier whose hair was caked with dirt and poured water gently over his head. They've been through a baptism of fire too—going to hell and back.

Late in the afternoon—exhausted, hungry, with arms aching—Magda was told she could leave on the truck to get a meal at the main building and report to her ward. She stripped off her soiled smock to be laundered in the hospital facility, and put on a clean one. After eating, she stood in the doorway of the amputee ward for several minutes, gathering strength as she gazed down the rows of over a dozen beds lining each side of the room. Her instinct might have been to focus on their limbs and gauge their losses, but instead she looked into every face. Was he Fred? No, no. But someone else's brother or son. What would he need from her? Would she be able to do this day after day, until the war's end?

The head nurse on the ward introduced herself as Matron Leister, in a manner more solicitous than abrupt, unlike most senior staff. "We're happy to have you here, my dear. All our volunteers are much appreciated, especially by the patients. I heard you've been sick. You must not overdo it these first few days on the job or you may relapse. Did they send you to the ship this morning? That was unwise—you should stay out of the chill. Go home to rest now and I'll explain your duties in the morning."

Whether from fatigue or emotional shock from the day, Magda thought she would start crying. Annoyed with herself, she shook her head. She needed to be strong and not a case for special treatment.

"Thank you, but I think I'd like to stay for a little while, if you're able to tell me now?" Since Matron Leister seemed sympathetic, she ventured further. "I was actually hoping that I might find out if my brother was sent here. We were told he'd been injured several weeks ago and would be recuperating in Baltimore. Is there any way to check the patient roster? I don't mean to interrupt work now, but is it possible?" She held her breath.

"Ah, do you know how many of us have family members we are looking for?" the woman replied with a deep sigh. "My second son. We haven't heard from him for months. I keep praying he'll be among the convalescents and not one of the missing. I think half of the staff here are wondering the same, hoping the same." She looked over the rows of beds, her face clouding. "You can ask in the office, they have the list of patients who've already come through McHenry. Several thousand, at least, since we entered the war. But they can't tell you the nature of the injuries. Perhaps they record the last ward where they were placed."

Magda wanted to hug the woman, who in that moment reminded her of Tilly. It felt better being able to share her worries. Almost everyone who cared deeply about a soldier was holding pain inside—or bracing for it. "What's your son's name? My brother is Fred Augustin. We can look out for both of them, maybe?"

MAGDA, STANDING

The matron smiled and patted Magda's arm. "John Leister, Navy seaman. But you go home now, I insist. You're still pale and we need our staff to be hale and hearty." With that, she turned around and headed back through the ward.

29

"Go to Bed 8!" a nurse barked to Magda as she reported to the ward the next day. The patient looked barely over twenty. He had lost one arm above the elbow and a wound on his forearm was exposed with open bandages above his wrist. A repulsive smell wafted from the wound and the skin surrounding it was blackened. A nurse and doctor were attending him.

"Gas gangrene. There's nothing we can do, it'll have to come off. This time below the elbow, hopefully. Prepare him for surgery," the doctor said to the nurse tersely, not looking at the boy who was clearly distraught.

"Take this over," the woman said to Magda, handing her a bottle of disinfectant and indicating where to use it. "I need to inform the surgery nurse."

"What's your name?" Magda asked him as she sat in the nurse's empty chair. She hadn't had time to check the chart on the bed and couldn't think of anything else to say. She took his hand, which was limp and cold.

MAGDA, STANDING

"Richard Wallace," he whispered, blinking back tears.

"I'm Magda. I have a brother Richard," she replied, as she applied a cold compress to his feverish head.

"Will you stay with me?"

"I don't know if they'll let me go into surgery with you, but I'll stay as long as I can." The boy threw his head back on the pillow and grimaced. She imagined what he must be thinking. Missing both hands, what would he do with the rest of his life? There was no time to contemplate as two orderlies approached the bed and, without a word, shifted him to a wheeled stretcher.

"Richard, I'll be here when you get back," Magda said softly. She didn't even know where he would be sent after the operation or what her schedule would allow, but he was her first patient and she wanted to keep her promise.

It proved almost a luxury to linger with a patient, as Magda mostly found herself running from one to another. Feeding them or helping them feed themselves, shaving them, and writing their letters if they requested were the most satisfying tasks. Many of the patients were withdrawn, but others thanked her effusively for the simplest attentions. She was happy when they asked her about herself, since it seemed they must feel a bit better to make that effort.

One of her favorites, Private Jim Fine, a self-declared farm boy from Virginia, was missing both feet but wheeled himself around the other patients and offered to help them during the day.

"You're a light to your buddies," Magda told him one evening as she prepared to leave. "I wish they could all have your strong spirit."

"In the middle of the night, I sometimes think of throwing myself down the stairs," he replied quietly. Magda paled.

She shook his shoulders gently. "Don't, don't, don't say or even think such a thing!" she said firmly, looking into his eyes. "We need you; your pals need you." But she resolved to tell Matron Leister and to return to the ward late some nights and check on him.

"You're new here, aren't you?" A doctor asked Magda one afternoon as he stood smoking a cigarette in the small kitchen off the ward.

She nodded. "There are several patients who've lost both legs. How did they survive the shock and blood loss in the field?"

He looked impressed by her question. "The dressing stations near the front are quite amazing. For all the terrible wounds that artillery causes over there, we have more capacity to save lives than in the past. But it doesn't make the toll less horrific. The better our medical advances, the fiercer the weapons."

"But what will happen with these patients when the stumps," she winced at the crude word, "have healed? I mean, when they don't need medical treatment any more, if they're lucky enough? You save their lives, but then—?"

"McHenry has rehabilitation activities on this campus. Teaching them how to get along with their amputations and to learn some way to make a living. The Red Cross is providing services for that too. But hopefully, most of them have families. It'll be tough—maybe impossible—to go it alone." He stamped out his cigarette in the sink. "We've never had so many amputees survive in the past," he acknowledged. "We'll all have to step up and help them when this is over." He made a gesture as if tipping a hat as he turned to leave. "And you are?"

"Magda Augustin. Thank you, Dr. Schmidt." The aides didn't get name tags, but his was stitched into his coat. She appreciated that he treated her almost like a colleague, not like low ranked staff.

She decided to explore the rehabilitation facilities when she found the time. And she would do some research of her own, with Con.

———

The weeks sped by, with Magda and the rest of the aides working at least twelve hours a day. They were to have one day off a week, but aside from sleeping late, washing her underthings, and writing letters, Magda couldn't find enough distractions to justify it, and often went back to the ward to keep her patients company. She had discovered that Richard, her first patient who'd lost both hands, was interested only in chess if someone moved the pieces for him, so she set up a schedule of games with his ward mates.

By late May, the weather was warm enough to sit outside on the house porch after dinner and catch a bit of fresh air. Magda and her housemates would have liked to go into the city to take their minds off the agonizing scenes they witnessed in the hospital, but they were too tired and could only share stories about their patients.

"We're seeing many cases of dysentery and measles," Lana remarked as she sat on a wooden rocker with a cup of tea. "Some of the boys are so weak when they get off the ship that they can barely make it down the ramp. I wonder if anyone cleans those ships at all between voyages." She reached for a slice of the dried apples that Jane's family had sent them. "Do you know we can give them fluids right into their veins when they're dehydrated? Through a hose and a bottle that drips saline directly into their arms."

"I've heard that can even be done with blood, passing from a healthy person to the patient, but it's more dangerous," Jane commented. "I haven't seen it yet—not in my ward, at least, where they call ours 'the walking wounded.' The boys may not even have any visible injury, but some of them just sit there and stare at the wall, and loud noises can make them frantic."

"What can be done for them?" Magda asked.

"We're told only time, rest, and convalescence somewhere quiet, calming, and close to nature. But how can that work, when there are thousands with this condition? I think they'll be sent back to their families, but I can't imagine living at home will help in every case. One boy comes from a family of twelve in the poorest part of Boston. There can't be any respite for him there."

"We have patients who are nonresponsive like that, but because their brains are so badly injured." Agnes wasn't freshly trained as a nurse's aide like the rest of them and had seen hospital duty before, but nothing like at McHenry. "Two in our ward have openings in their skulls that can't be closed fully, so they have to wear a special helmet. And some of them have lost half their faces. Can you believe the surgeons here are replacing jaws and noses? I've seen a few who were operated on a couple months ago and are getting ready to leave. They still look badly injured, but at least they may recover enough to eat and talk."

Magda appreciated her colleagues' sharing what they learned, since there was little time during the day to query the senior staff. "In our ward, most of the patients are recovering from their wounds, but their spirits are very low," she said. "Some say they wish they'd died, that their lives are over. They fear their wives or fiancées will reject them or that they'll never find someone to love them now."

MAGDA, STANDING

The aides nodded. The most widespread affliction in all the wards seemed to be emotional shock. "The senior nurse told us that we have to help the patients regain their will to live, after the army beat into them a will to die," said Lana in a soft voice. "That we need to be their mothers, their sisters, girlfriends, wives, and somehow make them know that we do care and that they're still worthy of love. But it's so hard when we're rushing from one patient to another all day."

"And when you lose one . . . " Agnes said, letting her words hang in the air. "It's just as well if you don't get too close to them." The women dispersed to their rooms without further conversation, feeling the weight of her words that they knew to be true.

After work the next day, Magda entered the boarding house to find a thick envelope from Willa on the table by the door. She raced upstairs to read it on her bed.

> may 20
>
> Dear Magda,
>   I'm enclosing a letter Fred addressed to you, that arrived only yesterday. I apologize for opening it but Papa insisted, since we haven't gotten a letter from him for so long. As you can see, Fred wrote it weeks ago, before he was injured, and it's been long delayed.
>   Even so, the tone is very grim—not at all the Fred we know. Papa was quite upset, as it confirms his opinion of this war. He says when the soldiers lose

faith in the cause they are fighting for, it makes every casualty that much less bearable.

Since you left, I still haven't heard from Johannes, nor have his parents. Con kindly wrote to say that he's been asking about the engineering unit, but the most he can determine is that it's somewhere in northern France. He's able to check casualty reports from the War Department and hasn't seen Johannes listed, thank goodness. All we can do is wait. Sometimes I tell myself that maybe he just hasn't had time to write, but I can't believe he would not have thought of my feelings, knowing how I worry. I realize the post is slow and unreliable. He can't know how many letters may be lost in transit. I write to Johannes as often as I can, and tell him all about how Caroline is growing—at least I can make him feel guilty!

We are doing well here, otherwise. Caroline is a very easy baby—good thing, since I came down with influenza shortly after you left and she stayed with my in-laws. None of the rest of us caught it.

I look forward to your letters. Do let us know more about your patients and what you are doing for them.

Lots of love,

Hilla

Magda's heart ached for Willa, who was so thoughtful of everyone. She couldn't believe Johannes would have been deliberately neglectful, but the alternative might be even more worrisome. She turned to Fred's letter, which had probably been delayed by censors.

March 25, France

Dear Magda, I don't have the energy to write to anyone else right now and I need to unburden to someone. For the past month, I've been assigned to stretcher duty with a British unit near a town here that was torn up by shelling almost 2 years ago. The BEF has been fighting close to 4 years already ███████████████████████, so we Yanks have to pitch in with them sometimes. I'm not a medic, I just carry injured and sick soldiers to the casualty clearing stations in the rear. ███████████. fresh blood spurting before they can be bandaged, or covered with a blanket when they're already dead. ████████ ████████████████████ Lots of bodies have been left for weeks in the fields between the lines, and there's no way to get them because of the snipers and machine guns.

The smell is getting worse as the weather gets milder. Another guy and I, he's from a place called Liverpool, have to run with the injured lying on a canvas between two poles we try to hold steady, ▮▮▮▮▮▮▮▮▮▮▮▮

▮▮▮ We leave them at the dressing stations. The nurses and orderlies there are running ragged too, but they're nice and offer us a tea sometimes. One of them told me the field hospital tries to patch up the guys who are less injured so they can be sent back to the front as quickly as possible. How insane.

▮▮▮▮▮▮▮▮▮▮▮ The German army is a killing machine and must be destroyed, but ▮▮▮▮▮▮▮ ▮▮▮▮▮▮▮▮▮▮ we're stalemated in a muddy hell. Another big offensive is expected ▮▮▮▮▮▮▮ A few guys say they're looking forward to it—anything to move us out of here. It's almost a year since I left, and I feel like I've aged 20 years. So far, I'm holding together, but don't think anyone can come through this without damage.

MAGDA, STANDING

> Sorry for this letter. I should tear it up since it will probably upset you if it gets through the censors, but I know you're tough and we've always been close. I'm so glad that at least this war isn't destroying our homes and cities. I don't think this part of Europe will ever recover.
>
> For what it's worth, since I can't feel much emotion these days, give love from me to the family. Please don't share this letter with them or with Elise.   Fred

Magda sat frozen. In his previous letter, Fred had sounded somber, as expected since he'd arrived at the front. But now he seemed so depressed and with little hope. She felt she could understand a bit better what her patients had been through, the awful memories and nightmares they must have. She wished Willa and her father hadn't read the letter, though she didn't blame them for having done so. The people left at home suffer their own kind of torment.

Tossing in bed and unable to put Fred's letter out of her mind, she knew she must find out if he had come through McHenry, or if he was even now somewhere in the vast reaches of the complex. She hadn't had a free moment to go to the intake office when it was open and request to see the patient roster. She had already asked all the aides to look out for his name, and they had given her some names too.

The following afternoon, she wheeled Private Fine back from his physical therapy in one of the dozens of outbuildings.

Her morning had been furiously busy, as several of the men had developed infections or needed further surgery. The mood in the ward was especially tense when the patients saw any of their mates going under the saw again. They all felt so vulnerable, and sometimes the only comfort Magda could give them was to not pretend that everything would be alright. She tried to say she understood their feelings and that their family and friends would understand too—though she didn't entirely believe that. Many of the patients didn't get any mail, but she wrote letters home for them anyway if they asked. Magda wasn't able to put on jolly airs, as a few of the newer aides tried to do—she found that irritating and almost disrespectful. Sitting with the most suffering patients and reading to them was the quiet kind of company that would have meant most to her if she were in their place.

Private Fine was visibly tired from the exercise, but as the day was beautifully sunny, he asked Magda to stroll around some of the walkways between the buildings, taking a long way back to the ward. They passed signs marking a wide variety of rehabilitation activities such as "Occupational Therapy": carpentry, tailoring, metalwork, telegraphy, auto repair, typing and shorthand. Other buildings held classrooms for academic studies.

"Look at that," he remarked, tilting his head back in her direction. "Do you think we can learn something here and get the work home? Would anyone hire me as a footless carpenter?"

"And why not, if you're skilled?" she asked. "Maybe you won't lead a barn raising, but you could make fine furniture! You'll be fitted with prosthetics before you leave here, and you can decide what you want to do. The doctor told you the other day you're about well enough to start some classes."

MAGDA, STANDING

As they approached the main hospital building, Magda stepped in front of the wheelchair and looked at him directly. "Would you mind if we took a small detour—just for a few minutes? I have a question for the administrator." She knew she wouldn't have another chance before the office closed, and didn't want to lose another day.

She entered and approached an elderly man behind the counter. "Is it possible to check the roster of patients? I'm looking for my brother, who may have been sent here."

He showed no surprise, as if he expected such a question from every staff member who bothered to speak to him. "Yes, but the list isn't alphabetical. Just name, date of entry and departure or death, and first ward assigned. Who are you looking for?" He opened a massive book with pages filled in a fine script.

"Frederick Augustin. He probably arrived after mid-April." That was over a month ago and she realized the search might take hours.

The man raised a bushy gray eyebrow. "I can't give you the book to look on your own, Miss, but I'll add him to the list." He fingered a slip of paper that evidently held other names requested. "If I find it, I'll send a note to you." He passed her a notepad to write her name and ward number.

She apologized to Private Fine for the delay and resumed their walk. "I wish my girl was looking for me," he said quietly. Magda knew he had written to her and received few letters in return. She patted his shoulder as she wheeled him into the ward.

"When you get home, many girls will be waiting," she said. "Even if you decide not to be a carpenter. Everyone will have missed you so much!"

While Magda didn't hear anything from the administrator, she did receive a piece of good news in a letter from Kitty.

May 30
New York City
Dearest Magda,

I'm happy to tell you that Walter and I are engaged! I called home to give Willa and Papa the news and told them to spread it among the Pittsburgh family and friends, but I wanted to write to you myself. Walter has been able to make several trips for work to the NYC area so we have spent enough time together in the past few months that we are certain of each other. As much as I would love to be married in Pittsburgh, given the war, we have decided to have a small ceremony here on June 15. I've given my notice and expect to move to Walter's house upstate by the end of June. My employers have been very kind and have given us a lovely china tea set and a generous money gift as well.

I'm sorry it's been so long since I've seen you. It's hard to imagine that you are an experienced nurse's aide now, doing very difficult work, I'm sure. Willa said you're looking for Fred. I do hope you find him and that he recovers quickly. Give him my love.

I'm getting sentimental these days. I will become the mother of two young boys soon, and I'm trying to imagine how that will be. I know I face a big adjustment, but my heart is big enough for Walter and his children, and I'm so looking forward to my new life!

MAGDA, STANDING

Well, I have to close now as there is too much to do before I leave. I need to interview and train my replacement and prepare the wedding (even a modest ceremony and reception take planning!). Willa has sweetly offered to make me a dress, but I know she doesn't have time for that.

I promise to send you a photo of the happy couple!

With warmest thoughts of you, little sister,
Kitty

30

As Magda sat down later that evening to write Kitty an enthusiastic response, Maude surprised her by running into the room, out of breath. They hadn't seen much of each other since Maude had transferred to McHenry only recently and took night duty on her ward—a rotation Magda had avoided so far.

"Is everything all right?" Magda asked, jumping up from the desk.

Maude came over and put her arm around Magda's shoulders. "I think your brother might be in my ward. We got about a dozen new patients today and I saw the name Fredrick on one of the charts, but the last name was obscured. We haven't had a Fred before. I wanted to let you know so I ran over here before signing in, but I need to get back right away. I can leave you a note tomorrow since we always miss each other in the morning."

"Oh, thank you!" Magda hugged her. "I have to know now. I won't be able to sleep. I'll come over with you." She pulled off her nightgown and grabbed the uniform she'd left hanging on a hook by her bed. It was never easy to put on quickly, with all the buttons and layers, but she knew that to enter a ward without authorization she needed, at least, to look professional.

"As you know, this is the ward with soldiers who've been gassed," Maude said quietly as she helped tie the smock in back. "Some cases recover enough over there, but the ones sent here . . . " Magda turned around, biting her lip. "They can be in pretty bad shape, especially in the first few weeks after they arrive. It's very difficult."

Magda grabbed her hand and they took the stairs in a rush.

The gas ward was on the second floor at the far side of the hospital, where Magda hadn't been before. She stood in the doorway, gathering her nerve. She could see that many of the patients had bandages over their eyes. The lights were dimmer than in other wards.

"Almost all have eye injuries," Maude whispered, "and they can't look at light."

They walked to the central station in the middle of the room where charts were kept, ordered by bed number. Holding a lantern over the charts, Magda moved a shaking hand from one to the other. Halfway through, she stopped—Fredrick Au. Something had been spilled on the paper, but it was enough.

She slowly walked down the central aisle to Bed 12. The upper half of the patient's face was covered down to his ears and there were other bandages on his chest, arms, and hands. His breath was ragged and his limbs jerked as he slept. She bent over him, placing a hand very gently on his shoulder. She felt sure that this was her brother. "Fred," she whispered. He didn't react. She stood there for a while, listening for any change in his breathing or sign of wakefulness. "I'll be back."

Magda tossed all night through a broken sleep, got up before dawn, and left without breakfast. Thankfully, Matron Leister was already in their ward.

"You're very early, Magda!"

"I found out last night that my brother is here in Gas Ward 14. I saw him last night but he was sleeping, so I wanted to go back first thing—and if he's awake, maybe talk to him." Her voice was shaking.

The woman placed her hand on Magda's arm. "I'm glad you found him. Of course, run over and see him. Just come back by nine o'clock; we have several new patients coming in today and I'll need all aides here."

Magda turned to go, then stopped. "Matron, have you heard anything about your son?"

"No," she said sadly. "He hasn't been on the listing downstairs. Perhaps in another hospital, but I haven't received any notice."

"I'm sorry! Maybe ... I hope ... " Again, Magda was struck that not knowing could be agonizing for loved ones. But she was also frightened at what she might soon find out.

"Go on now."

The lights in Ward 14 were still dimmed and paper blinds covered most of the windows, masking the early morning sun. Magda introduced herself to the supervisor, Nurse Irwin, not wanting to invite questions later.

"Patient 12? Let me check." Maude must have explained to her before leaving in the morning. The nurse looked through a separate listing by the door. "It says here Fredrick Augustin. Is he—"

"Yes!" Magda felt an equal surge of hope and fear that cramped her empty stomach. "May I sit with him? I only have two hours; I have to get back to the amputee ward."

MAGDA, STANDING

As she walked down the aisle toward Fred's bed, she glanced at the patients in his row. One moaned softly and another called out with a harsh croaking sound. A very young-looking patient was quivering uncontrollably. She saw two of the aides gently changing bandages over angry burns, while others spooned liquid into patients' mouths slowly.

She pulled up a chair next to her brother and bent low to his ear. "Fred? Freddie? It's Magda." His head and arms jerked. She saw that his lips were badly blistered and coated in salve. He tried to swallow and coughed roughly, trying to raise his head. She looked quickly to the closest nurse.

"May I give him water?" She'd learned that even the simplest action could cause distress for a patient, especially ones with internal injuries or those who were not fully conscious. The nurse signaled to use a straw.

"Fred, I'm going to hold your head up." Very gently, she lifted his head a couple inches and placed the straw to his lips. He took the water eagerly. A good sign, she thought. Then he resumed a deep wet cough that racked his chest.

He lay back and turned his head away from her. She still wasn't sure if he could hear, or was fully aware of who she was. "Do you know who's been asking about you every day? Richy!" He jerked his face back in her direction and returned a weak squeeze to her hand.

The head nurse and doctor approached the bed later, and Magda stepped back. Not being assigned to this ward, she couldn't insert herself into their conversation but stood close enough to watch and hear. They said little as the doctor studied Fred's chart and held the stethoscope to his chest while the nurse took other vital signs. He told the nurse to change his bandages and headed out of the ward. Magda followed him.

"Excuse me, Doctor? Doctor? That patient is my brother. Can you tell me—"

"I'm sorry." He turned and looked at her, deep bags under his eyes. She wasn't sure if he was apologizing for passing her hurriedly, or expressing sympathy.

"How badly is he injured? What's his prognosis? What can be done for him?"

The doctor stopped, motioning for them to sit on the wide windowsill in the corridor. "How much do you know about gas exposure?"

"Almost nothing. They didn't cover it in our training."

The doctor took a cigarette from his pocket, put it to his lips, then removed it. He stroked his fingers through his thinning hair. "We don't know the details, but given the timing, your brother probably faced a mustard gas attack. Was he infantry?"

She nodded. "His last letter said he was a stretcher bearer."

"The men down low in the trenches get it worst, since the gas is heavy. And those running and breathing hard. It doesn't typically kill its victims—just tortures them, I'm afraid." The doctor spoke in a monotone, looking away. "Most are blinded at first, but many can regain their sight. The blisters and burns to the skin, vocal cords, esophagus, windpipe and lungs may linger and become—"

Magda gulped and stood up abruptly, covering her mouth. For a moment she thought she would vomit. She took a very deep slow breath. "How ... How can all that be treated? And," she could hardly get the words out, "will he recover?"

The doctor rose and placed his hand momentarily on her shoulder. "Most of them will survive, that's all I can say. We can only offer morphine for the worst pain, along with poultices, hydration, and rest, what you nurses and aides are so good at offering. I'm afraid we doctors can't do much more. We weren't prepared for these gas injuries. Research is being done, but not fast enough." He paused while Magda closed her eyes and steadied her breathing. "I'm sorry, I have to go." He nodded to her, turned on his heel, and walked away before she could thank him.

It was almost time to return to her own ward. She went back to Fred, but he seemed asleep and, not being able to stay, she didn't want to disturb him now. She followed the supervisor to the end of the ward.

"Nurse, do you think, if I could get a transfer from my ward, might I be assigned here to take care of him?"

She looked at Magda kindly. "That's not recommended. It's hard enough caring for the patients we don't know. And we can't have favorites for our attention. But you're welcome to come see him as often as you can get away."

Magda wasn't surprised. It was like the military—no personal favors permitted. "I wonder how in the world these men made it through the voyage here, suffering like this?"

The nurse scanned the beds. "I suspect many did not. The nurses on board the ship have the toughest duty—worse than those in the dressing stations at the front, in my view. But they save many lives."

Magda walked to her ward as if in a trance. She was exhausted and hungry, but too anxious to rest or eat. She would find a way to get Fred back on his feet. He was strong, he would heal. She would make him better.

Back at the boarding house, Magda decided to call home to give them the news. It was important enough to spend the money.

"Papa!" She felt a surge of warmth hearing his voice. She fervently missed home at that moment. "I found Fred. He's here, at McHenry!"

"Tell me, how was he injured?"

She could hear Willa's voice in the background as she came close to the mouthpiece. "Magda, how is he?"

Magda weighed her words, not sure how much to tell them. "He's in a ward with patients exposed to mustard gas. I don't know yet his exact condition. He has bandages over his eyes, but he recognized my voice. The doctor says he will most likely recover." She chewed her cheek and wanted to cut the call short, afraid of further questions.

"Find out how long he needs to be in that hospital," Papa replied. "Can he come back to Pittsburgh so we can take care of him here?"

"I'll see, Papa. I'll visit him every day." She took a minute to ask Willa about Kitty and heard a few more details. "So happy for her!" they both said, almost in unison.

"I have to go now. Please tell the rest of the family about Fred. It's not too bad, I think!" Magda wasn't sure she was being entirely honest, since she knew so little. As she hung up, she decided, despite being dead tired, to write a short note to Con, since she wanted to hear what he might know. She would not tell Elise until she had more information. With Elise, Magda felt an obligation not to spare her feelings, but to be totally honest. The way she herself wanted to be treated.

Magda went to Fred's ward early every morning before her own shift, during her lunch break whenever she got one, and

MAGDA, STANDING

in the evenings. The staff accepted her as Fred's aide during her brief visits and left her tasks such as changing his dressings. She was there when his eye patches were removed the first time.

"Can you open your eyes, son?" the doctor asked. He'd explained to Magda that the gas targeted moist areas of the body, especially any that were exposed. Fred's eyes had been covered since he was taken to the field station. The biggest risk was that the eyelids might have fused.

They fluttered. Slowly, Fred opened his eyes. Magda could just see a sliver of white and blue. "Is that you, sis?" he croaked.

Magda's hands flew to her mouth and she gasped. "Yes, yes! And that's still you in there too!" she exclaimed, grabbing his free hand to kiss it.

The doctor stood straight and smiled. "This one will make it, I do believe," he said to her. "Private, you need to keep your eyes shielded from bright light for at least a month, and your skin away from sun, but get plenty of fresh air to heal those lungs. We might be able to get you out of here by summer's end."

"Could he go home before then?" The doctor shook his head slightly as he walked away. Magda realized it was the kind of naïve question a relative would ask, not a professional. And she had no idea of Fred's mental state. But she would make sure he recovered. She bent down and whispered, "I'll be back this evening and we'll plot your escape!" She thought he faintly patted her hand, but his eyes had closed again.

Con's telegram arrived within two days of her letter to him.

GLAD YOU FOUND FRED. ARRANGED TO WRITE ARTICLE ABOUT MCHENRY. WILL ARRIVE IN JULY. LOOK FORWARD TO SEEING YOU BOTH.

CHRISTINE FALLERT KESSIDES

⁓

Magda's spirits carried her aloft for the next couple weeks and she didn't feel as tired or saddened by her duties in the amputee ward. She found herself expressing an optimism she actually felt, and sometimes had to remind herself that not every patient appreciated it. But she was popular among the men, who started calling her Sis instead of Miss, and she was happy for that.

Fred slowly improved, although his voice was not much above a whisper and he wasn't yet able to swallow regular food. After helping him eat his breakfast of broth and powdered grain with milk ("baby food," he complained), she wheeled him outdoors and they sat on a shaded porch while she ate a sandwich and read to him. He said little and she often found him in the ward staring into space, sometimes with tears running onto his pillow. She knew that it was normal for patients to become depressed, especially as they faced their limitations. She prayed that Fred hadn't inherited weak nerves like Mama. Magda never would have imagined that before the war—not Fred.

As she wheeled him back to the ward one evening, careful to stay on the shaded paths, she heard her name and spun around. Con's long legs took him across the courtyard in a few steps, and she threw her arms around him. He bent down to Fred.

"Hey! You're back. All limbs present and accounted for?"

Fred smiled slightly, his lips still sore and cracked. With effort, he replied slowly, "You weren't . . . kidding about it . . . over there. Really . . . good to see you." He offered his hand, still partly bandaged, and Con held it gently.

MAGDA, STANDING

Magda arranged a day off and the three of them spent it together. Con told her about his interviews with McHenry's staff. "The War Department's censorship is so tight, they'll only allow positive stories about soldiers recovering due to the wonderful medical care," he told her. "That's important, but the public needs to know about the real toll too. There's another major deployment coming up and they're preparing a second draft, this time for ages eighteen to forty-five. About two million more men."

"Oh no! That means Tony too. And maybe even Kitty's husband."

"Well, with four children, Tony may not have to serve," Con replied.

"But knowing him, he'll insist on it if the draft includes his age. Poor Sabine."

Magda arranged for Con to meet some of her patients, hoping he might provide encouraging words on life after amputation. "As long as you still have your head on your shoulders, life is worth it," he told them. "You're worth it." He spent some time visiting her ward and played rounds of checkers and poker with the men.

Three days after his arrival, Con finished his interviews and article. Magda walked him to the exit gate after her shift. "Come to my hotel and I'll buy you a proper dinner," he said. "You've gotten skinny."

"Well, some of us don't have expense accounts for nice restaurants. But I'll take you up on that!" They approached the hotel and she hesitated. "I'm obliged to remind you that I don't visit gentlemen in their rooms. Just eat their food."

"Would I do anything to sully the reputation of a noble Red Cross volunteer?"

She blushed. "In fact, I'd like to change out of this uniform. I have nothing nice to wear to a restaurant, but—"

"I'll pick you up at seven. I just want to do one thing while you have it on—to show my respect."

He kissed his fingertips and stroked the badge resting on her breast. She raised her hand and tapped his cheek, then pulled down his chin for a proper kiss.

MAGDA, STANDING

3I

By late summer, Fred's vision had returned, although he found it tiring to read and needed eyeglasses. The blisters on his face and hands had healed, but left scars. "With spectacles and a neat beard, you look like a distinguished professor," Magda told him. Her greatest concerns were that his spirits remained very low and he became winded after brief walks around the grounds. But, with her encouragement, he started observing the classes in carpentry.

In early September, new patients started pouring into McHenry from among the cohort of recruits traveling from training camps to join the war. Many were falling sick as they arrived to the coast and had to be admitted to the hospital urgently; others were still directed to board ship if they could walk. Returning casualties, from all branches of the military, continued to arrive in larger than usual numbers. The new cases, both those coming from inland and those from abroad, showed a similar pattern of illness: high fevers and hacking coughs, difficulty breathing, extreme weakness, severe head-aches and joint pain. The numbers of reported deaths on board the ships had risen dramatically. Magda recognized some of the symptoms that she had experienced when she first arrived in Baltimore. But this disease struck with a ven-geance and these patients were much, much sicker.

After a few days, the medical director called all staff together, the first time in Magda's experience at McHenry. "We are experiencing an influx of grippe," he announced. "Our soldiers have apparently been exposed in France and by the time they arrive here, the illness has incubated. Some troops coming from certain camps, notably in Boston and the Midwest, have been infected as well. No cause for alarm. Influenza has struck our military before and it will pass without great incident, I'm certain, but we must take measures to minimize exposure to our weakest patients. Those presenting with symptoms will be moved to separate wards. And as of today, all staff must wear caps, masks, and protective gowns throughout the hospital."

When Magda mentioned the new conditions in her next letter to Con, he wrote back immediately.

> BE VERY CAREFUL. WE HAVE INFORMATION THAT A MAJOR OUTBREAK OF INFLUENZA HAS BEEN SPREADING THROUGH THE TRAINING CAMPS BOTH STATESIDE AND IN FRANCE. IT EVEN STRUCK THE GERMANS SO ACUTELY THAT IT'S BELIEVED TO HAVE CUT SHORT THEIR LATEST OFFENSIVE. IT'S BEEN REPORTED ALL THROUGH THE WAR ZONE, THREATENING OUR OWN RESERVES AND MEDICAL STAFF IN THE FIELD. THE GOVERNMENT WON'T LET US PUBLISH STORIES ABOUT IT, FEARING A LOSS OF MORALE JUST AS THE NEW TROOP SURGE IS GOING ABROAD. I'LL LET YOU KNOW IF I LEARN MORE.

Within a week, there were influenza cases in every ward; all beds were filled, and extra rows of cots were forced into any empty space, including corridors. Tents were set up outside, and in a matter of days they covered the grounds. It became more practical to move the non-symptomatic patients into a separate wing for their own protection, but every day more of them came down with a throttling cough, chills, and aches that made strong men moan.

"Keep them warm; feed them broth, juice, and tea; apply cool compresses; give aspirin to bring down the fever, and give codeine for cough." That was all the doctors could prescribe, and implementation was left to the nurses and aides. There was no medical treatment for influenza—if, indeed, that's what it was. The disease didn't look like the familiar seasonal infection, but something much more treacherous. Every day more patients were dying as their lungs filled with fluid, blood spurted from nostrils and ears, and they gagged on bloody sputum, unable to breathe. In the worst cases, their faces turned a deep red or purple and the poor souls suffocated within a matter of hours.

There were no more assemblies of staff for announcements, as they were instructed to avoid gathering even in small groups unless necessary for work. The matrons of each ward were the only source of information, but there was little to be had.

"Make them stay in bed, under covers, even if they feel better," Matron Leister told Magda and her colleagues. "They may think they've recovered when their fever goes down after a few days, but that's when they can relapse and get worse." But how to prevent patients from getting up and moving around if they wanted to, even if it meant infecting others? The staff could barely tend to those who were immobile.

Magda rarely got away from her ward during her shift, as increasing numbers of staff members were collapsing and there were none to take their place. She and her housemates who'd been sick in the spring weren't affected, but one morning neither Lana nor Agnes got up for work. The aides couldn't take time off to tend to them, but Mrs. Field kindly offered to help as she'd done for Magda and the others. Arriving at the boarding house a few evenings later, dragging their feet with fatigue, the aides encountered the landlady sobbing in the sitting room.

"That sweet girl. She's gone." The landlady whispered Lana's name.

It felt like a stomach punch. Until now, Magda hadn't imagined this flu would kill someone she knew well, especially not a friend. Now her greatest fear was for Fred; he'd been moved to a distant wing of the hospital where she thought he would be safe. With nursing shifts extending to more than sixteen hours, she hadn't been able to see him as frequently. "Don't go walking around," she warned him, when she quietly told him of Con's report. All classes had been suspended so she'd given him some books from the hospital library, but she doubted he was willing to comply as he healed.

It was almost midnight, but she turned suddenly and ran back to the hospital, up to Fred's ward. Putting on a fresh mask and gown, she walked in and saw that more than half the beds had been partially enclosed by sheets hanging from the ceiling—less a measure of effective quarantine than an attempt to give sufferers some privacy. She looked for Fred. He was behind the last sheet, sleeping. She felt his forehead and it was hot. His breathing was labored and raspy, the way it had been from the gas when he first arrived.

The ward supervisor approached her.

MAGDA, STANDING

"When did he develop the fever?" Magda asked, trying not to let her voice sound accusatory. The staff knew her so well, she would have expected someone to tell her—but then, no one had time for the normal considerations. And this nurse, like all the others, looked drained.

"Last evening. He complained of a sore throat, headache, and backache, but his breathing hasn't worsened today. His temperature was 102 degrees at least reading. He took water and a bit of nourishment before falling asleep." She moved on.

Normally, Magda knew better than to wake a sleeping patient if not necessary, but she wanted to speak with him. She sat on the edge of his bed and whispered, "Fred, it's me." He didn't stir. She felt his arms and torso. He wasn't sweaty from the fever, like so many of the flu patients, which could cause a dangerous chill. She decided to go home and try to sleep for a few hours, then visit again before her shift.

Shortly before dawn she forced herself awake, her heart sinking as she saw Lana's empty bed. Agnes seemed better, but Magda knew that one of the cruelest things about this disease was its capricious behavior.

As she approached the main hospital building, the shuttle that had brought her and the others to McHenry almost six months ago pulled up on the broad driveway. A half-dozen women stepped down, their white uniforms peeking out from under dark blue capes. She stopped, her hands flying to her mouth. Could they be reinforcements? Thank God, finally! As she got closer, she saw they were colored nurses, wearing Red Cross badges. She ran up to them.

"Welcome, oh, we're so happy to see you! Thank you, thank you for coming!"

The closest of them turned around. It was Sally.

CHRISTINE FALLERT KESSIDES

"Well, hello! My, you're looking thin. Don't they feed people here?"

Magda threw her arms around Sally, and kissed her on the cheek, then took several steps back in embarrassment. "Oh, I'm sorry, I forgot to put on my mask. I'm so excited to see you! You can't imagine how badly we need you here." She looked at the others but didn't recognize them.

"Well, the army finally decided to take a big chance with us," Sally replied with a sardonic tilt of her head. "This flu hit so many nurses they finally got down to us. It's an ill wind, as they say." Magda walked alongside the group and escorted them into the building.

"How are things at home in Pittsburgh?" she asked before leaving Sally.

"Not good. Mercy Hospital is full to bursting, but most sick people are staying home if they can. Schools, restaurants, theaters, even churches all closed last week."

When Magda arrived at Fred's ward, he was propped up on his pillow. He felt less feverish, but his cough was frightening as it shook his whole body and left a trail of blood from his nose and down the corner of his mouth. The skin around his eyes and ears was dark, bluish. He looked at her and gave a weak smile.

"What now, Fred?" she asked gently. "We were going to leave here soon, remember? You're not allowed to be sick like this. We're planning to go home!" She wiped his face with a damp cloth and held a spoonful of water to his mouth, but he had trouble swallowing it.

"Beer. I want beer. Cigarette." He seemed delirious.

"I don't think so, brother! I'm going to get you broth or milk. You need to fight this." Magda walked quickly to the small

MAGDA, STANDING

kitchen. The stove was on, but the pan had burned dry. She would have to go to another floor.

She wanted to avoid her own ward, but several of the kitchens and pantries were nearly empty, and no one was preparing food—usually the task of the most junior aides or orderlies. Everything appeared to be falling apart, she thought; nothing was as it should be, no one could keep up. The only thing to be glad about was the arrival of more nurses.

Finally, she filled half a cup with some warm milk and headed back up the two flights of stairs and down the long corridor. At the end, outside the entry to Fred's ward, she saw the senior nurse, who turned at Magda's steps. The woman looked up and shook her head, came closer and put her arms out.

"No." Magda whispered.

"I'm so sorry..."

"No!" She screamed and pushed the woman away.

The mug shattered on the hard floor.

Magda sat on the edge of Fred's bed and cupped his face with her hands. His mouth was twisted, as if he had died in the middle of a cough, and his brow was furrowed. She smoothed his forehead, lips, and cheeks with her thumbs, making the sign of the cross. Then she kissed his hands. She turned at a sudden sound and saw the orderlies approaching with a stretcher. Beds were in such demand, she knew, that they removed the bodies almost immediately for the next patient. Unable to watch them cover Fred and transfer his lifeless form, she ran out of the ward and down the stairs.

Magda wandered off the grounds and down to the riverbank. A chilly breeze cut through her uniform, still covered with the bloody gown. She pulled off her mask and cap and let them blow towards the water. She couldn't feel anything. Fred had been her protector and hero since she was a little girl. But she couldn't protect him. God was too cruel—first, to Mama, now to Fred.

She ran back to the boarding house, not stopping at her ward. She couldn't face her supervisor at this moment, or her colleagues; she didn't want to hear sympathy or the cries of the other patients.

How would she tell her family? In her last letter she had said that Fred was recovering and that he could probably go home soon. How could she tell them now how wrong, how stupid, how careless she had been, to let him die?

She tried to call Con first. On the phone, the hotel concierge said that Con wasn't picking up his messages and they hadn't seen him for days. Probably on an assignment, she thought. She left a note that she'd called. Now there was no way to put off talking to Papa and Willa.

She pulled herself up the stairs to her room and removed her soiled uniform. A letter for her from Willa sat on her bed. She tore it open.

September 30

Dear Magda,
It has been difficult to find a minute to write since so many people are falling sick with what everyone is calling Spanish flu. Those of us not sick—or at least not yet—are working

round the clock to care for the others.
First, Jilly had a bad spell of it, but
she has mostly recovered. Minnie, who
tended her, seems untouched. Jony was
about to head out Sept. 15 by train
to camp Devens in Boston but got word
to detour to a different camp. Then
he fell ill before departure and was
unable to leave. Sabine is also sick.
Their children are well, so far at least,
and staying with her parents. I've been
nursing her and Jony at their house
and I think they are out of danger.

Magda could hardly take it all in. And what about Richy?

caroline and Richy are with Johannes'
family for now. I'm not happy about
leaving them there as I can't be
sure they are safe anywhere, but the
children seem healthy. God willing they
stay that way. The play-school has been
closed, of course, and almost all public
places. I seem to be the strongest one
at the moment, along with Minnie, God
love her, who still has all her energy
and drives to the grocer, the pharmacy,
and the doctor for whatever anyone
needs, and makes sure Papa eats.
I hope you and Fred are staying
safe, but I worry about you both until
you can leave the hospital and come
home. We need you both here.

The only good news I can give you is that Kitty writes that she is pregnant! Already three months along.

Please ask Fred to write to Papa as soon as he is able. He is aging before our very eyes. Some people are saying this flu was caused by Germany as another weapon against the Allies and this upsets him too, although, of course, we don't believe it.

I did finally receive a letter from Johannes, thank God, from France, where the engineers have been repairing bridges and roads. He was also very sick with something like this flu in the summer and couldn't write, but fortunately says he has recovered.

much love,
Hilla

Magda decided to write the terrible news, telling herself that no one might be home if she called. She didn't think she could bear to speak the words.

October 10

Dearest Papa, Willa, Tony, Sabine, Tilly and Minnie,

It is with the heaviest heart I have ever borne that I have to tell you the most tragic news. Our Fred, dear, dear Fred, passed *away of the influenza early this morning. He had been doing well, recovering from the gas attack, and I was so hopeful. He was in a ward that shouldn't have exposed him to flu cases, but there is no corner of this hospital that has been spared. And his lungs were still weak. He didn't suffer long. I was able to speak to him a short while before he died and he recognized me. He said—*

She stopped. So many of her patients had asked her to write to their families and loved ones with last messages, and she had done so, sometimes after their death. Fred hadn't given any last words. Should she say he asked for beer and cigarettes? However delusional, it almost made her smile— it was very like him. But she hadn't imagined, nor had he if he was thinking clearly, that he could die of this disease after surviving the horrible months at the front. How could it be?

—that he loved all of you, that he doesn't want you to feel sad, and that he will keep Mama company in heaven until we all have a family reunion there.

She knew it didn't sound like Fred, but she didn't have the strength to tear up the letter and write another. She had to inform Elise, too, and it wouldn't be fair to wait longer. She added a postscript.

CHRISTINE FALLERT KESSIDES

Willa — Please can you write Elise Freund and tell her on my behalf? She and Fred had become close, and while it's my responsibility as her friend first, I can't write to her yet.

Magda felt numb and unable to think another word. She knew she should also be the one to tell Richy, but Willa would be better able to do that now, in person. She sealed the envelope and left it in the basket by the door. Then suddenly, she remembered something. Running back to the bedroom, she drew Richy's baseball and toy car out of her valise, realizing that she had never shown them to Fred. He would have been amused. And Elise's gift! She had been keeping it until his eyes improved and planned to give it to him soon, but in the rush of work she had forgotten about it. Did she deny him whatever blessings the scapular might have brought him? She pressed the soft embroidered cross to her heart as she curled up on her bed, and cried herself to sleep.

MAGDA, STANDING

32

Waking late in the afternoon, Magda went back downstairs to call Con's hotel. The same answer: the desk staff hadn't seen him for days. It was very unlike him not to write or send her a telegram, especially after the concern he'd expressed about the epidemic.

"Can you please knock on his door? This is an emergency!"

Grudgingly, the clerk told her he'd call back after checking. Within ten minutes the line rang.

"Miss? The maid says Mr. Hecht ordered soup and tea from the restaurant the day before yesterday, but she hasn't been in the room for a week. She thinks he's sick and she's afraid to go in."

Magda's stomach dropped.

Willa had said their own family members had gotten flu but they were improving, and that she and Minnie were taking care of them.

But Con had no family. No one to care for him. She needed to go to him.

Before dawn the next morning, she headed to her ward, determined to tell Matron Leister that she must leave for a personal emergency. She didn't expect to get official permission, since almost everyone was experiencing family crises, but, short of being arrested, she wouldn't be held back.

The ward was even more crowded than it had been two days earlier. The matron hadn't arrived yet, which was unusual. Magda was surprised to see Sally, who'd been assigned to the floor.

"What's wrong, Magda? Aside from everything, that is. You look like the devil is on your back."

Magda told her about Fred—only the second time she had voiced it out loud, after telling her housemates. Her voice shook but her tears had run dry. Then she told her about Con.

"You sweet on that boy?"

"Yes, and he needs me now. He really has no one—no family. No one to care, or even to check on him."

"Go on, then. You look too tired to be much good here. Maybe it will be better taking care of one patient, not dozens. You might have trouble finding transport to DC, though. Buses are not running as usual. Not sure about the trains. You have money?"

Magda hadn't even thought about the practicalities. She had enough for one-way fare at least, she thought, since she hadn't spent anything. She ran down to the administrator's office and asked the old man there how to get to Washington in a hurry. He squinted at her over his eyeglasses.

"Only essential transport going out or coming in. Trucks leave from the depot at the end of the yard." He consulted one of his large ledgers. "Food supplies arrived early this morning. That truck will be heading back, soon probably." He could see her desperation. "I can call over to the depot and ask them to wait, if you want."

"Yes, please!"

He made the call, then pointed out the window, beyond the billowing white tents. Magda had barely an hour to go back to the boardinghouse, tell Mrs. Field of her plans, and pick up a change of clothes and her money.

The driver questioned her, "What's this about, Miss? I'm not allowed to take passengers. Especially now, because of the infection."

"I'll sit with the boxes in back," she replied. She was close to tears but felt she'd have a better chance being assertive, like Minnie. "No" wasn't an answer. "I can pay you for your kindness," she insisted, putting a couple dollars in his hand. "Bless you, sir!" She would have given him more, but she had no idea how much she would have to spend in Washington.

⌒

Two hours later, the driver dropped her off a few streets from the address on Con's letters. The lobby of the hotel was well-appointed but unkempt, a clear sign the housekeeping staff were not on duty. The desk clerk scrutinized Magda when she asked for the key to Con's room. "I'm his cousin, his only family!" she insisted. Since she didn't share his surname, she didn't want to get into a further argument about proof, but held her ground. He waved her upstairs.

Magda stood outside his room, her heart beating so hard she felt her pulse in her fingertips. Two, three knocks, no answer. Of course, he must be asleep. She opened the door.

CHRISTINE FALLERT KESSIDES

The dark room was tiny: a narrow bed, washstand, desk with typewriter, a window with curtains drawn. Con was lying still in the rumpled bed. There was a strong odor of sweat, urine, and vomit. In three steps, she grabbed the lamp from the desk and turned it on, crossed to him and, bending over, took his hand. He was feverish, but thank God, he was alive. His breathing was low, but steady. She knew by now how to gauge the many signs and stages of this flu. The most important thing was that his lungs sounded clear, although she could only put her ear to his chest. His hands and face were dry as paper—and dehydration alone could kill.

"Con, Con! Can you hear me? It's Magda." He gave a slight moan. He was unconscious, not merely sleeping.

Magda looked into the corridor for a maid, but didn't see anyone—it was early evening, after all. She ran downstairs to ask the clerk to have the restaurant send tea, soup, bread, and a pitcher of clean water to the room.

"And can you call the housekeeper?" she asked, "He needs clean sheets. And where can I dispose of soiled ones?" He gave her a look of extreme distaste and pointed to a back room with laundry tubs and wringers. The shelves of the supply closet next to it were nearly empty, but she grabbed two sheets and towels, the one remaining blanket, a bucket, and a cake of soap.

Back in Con's room she was torn between cleaning him or trying to hydrate him. She decided to wash him first, the way she'd been taught—one small part of the body at a time, so the patient didn't suffer further chill. If it woke him, all the better so she could try to feed him something. Quickly but gently, she pulled off the soiled sheets, then took a penknife from the desk and cut away his filthy pajamas. She rolled the cloths into a ball and left them in the small bathroom down the hall, to

MAGDA, STANDING

be dealt with later. She couldn't lift him, but rolled him just enough to slip a clean sheet partially under him, and covered him with another sheet and blanket. He did wake, but seemed to be hallucinating and didn't recognize her. She got only a few sips of liquid into him before he fell unconscious again.

Magda worried that Con's breathing was sounding more labored. She ran down to the clerk again and asked if she could place a call to a doctor.

"A doctor? They're scarce now. Most of them are away with the army, and the ones left are mainly at the hospitals. But here are the numbers to the hospitals; you can try calling."

After repeated ringing at the first number, the switchboard operator answered. "We can't take calls now, Miss. No doctor is available here. Try tomorrow."

Magda tried the second number, and after further delay and transfers, an authoritative-sounding woman took the call, introducing herself as a nurse matron. Magda quickly explained that she was a trained Red Cross nurse's aide and was caring for a family member at his hotel. She described his symptoms. "Is there anything more I can do myself, or should I try to bring him to the hospital for evaluation?" she asked, breathlessly. She looked over her shoulder and saw the clerk hanging on her words.

"It's fortunate for your relative that you're there," the woman replied in a kind voice. "We have no beds and it would be risky to transport him here in his condition. And frankly, there is little the doctors would do. If he makes it, it will be due to your care."

The nurse continued. "Wake him at frequent intervals and try to get him to take fluids. Cold compresses for the fever, and aspirin if he can swallow it. Try to get him to sit up as soon as possible, to keep the lungs clear. Leave a window open for fresh air, but don't let him get chilled." The matron also warned Magda to watch for signs of pneumonia, the most dangerous path of the flu. "Good luck," she added.

Magda felt a momentary flush of pride, followed by greater anxiety. She returned to Con's room, felt his forehead and pulse, and listened again to his chest. He seemed unchanged. She wrung out a cool washcloth and placed it on his head, then dipped her fingertips into a cup of warm water and, parting his lips, let drops fall slowly into his mouth. She needed to stay alert to any change in his condition. knowing this disease could shift from dangerous to deadly in a matter of hours. But it was very late, and she had barely slept for two days.

Most of all, she wanted to protect him with her own body. She needed to hold him tight, and press her head to his, with her hand to his heart. She didn't know if he would live or die in the night, but for now she wanted to be close and feel any changes in his breathing, and hear any words he might whisper.

She took off her uniform and in her underdress, covered by a light sweater, she slipped into his bed and lay close behind him, warming him with her arms and legs. They both slept till just before dawn.

Later in the morning, Magda met the two remaining hotel maids, who brought her a cot to sleep on, and the cook, who kept her supplied with fresh tea and broth for Con. He had regained consciousness briefly, but remained quiet and seemed confused. She tried to talk to him when he was awake.

"Con, it's Magda." He only looked at her vaguely and said nothing. He lay curled up with his hand on his head and moaned softly. He was clearly in pain, and he'd started coughing.

MAGDA, STANDING

On the third day, remembering what she'd witnessed at McHenry and what the hospital nurse had told her, she dared to hope that Con was out of the gravest danger, as his lung congestion didn't seem to have worsened. But she knew his fever might continue for some time, as well as his confusion, which became her biggest worry. She bought some aspirin after stopping at three different pharmacies, and tried to get him to take it.

On the next day, a heavy-set young man knocked on the door and told her that he was from Con's newspaper. She introduced herself as Con's cousin, and they looked at each other with suspicion.

"He hasn't been responding to our calls," the man said, rather petulantly. "Has he been ill?"

"You didn't wonder about that before now?" she asked, not even trying to sound polite. "It's fortunate I came to check on him when I did. Yes, he's got influenza. But his condition is stable."

The man backed away.

"Could you please advance the funds for his room and food?" She followed the man into the hall. "The desk clerk says his account is due and Con obviously hasn't been able to pick up his wages for the past week."

The man opened his mouth to object. Magda lowered her eyebrows. "Con was hard at work for your paper and obviously didn't shirk from exposure to the flu in his duties. I will pay you back if he doesn't return to work. I'm confident he'll recover, but he needs more time." She paused for effect. "You can pay downstairs, or give it to me." That settled it. The man took out a notebook, consulted it and pulled out a folio. He counted some bills into Magda's hand, then disappeared down the corridor.

By the end of the week, Con was able to walk around the room slowly, eat a little solid food, and take a bath on his own.

He recognized her, but spoke little—as if they were almost strangers. She read to him, trimmed his beard, and massaged his limbs and back in the few hours while he was awake. She couldn't resist napping while he slept, as she still felt exhausted from work. Finally, five days after she had arrived, she knew he was recovering well when he spoke to her upon awakening while she lay in her cot.

"Magda, have you moved in with me? Does your father know?" He grinned for the first time since she'd arrived.

She leaped up from her cot and sat on the edge of his bed. "I've even bathed and dressed you, but don't think anything of it! I'm just your nurse." He reached out and held her waist while she wrapped her arms around him.

"I can't thank you enough. I . . . didn't think . . . I thought . . ." His tears ran down her neck.

"Don't thank me. The best thing you've done for me is come back to the living. I thought I was going to lose you." She took his hand and pressed her lips to his palm.

"How did you get away from McHenry? And how is Fred? What about the rest of your family?"

She wondered if he was well enough to hear it. But her face gave it away. He sat up and she curled next to him. She told him in a whisper about Fred's last hours, and how she had failed him.

"No way, dear one. You couldn't stop this monster, especially with his lungs so damaged. But your family—maybe they need you there. What about Willa and your father? What about Richy?"

Magda realized with a shock that she hadn't even written home after leaving McHenry. Letters to her there may have even been sent back, which would cause a panic. "I need to call them! I've been so distracted, and lost track of time."

MAGDA, STANDING

Con got up and gripped her shoulder. "You've done enough for me. Call them from downstairs right now. I'm going to pay for your train ticket. You should head home."

"I left McHenry and my duties there without permission, or even giving proper notice," Magda explained. "I may be dismissed from the Red Cross for dereliction."

"Write to them and explain. You're only a volunteer, after all—they won't court-martial you. And if they try, I'll testify you're the very angel of mercy. Don't think any more about it."

She hugged him and went downstairs to call home. Papa answered.

"My child, where are you? We tried to reach you at that boarding house when we got your letter. You should have called us. We have been trying to have Fred's body sent home, but it's been impossible to get answers from anyone at that hospital. They tell us the military will arrange his burial." His voice was shaking.

Through tears, Magda managed to explain that she had left Baltimore suddenly because Con had fallen ill in Washington, and that he was recovering. She asked about the rest of the family. Papa said little, which she took to be no more bad news, but his mind was only on Fred. There were not enough coffins in the city now, he fretted, so they would have to wait for the army to bury him. She promised to come home on the next available train.

Union Station was nearly deserted, apart from clusters of fresh troops still headed to embarkation points for Europe. Only two civilian cars were running and there were few passengers who, like Magda, sat as far from each other as possible, fully masked. She couldn't have conversed anyway, her heart filled with hope, fear, and sorrow.

Minnie picked her up in Pittsburgh. They held each other for a long while. Minnie looked more angular than before, but she bustled Magda into the motorcar as if she were a patient too.

"I'm so sorry, my dear, for what you have been through, tending poor Fred through his terrible injuries and final illness. I know you must feel not only great sadness but also guilt—I know because it was like that when we lost our younger brother. I blamed myself for months, that I hadn't found some way to restore him. I'm so sorry you were alone."

Magda looked out the window at the dingy sky of midday. It matched her mood. On the whole ride, she'd been tense with worry about what she might find at home. The car passed through residential streets with black crepe hanging over many doors. It marked houses that had lost someone to the flu, Minnie explained.

"How's Aunt Tilly?"

"She escaped pneumonia, but hasn't gotten her old energy back and has not left the house these past few weeks. But she is eager to see you."

"Sabine and Tony, have they recovered? And how are the children?"

"Thankfully, they are regaining strength. None of our own children, nor any in the play-school as far as I know, has fallen sick with the flu and we hope to God they won't, although it is still striking families every day. But the little ones have suffered, poor dears, being moved around among the relatives and sensing the worry that is on every face.

MAGDA, STANDING

The children can't go outside or to school, or to play with each other, and the adults don't have time for them, too busy caring for the sick."

Magda sat silently. It was for Richy that she felt a surge of guilt now.

Only Papa and Willa were at the house when they arrived. There were many tears and embraces—he seemed to have lost his traditional reserve and clung to her. "We will get your brother home, I will insist on it, to lie next to your mother."

Minnie left to fetch Tilly, who wanted to see Magda right away. When they returned, she appeared frailer than Magda had ever known her, but her face lit up as they sat on the sofa together, arm in arm. Over dinner, Magda talked about Fred going to the carpentry class. They tried to share stories about his life, but it seemed that each one only widened the deep bruise on their hearts. No one expressed the thought that remained paramount in Magda's mind—the flagrant cruelty of it—Fred dying of a random disease after fighting his way back from near death.

"When will you bring Caroline and Richy home?" Magda asked Willa after the aunts left.

"Now that you're here, I'm hoping you can help me do that. I've been spending every day with Tony and Sabine, but I think they can manage now. Tony feels ready to report back to the army, he says. Sabine isn't strong enough to take care of the children on her own just yet, but hopefully they can all be together in a few more days."

Magda was eager to help, but it weighed on her mind that she had deserted her patients in Baltimore. She especially worried about Private Fine with his dark moods, so she decided to write to him. She would stay at home long enough to be sure her family was sufficiently recovered, then go back to her Red Cross duties.

The phone rang, despite the late hour. Magda thought it might be Con, and remembered that she'd promised to call him after she arrived. She didn't recognize the male voice at the other end.

"I am Walter Lang. Is this the Augustin residence?"

"Yes!" Magda started—it was Kitty's husband. Why wasn't she calling? She turned to signal to Willa to come to the phone. "Mr. Lang, I'm Magda, Kitty's youngest sister."

She could hear him trying to catch his breath and clear his throat. "My beloved Kitty... your sister... the flu has taken her. The doctor said she was weakened, because she was expecting." His voice broke.

Magda nearly dropped the earpiece and Willa picked it up. She had overheard. "This is Willa. When? How long was she sick?" Willa was gasping and looked like she was about to faint. Magda grasped her tightly.

"My Kitty was doing well. She was so happy to be expecting our child. She cooked us dinner two days ago and went to bed, but during that night she started coughing severely and told me her head hurt terribly. By the time the doctor arrived last night, she was unconscious. She didn't wake again." He was sobbing now. "We had no time to tell each other—"

After a few more moments, he continued, "I'm so sorry. I feel I failed you, too, for not protecting her. She loved you all. I will write a letter to your father when I am able. Goodbye."

Magda and Willa stood staring at the phone, twisting the cord. Their shared thoughts were unspoken. How could Kitty have been taken too? She was so strong and animated—so much in charge—and everyone depended on her. She had

MAGDA, STANDING

been an anchor of their family, and of her employers' family, and would have been so for Walter. Being pregnant made her weak? Surely not Kitty. She was so contented, having found her love and the life she wanted.

Willa was near collapse, and Magda helped her to bed. She wouldn't wake Papa to tell him the awful news, or call the aunts at this hour. Magda wanted to break something, to scream at someone, and to curse whatever spirits were supposed to be watching over their family.

In a panic, she dialed Con's hotel. The man who had worked there throughout her stay didn't answer the phone—it was someone else.

"Can you please take a message to Mr. Hecht for me? He's recovering from illness and might not be able to come down to the lobby. Tell him Magda arrived safely but asks him to call when he's feeling well. And," she pressed on, "can you please call me if you don't see or hear from him by tomorrow?" She couldn't be sure of anything. There was no way to feel confident about his condition, since relapses were common.

She felt braced for the worst, from any direction. Nature was turning on itself, she thought. Nothing could be trusted anymore. Only the worst seemed possible. She thought she and Willa must be immune to the flu, but could she have brought more infection into the house with her arrival? The family depended on her now, but would she be a source of well-being, or new sickness and death?

33

The only source of happiness the next day was the return of Caroline and Richy. Willa had insisted she needed her daughter with her, despite her wrenching grief and the continuing fear they all felt. Richy seemed almost hostile towards Magda.

"Where's Fred?" he asked her. "He said he'd come back. You said he'd come back!"

She sat down beside him on the sofa, but he moved several feet away. "I couldn't make him well," she said softly. "He was so brave. He was hurt in the war and was getting better. He wanted so much to come home, but he . . . had trouble breathing, and the doctors couldn't heal him." She started to say, "like Kitty," but it was too much for him to know that. Kitty also hadn't been home for many months, but Richy wasn't as close to her as to Fred. The adults decided not to tell the children yet, despite the fresh sadness they couldn't hide.

MAGDA, STANDING

"Will you die too?" he asked her, accusingly. "And Willa? And Caroline? And . . . me?"

"No." She challenged Death with a statement she couldn't guarantee. "Most people, especially little children, don't even get sick. And you will always have your family to take care of you." She could see that he didn't believe or trust her anymore. He ran to Willa and refused to let Magda touch him.

Con called later that day. He said he didn't have any new symptoms, that the aches and dizziness were subsiding, and that he'd even been able to do a bit of writing. He would stay in his room until his cough was gone. She teared up.

"Your recovery is the only reason I have to thank God at the moment," she replied, daring the blasphemy. Since there was no privacy around the phone, she covered the mouthpiece and whispered the news of Kitty's death.

When she recovered her voice, she said, "I need you to do one thing. Would you talk to Richy and tell him about your visit with Fred? He needs to hear from someone else who was close to him. He's heartbroken and won't talk to me."

Richy came over willingly, as he was always fascinated by the telephone. He stood on a chair with Magda behind him. As he listened to Con, she saw his little hand tighten into a fist, then relax slowly.

"Can you take me to a baseball game?" Richy asked Con suddenly. "I want to throw Fred's baseball there. And go see the dinosaurs? I want . . . I want . . . to pick one for Fred." He paused, listening further, and turned to hand the receiver back to Magda. "As soon as he can," Richy told her, and jumped down.

"As soon as I can come back to you both, I will," Con promised her. She looked over at Richy, who had a slight smile on his face as he stroked Willa's cat. A tiny, momentary flash of light.

CHRISTINE FALLERT KESSIDES

———

Magda wrote to the Red Cross supervisor at McHenry to explain her departure the day after Fred's death, about nursing Con, and then returning home to help her family, only to find an older sister struck down. She offered to return either to Baltimore or to any other duty station where she was needed, if they still wanted her. Waiting for the reply, she wasn't sure where her greatest obligation lay, but she felt wasted, emotionally and physically.

Although social visits had been discouraged for weeks, Magda had to see Elise. When she arrived at her door, forgetting the advice not to get near people outside one's family, they embraced eagerly and wet each other's faces with their tears.

"I will always remember Fred with love. We had a rather hurried courtship, if one could even call it that. I think going to war hastened his expression of feelings, as it did for me."

Magda thought that, too, especially since Fred hadn't said anything to her before he left. But his letters had expressed his genuine emotions.

Elise continued, speaking slowly. "I have suffered another loss. My sister-in-law—I told you about her—passed away from the flu last week. I'm taking care of her daughters. She asked me to keep them, if Emil doesn't return." She spoke impassively, as if she expected it. "Now, you see, I have no time to feel sorry for myself. I hardly got to know her, but God has given me more purpose. And that's all I can think about now."

As Magda left, she marveled at how Elise seemed to accept her fate. Maybe caring for children made you do that, she

MAGDA, STANDING

thought—although, Mama had never been fully restored by the children life had given her.

Passing Lucia's family store, Magda was shocked to see black crepe hanging above the door. She hadn't gotten a letter from Lucia in weeks—nor had she sent one, she realized. She ran the few blocks to Lucia's house and knocked loudly.

As Lucia came to the door, Magda threw her arms around her. "Lu—you're here! I just saw the store!"

Again, the friends clung to each other, thinking only of comfort, not risk. "My mother," Lucia barely got the words out and was unable to continue for several minutes. Magda held on to her as they sat down on a bench in the entryway. "She had refused to close the shop, insisting that families needed food and supplies. When she saw that mainly young people were being stricken with this flu, she wanted me to stay home. My father and grandfather continued to make deliveries." Her voice broke again. "Mama came home on Sunday after taking food to some customers nearby, and went straight to bed. By Tuesday morning she was gone." Lucia put her fists to her head and pulled her hair. "I argued with her so many times. I should have insisted she stay home, too, Magda!"

They sat close together, arm in arm, until nearly dusk. Lucia hadn't asked about Magda's experiences since she left Pittsburgh, and Magda didn't want to talk about herself. They only recounted losses. Fred, then Kitty. Lucia told Magda of their old school friends who had been killed or maimed in the war—that is, the boys she knew about so far. Magda was more shocked to hear that Mary Alice had died of the flu over a month ago, nursing in France. She remembered how excited her fellow trainees had been, and how jealous she felt when they were sent there.

Magda had never felt so vulnerable. It seemed that if one thought too much about loving someone, they would soon be gone.

She didn't want to read the newspapers or listen to the radio, as nothing sounded encouraging, and the censorship Con had told her about made it impossible to believe any good news. He wrote to her that the AEF was pursuing a major offensive in the Argonne Forest that was expected to be definitive; virtually all troops who were able-bodied were deployed in it. The battle was not just a last grasp at victory, but a maelstrom sucking hundreds of thousands more soldiers into its maw.

Magda realized that Johannes was most likely in the throes of that battle.

On November 11, bells tolled across the country for the Armistice, the end of the world's worst and largest war to that time—and, as everyone could only imagine and hope, for all time. Hundreds of people poured out of their houses and joined parades, risking the proximity that could provoke more infections. But in many hearts, there was little room for celebration. Families were too exhausted, devastated, and depleted to believe that even this long-awaited event meant they had reached an end to suffering and had won the chance for happiness again.

Magda spent most of her days with Richy and Caroline, trying to relieve Willa, who waited in agony for word from Johannes. Finally, she received a telegram. Magda held an arm firmly around Willa's shoulders as she opened the message.

MAGDA, STANDING

"It's from him! He's coming back!" Willa was laughing, crying, screaming at once. Magda grabbed Richy and spun him around; words couldn't express her relief.

A few days later, Magda took the children to see Minnie and Tilly. Tilly was napping—unusual in the middle of the day—while Minnie was alone in the kitchen, cutting vegetables for dinner.

The news of Kitty's death had struck the aunts even harder than Fred's. Kitty was the first of their nieces, so able and self-reliant, like the aunts themselves.

"We were somewhat prepared for Fred's loss," Minnie said quietly, as she and Magda watched Richy playing in the yard outside and the baby toddling at their feet. "He was a soldier, and we knew he had been injured badly, so we braced ourselves. But Kitty—how could any of us have imagined that? And recently married, expecting her first child! Oh, it is bitter."

Magda couldn't hold back her thoughts. If Kitty could die, without warning, from this fickle, pitiless, malicious influenza—not to mention all the other young men, women and children struck down by the war and its deprivation—then there was nothing safe or secure in life any more, she told her aunt.

"Is it worse that I feel that way?" she asked Minnie. "The priests told us that despair is a sin against God, against hope and faith. How can we have faith now? How can we still have hope? It seems a lot of foolish and empty promises." Breathing rapidly, she dug her nails into her arms. "At least Kitty didn't suffer long, although the future she lost was the deepest cut. But in the hospital, I saw boys my own age without arms, without faces, unable to talk—all because of the arrogance of some generals. And then, just when they might have gotten back their lives and started anew, like Fred ... and Kitty!" She covered her face with her hands, but had no more sobs left.

Minnie patted her back. "If all we can see is the suffering and evil, there is indeed cause for despair. There is no excuse for the destruction of man by man. But know, too, that in the midst of it there is still good and there is still love. You and the other volunteers acted with selfless generosity to help those boys, and you saved lives, you can be sure of that. Children are always a cause for hope. They bring us back to the present and give us a future. The people we love who are still here with us, they're the reason we go on, for their sakes."

They sat quietly for a little while, then walked outside to stand in the rare November sun.

"We need to think of more than our sorrow and grief," Minnie suddenly spoke briskly, as if shedding a heavy veil. "There is so much to be done, now that the war is finally over. The men who come back will need education and training. Especially if they are maimed, they will need to use their minds. So many children have lost fathers, and now mothers as well." She took Caroline, who was getting restless, from Magda's arms and bounced her gently.

"Have you thought about what you'll do now that you're back? Do you want to go to nursing school and get fully qualified? Or how about university? Almost a third of the students at Pitt are women, and Duquesne has female graduates now. And then perhaps medical school—you're smart enough to become a doctor."

Magda looked at Minnie with a stir of the old discomfort that she'd been given an assignment she hadn't finished, or a test she wasn't ready for. "I ... I don't know, *Tante*. I haven't thought even a day ahead lately. I don't have any money to pay for nursing school, let alone university. Maybe . . . well, it's all so hard to imagine right now."

Minnie called Richy to come inside. "Let's think about it," she replied as she led him to the table for lunch and placed Caroline in the highchair.

Magda took a tray up to Tilly, who was awake but still in bed and had pushed herself into a sitting position.

"My dear, I'm ashamed for you to see me like this, lounging away a perfectly good afternoon."

"Don't you dare say that! We need to be certain you've beaten this flu, so it won't come back. The best thing is rest and plenty of hot fluids." Magda poured her a cup of tea, adding a little milk and honey the way Tilly liked it.

"Did you find your calling in nursing?" Tilly asked.

"I thought I might, but my mind is churning," Magda answered, nibbling on a piece of bread. "I was very glad to have worked in the hospital, and I want to go back to serve out my assignment, whatever that may be, but I don't think I'm interested in spending three years to become certified." She paused. "Minnie was just asking me about that."

"And what about that young man you tended in Washington? I remember meeting him at your house last year. He seemed very fine. And clearly even then, he was quite impressed with you."

Magda smiled broadly.

"And you with him, no doubt, since you left your job to take care of him."

"He was all alone, and might have died like that. And yes, I . . . I might even say, I do love him. But I'm a little afraid, *Tante*. Does that mean I should be ready to drop everything and marry him, and have as many babies as . . . well, as many as

Mama had, or more?" She shook her head slightly and chewed her cheeks. "I'm getting ahead of myself, we've never talked about being together after all this. But I don't see clearly yet what I should do with my life now. There are so many uncertainties. The family still needs me, especially Richy."

"My dear," Tilly replied, pushing the tray aside and taking Magda's hand. "You don't need to rush into anything. Take your time. I think it would be wonderful if you continue your education and go to college—oh yes, Minnie and I talked about that a few times, and we do hope so." She smiled. "The future is open, it is yours for the taking. We will not let you simply give up on yourself. We didn't before, and we won't now."

"But," she continued after a pause, smoothing the bedspread, "you can listen to both your head and your heart. I can tell you that as satisfying as my life has been, I think of my Basil often. And I still feel that if he had not died and we could have been together … if I were given that choice even now, I would take it. It would have been a different life, especially if we had stayed in Germany, but I still feel that we would have been a great pair. And we could have faced whatever came, together." Tilly's expression softened as she looked at Magda, their eyes moist.

They both rose with a start as Minnie called from downstairs, "The little ones are ready to go home!" Magda and Tilly smiled at each other. "We mustn't test her patience too much," Tilly whispered as she stood. "I feel strong enough to walk with you a few blocks, I think. A bit of sun will do me good."

That momentary flash of light again, Magda thought. Lasting a bit longer this time.

MAGDA, STANDING

1919

34

For the first time in months, the wide path beside the Allegheny River was crowded with people. Couples of all ages, young people on scooters, and children moseyed among each other and stood elbow to elbow on the railings overlooking the water. The weather was unusually bright for February. The steel and iron mills had banked their furnaces during the worst weeks of the pandemic, mainly in response to the absence of workforce, so the usual dirty air had receded a little, allowing the sun to venture out in place of the resident winter gloom. Magda could see that everyone's mood was lighter and brighter, more than during the Christmas holiday when families had still huddled in fear and grief, unable to gather freely. Surely, they all deserved a more hopeful year.

Con cast his strong arm over her shoulders and gave her a gentle squeeze. She raised her right arm and circled his back, tugging her fingertips into the edge of his coat pocket.

MAGDA, STANDING

Up ahead, Magda suddenly recognized her old classmate from high school and training, Margaret, strolling with Christoph. She was surprised they were still together.

Magda broke away and ran up to Margaret, who beamed as they exchanged a warm hug, "It's good to see you," she cried.

"I'm so glad you're back safely!" Then Magda's face dropped. "I heard from Lucia about Mary Alice."

"I heard, too, only when I returned," Margaret said. "We were separated when we arrived in France; she was closer to the front."

Magda turned and beckoned to Con to join them. She introduced him to her old friends—or so they seemed now, her past feelings of jealousy and competition forgotten. She noticed that Christoph had a long scar on one side of his face and around his neck, and he didn't speak except to nod thanks to Magda for congratulating them on their marriage.

The couples moved on. Passing a bench facing the river, Con said, "Let's sit a while." Magda looked at him quickly to check if he seemed tired. She knew that some flu survivors experienced lingering effects of weakness, but his color was good—the fresh air helped with that.

Con hadn't said whether his trip to Pittsburgh was just a visit or to stay. Her overwhelming sense of relief that they could at last walk together in a crowd made her want to focus on the present. They had been through so much. Everyone had, and nothing would ever be the same.

"I'm starting a new assignment for the *Pittsburgh Press* next week," he announced, "but again in Washington."

"Will you be traveling around from there? Will it be safe?" Magda asked. She didn't want to ask: Are you strong enough?

"Safe enough for me," Con replied, and added with feeling, "The few reporters who stayed here held the Press together, but barely. There are so many stories left to tell. With the contacts I made in Washington, I can take the lead covering the peace process and postwar diplomacy. And I know there are new opportunities opening at bigger papers too. I've seen notices from New York, Philadelphia, and even Chicago. I want to be out in front. If I can get a few major bylines in the next few months, I think I'd have a good chance with a larger market."

Magda sat back and gazed at the flowing water below, dark but speckled with the sun's rays. She tucked in her feet, feeling a chill, and drew a ragged breath.

Con reached across and covered her closest hand with his. He tugged it and leaned in close.

"Of course, I don't want you to think…" He coughed. "Magda, may I ask you a very important question?"

She gently pulled away and turned to face him.

"I have something I want to tell you too," she murmured. She looked into his warm eyes. She felt a pang of guilt that she'd interrupted what he was going to say, but she was afraid of it. Afraid of what he would ask and what she might reply.

"I've decided to apply to university, here in Pittsburgh. I didn't want to say anything unless I was accepted. I just found out I can start at Pitt in the spring, as soon as I terminate with the Red Cross."

"That's wonderful!" Con looked genuinely pleased, although surprised.

"I still have to work out how to pay for it," she said. "They gave me a scholarship, and my aunts have offered to lend me some funding at least for the first two years. I will live at home since I want to be close to Richy; he'll be starting kindergarten."

"Of course. But what do you want to do with a degree? Teach?"

"I'd like to help the returning soldiers somehow."

"You can do that even now. Tutor them to get their diplomas, as your aunts did for you."

"Well, I might like to set up something more formal, eventually. You said I was good at organization. Perhaps start my own school for rehabilitation of the handicapped or blind. The government is supporting vocational training of disabled soldiers, and the Red Cross started an institute for that in New York last year. The needs are so great and will be for years. I may be able to do something like that here." She looked down, feeling slightly embarrassed. "Big ideas."

Con looked out at the river. "Not too big for you, if that's what you want."

She couldn't leave the conversation like this. "Con, what did you want to ask me?" She knew, and he knew, but they didn't want anything left unsaid.

He looked down, then held her gaze. "I've always been impressed by your ambition, and your dedication to your family as well—the first things I loved about you. I have ambition too. But I don't have a family to need me, to make claims on me—someone, *someones* to bring it all back to at the end of the day."

Magda locked her fingers with his. "I don't want you to be alone. But I just don't know if I'm ready—" She took a deep breath. "Just thinking about the commitment I'm making to the university, deciding what to study, and managing all that—it seems so much already."

Con smiled. "You aren't likely to become overwhelmed by anything."

"I just need more time, I think."

He stood up and pulled her to her feet for a tight hug. "I'll be in Washington at least through the summer," he said. "You

get going at Pitt. I'll know where to find you, and you me."
Magda nodded. She couldn't make a promise, but she rose
unsteadily on her tiptoes to give him a lingering kiss. Why
was she always the first to do that? she wondered later. And
would he always wait for it?

Would he wait for her?

Throughout the winter and spring, the Spanish flu continued
to strike randomly, especially young adults, but with fewer
numbers and weaker cases. It finally dissipated with the warm
weather, as suddenly as it had appeared the year before. Life
started to resume. Businesses, schools, and places of entertain-
ment restored their original schedules, but with a noticeable
shortage of strong, healthy young men. Magda started her first
term at university, where it was particularly evident that her
generation was missing brothers, friends, and lovers.

The family was moving on too. Tony was hired as a photographer for the *Pittsburgh Press*, a job he'd dreamed of,
although Sabine was not happy with his longer and more
irregular hours. Papa started seeing a widow, Mrs. Salzmann,
a cheerful and kindly woman who was about his age and well
known in the parish community. She had also lost a son in
the war.

"It's hard to get used to, but I think she's good for him," Willa
said to Magda one evening, as they watched Papa leave the
house in his best suit, looking ten years younger. Magda agreed.

The play-school was doing well, and Molly had even managed to recruit a few more families. "I was wanting to bring in
some who'd lost a dad or mum, poor little ones," she said, when

Magda stopped to see her after it reopened. "We raised some money through the church." The aunts continued to provide advice and were very pleased with its progress. "The Montessori approach is really just common sense, but one more of those things that people didn't see until a wise woman put it in front of them," Minnie declared.

Minnie had thrown herself into other activities as well. In addition to tutoring a few hours weekly at a Red Cross class for returning soldiers, Minnie enlisted in the resurgent letter-writing effort to get the woman's suffrage amendment ratified by more states, following Pennsylvania's early lead in June. "If there's anything that should impress on politicians the need for women to vote, it's the absolute mess men have made of things!" she fumed.

Tilly started volunteering with a group promoting public education on birth control, following the lead of Margaret Sanger. "I'm too old to challenge the law and go to prison like she did," Tilly declared, "but I'll gladly distribute the information she gathered in her research. Women have shown we can run the offices and factories if we're not tied down. We should have the right to determine how many children to have."

"Does Father Magnus know about this, and what does he say?" Magda asked with a grin, already sure of the answers.

"The Church's guidance is always welcome, but not in the bedroom," Tilly replied tersely. Magda hadn't seen her so fired up before, except during the suffrage marches. She, Willa, and Sabine eagerly endorsed the cause, but didn't have much time to join the meetings.

Johannes had lost an eye in the final battle of the war, which kept him from returning to his previous job. He was able to find another in the mill, though it didn't pay as well, so Willa resumed her work as a seamstress part-time. Styles were changing and the demand for her skills was rising as fast as the hemlines.

—

Six months later, Magda was on the train again heading to Baltimore, this time with her father and Richy, Willa, Johannes, and Caroline. They had gotten word that Fred had been buried at one of the national military cemeteries there, and families were invited for a collective ceremony. It was a significant expense, but Papa decided it was the best way to honor Fred. Minnie and Tilly stayed at home, as did Tony and Sabine with their children. Con told Magda that he would meet them in Baltimore.

The graveside ceremony was solemn, but the company of hundreds of families made it more comforting. Afterwards, while the others headed back to the hotel, Magda and Con, with Richy clutching the folded flag, decided to stroll through the cemetery.

"Fred was my best friend," Con said thoughtfully.

"Mine too," said Magda.

"Everyone loved him and that's how we'll always remember him. We should all be so fortunate, in a way, to leave that kind of legacy." Con put his arm around Magda and she did the same to him and Richy. They walked on, three abreast.

"I've something to tell you. I got another promotion from the *Pittsburgh Press*," Con said, "to be assistant editor of the politics section. And, just yesterday, the *New York World* offered me a job covering the Washington politics beat. If I worked for them, I would probably have to divide my time between New York and DC."

"I'm proud of you!" Magda replied. But she couldn't make herself smile at the news.

"I have to decide soon," Con continued. "I know the *Press* best and I could exert a lot of influence there. The *World* offers better pay and national exposure, of course." He paused, looking over the field of tombstones. "But the work itself is only one consideration—"

"Pittsburgh is much less exciting than New York or Washington, I'm sure." She looked down and her voice started to fade.

"You know there's another factor that would tip the scales for my decision." He stopped and lifted her chin, looking into her eyes. "Do you want me to be wherever you are? Because I do."

"Yes, I do!" she replied. They burst out laughing. "Did we just exchange vows before the proposal?" she asked. Richy laughed along, without knowing why.

They had reached the outer gate of the cemetery. There was an ice cream vendor on the sidewalk. Richy looked up to them with a silent appeal.

"I think we can celebrate!" Con bought a cone for each of them.

"Lovely family," the vendor called in thanks.

"Yes, we are!" Magda replied. She beamed at Con.

And this time she didn't have to stand on her tiptoes.

AUTHOR'S NOTE

MAGDA, STANDING IS about the long arm of family—both the one we're born into, and ones we choose—and its inescapable reach that envelopes us and grips our hearts, bringing many of our deepest joys and sorrows. Family may also be the first place where girls encounter expectations that confine their dreams and dictate what they can be and do in life. I was fortunate that my family let me fly. I hope that reading about Magda encourages more girls to "never take 'No' for an answer."

This story was inspired by many aspects of my own heritage and the experiences of older German-American relatives in Pittsburgh. In her teens, my mother and her older sister cared for their younger brothers for an extended period while their mother, my grandmother, was hospitalized for a so-called "nervous breakdown"—what today would probably be termed clinical depression but was rarely discussed at the time. Her condition was possibly provoked by the loss of two infants. Fortunately, my mother didn't have to leave school, but she and her siblings did receive strong support from two great-aunts who were unmarried school teachers and headmistresses. The models for Minnie and Tilly, these women mentored and inspired my mother to pursue an advanced education and start a career when that was still rather rare for women.

The 1918–19 Spanish flu* epidemic left a deep scar on my grandparents' families. My paternal grandfather died at thirty-three within a couple days of falling ill, leaving my grandmother (who had started nursing training before marriage) to raise three young children alone, including my father. Two of my maternal grandmother's siblings also died of that flu in their twenties—a sister who was a housekeeper and a brother at an army base. Pittsburgh suffered one of the highest fatality rates from Spanish flu among major US cities, with most of the deaths, like those of my relatives, striking in October and November of 1918.

---

*   This moniker became current because the disease was first reported in Spain, which didn't have the wartime censorship of most other countries.

CHRISTINE FALLERT KESSIDES

HISTORICAL NOTE & SOURCES

WRITING THIS BOOK gave me an opportunity to research many elements of this story. First, about German heritage. Immigration of Germans to the United States surged in the second half of the 1800s through the turn of the last century, and German is still by far the largest self-declared nationality in America today, according to the US Census Bureau. German immigrants tended to be literate and better educated than most other newcomers of the era. They also cultivated strong cultural ties, supporting 500 German-language newspapers across the US at the start of World War One. As the US became involved in the war, public sentiment turned against them, sometimes violently, out of jingoistic fears that the German immigrants held divided loyalties and might even harbor spies. In response, many German-Americans, as my older relatives reported, avoided open expression of their culture and language, and some even changed their names. The German-American Heritage Museum in Washington, DC, is a helpful resource on this history. I found there two informative books by Astrid Adler on the stories of some immigrants: *Our Ancestors Were German* and *Goodbye Forever—Life Beyond Germany*.

Among the many works about WWI that convey the human cost, both on the home front and to the soldiers, I found most revealing Vera Brittain's *Letters from a Lost Generation: First World War Letters of Vera Brittain and Four Friends*, and Brittain's memoir, *Testament of Youth*; and David Laskin's *The Long Way Home: An American Journey from Ellis Island to the Great War*. The classic novel by Erich Maria Remarque, *All Quiet on the Western Front*, Pat Barker's *Regeneration* trilogy, and *World War One Short Stories* edited by Bob Blaisdell, are memorable fictionalized accounts.

To understand the role of the American Red Cross in the lead up to and during the Great War, I referred to Marian Moser Jones' history, *The American Red Cross from Clara Barton to the New Deal*. I learned graphic details about the practical challenges of nursing in the time of industrialized trench warfare from Kirsty Harris, *More than Bombs and Bandages: Australian Army Nurses at Work in World War I*; Julia C. Stimson, *Finding Themselves: The Letters of an American Army Chief Nurse in a British Hospital in France, 1918*; and *Into the Breach: American Women Overseas in World War I*, by Dorothy and Carl J. Schneider.

I started planning to write this novel when the 100th anniversary of the Spanish flu pandemic was approaching and wrote most of it during the unanticipated COVID-19 pandemic. While there are many similarities in how governments and populations responded to both pandemics—with disbelief, fear, misunderstanding, resentment of restrictions, and wild ideas of home remedies when no scientific treatment was available—the 1918–19 epidemic is still unprecedented. John M. Barry's authoritative history, *The Great Influenza*, as well as Catherine Arnold's *Pandemic 1918* and Laura Spinney's *Pale Rider* give richly detailed accounts. These analyses permit a comparison of the two pandemics (using also current World Health Organization data) as follows:

SCOPE   The Spanish flu killed from 50–100 million people worldwide (the upper figure extrapolated from incomplete records), representing about 2.5–5 percent of a global population below 2 billion. In contrast, from 2020 through 2022, COVID-19 accounted for 6.7 million deaths in a global population of almost 8 billion (a 0.08 percent fatality rate). In the US alone, 675,000 died from Spanish flu when the country's population was 105 million (0.6 percent), while COVID-19 killed 1.1 million of the 338 million American residents as of end-2022 (0.3 percent).*

SPEED   COVID-19 has remained active across the globe for almost three years at the time of this writing, most virulently in the first year before the development of vaccines. Although the Spanish flu appeared in three waves from early 1918 to mid-1919, most cases and deaths occurred during just twelve weeks in the fall of 1918 while the world endured the Great War's last major battles.

IMPACT   Typical spells of seasonal influenza, and COVID-19, affect mainly seniors and people with chronic health conditions. The Spanish flu targeted healthy young adults, with the

---

*   Next to the toll of the Spanish flu, deaths among mobilized forces in World War I pale in number (9.7 million among all combatant countries, and 117,000 for the US alone).

highest mortality among those aged 21–30. These were the soldiers, their siblings and spouses, parents of young families, and the most educated labor force. The personal toll, and the manifold losses to society, of the 1918–19 pandemic are difficult to comprehend.

The websites and online resources of the National Institutes of Health, Library of Congress, and World Health Organization were also useful on many points of my research. Any factual errors in the novel are, of course, my own.

ACKNOWLEDGMENTS

I WOULD PROBABLY still be buried in some obscure history book if I hadn't been awakened to the novelist's craft by the very helpful staff and members of The Writers Center in Bethesda, Maryland; the Maryland Writers' Association; and by several online writers' communities that shared freely their knowledge and encouragement. I am especially grateful for instruction and coaching from Caela Carter, Meg Eden, Tammy Greenwood, and Jennifer Jacobson, and for helpful editorial suggestions from Amy Ewing. A warm thanks to my early readers who were brave to venture into raw text, including Jeanne Crowley and Celia Csonnabend; writing group partners Viviana Acosta, Katrina Ballard, Amy Bell, and Heather Davis; Judy Bailey, Anita Krichmar, and Constance Guimbert; as well as my extended family members Mary Anne Blackwood, Norm and Jean Leister, and Joey Geisinger. Special appreciation goes to Katja Sipple, Executive Director of the German-American Heritage Museum, for checking the authenticity of cultural and language references. A big hug to my three daughters, Maria, Lara and Eleni, each of whom is represented within Magda and who humored me by reading the earliest draft. Thanks also to my doctor son, Nick, who answered some medical questions and who shares my German ancestors' insistence to never waste leftovers, especially those cooked at home.

Chronologically last but not least, Magda and I would not be here for other readers without the faith placed in us by Emily Barrosse, CEO of Bold Story Press, and her expert team: Karen Gulliver, who provided invaluable editorial guidance; Julianna Scott Fein, the production manager, who kept us all on track, and Karen Polaski, whose design of the cover and interior made it all look beautiful.

First, last, and always, thank you to my husband, Ioannis, who found me in a college reading room many years ago and still provides daily inspiration, best-friendship, and great Greek meals.

ABOUT THE AUTHOR

CHRISTINE FALLERT KESSIDES was born and raised in Pittsburgh, Pennsylvania, and was always interested that all her ancestors were from Germany. After reviewing the family genealogy and reflecting on some of her relatives' experiences, she was inspired to write Magda's story.

Christine attended college and graduate school at Northwestern University and Princeton University, respectively. She had a career at the World Bank in Washington, DC, writing policy reports in international development. Reading, especially historical fiction, has always been a passion. She lives in suburban Maryland with her husband, and sees their four children and grandchild, along with two dogs, as often as possible. *Magda, Standing* is her first novel.

ABOUT BOLD STORY PRESS

BOLD STORY PRESS is a curated, woman-owned hybrid publishing company with a mission of publishing well-written stories by women. If your book is chosen for publication, our team of expert editors and designers will work with you to publish a professionally edited and designed book. Every woman has a story to tell. If you have written yours and want to explore publishing with Bold Story Press, contact us at https://boldstorypress.com.

**BOLD
STORY
PRESS**

The Bold Story Press logo, designed by Grace Arsenault, was inspired by the nom de plume, or pen name, a sad necessity at one time for female authors who wanted to publish. The woman's face hidden in the quill is the profile of Virginia Woolf, who, in addition to being an early feminist writer, founded and ran her own publishing company, Hogarth Press.